Bound by Duty

Stormy Smith

Cover design by Toni Sarcone
Editing by Monica Black (Word Nerd Editing)
Formatting by Polgarus Studio

For more information about this book and the author visit:
www.stormysmith.com

To Abe

For inspiring me every day.
I could never write a love story better than ours.

And, "Hi, Dad!"
Just like I promised.

Prologue

Her stark white hair fell down around her face. For the first time in one hundred years it wasn't pulled back in a waist-length braid. Her crimson robes were torn and stained. She bit back a groan, her lips a tight line as the pain ripped through her once again. The invisible knife raked its way up her back as wounds no one could see flayed her skin and weakened her resolve. It had been days of this and she wasn't sure if she could continue. As she looked up and met the queen's eyes, Lavignia pushed the anger down and forced compassion to rise yet again.

"What is it you hope to learn, Julia? What is it you think you have to gain from all of this?" she asked weakly as she tugged on the restraints that kept her tethered to the heavy wooden chair. Her power was already weak when the Hunters had found her, and the enchanted chamber had dampened what remained to a tiny flame.

The room was dark, but the sun was slowly rising. An orange and pink glow filtered through the small window above Julia's head. The colorful rays that should have resembled hope of a new day only shed light on the reality that Lavignia would never leave this room alive.

Julia stepped from the shadows and walked slowly toward Lavignia. She stopped and crouched down, putting herself at eye level.

"Oh, Livvy, dear. Don't do that," she said, her tone patronizing as her ice crystal eyes narrowed. "Don't pretend you can still look down on me from your Elder tower. Don't pretend you can utter your polite words and suddenly I'll remember who you are versus who I am. I know exactly who I am. I am the one who rules them all. I am the one they will bow down to and worship. I am the Queen. Not you. Or your sisters. Your time is done."

She looked back over her shoulder to the Hunter who stood in the still dark corner of the room and nodded. The Hunter's eyes burned bright orange as Lavignia's screams echoed off the walls. Julia raised her hand and the screams dropped to whimpers. With that same hand, she reached out and took Lavignia's.

"Livvy, look at me," she commanded. Dazed, dim violet eyes struggled to focus and find hers. Julia tightened her grip, digging her scarlet nails into Lavignia's already tender flesh, making her yelp and their eyes connect.

"Livvy, you need to tell me," she said. "I know you see it. You knew this day would come and you know I won't stop until you tell me. I scoured the lands for you. I know there are others left, but they can be saved. You can save them, old friend. You just have to tell me." Her tone was persuasive and gentle, but the frantic look that passed through her eyes told Lavignia the truth the queen couldn't hide — she was scared.

"You won't harm the others? You will let them live out their lives hidden and free? You will swear an oath?" Her words trailed off and Lavignia's eyes closed, the torture of the last few days taking its toll. She could only hope the oath would keep her people safe.

She didn't see the triumph that straightened Julia's posture or the sneer that twisted her thin, painted lips. "Of course, my dear. I swear to you that I will not seek out and harm the remaining Elders. I swear that I will not take their freedom."

"Your blood," Lavignia said, her words barely audible.

Julia removed a small dirk from the folds of her skirts and repeated the words as she slid the blade down her palm. As the deep red drop hit the floor, she sent a small wave of power through to heal the wound, reveling in the knowledge that she had won.

"Now, Livvy, darling, you must tell me." When Lavignia didn't respond, Julia whipped back around to the still silent Hunter. "Help her. Give her what she needs. NOW!" she commanded, panic finally breaking through her controlled facade.

The Hunter flicked a wrist at Lavignia and she suddenly straightened, her eyes luminescent and shining at the welcome invasion of power that flooded her system, giving her renewed life for a few precious seconds.

With sudden clarity, she saw the future that had eluded her. She looked down on Julia with authority and pity as the words that would cement the queen's fate fell from her lips.

"You will have your time, but it will end. She will be born to the one who got away. Inside her, the five families will merge and only a man who is both king and companion will tame the wild and set her free. She will be your undoing. She will lead them all."

Julia reared back, Lavignia's words not the ones she expected. Seconds later, her dirk was buried deep in Lavignia's chest. Lavignia collapsed back against the chair, a content smile mocking the queen from her lifeless face.

Julia's breath heaved in and out in short bursts as she turned to the Hunter. "I made an oath. You did not. Find them. Kill them all."

Chapter 1

Last night's dream had been different. More vivid than normal. Even now, as I sat on the picnic table bench on campus, I couldn't stop seeing my father's eyes. My dreams had always been constant and the emotions I awoke with varied from anger, to sobbing, to complete fear. Waking up peaceful was a rarity for me. It was only recently that I could actually recall my dreams hours later. Before, they'd disappear as soon as I woke up. Now, they haunt me.

My hands still ached from clutching the pillow to my chest as I tossed and turned throughout the night. I didn't have to close my eyes to see the scene replay for the hundredth time today. There I was, standing in my living room, nine years old again, wondering which of my father's personalities would take the five steps from his study and turn the corner to stand before me. As soon as I saw his wide eyes, his twisted scowl, and his tense, rigid posture, I knew this night wouldn't end with bedtime stories. So few nights actually did.

I wanted to back away but had learned it only made things worse when I showed my fear. I had to keep myself from searching the room for Rynna. I knew my nanny was gone. It was just me and my father, and he knew. He always knew when I had lost control, as I had just minutes before. Before I could react, he hoisted me off the ground, his palms cupping under my arms. He held me at eye level, his frantic stare making it hard for me to keep eye contact. I was afraid of my father in these moments; in the times where he didn't feel at all like himself and I was nothing but a failure to him. For a split second, I thought I saw his eyes soften and an apology flit across his features, then all I saw was the flash of orange in his eyes before he dropped me to the ground and ran out the back door.

That was the part that made no sense. My father's power source was green. One of the many colors associated with Witch power. Orange was the power of Hunters — of killers — and I'd seen my father release his power enough times to know that he was no Hunter. I was in mid-thought, wondering why my dreams never made any sense, when Bethany plopped down beside me with a, "Hiya!"

Her peppy, southern drawl interrupted my latest round of introspection and I was thankful for it. Bethany was one of those people you couldn't resist talking to. Nice in the most sincere way, even though no one could imagine where all that positivity came from. In her short sundress covered in multi-colored bird silhouettes and her cardigan that she somehow managed to make look fresh and trendy, I wasn't sure how I managed to win the lottery of college roommates. My messy top-knot, ripped Capri, and basic tee weren't winning any fashion awards today, but she probably slept last night. I didn't.

"Hey B. What's up?" I asked as I popped my ear buds out of my ears. I could tell by the look in her eyes that she was dragging me out tonight. Some guy, somewhere, was having a party that we, "Just had to go to!" College was supposed to be a non-stop party, but I didn't drink for fear of losing control, so I generally ended up being the DD. My father had managed to make the words "lose control" into the most terrible, gut-wrenching eleven letters the alphabet could string together, and, so far, I hadn't dared stepping out of line. Even though he was hundreds of miles away, some things just stuck.

"Soooooo," she started off slowly, her accent making it sound more country song and less *you're going to hate this*. "There's a party outside of town. A bunch of guys have a beach house they rented and it's invite only," she said. Her face was flushing, she was talking fast, and I knew what was coming next. "And… Micah's going to be there!" She almost squealed as she smacked her palms together and looked at me with ecstatic, begging eyes.

Bethany has had a thing for Micah Clair since classes started. I keep telling her that I don't think he's the best news. I get the weirdest vibe every time he's around, but

I've continued to listen to her go on and on about his European accent and male model looks.

I was done for. Somehow, some way, this southern belle had become my first real friend and I couldn't bring myself to say no even though it was the last place I wanted to be.

I guess this means I'm going to a party.

Great.

The music was shaking the walls. The green, yellow, and pink neon lights that probably once graced the walls of a bar somewhere in Brighton looked like they were going to come crashing down at any minute. Maroon 5 was going on about having moves like Jagger as people who might have been able to dance hours ago were now just falling all over each other.

Bethany grabbed my hand, dragging me through the crowd. Her head whipped back and forth, surveying the scene. The moment she spotted Micah, she stopped and I almost tripped over her. All of a sudden she turned and shoved me in the opposite direction, away from him.

"Does my hair look okay? Are you sure these shoes go with this dress? Is my eyeliner smudged?" She was smoothing her skirt and fluffing her hair, talking rapid fire.

With her olive skin and bright blond hair, Bethany looked like she had grown up on the California beaches. She adored dresses, her hair was always flat-ironed to perfection, and you wouldn't catch her outside of our apartment without makeup. She firmly believed girls had no business going without eyeliner and mascara, at the very least. Though, oddly enough, she was anything but a girly-girl. She grew up on a farm raising chickens, riding horses, and doing whatever else it is people do in the middle of nowhere Mississippi. I knew she *could* get dirty, she just wasn't really interested.

"Seriously, B, you're fine. You look amazing," I reassured her.

I glanced over her shoulder to see Micah looking our way. He stood in the corner of the room with a few other guys. I couldn't help but acknowledge he was attractive, even if he wasn't my type. His hair was a sandy blond and he wore it longer than most guys would dare. He had it tied at the back of his neck with some kind of leather strap. His polo and dark wash jeans seemed out of place with his Viking looks — shockingly blue eyes and long hair — but you couldn't deny it was working.

Micah continued looking her up and down appreciatively, not realizing she was bordering a panic attack in his name.

"Besides," I reassured her, "he obviously likes you from the back. Just get over there." I turned her around with the intention of giving her a small shove but Micah was already parting the crowds coming our way. His eyes were locked on Bethany's, a slow smile appearing as he got closer. I took this as my opportunity to get away and pushed my way through the throngs of people still bumping and grinding. Right before I stepped through the patio door, I turned back one last time to make sure Bethany was still comfortable. She had her back to me, so I couldn't get a good look at her face. Instead, I found myself locking eyes with Micah. An internal warning bell went off and I recoiled, quickly turning away from them. I'd learned long ago that my instincts knew far more than my brain. I just wish I could pinpoint what it was about that guy that was setting me off.

As soon as I stepped out on the giant deck, the sea air hit my face. It tangled in my hair, whipping it around my shoulders as if playing hide and seek in the dark strands. I exhaled, not realizing I had been holding my breath.

I stood there a moment, just listening to the waves beat against the sand as the tide came in. The full moon came out from behind the clouds, brightening my path and leading me to the stairs that would take me down to the beach. I didn't hesitate. Almost leaping to the bottom, I kicked my gladiator sandals off as soon as I hit the sand and ran toward the water. Just as the tide touched my toes, the hair on the back of my neck stood up.

Someone was there.

Instantly, a jolt of power raced through my veins. I tried frantically to calm it back down, to maintain control. But, against all effort, I'm sure my eyes went from their normal hazel to bright violet, as they always do when my power takes over. I stood there, staring out at the sea, trying to decide how to react. I couldn't draw attention to myself, but I could protect myself if I had to — I had learned that much. I felt my power build; like small pinpricks of electricity racing through my veins, filling my blood inch by inch. I forced myself to soften my stiff posture, but kept my right hand open and out in front of me in case I needed to use it.

Since moving to Brighton, I'd been working to actually use my magic, but it still felt like a second person trapped inside me that I couldn't force into compliance. Sometimes it worked with me, sometimes not. We've been fighting this battle for as long as I can remember and in times like these, when I didn't know what I was dealing with, I trusted it more than myself. I stood there, my body still as my power rippled beneath the surface and cautiously probed around me, just waiting to be unleashed.

I slowly started to turn around when he said, "Oh, so you're hiding from them too, huh?"

His voice was smooth and almost melodic, with just a little fire behind it. I somehow knew he was smirking even though I couldn't see him. The moonlight hadn't breached the shadow from the deck where I could see his outline sitting on a picnic table. He was sitting on the top with his feet on the bench and elbows on his knees. I heard the old, weather-beaten table creak and groan as he set his feet on the ground. A shiver ran through me; he looked dangerous.

"Do I know you?" Something told me I'd seen him before. The fear that had ignited my magic instantly turned to curiosity, the danger melting to intrigue. I could actually see the thready, purple wisps spreading out, poking around, trying to get a read on him. It's a good thing humans don't actually see our power unless we let them. Abruptly, I turned back toward the ocean, kicking myself as I mentally drew it back in.

What am I doing?! I don't even KNOW this guy. What if he's...?

"You don't have anything to worry about," he interrupted, as if reading my thoughts. I could hear his voice coming closer, a little tentative, feeling me out.

I'm sure he thinks I'm nutcakes. Well done, Amelia. You are here to blend in, not prompt people to think you're a freak a month into the semester.

I sighed, took a breath, and turned to face him, not realizing how close to me he now was. The full moon cast light and shadow across his body as he stood just feet from me, silent, sizing me up as I did the same to him. I drew in a quick breath as all my thoughts came together in just two words. *He's gorgeous.*

I couldn't stop my eyes from roaming. There was something tortured about him, I could feel it as easily as I felt my own curiosity building. He stood just a few feet from me, clearly trying not to be intimidating. But, between the hints of a tattoo peeking out from under his black T-shirt and the leather cuffs on his wrists, there was an intensity he couldn't hide. He had big eyes with long lashes a girl would kill for. As my gaze followed the strong, angular features of his face, I realized he had a dimple, just on the one side that must only come out when that corner of his mouth lifted into the smirk I had heard in his voice earlier. The one he was wearing now as he watched me watching him. For some reason, that dimple changed everything; transformed him in my mind to just being a boy on a beach.

"Hello?" I watched his lips move, turning into a full-fledged laugh as he waved his hand in front of my face, bringing me back to the present.

Oh, crap. And just like that, I reverted to the outcast kid that knew she didn't belong.

"Um. Hi. So, yeah, do I know you? I don't think I know you. I mean, I've only lived here a few months and classes just started. B — I mean Bethany Jackson — dragged me to this thing. She really just wants to see Micah and I couldn't deal with all the people and the dancing and the booze and…" I was floundering, looking in every direction but at him. I was doing the motor-mouth thing I do when I don't know what else to do. I hate meeting new people, especially people that feel way too familiar to be strangers.

"So, I'm just gonna go. Um…have a nice night," I stuttered as I tried to move around him. Mentally, I couldn't figure out why he was even still standing there after all of my rambling. Then, he grabbed my arm. Not hard, but enough to stop my sloshing through the rising surf. Just the contact of his fingers flared my power in a way I'd never experienced. It was like Pop Rocks under my skin, fizzing and bursting in small explosions beneath his fingertips. I quickly balled my hand into a fist and willed the rising power down. I could already feel the pressure and my energy level intensifying. I had to get control. I had to get out of here.

"Wait. Just, wait." His voice was quiet and I could feel his curiosity. His emotions were so clear to me. I stopped and met his eyes. It was dark and I still couldn't tell what color they were. For some reason, I was dying to know.

"I've seen you before. You're Amelia, right?" He looked me straight in the eyes, still holding onto my arm, making it hard to think.

I nodded, "Yeah." *Brilliant response, Ame. Just brilliant.*

"We have a couple classes together, but you always sit in the back and never say anything."

My eyes squeezed shut. I was ashamed of my inability to make new friends and blend in. My deep-seated need to stay under the radar. *This is fabulous.* I went to move away from him again as he stuttered, "Oh. That was dumb. I'm sorry. Anyway, I'm Aidan. Aidan Montgomery."

That's when he finally let go of my arm, only to trail his fingers down my forearm and grasp my hand in his, leaving pinpricks of heat everywhere he touched as he attempted to shake my hand. He gave me his first full-on smile and the corners of his eyes crinkled. I saw the adorable gap between his teeth, and ran.

I had to restrain the energy pumping through me, keeping myself at normal speed as I scooped up my sandals and bounded up the stairs. I pushed back through the crowd, shoving and elbowing the drunken partiers out of my way as I went out the front door and to my car. I would text Bethany to let her know I was leaving and could come back for her later. I sincerely doubted she'd even notice my absence since I saw her laughing with Micah as I ran through the house. I jumped in to the old Buick, locked the doors, and finally exhaled. I could still feel the exact indents his fingertips had made on my arm, the electricity still bubbling and some part of me already missing him.

Holy crap. Who was that guy?

Chapter 2

I was lying in bed the next morning, my arm thrown across my eyes, my hair tangled and spread across the pillow. I probably shouldn't call it a bed. Really, it was a twin mattress thrown in the corner of my room, but it was there and I was trying to convince myself I could still sleep. Last night's dream hovered on the edges of my mind, but I was used to being able to block out the hazy ones. Hazy nights were the best nights because it meant I actually slept. This morning's problem was that every time I closed my eyes all I could see was him. *Aidan*.

I had a hundred questions I wanted to ask him but had no idea why. More than anything, I wanted to know how he was the first boy I'd ever met to make me feel like this; like I'd been lit on fire from the inside out. Even though I've never had a real boyfriend, I have had crushes before, but no one had ever stopped me in my tracks like he did. My curiosity about him almost outweighed how hot he was. Almost.

Finally, I gave up, forcing myself out of the bed and into the bathroom. The hot water would soothe out the tension and the coffee pot in the kitchen would do the rest. Of course, as I padded into the kitchen after my shower, Bethany was already holding my mug out toward me as she stood at the counter stirring her own. She was an early riser and already cheery at this ungodly hour, even though she'd been out late last night and had been dropped off by none other than Micah himself. I had heard their futile attempts at whispering as I stared at the ceiling hoping for sleep.

"Ame, you know I was right, right? That party was exactly what we needed. Girl, you've got to get out more. Meet a guy like Micah!" She bumped me with her hip and tried to hide her Cheshire smile behind her coffee mug.

I harrumphed a little and rolled my eyes.

"Oh, no you don't, honey. You aren't raining on my parade today. I'm riding high and I have his number to prove it!" Bethany sauntered into the living room like she was walking a pageant floor. She had a box full of trophies claiming her title of Miss Sweet Pea, Miss Rankin County, and a host of other things, so she strutted like a superstar. As she settled into the couch, I was met with a perfectly-sculpted arched eyebrow and the question I dreaded most. "So, where exactly did you run off to last night? Did you meet a guy? You're holding out on me, aren't you?"

I hated how excited she looked at the prospect and how well she could already read me. But, for whatever reason, I just couldn't tell her about Aidan. I didn't know exactly what to say; how to describe the oddest encounter I'd ever had with a guy. How to explain that someone who initially seemed so dangerous didn't feel that way at all. I just knew I would sound like an idiot.

"You know me. I wandered around for a while, got bored, walked the beach, and then headed home. I wasn't actually feeling the greatest and I didn't want to bust up your moment with Micah." I hated lying. I hated how necessary lying was.

"Really? Another migraine? Well, that sucks. Next time I won't bail on you. Pinky swear. We'll make the rounds together and see if we can find you a matching cutie so we can do doubles!" Bethany dropped back into the couch with a wide grin.

I could only shake my head and laugh as I headed back to my room, leaving her to reminisce about last night. Curled into my beloved chocolate brown papasan chair, I tried to relax as my fingers slipped and slid across the satin edges of the blanket that hung over the side. Even after months spent with Bethany and realizing that she was the first real friend I've ever had, my first true best friend on top of that, I was afraid of her judgment. There was so much I wanted to share with her, but it just wasn't possible.

Early on, I had tried to explain some of my background and why I am the way that I am, but it wasn't like I could explain my powers and where I really came from. I told her about my mom and tried to explain to her that my relationship with my father was rocky at best, and basically non-existent at worst. That my only real friend growing up was my nanny Rynna, who had been my mom's best friend.

It wasn't always this way. At least, that's what my brother, Cole, would tell me before he left me to handle my Dad and his paranoia on my own when I was ten. There was apparently a time when my family was whole and my dad wasn't crazy, but that was before my mom died, which also happened to be the day I was born.

Moving to Brighton had never felt like a choice to me. It was where Cole finally settled after traveling the US for years. When he left, we had made a promise to be together again, and I had clung to that promise every day. It was what kept me going. Cole had opened a MMA gym a few years ago and, between the college kids and the locals, it was doing really well. He also had an amazing apartment and said he would help me out with anything the scholarships wouldn't cover. So, when I turned eighteen the summer after I graduated high school, I told my father I was leaving.

"What do you mean you're going to live with your brother? Just out there, for the whole world to see you? Haven't you listened to me at all?" my father said, his arms an animated swirl around him, gestures punctuating every question.

We were sitting at the kitchen table in a rare moment where my father had left his study and seemed lucid, and I couldn't stop fidgeting with my coffee cup as I tried to hold his gaze and be the adult I thought I already was. It would have helped if the questions he asked were rational, or if his too-long dark hair wasn't sticking up in every direction. If the glasses he shouldn't need weren't smudged and his eyes weren't wide and looking a little too wild. I knew this look and where our conversation was headed before I even answered, but I also knew it was time. I had played my part. I made sure he ate, I got good enough grades to get scholarships, and more than anything, suffered through his endless rants about how it didn't matter what he'd said eighteen years ago, I wasn't going to marry the prince and "they could never have me".

I tried to speak softly, but firmly. It was as if I were the one talking to their child, instead of the other way around. "Dad, I did listen to you. I've heard everything you've said. But, I have to do this. No matter what happens, I know that I have this time — just three years — to myself. The queen has kept the prince as far from me as you've kept me from him. You won't even tell me his name. I can't keep watching the years waste away, Dad. I've got to have some of my own life before this betrothal goes into full effect. And, I'm going to be near Cole, I'll still have family close."

I winced as he slammed his palm on the wooden tabletop. "Don't you talk to me about *him*! You know that I regret that moment. If I could take it all back, I would. You shouldn't do this, Amelia."

I sighed and tried to put my hand over his, cursing myself for bringing up Cole and aggravating the situation further.

"I know, Dad. It's just...well, I'm not asking. I'm telling you that I'm doing this." I tried to hold his confused stare but couldn't. "I just want you to know that I won't be alone, Dad. I'll be okay. I'll make friends — human friends. It will be everything you ever wanted for me."

"No, Amelia," he said, sounding defeated. "This is nothing that I wanted for you. I wanted to go away from here. I wanted to take you far, far away, but I...I just...couldn't." I watched his pupils dilate and the flash of green that meant he was losing control again.

"They are watching, Amelia. They are always watching. They can't believe it; they can't believe you have what they want," he said.

He was looking around the room as if Queen Julia's Hunters were right there, listening behind the pantry door. I couldn't take it when he got like this. "They'll leave you alone, you know that, right? You just have to try a little harder to convince them. You have to stay in *control*, Amelia."

I had grown to hate the word "control" more than anything in the world. I was a constant failure at it, and that one word was the source of almost every argument my father and I had ever had. Taking a deep breath, I tried to placate him, to stop his hands from shaking as his emotions swelled and the pressure in the room grew. It was a struggle to maintain my own power as it fed off of his, my emotions rising in reaction to the despair I heard in my father's voice. I had long-accepted his eccentricities but it wasn't often that his anger gave way to fear, as it was doing now.

"It's okay, Dad. I'm going to be okay. I'll do everything you taught me. I won't use my power. I'll stay under the radar. I'm going to be fine, Dad, do you believe me?" His fingers tightened on mine as he nodded a little too frantically. Standing, he yanked me in for a rare hug. "Just watch for them, Amelia. They are everywhere. Watch for them and stay in control."

The weight of my lies were a stone on my chest as I tried to relish our short embrace, nodding into his shoulder at the appropriate times. I was going to Brighton to experience a normal life — that part was true — but I was also going to try to figure out exactly who I was. I never believed I could get out of the betrothal, but at least I could go in prepared — something my father refused to do for me. There had to be someone out there that could explain what being an Elder meant and how to control the power that was growing faster than I knew how to handle.

I moved through the morning in a bit of a haze. I went to class and took my notes, but never really contributed. With everything my father had ingrained into me, I still didn't like to draw attention to myself even though my almost-black hair, hazel eyes, and slim figure would always make me more noticeable. Realizing that I would likely run into Aidan today, I had put in a little more effort than my normal thrown together outfit. It shouldn't matter — he shouldn't matter — but I was still a girl and he was still gorgeous. I don't know how I'd never really noticed him before, but a lot of our classes were seminars with tons of people in them and I never made efforts to seek out new friends.

Before I stepped a foot in the door of Composition, I knew Aidan was there. From outside the room, I could feel my internal reaction. It was as if we were back on that beach and the pads of his fingers were burning their marks into my skin. It was uncomfortable and exhilarating, my body reacting to just the nearness of him. As I walked into the room trying to reconcile myself with the heat in my veins, there he was, the guy setting the fire, sitting right there in my normal back row seat.

I stood awkwardly for a minute staring at the back of his head, not sure what to do. He was fully immersed in conversation with a guy one seat over, fist-bumping and laughing over some story being told. I caught just the slightest stiffening of his back as I moved through the doorway. He knew I was there too, but didn't even acknowledge me as I walked past him and sat a few rows up and to the left. My annoyed stare could have bored holes in the back of his head as I walked past, even though I realized that he very well could have chosen my seat without realizing it. It was ridiculous that I was so irritated, and just the fact that he could get me worked up was making it worse. I couldn't stand how much I wanted to know more about him.

I got myself settled, already hating my middle seat but pulling out my notebook and our poetry assignment for today's class anyway. As I was leaning up from my backpack on the floor, I stole a glance in Aidan's direction through the hair that had fallen in my face, only to find myself locking eyes with him. He was staring right at me — his chin in his hand and a slow smile creeping across his face, not even remotely trying to be subtle. I couldn't move. As if in slow motion, I saw his right eyebrow raise and humor shine through his eyes. It was no coincidence that he had taken my seat today. He was issuing a direct challenge and I was having a hard time backing down. I narrowed my eyes as if to ask him what he wanted, and he did the damnedest thing — he winked at me.

That tiny motion brought me back to myself. I whipped back around and started straightening my papers, fidgeting in my seat. I heard a low chuckle from behind me and just *knew* it was him. It reverberated through me and sent a burst of heat to my cheeks. Apparently, the good-guy act from last night was just that. This guy was a player. *Great. Just what I need.*

The classroom door slammed and we all turned in surprise to find a man standing just inside the room. He looked uncomfortable in his wool cardigan, dress slacks, and Buddy Holly glasses. I couldn't tell if he was going for Mr. Rogers or a failed attempt at hipster, but thankfully he broke the silence as he surveyed the class. "Ms. Brown is ill, so today's class is canceled." I was disturbed by how his eyes seemed to linger on me, but he finally turned on his heel and left.

I quickly gathered my things and bolted out the door. The hallway was empty since the other classes were already in session, making it a quick jaunt out into the commons and toward my car. I was just cutting across the last patch of grass when I heard footsteps clearly running to catch up.

"What's your hurry, doll? We never got to finish our conversation last night." Aidan fell in step with me, the dry grass crunching under his flip-flops. With all of the contempt that I could muster, I glanced his way only to find him giving me a cocky half-smile. I stopped short, finally noticing the eyes I found so intriguing last night were actually gray. It was like staring into smoke and I was caught off guard by the flecks of bright blue scattered throughout his iris.

"W-we weren't having a conversation last night," I stuttered. "You surprised me, and then I realized I had somewhere to be." I tried my best to sound distant, pulling my posture up to at least pretend I could look down at him as if he didn't have me by at least a few inches. I finished with, "I've got no real interest in knowing you. I've seen your type." I don't know why I said that. It sounded weak and silly and I didn't even mean it, but Aidan was just unnerving.

That eyebrow rose again but he didn't comment on my ridiculous statement. "You had somewhere to be? At midnight on a Thursday? In the middle of a party you were clearly trying to escape?" I could feel him holding in his laughter. Damn it, this guy irritated me.

"Yes," I snapped. "And, what I do or don't do is absolutely none of your business." With that, I hit the keyless entry, tossed my backpack and purse in my car, and climbed in. I gave a fake wave, complete with a roll of my eyes, and backed out of the spot. In my rear view mirror, Aidan stood in the grass looking confused and mildly amused with his hands in his shorts pockets and head cocked to one side. I had to force myself to pull my eyes away and put the car into drive, but that didn't stop me from glancing up a few more times as I pulled away.

Chapter 3

I was making a half-hearted attempt at my algebra homework when my phone rang. Rynna was calling for a check-in and I was glad for the official distraction. My mind had been constantly wandering off since I got home. All avenues pointed to Aidan and what I should have said differently, or how I could have made myself look any more foolish. I sighed as I slid my finger across the screen.

"Hey, Ryn!" I couldn't help but smile as I answered. Rynna had been my rock during the rough years after Cole left, and I fully credit her with me being as functional as I am today. She also provided a constant connection to my father since he refused to use telephones. Just another one of his wonderful eccentricities.

"Amelia, I wasn't sure if you'd pick up. I just wanted to let you know that things are going…okay." Rynna's soft, proper voice floated through the speaker but I heard the muted panic behind her words.

"Is he eating? Will he even talk to you yet? Ryn, I've been gone for two months. Please tell me he's at least talking to you?" My father had never engaged with Rynna. Since my mom had died, he hadn't spoken a single word to her. My father was an odd man. On the worst days, he was outright mean. She had been my mother's best friend and they had all grown up together, yet he refused to acknowledge her existence. He hadn't actually even hired her to be our nanny, she just took it upon herself and continued to show up. For years she cooked, cleaned, and helped with homework for free. She always said mom would have done it for her if the situations were reversed.

She sighed and I knew she was holding back. "Come on, Ryn. Just tell me. Did he light the barn on fire again? Finally kill the neighbor's dog?" I had to make light of the situation because there were so many worse things my father could have done.

"You know I try to keep you out of these things, Amelia. Your father...he's just having a hard time. He's...lonely." Her hesitation only made my reaction worse.

"LONELY?" My blood pressure skyrocketed and, with it, my power bounded through me. A headache started to take hold at the base of my neck. It was the one I always got when too much power let loose too fast. "Rynna, you honestly think he's lonely? I spent years under that roof and was lucky if he spoke to me once a day. You think *he* is the *lonely* one? I have one friend here and can barely

28

manage stringing a coherent sentence together around new people."

The temperature in the room rose and I knew I had to get myself under control. No one could send me into a tailspin like my father, and Rynna knew that. All those years of me desperately trying to make him show me an ounce of affection, even knowing he was the one who gave my future away.

"Now, Amelia, calm down. Honey, be fair. You know that your father hasn't been himself. Your leaving has just been…a transition." Her quiet patience was doing nothing to tamp down my anger. My *guilt*. I knew when I left that he wouldn't take it well, but I only had these few precious years to myself.

"Just tell me," I gritted the words through clenched teeth, trying to hold back tears, already expecting the worst.

Another sigh. "Well. He left. He moved out into the woods. He said that with you and your brother gone, he doesn't have to do it anymore. That he can be free, whatever that means. I don't think he really means it, honey, I just think he's hurting. You know how his delusions take hold. We just need to wait him out a little bit. I won't let him go far, you know that, right?"

Rynna continued on, trying to smooth over the words she knew cut me to the core. Hurt flooded my heart and my mind. *He can be free.* I dropped to my bed as the tears threatened and Rynna's voice faded into the background. I bit the inside of my lip, the metallic taste and the shot of pain stopping the onslaught of emotions. I was on my own. *I've always been on my own*, I reminded myself. Swallowing down emotions I didn't want to acknowledge, I hung up the phone, not caring if Rynna was still on the other end.

After my conversation with Rynna, I tried and failed multiple times to focus on my homework. The longer I sat there, hearing her words inside my head, the more my power spun and built inside me. From the deepest corners of my heart, the hurt bubbled over and my power was quick to respond. Ever my internal champion, it warred with the pain — pushing, shoving, and growing in response. I was a war-torn battlefield of emotion. My gut ached, my anxiety built, and the power vibrated through every cell. Something was going to have to give. There was only one place I could go, one person who would understand what I was dealing with.

As I pulled up to Cole's gym, I felt ready to burst. All of the pain and anger my father's words had stirred up inside me were snowballing into something near hysteria. My power and emotions were so closely tied that I couldn't control either. I needed Cole and needed him quickly. I had to keep myself from running into the training room looking as frantic as I felt. Luckily, I didn't even have to get all the way through the doors before Cole was pulling me into a hug.

In a split second, all of his strength and soothing emotion enveloped me and the swirling inferno slowed. This was Cole's gift, his ability to calm the raging storm of my emotions, and thus my power. Before he left, from the time I was a baby until I was ten, he would be the one to pull me out of my nightmares and allow me to sleep. He was also the one to help me keep my power in check, to stop the surge before my father sensed it and locked me in my room again. Dad always claimed it was for my own protection, so *they* wouldn't see. So *they* couldn't know what I was. But, they had to know. The Hunters had arrived just after mom died and they knew I was an Elder. The Hunter knew exactly what he was doing when he demanded my betrothal to the prince.

Cole's strained voice broke my train of thought. "Hey, there. It's okay. Ame, what happened?" He had my head tucked under his chin and I had to turn it to the side to stop my voice from being muffled by his shirt.

"It's Dad. Rynna says he took off. Since we're gone, he can finally *be free*." I punctuated those words with as much sarcasm as I could before tears filled my eyes and a sob filled my chest. Cole was the only other person in the world who understood what our father could do to a person's self-esteem; what spending a childhood with him could do to you. It was why he left when I was ten and he was eighteen. At that point, I wanted to hate him for it. Now, I understood. Even then, I understood that it was because of me that he had to leave. I was born and mom died. Mom died and dad went crazy. It was all because of me.

I pulled away, furiously swiping at the tears on my cheeks and feeling even more ashamed for needing my brother, yet again, to save me from myself. "I'm sorry, Cole. I shouldn't be here. I shouldn't be putting this on you. I don't know why he does this to me. Why I let him."

Cole's aura changed from soothing to angry. He wasn't trying to help me anymore. He was pissed. "Damn it, Amelia. Don't *do* this to yourself. How many times do I have to tell you this isn't your fault? None of it is. If you need me, you come to me. That's our agreement."

Cole lightly gripped my chin between his finger and thumb and forced my head up to meet his eyes, his voice softening to a whisper. "Right, Ame? That's our agreement. That's why you're here, so I can help you. You know that's what I've been trying to do ever since I left."

The anger had melted away and I saw his own guilt over leaving me; felt him showing it to me. I sighed and moved in for another hug. "You're right," I mumbled into his chest. "And, it's not your fault either. God, I hate how screwed up he's made us."

"Speak for yourself, half-pint, I'm doing just fine." A laugh rumbled in Cole's chest and I pulled away smiling, blinking back unshed tears. Cole ruffled my hair and slung his arm over my shoulder. "You look like hell, Ame. How about you go get cleaned up and I'll buy you some dinner. Unless, you want to take a turn in the training room? It might do you some good."

I seriously considered it for a second, but right now I needed food more than a heavy bag. "Nah, soon though. I'll come in and have at it. And really, Cole, at least I don't smell like a mix of sweaty boy and dog," I said with a snort. "Did you and Charlie work out together today, because pheeww! Besides, you know I can't turn down a free meal." Trying to get things back to normal, I stuck my tongue out at him for the full effect and got a poke in the ribs for my sass.

"You leave my dog out of it. Charlie might be a brute of a dog but he's worth every gnawed table leg and new pair of running shoes I've had to replace," Cole said. The vision of his giant Great Dane snacking on his table leg gave me a chuckle.

I know Cole will never see me as an adult, but I can't help but play the part of the younger sister. I'd missed him. Even though we only spoke through letters and emails, Cole never let his "big brother" status slip.

I made a pit stop in the bathroom and spent a few minutes staring in the mirror. Focusing, I was able to concentrate on my red, puffy eyes until my power finally responded to my command and moved to that area. I watched my eyes brighten and the dark circles fade, feeling pleased with what I could accomplish. It was still a work in progress, but I was slowly figuring out how to conquer the basics. I'd been blowing things up in bursts of power for years, but even Rynna hadn't been allowed to explain the little things.

We left the gym and headed out to the boardwalk. The waves crashed in the background as we walked silently toward our traditional dinner stop — Mariano's. We both loved Italian and Cole was forever carb-loading with all of the time he spent in the gym.

I turned to look at him as we walked. Of course, my brother was a good-looking guy. Any decent sister could admit that. But, over the years, it's been so interesting to see him change through pictures, and then to see him now in person. He's different. He tries to hide his own anger and pain, but I can feel it. I still don't know exactly what he went through in the time since we'd last seen each other, but he promised that one day he'd tell me. Still, there are times when I'm shocked that I can walk up and hug him.

Cole was on the shorter side, though still taller than me, with really broad shoulders and a trim waist. His hair was a little longer, just brushing his ears, thick and dark like mine, but more brown than black. With his powers suppressed, his eyes were the darkest brown, like Dad's. He had kind of a big nose, which once I realized, stirred a memory inside of me I had long forgotten. I stifled a giggle, remembering an instance where Cole had picked me up to carry me inside after I'd scraped my knee. I looked up to say something and found it hysterical that he had such a big nose. My six-year-old self couldn't contain her laughter and he had blushed the darkest shade of red.

"What's so funny over there, eh? What are you staring at?" Cole gave me a shove as I pointed my finger at my nose and gave him a look that made him realize exactly what I meant.

"You're pushing it tonight, girl. It might be bread and water for you!" He crossed his arms, his biceps looking like they might actually burst, and tried his best to give me a haughty look. He totally failed.

"Right, Cole, you'd leave your only darling sister to starve?" I clutched his arm and leaned my weight into him, acting as if I would die without food that moment. Two seconds later, his arm was wrapped around my head. Putting me in a choke hold, he ground a noogie into my hair and shoved me toward the door of Mariano's with a laugh. "Get in there, half-pint. Let's eat."

Later, I took a break from shoveling pasta into my mouth to ask the question that had been burning in my mind, the one I asked every week when we had dinner. "Have you learned anything new lately?" I tried not to look hopeful, but knew I failed miserably when Cole laughed at my expression.

"Not really. I just can't believe that no one will even talk about who and what the Elders used to be. I understand that Queen Julia and her Hunters have scared the crap out of every Immortal out there, but there has to be somebody that can tell us what's happening to you."

Cole looked defeated. His eyebrows were drawn together and his scowl deepened the longer he thought about it.

"I know Cole, I'm frustrated, too." I tried to sound reassuring, "But, you've been asking questions for years. I know that has to be part of why you moved around so much while you were gone. Maybe we should stop pushing. I'm going to have to do this no matter what. The queen wants a magical puppet for her prince and I drew the short straw." It was just the reality of the situation, no matter how much we both hated it.

"No, Amelia. I won't. I won't stop until I figure out how we can either get you out of this betrothal or at least get you prepared to handle it. We've talked about some of what I've learned, but there are a lot of things I've never told you; things I didn't want to have to tell you. It's probably time. You need to understand what you're up against and the deadline is only coming closer. The queen will come to collect."

There was a different emotion in his voice this time — fear. Just the edges of his irises were turning green and I could feel the change in the air around us. I grabbed Cole's hand. "Hey. Hey, Cole. Not here." He was lost in his own thoughts and I wondered what it was he was seeing behind those eyes. What memories were replaying in his mind to take him out of our conversation and somewhere else entirely? I gave him a few more seconds, but when I couldn't seem to get his attention with my hushed whispers, I kicked him under the table. I hadn't thought it all the way through and my Cherry Pepsi was almost upended as my foot not only connected with his shin but also the table leg. Cole came out of his trance and reached out faster than he should have to stop it from tipping over. He quickly glanced around to make sure no one was watching and then scowled at me. I shrugged.

"What'd you want me to do? You just disappeared over there."

Shaking his head, Cole gestured for me to continue eating. We ate in strained silence as I continued to wonder what he wasn't telling me, and Cole maintained a look that told me his mind was elsewhere. Finally, he paid the bill and led me outside. We walked silently along the beach for a few minutes until he plopped down in the sand and gestured for me to join him. After a few more moments of silence, he finally spoke.

"You know that when I left and told you that I had to get away from Dad, it was really so I could help you, right?"

"Of course, Cole. I mean, no, I didn't know that right away, but eventually it made sense. And, I knew Dad was too much for you. After knowing him and Mom before…well, before me, you knew what you were missing. I never did," I said.

"Don't do that. Just don't," he said, turning to me to make his annoyance clear. "We aren't going there today. I left because Dad was never going to help you and you were finally old enough to keep yourself together while I was gone. I knew that Ryn would be there, too. I thought there had to be people out there — our people — who knew what you were going through. It wasn't right that he handed your future off and then refused to teach you what to do with what you had.

"I started out young and stupid and way too obvious. I knew that some of the larger Mage populations in North

America were in the North West and the upper Midwest. It wasn't hard to find them once I got close — I could feel their power like I do yours. But, when I outright asked other Immortals about the Elders, they would just turn and walk away from me, refusing to acknowledge the question. So, I got a little stealthier in my approach. I had to give myself time to become part of their community and not just some stranger off the street. I did a lot of odd jobs. I found myself in conversations where after a few drinks, it was easier to pull out a few details here and there. I kept journals of everything I learned so I could connect the dots later. And, I always tried to find out where the next closest community was before I started in about the queen or the Elders, in case I needed to move on."

It was odd to reconcile the stiffness of Cole's posture with the easy-going flow of his words. There had to be so much more he wasn't saying. So, I sat silently, waiting.

"I actually focused a lot during those first few years on the queen. It was just as hard to get people to talk about her, but once I found the right person and we were in the right environment, they'd let loose for hours. Like I said, give them a few drinks out by the lake where no one else was around, and all these Mages wanted was someone to listen. They had lost family or friends to her demented plans. Damn it, Amelia, I never even wanted you to know this stuff." Cole dragged a hand through his hair and finally looked over at me. "I was so naive and I thought I was going to find some hidden answer. Some way to either get you out of this betrothal or to unlock whatever power you have that she wants. To give you time to use it, master it, and go in there with a fighting chance."

I looped my arm awkwardly around his neck for a half-hug. "I know," I said. "It just isn't that simple, Cole. It never has been. And, given the way my crazy power has been acting, I don't know if I want any more of it unlocked." He patted my hand, nodding. I settled myself next to him again and he continued.

"You know the basic history. You understand how the Hunters work for the queen and the AniMages have been exiled. You know about how Elders used to be in positions of power working with Queen Julia. But, nobody talks about how or why that changed. That's what these people told me. They told me both how and why. Somehow, Julia found out how she would die, so she started taking out anyone who could possibly be involved. She didn't know when it would happen, so her plans were mindless and insane. Some of the people I spoke to even shared their memories, the same way dad has before. The first time it happened I was talking to an older man who had lost his wife to one of Julia's raids. Mid-sentence he couldn't speak anymore, so he just reached over and touched my temple. His memories will forever be burned in my mind."

Cole shook his head quickly back and forth, as if he were trying to change the channel in his head and make those scenes stop. I wasn't sure how much more of this I truly wanted to know. Even though I needed to, I refused to ask for more details. Not yet.

Cole carried on. "Okay, remember the history lessons from when we were little? Our races have been around for hundreds of years. We can be traced back to the Fertile Crescent and Rynna told us our parents grew up in Syria where the main castle and communities stood. What we weren't taught was that there was a time when the queen was nothing more than a figurehead. Everyone always talked about Elders being so powerful, but from what I understand, it's so much more than that, Amelia. Elders weren't just powerful Mages. Elders were *the most powerful* Mages. They led us all. And by *all*, I mean that in the beginning, all races were equal. The Elders oversaw Mages, Hunters, and AniMages alike. It was Queen Julia who changed everything, and she was also the one who forced the silence about what really happened. She put a fear into the hearts of all Immortals so deep, she was sure no one would defy her." The way his face pinched together, his lips a thin line as the tendons in his neck protruded, made it clear that my brother's hatred for the queen went far beyond the conversation we were now having.

"There used to be a group of Elders," he continued. "Five families made up the Elder lines and only the women could pass on the Elder power. Female Elders were revered. They were the ones who foresaw the future and ruled our people. The male Elders had power, but nothing like the women. It's like you and me. I have some extra power, but what you have is far beyond normal. You have the trademark purple Elder magic. I just have Mage green. Anyway, the oldest female in each family served on the High Council and their wishes were carried out by the queen. She got jealous. She couldn't take being ordered to carry out the whims of women she felt superior to; orders she disagreed with at every turn. She started plotting out ways to overthrow the Elders and take control. But, she needed help.

"Julia was smart. She knew the Hunters were more powerful than even she was. They can track the other races, have extremely powerful attacks, and seem to have very little emotion, so doing Julia's evil bidding never seemed to bother the Hunters she initially recruited. Realizing what a partnership with the Hunters could do for her coup to take over the realm, Julia began polluting their minds with stories of blood line pollution, weakening races, and the inevitable death of their clans if they didn't act. She was smart enough to allow her recruits to spread her stories to their clan leaders and it didn't take long for them to call a meeting. Not everyone bought her story but Julia continued to make her case, charming the leaders in whatever way she needed to. Finally, the clan leaders voted and though it wasn't unanimous, it was decided that the Hunters would align with the queen. Problem was, Julia had found a way to trick them into making an oath of servitude. In one fell swoop, the Hunters became her Royal Guard and captives to the crown.

"The Hunters brought in anyone who could give Julia information on the Elders' weaknesses — whether the captives wanted to contribute to her plan or not. That was a lot of what people talked about — the kidnappings and interrogations. Eventually, the queen figured out that if the Elder families were separated, especially when the female Elders were separated from their mates, their power dwindled. As their power lessened, she was eventually able to kill them. No one is entirely sure how she did it or, more likely, how her Hunters did it, but Elders who were caught were never seen again."

Chapter 4

"So, how do mom and dad factor into this then, Cole?" I finally asked. "Mom was an Elder. They got away. How did they manage to survive?"

Cole kept his gaze fixed on the water. "I don't know, Ame. But, I heard stories; stories of an Elder who got away. Of one who could see the future and had the power to make a difference. Any time I asked if people knew of Elders still out there, she was who they talked about. I think it was Mom. And, if what they tell me is right, she was it. She was the last Elder left alive."

"Until me." It wasn't a question.

"Until you," he responded quietly.

"That means there isn't a group of Elders for me to find. No one who understands. You and I are it. Dad isn't an Elder, it's just us." I dropped back into the sand as the thoughts kept coming. "There aren't any more answers... I'll never know what this power is, what it can do, what it shouldn't do. The queen will come for me. I'm bound,

Cole. I'm bound to this betrothal, for better or for worse."
My breathing was labored as I recovered from the hurried
rush of words that had tumbled from my mouth.
Questions rose in my mind, popping like bubbles only to
give way to more.

What does Julia want with me?
What can she do with me?
What can I do to stop her?
I am the only one.

From what Cole had said tonight, the entire Immortal
community was terrified of Julia and her Hunters. How
was I going to be any kind of match for her? I didn't even
know what I could do, let alone what she could make me
do. The fear overtook me so quickly it was like a punch to
the gut. My power rose in tandem with the onslaught of
emotion and the two fed off of each other. My hands
started to shake as violet threads of smoke swirled and
grew around them.

"Cole," I whispered, pled. I could feel what this was
about to become and we were out in the open. No one
could see the violet ball of crackling light building around
my palms, but they would see the damage it did and I
didn't have the presence of mind to stop it.

Cole took a few deep breaths, quickly trying to calm
himself, and then swept me up into a fireman's carry. As
quickly as my power had grown, it scaled back down. I
could feel how angry it was, knowing it was so close to
being let off its leash. Thankfully Cole was here for me this
time. I was wrapped in his green blanket of calm energy

and it seemed to smother the bright purple veil pulsing around me. These times were happening more frequently, and I was afraid of what would happen if I lost control when Cole wasn't around to stop it.

It was awkward being eighteen and held like this by your brother, but it was literally the only thing we knew to do. And, the worse the episode was, the more contact we needed to calm it down quickly. I'd been able to keep a fairly decent hold on it for a while now but, in the last few weeks, it seemed like all of my signals were scrambled and I never knew what might happen. Not to mention, I just kept learning more about my past and my future, and not much of it was feeling too positive. Well, except maybe Aidan. Thinking of him helped me even out my frantic breaths and added another layer of calm. As soon as Cole felt me return to normal, he set me beside him, and we scooted apart.

"You know we can't do this forever, right?" I asked the question, but knew neither of us had the answer. He nodded. "Yeah, I know. I'm going to start reaching out again. There are a few people I haven't been able to find who could help. You might be the only female Elder, but you're not the only Elder, I won't let you face this alone."

As I pulled into the parking spot reserved for my afternoon classes, Aidan was on my mind again. I didn't want him to be... but I couldn't help that he was. It was the same internal struggle that I had been experiencing daily. I was drawn to him. By what exactly, I didn't know. I wanted to know more about him and the way he affected me, yet, when he tried to engage me, I bristled and tried to push him away, hearing Cole's words in my mind about who Queen Julia was and the realization of what being an Elder truly meant. What being the *only* Elders could mean. And then there was the betrothal, which was ridiculous, but still a factor. I didn't know what my destiny was, but it didn't seem right to drag him into it. However, the fact that I couldn't get him off my mind had to mean something. I was still pondering the oddity of the situation as I entered the building and found him sitting outside my seminar.

"You've got to be joking," I said with a hand on my hip, trying to sound irritated when I was truly thrilled to see him again. Every time I was near him my heart raced and giddiness spread through my veins. All of my concern over the queen and my future just dropped away in those few moments I was with Aidan. I stood over him as he reclined on the bench outside the door to my class, looking far too calm for how worked up I was. His hair was disheveled and just the front of his red polo was tucked into his dark jeans. The black ink of his tattoo drew my eyes away from his, to his impressive bicep, and I had to force them back. I waited for a reaction as he quirked an eyebrow and shoved his phone down into his front pocket.

"You know, Amelia, you really need to relax. Everything isn't just about you." Aidan's face reflected the humor in his tone, his eyes laughing.

"Really? Somehow you've managed to just appear in not one, but two of my classes?"

"Actually," he said slowly, giving me a look of mild annoyance, "we have three classes together. And have for the last month. So glad to know I'm so easy to miss."

He pushed himself off the bench and tossed his backpack over his shoulder, meeting me eye-to-eye. I couldn't help but take a step back. I was afraid he'd hear the thunderous pounding of my heart, yet I couldn't hide the red flush creeping across my face.

"Do I make you uncomfortable, Amelia?" His voice was low as he matched my backward step with a forward one. The look in his eyes made it clear that if I were running, he'd be giving chase.

I swallowed and tried to project a confidence I didn't feel. "You wish, Montgomery. You just seem to irritate the crap out of me."

I turned on my heel, felt his eyes on my back, and struggled not to react to his deep chuckle as I rushed away and into the room. Trying to calm my frantic heartbeat and the electricity that came with every one of our interactions, I took a seat in the back corner, as I usually did. I was comforted by the fact that I could see him, but he had to make it obvious he was watching me. Unfortunately, he didn't seem concerned over making his interest obvious and turned in his seat multiple times throughout the lecture to catch my eye. I wanted to look away, but I found myself holding his stare every time, memorizing the dimple that came along with his smirk of self-confidence.

As we were dismissed, I tried to get out quickly, to avoid Aidan completely and get myself together, but just as I pushed through the double doors outside, he caught up to me. "Hey, doll, you're running off again. You can't avoid me forever, you know?"

I kept walking. "Can't I? You don't quite seem to be getting the hint. Or haven't you noticed that I just keep walking away?"

I slipped my sunglasses on, feeling smug as I turned to do just that — and ran straight into a wall. Of muscle. Of Aidan. He had cut off my escape. As I not-so-gracefully tried to keep myself from falling over and then attempted a glare up at him, I found Aidan smiling down at me. "Well, that stopped you, now didn't it?"

We both looked down and I realized I still had both hands pressed against his chest. In that same instant I both heard and felt a familiar *crackle* and *pop* and we recoiled from each other.

"What the hell?" he yelped. Aidan stood rubbing his chest as I stumbled for words. "That was some… uh, static shock. What did I tell you? You should just leave me alone." I tried to sound nonchalant and failed miserably.

"I don't know why you seem so offended that I'm interested in you, Amelia." He stepped forward again, thankfully not noticing the small burn hole in his T-shirt.

I struggled to maintain my position, not wanting to give him an inch but afraid of my potential reaction doing more than burning his shirt if I touched him again.

"I can read you, doll. I can see that you aren't as offended as you want me to think." I stuck my chin out defiantly but got caught in Aidan's stare. The gray in his eyes deepened from smoke to ash and I was sure he could see right through me. "Again, Montgomery, you're out of your league. You don't know a thing about me or what I want. You're going to need more than a wink and pretty smile to make this happen."

I stepped around him as he clutched his chest, saying, "Ow, now that one hurt. Insulting a man's pride is just too far."

"This is what I'm saying. You don't want to take me on." I tossed him a smile that was more confident than I felt as I strode away, fervently trying to maintain a normal pace and not sprint to my car, all the while wishing I had a reason to look back and see if he was watching me go.

This continued with Aidan; him popping up before and after my classes. He was never intimidating or creepy, but made it obvious that he was interested and thoroughly enjoyed rattling me. I'd never really done this dance with a guy and my reactions were varied. I generally ended up berating myself as I walked away from him for the latest dumb thing I said, or reminding myself for the billionth time that this game was a terrible idea and that I should just walk away. We both could get hurt and I had a commitment that included both a crazy queen who wanted to abuse my power and an unknown prince who was likely just as deranged. But, with each interaction, I found myself smiling more, laughing with him, and hoping these encounters wouldn't end. We were slowly building the base of a friendship, learning more about each other — our interests and our pasts.

Given all of that, I wasn't too surprised to find him sitting underneath a tree near where my car was parked after classes one day.

"You understand this is bordering on stalking, right? I could probably convince someone a restraining order is necessary." I couldn't help but smile as I said it. Over the last week, I had actually found myself looking forward to our sarcasm-laced interactions.

He didn't miss a beat. "Well, if you'd stick around for more than two minutes at a time, you'd figure out that I'm not a bad guy. And, you could just face the fact that you've been waiting for me to ask you out."

His cocky grin did me in and I couldn't stop the laugh that erupted. "Oh, really, is that all I need to do? Give in to your manly prowess? Just accept my fate as your next conquest? You really haven't learned anything about me, Montgomery, have you? Try again."

I flipped my sunglasses down from on top of my head, but not before I sent him a saucy wink of my own. I was finally getting used to this game, but I wasn't ready to give in just yet. I should stop, but it was just too much fun.

I turned to toss my backpack into my car and heard my name from across the parking lot. Looking up, Bethany was waving her arms and beckoning me over. I tossed a, "Later, Montgomery," over my shoulder as I strode back toward the main building. "There will definitely be a later, Amelia." He hadn't said the words loudly, but they echoed through my system and I couldn't stop the little shiver that went up my spine. The electric fire that shot through me every time he was around put an extra pep in my step and I almost skipped across the parking lot.

As I approach Bethany, she immediately looped her arm through mine. "What's up, buttercup?" I joked as she pulled me toward the campus coffee shop.

"Oh no you don't, Amelia Bradbury. You're not changing the subject on me. I want to know who that lovely hunk of tall, dark, and steamy was you were talking to. That's Aidan, right? From Humanities?"

It had taken me a month to realize he was in the same class as me. How exactly is it that everyone seemed to notice this guy but me? Was I that socially awkward in our first month of classes?

Without Rynna and then Bethany, I would have hit rock bottom in my downward spiral of social awkwardness. Growing up, Rynna always pushed me to try to make friends, while my father strictly forbade it. In my high school years, I went full rebel and signed up for public school. In that experience, I found a few girls willing to take pity on me and let me sit at their lunch table. In those uncomfortable years, I learned quickly that if I found a way to make things funny, people would pay attention to me in a positive way. When I met Bethany, I was the person I had grown to be — the sarcastic version of my former self — and we instantly clicked. She also took over where Rynna left off, forcing me to constantly interact with people. That first month of class was rough, though. I basically hid in the back of every class and tried to stay under the radar, but Bethany made me branch out of my comfort zone once more.

I shook my head to clear my thoughts, but confirmed her question. "Yep, that's Aidan. He's been… uh, hanging around lately." I hadn't explained any of my interactions with Aidan to Bethany yet. She was caught up in her budding romance with Micah, and I was still trying to figure out exactly what Aidan and I were doing.

"Sweetie, you've got to get with the program." Bethany gave me an exasperated look and an exaggerated sigh. "I know this is new to you, but besties tell each other *everything*. You're holding back and I can feel it, so give it up." Bethany pulled me to a stop and crossed her arms, making it clear we weren't going to get that caramel latte I really wanted until I started the story.

"Okay, *okay*!" I laughed as I put both hands up in surrender. "Coffee first, story second."

"HA! I knew it!" She clapped her hands together as if she'd actually won a prize. "I knew you'd been too quiet lately. You do that, you know? You clam up when things are brewing. I can always tell." I had to laugh at her self-assured tone and serious look. She was right, she knew me better than most and I didn't know how to not be an open book. It had caused problems between my dad and I for years because I couldn't hide the fact that I couldn't control my powers, and sometimes I didn't want to.

I was able to order my latte in peace, but as soon as we were tucked into our favorite overstuffed chairs in the back corner of the coffee shop, Bethany demanded the full story. It was hard to figure out which words to use with her. I wanted so desperately to explain the strange feelings Aidan stirred in me, but that would take explaining my powers. Some of dear old dad's lessons stuck with me and I wouldn't expose Bethany to a world that could hurt her. But, I seriously wanted to tell her that every time Aidan got within fifty feet of me, I felt this buzzing in my blood, as if my body were just waiting dormant for him and once I could see him, I came alive. That Pop Rocks feeling would bloom and spread, his touch like fire on my skin. Not the burning kind, but the kind you wanted to lean toward and soak in. If this was lust, I wasn't complaining.

So, I sat there for a few seconds, sipping my latte and trying to determine where to start. I had just opened my mouth when I saw Bethany's eyes go wide and light up. "Well, hiya, Micah! Fancy meeting you here!" Micah came around the back of my chair and sat on the arm of hers.

"Well, hello, ladies. How are you both today?" Micah was oddly formal. From what I had learned about him from class and Bethany, he was born in Europe somewhere, raised in boarding schools, and had pulled a typical rich-kid rebellion by moving to California and going to a community college instead of the prestigious Ivy League schools I'm sure he was accepted into. I'm certain his parents were thrilled.

While Micah and Bethany engaged in small talk, I picked up a magazine from the table next to us and began absently flipping through. My mind actually on Aidan and not seeing a single word, I missed it entirely when Micah addressed me directly.

"Amelia? Hello?" I quickly raised my gaze to his, trying to figure out what I had just missed, but something was off. I quickly stood and looked around. I could feel it. A strange pulling in the back of my mind. I'd never had that sensation before, but it was like I could feel someone trying to communicate with me, trying to tell me something. It's that same feeling you have when you're sure someone called your name but you don't see anyone you know. I don't know exactly what I was searching for, but I kept scanning the coffee shop.

"Ame, honey, what the heck are you doing? You look a little crazy right now." Bethany's quiet concern brought me out of my trance and I noticed a quick look of surprise flash in Micah's eyes before he stood as well.

"Um. Sorry, guys. I swear I heard someone looking for me or something," I said as I took one last look around. Bethany laughed and said, "Your ears are burning, huh? That's what my mama would say."

Micah gave me the strangest look that disappeared as he turned to Bethany with a smile. "It seems as if I've interrupted something. I'll let you two get back to it.

Bethany, I'll be in touch later to set up dinner this weekend, if you'd like."

She was glowing. "I'd love that, Micah." A few bats of her eyelashes and I actually watched him soften a little as he took her hand and kissed it. I thought it was over the top. She, on the other hand, melted. "Until then," he said, and walked away stiffly without another word to me. Bethany actually sighed.

"Oh, B. Really?" I teased. She tossed her balled up napkin at me in protest.

"You just shush, Amelia. Just because I enjoy a little romance to go along with my Viking hottie, doesn't make me any less of a woman." I couldn't stop it this time, I doubled over as the laughter overtook me. Then, Bethany was laughing too. We were like five-year-olds, both red-faced with tears leaking from the corners of our eyes. I was struggling to catch my breath as we calmed down, but I couldn't help taking one last dig. "Watch out B, he might call your daddy for permission to take you out to dinner." That got me a good kick in the shin as we both laughed some more.

She did end up getting the Aidan story out of me, just a very short and condensed version. She was pissed that I hadn't told her about our night on the beach before now, but got over it as she went into match-making mode after I told her about his continued quest to take me out.

"Amelia," she gushed as she leaned in toward me, almost whispering, "You need to do this. You need to let this thing with Aidan happen. You told me you came to

Brighton because you wanted to really experience life outside of where you're from, away from your crazy dad. I know your brother is here and it's awesome you guys are catching up, but you deserve a little romance. College is when you figure out who you are. Maybe Aidan can help!" She made a suggestive face and gesture that had me muttering about her southern propriety, or lack thereof, as we tossed our coffee cups and went to go our separate ways.

"I'll think about it, B. I just don't know yet."

She gave me a quick hug and said, "Honey, maybe that's what you really need. A little bit of 'don't know' to liven things up."

If she only knew how much my life was a constant stream of "don't know", she might have suggested otherwise.

Chapter 5

Bethany and I only shared one class, a class Micah was also in given the googly-eyes I watched her make at him for an hour and fifty minutes twice a week. Humanities was also the third class I shared with Aidan. I smiled a little when I walked in. He was at least sitting *next* to my normal back row seat, instead of in it, which had been his M.O. lately.

"I wanted to make sure you didn't miss me this time, doll, so I saved your seat." His mouth turned up as he tried not to smile.

"Well, aren't you a gentleman," I said as I rolled my eyes and scooted around him, "and I'm not your doll. I'm not anyone's *doll*." As I tossed my bag in the seat to my right, I saw a small, white daisy sitting on the built-in desk portion of my seat. I couldn't move, I just stood there awkwardly staring at the dainty, beautiful flower. The whole flower head was maybe the size of a golf ball, it was no dozen roses, but it was the first time anyone had ever given me flowers... or one flower. Ever.

Aidan reacted instantly to my stricken face, his hopeful look disappearing as he misjudged my emotion for disdain. He stood and tried to grab for the stem, but I simultaneously leapt for it, yelling, "No!" As skin met skin and our hands collided, I heard a *crack* like lightning hitting the ground and I flew backward, catapulting a few rows of seats below us.

As I came to, the first voice I heard wasn't one I expected. But, I knew that formal tone and squinted, my eyes opening to confirm Micah's scowling face inches from mine. "Amelia, we do not have much time before Aidan and Bethany get back with a nurse. You've got to get some control. I have no idea why you would expose yourself like you just did, especially to a human, but reign yourself back in. And for goodness sakes, change your eyes back!"

Through my foggy state I watched Micah's eyes blaze red for a split-second before they reverted back to blue. As what he'd just said and done sunk in and I realized what that meant, I couldn't stop myself — I fainted.

"Ame, come back to me, honey." I heard Bethany's soft southern lilt as something cool was placed on my forehead. I struggled to open my eyes and then snapped them shut again, remembering Micah's warning. Doing my best to shove the power pulsing through me back into the little corner it hated, I hoped my eyes were back to their normal color. As I slowly opened them again, I first saw Bethany hovering over me with a relieved smile as her eyes connected with mine, and then Micah and Aidan in the background.

We were in the hallway outside the lecture hall and I was lying on the same bench Aidan had been occupying yesterday. Bethany was holding my hand. "Cheese and rice, girl, you had me worried. One second I'm laughing at Micah and the next you're flying into the back of our seats. I know you're a klutz, but how in the heck did you manage that?" Her accent was more prominent when she got upset, and the words came out as one hurried sentence.

Before I even had a chance to respond, Aidan spoke. My head was still throbbing and I was afraid to even attempt to heal myself given what had just happened. I tried to look toward him, but couldn't focus between the slices of pain that accompanied every breath.

"Apparently she doesn't like daisies." I could hear his sarcasm, but what I felt was something else altogether. I could see the angry red aura pulsing around him, but his hurt and embarrassment radiated just as strongly. Before I could argue and explain, Micah stepped toward Aidan and put one hand on his chest, pushing him backward. "Montgomery, do you really think that's what she needs right now? Do you think the best plan is to further insult a girl who went so far as to do herself harm to get away from you? Maybe you should just take the hint."

I had to squint to focus through the pulsing pain but I saw Aidan's face transform. He looked down at Micah's hand and then slowly back up to his face. He stepped toward Micah, simultaneously wrapping his hand around Micah's wrist. Each movement slow and deliberate. Then, he shoved Micah backward, pushing at him with his own arm.

His voice was menacing and the threat in his words was palpable in the air. "You don't touch me. Ever. And—"

"Why don't you just get out of here, Aidan?" Micah interrupted, stepping back into Aidan's face. "What good are you really doing?" Micah gestured back toward me at the same moment I winced from the loudness of their exchange.

I watched Aidan start to speak, opening and then closing his mouth as he looked from me to Micah and back again. His posture stiffened, his fists clenched, and I saw exactly when he decided it wasn't worth the fight. That I wasn't worth the fight. Without another sound, he turned on his heel and stalked away.

I wanted to stop him, to explain somehow, even knowing I couldn't. But, Bethany put one hand on my chest as I made a pathetic attempt to sit up, effectively stopping any movement.

"Nuh-uh, sister. You let him have his snit. You're going home," she commanded.

I refused to let Micah carry me, shoving his hand away and glaring at him with all the contempt I could muster through my throbbing skull. Instead, I leaned heavily on Bethany as she led me out to the car. I laid down in the back seat, willing us to be home so I could stop my head from pounding and the nausea rolling through my system.

Closing my eyes against the pain, I thought, *Why would Micah care about me?* Before I could ponder that question, the darkness that had been threatening to pull me under since I had awoken finally won, and I passed out again.

Later that night, after I had been able to lock myself in my room and heal my physical ailments, I stared at the computer screen trying to do homework. It was pointless. All I saw was Aidan's face as Micah basically told him this was all his fault and I wasn't interested. I replayed each second in my mind as he decided that Micah was right; he didn't even ask me, didn't even confirm what I thought. Why hadn't I just spoken up? Shoved Bethany aside and forced my way between them? I was pissed off and my heart hurt — too bad I couldn't fix that pain.

I wanted to call Aidan, but I didn't have his number. I thought about emailing him, but explaining that I wanted him more than I had ever let on didn't seem like something I should do over email. Frustrated, I slammed my hand down on my desk and watched the violet streaks shoot out like sparks, burning the wood.

I was so confused. I wanted Aidan. I didn't want to want him, but was it so bad that I did? I mean, why couldn't I want him? Why couldn't I have anything of my own? I'd never had a boyfriend; I'd never even really had friends until now. Everyone in my life had either walked out on me or constantly reminded me of my failings. What about me was so terrible? Why did everyone feel so entitled to tell me how I needed to live? And, who in the hell just offers their daughter's future to a queen everyone hates and her devil spawn?

"Dammit. Just DAMMIT! What about what I want?" I couldn't stop myself from yelling the words. Bethany was at the library and, without truly thinking about it, I had given my power license to run rampant through my veins. I could feel the buzzing build from the ends of my hair to the tips of my toes as it flooded my system, going full throttle.

I needed a release. I stared down as the wisps of violet floated around my fingertips, curling around each digit and waiting to be sent somewhere. This was not going to be a night where I could shove it back down. I had never let my power loose of my own accord, but in that moment, I decided tonight was the night.

I grabbed an old sweatshirt, pulled my purse over and across my body, and let the front door slam behind me. The pent-up emotion I shouldn't be letting get the best of me demanded loud and dramatic acts. I stomped down the stairs, my tennis shoes making a distinct *thud* on each step and echoing as I strode down the hall and toward the back door with purpose. Without even caring who saw me, I shot a blast and sent the door flying open. I allowed a wry smile as I walked through the door and saw the charred section where I'd struck. I was just getting started.

I walked the trails behind our complex, feeling as if I were floating. The dry dirt barely responded to my footfalls and the brush seemed to bend away from me. The release I needed would cause a scene and I needed some privacy. But, with every step I took, every second longer my power was off its leash, it seemed to double and triple in intensity, growing well past my ability to stop its trajectory.

I was aware, but I wasn't. I made conscious decisions but then chose trails without knowing why. Thoughts continued to spin and swirl in my mind. Those, meshed with the emotions I couldn't control and power I'd never felt, were a dangerous combination.

Aidan's eyes flashed in my mind.

I want him. I want to know him. I want him to kiss me.

My hair was floating as if static electricity coursed through every strand, creating a popping cacophony as it danced around my head.

This is my life. I'm eighteen. Why can't I want him?

I began to walk faster and the muscles in my legs started to burn. The ache was welcome, it brought me back to myself for a brief moment.

He doesn't know or care what I am, and he still wants me.

I found myself pushing into the trees and off the formal trail — looking for what; I wasn't sure — but knowing I was going where I needed to.

I heard my father's voice in my mind. *You can't have him. The decision's been made.*

I let a scream of frustration out into the night, hearing the anguish echo softly back to me in the light breeze. Allowing my fingers to graze the solid tree trunks, I tried to let the sounds of the night overtake me. Soothe me. Calm me.

The choice isn't yours. It never has been. It never will be.

I bit the inside of my lip, attempting to focus on the salty iron-tasting liquid and not my raging mind. I failed miserably.

Why? Why isn't it mine? Why is no decision mine to make? Why isn't he allowed to choose me?

I swallowed back the tears forcing themselves to the surface. I walked and walked, finding myself on the rocky ledge overlooking the water. I had no idea how far I'd gone but the walk had only increased my fury, not dampened it as I'd hoped.

But, he wants me. He's choosing me.

As I stood on that ledge, I closed my eyes and let the waves of energy thrum through my system. I heard each heartbeat *whoosh* in my ears and was more alert and alive than I had ever been. Yet, I felt nothing like myself. The tingles in my fingertips told me it was time to let it loose. Energy pushed from the inside out and I expected my skin to stretch and bulge from the pressure trying to force its way from me. In that moment, I allowed myself not to care. For just one minute, I decided to do what felt right. As I stood on that ledge, I closed my eyes and let the As my hair floated in a dark cloud around me and the breeze whipped around my body, I simply let go. I allowed every wall I had built, every fence I had erected to come crashing down. I pulled from the darkest recesses of my soul and gathered each molecule of power I had denied.

No one was watching. No one was judging. There was no one on this deserted stretch of rock but me. I opened my eyes to see violet streams pouring from my palms. White slashes shot through the purple blast, blending with the current connecting to the rocks below me. They shattered. Boulders the size of beach balls were obliterated into clouds of dust that disappeared as each wave hit and dragged the bits and pieces back out into the black water.

I couldn't help but laugh as I moved my hands and directed the bursts. The beach slowly grew larger as the rock piles disappeared. I had created my own symphony of light as I tried to vary the intensity and destruction of each blast. The sky was lit in violet and glowing white. The clarity and crispness I saw in everything around me was breathtaking. I held my hands in front of me and saw the shifting violet smoke weave its way up my arms and around my torso.

I'd never known this feeling. The only releases I'd ever experienced were the ones I failed to stop and those were wrought with shame and fear of the consequences.

Tonight, though — tonight was mine. I stood on those cliffs for as long as my body would let me blow the rocks below to smithereens. Shooting blasts out into the water and watching it erupt as if it were the Bellagio water show. Violet bursts of light flew from my palms, growing and shrinking in tandem with the mental commands I was giving. I couldn't believe how freeing it was to push all of that energy out of me. To allow it to freely move within me and around me, guiding my thoughts and actions. In the same moment, I saw through my own eyes and those of an outsider peering back at me. I felt whole and powerful. While I wanted to continue on forever, I knew I had to stop. Reigning my ecstatic power back in, I felt satisfied.

I regretted the act, but it was necessary to pull the strands back toward my core, escorting them back to the safety of their little corner inside me. I could feel the frustration, how much it hated being tied down and not allowed to accompany me in the way we just had, but I was tired.

Feeling the last rogue bits of energy resign to their corner, my body became solely my own once again and I was suddenly overtaken with fatigue. I slowly dropped to the ground. Folding in half and then falling to my knees, each one of my muscles seemed to give way at the same time. I tried to reach out and steady myself on a nearby tree but my vision wobbled, zooming in and out. My arm and hand appeared as one, then four, then two, and back to one again. As I tried to find my balance and push myself up, the dark veil of exhaustion reached up and took hold, collapsing me into the dirt.

I awoke hours later. The sun was starting to come up and as the light hit the water, the sky bloomed in oranges and pinks, the water reflecting the start of a new day. I struggled to open my eyes and felt the grit of the sand on my cheek. My arm was still outstretched and every muscle in my body moaned as I struggled to sit up. I managed to pull myself to a seated position and sat with my knees drawn and my arms folded on top of them. I stared out at the sea. I was dirty and tired but actually at peace.

I thought back on my rage and what I was able to do with my power. The night seemed like it had happened to someone else, like I was seeing my memories playing on someone else's TV. And, though the catalyst was Aidan, the real source of my angst rested with my father. It was laced in our every interaction, in every moment I failed to maintain control and he withheld the only thing I needed from him because of it. He had walked away from me again and again, leaving me to fend for myself; to close myself off and distance myself from the power that sat at the core of who I was. After tonight, I knew for certain that I had no idea who I truly was.

I was an Elder. The only female Elder, apparently. My destiny was set, based on power I barely understood. Power that could be used to cause more harm to our people. Maybe I could stop the queen; maybe nights like tonight were just the beginning. I hadn't chosen this, but it had chosen me.

With a sigh, I pushed myself to stand, knowing that what I wanted still didn't matter. Just like I always had, I would make the choices I'd been told to make. Realizing I would have to push Aidan away caused a deep ache to pulse inside of me, my gut clenching in physical response. Our game couldn't continue. Soon, I wouldn't be strong enough to walk away. It wasn't an option to stay.

I snuck back in to the apartment and was, thankfully, able to drop onto my bed just before Bethany's alarm went off in the next room. I was exhausted but knew what needed to happen. My father was on my mind, so I shot Rynna a quick text asking for an update. I wanted to not care, but I'd been bound by duty for too long.

Chapter 6

All day long I was well aware that Comp class was coming and I was dreading it. I didn't know how to handle Aidan. It wasn't like we were officially dating, but there was clearly something there. There was more than casual banter and we both knew it. Now, I had to stop it. I was essentially breaking up with him before we started dating.

I worried that I would see that look again, the one he'd worn as he walked away from me last week. Under my own constant waffling, I could feel my power fizzing and popping angrily in its little corner, threatening to burst out. While being around Aidan set my magic off in an entirely different way than I had ever known, it had never been negative. I always walked away from him feeling a sense of happiness I had never found anywhere else.

I was sitting on a picnic table outside, lost in my own thoughts. I hated knowing what was coming. Knowing that even though it technically was my choice to walk away, it didn't feel like one. It wasn't the choice I wanted.

Suddenly, I heard a loud *thwack* and a backpack landed next to me. Micah plopped down at the table, sitting opposite of me.

"Um, can I help you?" I had successfully avoided him and his prying questions for a few days, but I couldn't outrun him forever.

"I have been looking for you, Amelia." He cocked his head, his blond hair getting a little wind-blown since it wasn't tied back. He shoved a hand through it, putting me directly in the path of his bright blue eyes. "We need to talk. I think you have some explaining to do."

I honestly had no idea what to say. I just stared at him, wondering what to do next. I was shocked when he leaned in with a mischievous gleam in his eyes and whispered, "We Mages have to stick together, you know." My jaw dropped and was still hanging open when Bethany swooped in moments later. By the look of it, she knew Micah would be finding us at lunch today. She was in her favorite skinny jeans with the sparkly design on the butt, a flowing electric-pink top, and four-inch stilettos. I had never been happier to see her than in that moment. Micah didn't miss a beat, he scooted over and gave her a killer smile.

"I swear I'm going to fail French," she whined as she tossed her silver Coach handbag on the seat next to her. It was more of a luggage piece with handles, but "a girl could never be unprepared". I was fairly certain she could save a small country with what's in that bag. I focused in on Bethany, refusing to acknowledge Micah and his blatant admission. I'd seen his eyes after the incident with Aidan and I'd assumed he was also a Mage, but I'd never known a Mage to just out themselves like that.

"The instructor hates me," she continued. "I don't understand all the verb tenses and I can't even figure out how to ask where the bathroom is. Does she not understand growing up in Mississippi means I've already mastered what most consider a foreign language?" Bethany dropped her head back and groaned loudly, pulling me out of my own head as I stifled a laugh at her theatrics.

Micah also chuckled as he turned to face her. I wanted to be happy that he was giving her so much attention, but I had to keep myself from scowling at him as I wondered what he was doing with a human. How was it that he was lucky enough to get to make his own choices? Then, as Aidan crept into my head once again, I realized that was the pot calling the kettle black. I couldn't stick around to witness him being able to have the thing I was about to give up.

"Well, I'm going to let you guys sort this out. I've gotta get going anyway. Later!" I couldn't move to grab my backpack and untangle myself from the table fast enough. As I turned to walk away, I caught a look from Micah that clearly told me our conversation wasn't over. Bethany gave him a shove and demanded his attention again, taking his focus off of me. God love her, I was so happy she could keep him occupied. "Bye, Ame! See ya later," she chirped. The last thing I heard was her giggle as I hurried away.

He's here. *He is here. Dammit, he's already here!* I couldn't believe my eyes as I walked into class and found Aidan, once again, in my seat. This time though, he was the only one in the room. He turned around, as if he were simply biding his time, waiting for me to arrive. He stood and gestured to the seat he had just vacated. "I was just making sure no one else took it. I didn't want to cause any more issues." I'm sure he meant it to be funny, to make it easier to broach the topic of what had happened last week, but him making the incident a big joke just sent me over the edge.

"Can you just stop? I mean, for once, Aidan, can you just stop with all the funny-guy flirting? Didn't you get the message the other day? I'm not interested. We're not doing this...this thing we've been doing...anymore. So just stop." My voice was cold and callous as my insides were shredded and my power flared in response to my words, sending a clear message that it disagreed with my choice. Lightning zipped through me, trying to push out and reach toward Aidan. I dropped my backpack to the ground and crossed my arms across my chest, trying to protect myself from my own undoing.

I had known what I wanted to say, but I hadn't intended to just blurt it out like that or use those exact words. I hadn't meant to sound like a rude and intolerable bitch. But, I did and I had, and the expression on his face made me regret every syllable. His smile instantly disappeared and the laughter in his eyes died, replaced by hurt and anger.

"So that's it then, you just decided?" he exploded. "That's just great. I was going to apologize for being a jerk the other day, for what it's worth." With that, he picked up his backpack, moved to the front of the room and didn't speak again. After class, I wanted to stay and apologize. I tried to reach out to him as he walked by but he looked down at me with so much disdain, I couldn't find the words.

"Don't do that," he said with a snarl. "Don't apologize to me. Just own it, Amelia." He rarely used my name and that one word held so much contempt, I hoped to never hear it again. He stalked away and I stayed in that seat for much longer than I anticipated, waiting for the threatening tears to pass. I had mistakenly thought we could just flirt and play and no one had to get hurt. Unfortunately, now we both were. He just didn't know it.

"What happened? Honey, you're forgetting again." Bethany held up her pinkie as a reminder that I was withholding information yet again. She settled herself on the opposite end of the couch from me and crossed her legs over each other, the look on her face relaying that she didn't hold much patience in waiting for me to start spilling my guts.

I wanted to talk about it, I wanted to share every last detail and be the best friend I was supposed to be, but all I had thought about all day long was how dangerous this world was for humans. How my own selfish wants to be "normal" and "have my own life" really meant that I would drag people into my crazy world who didn't belong there. But, I had to say something. I *wanted* to say something.

"I don't know, B." She was glaring at me when I looked up, daring me to lie. "I just...I mean...just, dammit." I rubbed my hands over my face and yanked my hair back, using the band around my wrist to control the tangled mess. "The Aidan thing is done."

As the word "done" left my lips, it held such a finality in my mind that the tears I had been pushing back all day let loose with fervor. Before I could stop it, I was sobbing uncontrollably. I'm sure it made no sense for me to be losing it over a guy I'd never even been on a date with, but Bethany would never know the depth of where those tears came from, of everything I'd never had that I'd already given up.

The wonderful part was that she didn't ask and didn't seem to care. Instead, she scooted to my side and pulled me in, letting my tears soak her shirt and rubbing my back while she whispered soothing words. As the tears slowed and I could breathe again, I started to apologize. Bethany shushed me immediately. Taking my hands in her own, she said, "That's the thing about best friends, sweetie. We're here when you need to cry it out, even when the reasons don't always make sense.

"Honey, are you sure it really has to be over?" She tilted her head, pausing before she spoke again. "I mean, it seemed like you really liked him and things were just getting started. What happened?"

I was still sniffling and the heavy weight in my chest threatened to release another flow of tears as I tried to pull the right words forward. I used an old trick Rynna had taught me growing up when my father was having a particularly bad day. I pictured all of my sadness over walking away from Aidan as a ball inside of me. I rolled the ball of emotions tighter and tighter together until it went from feeling like a basketball down to a ping pong ball. Then, I mentally put it in a closet and walked away. It took all of ten seconds to do this in my head but when I opened my eyes, I felt like I could breathe. Like I could actually explain myself.

Bethany was still holding my hands in hers and she gave them a comforting squeeze as I opened my mouth to speak. "It's complicated, B. But, it just wasn't meant to be. I mean, you saw how he just walked away the other day. He's just a player. He just wanted a new shiny thing to play with and I was the flavor of the month." I wanted my words to be true. I said them with a confidence I absolutely didn't feel and Bethany seemed to have her own issues reconciling the words.

"Are you sure, Ame? He really seemed into you from what I saw. Maybe you're reacting a little too strongly on this one. I know guy stuff is kind of new to you, but maybe you need to give him a chance. Clearly you aren't happy about this decision."

She just wanted to help, for me to be happy, but if I kept debating this with her I would either break down again or I would end up telling her the truth.

"Look, B, I know you mean well, but this is one of those things I need you to just stay out of." I pulled my hands from hers and tried not to wince at the shock on her face. Her southern propriety took over a split-second later and she plastered a fake smile on her face. "Well, okie doke. This one's your call, girl. I'm just gonna stay out of it." Her voice was too chipper and I immediately knew I had hurt her feelings.

"B. Damn it. I'm sorry. I didn't —" She cut me off before I could even finish. "Nope. Don't even do it. It's fine, girl." She waved it away as if it were an annoying fly buzzing around her. "It's just fine," she said. "But, I need to head out to the library. I'll just see you later."

Within minutes, she was gone, and I felt more alone than I had in weeks.

I had a day without Aidan in my classes and the reprieve was better than I had imagined. I hadn't stopped thinking about him for a moment, but not having to stare at the back of his head and watch him walk past me without even acknowledging my existence was something I needed. Unfortunately, I couldn't seem to get a reprieve from Micah, who was driving me crazy.

"You realize we still need to have a conversation, right?" he asked for the fifth time this week. I groaned in response.

"Yes, Micah. Yes, I've heard you each and every time you've asked. But, I'm not ready to have that conversation and I have bigger stuff going on right now than having a bonding session with you over things we shouldn't be talking about in public anyway." Part of me knew this conversation with Micah was the reason I was here. All I had wanted was to have someone explain to me what was happening inside me. Micah though, I didn't trust him. I hadn't trusted him when I thought he was just a guy and I surely didn't trust him knowing he was a Mage. I was just going to have to find my answers elsewhere.

"You do realize he isn't good enough for you, right? That you can do better?" His words were sharp and cut me to the quick. Fire raced through my veins and I turned on him.

Pushing one finger into his chest and shoving him backwards, I said, "You don't know me, Micah. You don't know anything about me. Don't you dare presume to know who is or isn't good enough for me just because we share this ridiculous *thing*. I didn't ask for this and I don't want it. I'm just stuck with it. I don't want to talk to you about it and you can't make me, no matter how long you follow me around." The violet strands that wrapped around my outstretched finger pulsed brighter and brighter. Micah's eyes widened as my eyes changed to match the magic building around me.

It took me a moment to realize everything had stopped. As I glanced back and forth in the hall, everything was frozen and the fear in Micah's eyes was apparent as he, too, couldn't move. I closed my eyes and tried to breathe. There had been just one other time where I had done this, I was about twelve and my father caught me trying to use my power to heal a bird I had found with a broken wing. He came storming out of the house as I was gingerly holding the small bird amid the swirling violet smoke and whispering, "Heal his wing, heal his wing, heal his wing." Even though I thought I had been hiding in the barn, he somehow always knew when I was using my power and snatched the tiny creature from my even smaller hands. Based on the look in his eyes, the frantic "hide the truth" look I always saw when he stopped me from using my power, I just knew he would kill it to stop me from trying to help it.

I screamed as I reached out with both hands and it all stopped. Though his eyes flashed green and stayed that way, my father was completely frozen. So, I carefully took the bird from his frozen palm and ran off. I didn't come back home for hours, terrified of how long I might be locked in my room this time, but he never spoke of it again. He did, however, give me a wide berth for a few weeks.

I looked around at the immobilized students in the hallway, took another deep breath, and whispered to myself, "Let them go, let them go, let them go." The only thing I could think to do was tell my rogue power what I hoped it would do. It was only a few more seconds before the noises resumed and everyone continued on as if nothing had happened. Micah, on the other hand, looked a little wary. Clearing his throat, he stammered, "Well, that was, um, interesting. You, uh, might want to reign that in if you don't want every Immortal within a hundred miles making a beeline for you."

I simply stood there, feeling ashamed and frustrated, not even fully grasping what Micah had said until he walked away. *Why would I be drawing anyone to me? Couldn't everyone do this stuff?*

Chapter 7

That was two. Between the night on the cliffs and my run-in with Micah, that was two major magical outbursts and Cole had to be looped in. He'd been my constant, even when he was gone, and I always told him when I learned something new about myself. He had been mentally cataloging all of my random acts for years and trying to figure out why my power was so different from everyone else's while he traveled the country. We knew we were Elders and that Elders were supposed to be pretty powerful, but now knowing Queen Julia killed them all, it made sense that they were another thing no one talked about. Just like AniMages. So, there were no records specifically of the female Elders' scope of power, no stories told at school or history lessons on the heroines of our time. My violet eyes were a dead giveaway for anyone who at least knew that much about Elders, but even those people seemed few and far between. The Mages I had grown up with never saw me lose control, so they never commented on my distinctive power color.

I walked into the gym to find Cole in his office. I didn't knock; instead, I just dropped into the seat in front of his desk. Without even looking up, Cole said, "You have something to tell me?"

I was standing there, mouth agape. "How do you do that, Cole? How do you always know?" I never got used to him being able to read me like that.

He finally looked up and his eyes gave away the concern he had been trying to hide. "Ame, I felt you before you even walked in the door. Something happened that you didn't like and it's hurting you. I can feel it all." He shook his head in clear exasperation. "We've got to find someone who can help you start to hide that stuff. I just wish I knew how to help," he sighed, also constantly frustrated that his own power wasn't consistent or easy to explain.

"It's happening again," I said. "The random stuff I don't mean to do. Well, I guess one of the times I meant to, but then I was blasting rocks apart and it felt really good. But, today...today I froze a hallway of people. All of them, Cole."

I went from remembering the high of being out on those cliffs to the low of knowing I had affected so many people unintentionally. I know I didn't hurt them, but I shouldn't be able to just do this kind of stuff on accident.

"Oh, and after the rock blasting thing, I passed out. Like, completely dropped to the ground and lost a few hours." Those words were a little more subdued. I looked up from under my lashes, a little afraid of his response. Knowing Cole was always concerned, I wasn't shocked to find him staring at me open-mouthed.

"Just gonna toss that one out there, huh? No big deal? You passed out after blasting rocks apart on a cliff and that's just typical Amelia, right? Froze a bunch of humans on accident. Standard week, eh?" The sentence got louder with every word and he was hollering at me by the end. I shrunk a little in my seat. "It's one thing when you're trying to keep a lid on your power until we figure it out. But, really, Amelia, what do you want me to do? You completely lost control and woke up hours later on some cliffs? What if something had happened to you? How am I supposed to react when you tell me about this stuff?"

His accusing tone set me off in the complete opposite direction and I stood up to do some yelling of my own. "You? How are *you* supposed to react? I don't know, Cole, I'm not sure how *I* am supposed to react. I froze those people today in the hall while Micah was yelling at me about 'us Mages needing to stick together' for the umpteenth time and I couldn't unfreeze them. I didn't *know* how to unfreeze them because I didn't actually mean to freeze them in the first place. And, on the cliffs? That... that was amazing. That was the first time I've ever gotten to use my power the way I wanted to and it felt great. I felt whole and alive and real. And then, I crumpled. I couldn't even stay awake. So, you want to talk to me about what you're supposed to do? I don't give a damn what you're supposed to do. You just drop the bomb on me that I'm the last female Elder and, in all likelihood, I'm going to get used and abused by some psychopath, and I'm supposed to worry about how you're reacting?" I could only take shallow breaths as I struggled to tamp down the panic building inside me.

Cole put one hand up. Paired with the shock on his face, I just stopped talking. "Micah? Who is Micah? And how does he know you're a Mage? And what the hell are you doing hanging out with other Mages, Amelia?"

Ah, crap. I hadn't meant to tell Cole about Micah in this way but my big mouth never ceased to cause trouble. "Um. Well. First, let's be clear that I don't hang out with other Mages. He's dating B and he's just always around. It's not my choice."

Cole snorted and I knew what was coming. He was forever making fun of Bethany or complaining about how prissy she was. "Of course, your pageant queen roommate would find herself dating a Mage. Of course."

"I don't know why she bothers you so much, Cole. Bethany is seriously my only friend and she's great. I don't know what I'd do without her. Anyway, there was an incident in class one day where I, uh, fell over some chairs and when I woke up, Micah was there and my eyes had changed. We realized we had something in common and he's been bugging me about it ever since. Wanting to help me or something, but I don't know what he means." I selectively chose to leave out all of the parts having to do with Aidan. I'd made my choice, so there was no real need to explain him to Cole. "I'm just happy I finally figured out what it was about him that kept setting off my internal alarms. I guess I always knew there was something different about him, now I know what." I shrugged even though, in my mind, I felt like there was something I was still missing about the situation.

"Wait, Amelia. What do you mean you *knew*?" Cole looked confused, but I could tell his own wheels were turning. Before I could respond, he smacked his palm down onto the desk with a grin. "Yes! I remember hearing about this! This is one of those Elder powers. You can sense other Immortals. Everyone's radar is a bit different, but that's one of your gifts. What did it feel like? How did you know?"

Cole was still leaned across his desk, both hands resting on the top, eagerly waiting for me to tell him some great story. Unfortunately, the reality was much less entertaining. "I don't really know. I can feel him, and he feels weird. Whenever he's around, I feel like someone is watching me. Like I want to get away from him. I don't know. Maybe my radar is broken?"

I started braiding my hair as I thought back on all of my interactions with Micah. It was a nervous tick of mine to twirl the strands together while I pieced things together in my head. "Come to think of it, a lot of my outbursts have been when he was around. I think maybe my power recognizes that there's other power around or something."

I looked back across the desk and realized Cole wasn't even listening. He had sat back down in his desk chair and was using his feet to toss himself left and right. I could see he was deep in thought but my curiosity outweighed any politeness I should have had. "Hey! You! Cole!" I barked out the words and he jumped in the chair. "What's going on up there?" I asked, tapping my temple.

A slow smile spread across Cole's face. "Micah. He's our solution. We need to find out what he knows and see if he can help you!"

I jumped to my feet. "NO! No, Cole. I know what you're thinking and I'm not going to manipulate him. I can barely even stand the guy and you want me to cozy up to him? And what about B? How am I supposed to explain why I'm spending time with her boyfriend, huh?"

"Tell the princess you need a tutor or something. I don't care what you tell her. Amelia, we need more help than we even know. Maybe this kid can do something we haven't been able to do ourselves. At the very least, maybe he can introduce us to other people in the area. You don't know how hard it is to break into these ranks of people. We don't belong anywhere. We don't have family lines we can point to without giving away our Elder ties. We need an in. He could be our in!"

I started to pace the length of Cole's office. I saw his point. I didn't understand what he had gone through to get the information he had, but I knew it wasn't easy. If Micah could help us at all, it could really get us somewhere. I just don't like the guy. But, he treats Bethany well and she obviously thinks he's great, so there's got to be something there. I continued my internal argument for a few more passes of the office while Cole patiently watched me, waiting for me to process. Finally, I stopped and sat back down in the chair across from him.

"I'll try to make friends with him. I won't lie to him. I won't manipulate him. But, I'll see what he has to say." Cole tried to speak but I stopped him, pointing a finger and glaring until he closed his mouth again. "I'm sick of lying, Cole. I'm sick of half-truths and hurting people in the name of secrets. Hell, I'm sick of being hurt by all the secrets. So, I'm going to really try to be his friend. If it works, great. If it doesn't, he wasn't meant to help us."

He nodded and I knew he wouldn't fight me any further. "Alight, Ame, do it your way. I get it. You're probably right to want to do it this way. I'm too used to the secrets and having to manipulate people to get what I need out of them. Speaking of, I don't want to get into it now, but let's do dinner again soon so I can do some more explaining. I know you want to know everything right now, but it's easier for me to do in pieces." At that moment, I saw how tired he actually looked. I hadn't seen it when I walked in, but every time he talked about Queen Julia and the stories he needed to tell me, it was as if I watched him age right before my eyes.

"Okay, Not now, but soon. I've gotta go anyway, but I'll let you know how things are going. And, I know you don't really care, but I'm going to call Ryn tonight too so I'll let you know if Dad's back home yet." I glanced up, hoping I would see some sort of emotion, but all I saw was indifference in his eyes. He shrugged and came around to give me a quick hug. "Just don't let him get to you, Ame. It's not worth it. Ever." The words were quiet but the anguish behind them was a thick cloud of emotion between us.

As I walked back out to my car, I wondered what had really happened between my father and my brother. On further thought, maybe I didn't want to know.

The nightmares have been terrible this week. I walked around in a daze of exhaustion from nights spent lost. Literally. Every night it was the same bits and pieces that I could barely recall. Fog everywhere, surrounded by trees, me calling out constantly, and gray eyes with blue flecks. It was always just his eyes, but they were everywhere. As soon as I called his name and turned toward him, they would disappear.

I hadn't expected it to hurt this much. I hadn't thought that stopping a relationship that had never started would feel like I was being ripped open every time Aidan walked by. He still wouldn't speak to me, but I caught him watching me like he had in the beginning. He wasn't hiding it. There was no anger like I thought there would be, like there had been that first day. He just simply stared while I made every attempt to not acknowledge it, to keep myself from locking eyes with him and falling directly into the smoky gray depths that wouldn't let me back out. He was blatantly telling me without words that he wasn't going away and I couldn't even let myself think about what that meant.

I was stronger than this. I had to be. Cole and I had dinner last night and, after another story-telling session, I was even more convinced that I had to remain on course. I still didn't understand what deal my father had struck to allow me to stay with him and not be taken directly to Queen Julia. She could force me into this marriage but hopefully I could do something good with it. I sighed as I heard Cole's story rolling through my head once again. He spoke of torture chambers, of Hunters forcing themselves into people's mind and extracting the information they wanted. He spent a good deal of time going through the exile of the AniMages.

"Amelia, did you know that AniMages were once respected by all Immortals? That their ability to become any animal, to commune so closely with nature, was something we actually celebrated, not persecuted?" Cole looked so sad as he spoke and I wondered if this was one of those memories he'd been given that wouldn't go away. I simply shook my head and he continued. "No one really understands what exactly set the Queen on her rampage against AniMages, but one day they were a part of the council and the next they were being banished. Whole communities of AniMages were flushed out by the Hunters. The Queen ordered them out of the castle, off the lands that had been their hunting grounds for centuries. When villages weren't disbanded fast enough, the Hunters went in and forced the issue. She tried to tell people she never killed them, only forced them out. But, I've seen it, Amelia. Women. Children. Grandparents. Dead."

We were both quiet a moment as his words sunk in. I was sure visions of the massacre others had passed on to him were pushing through his mind as his eyes took on a far-off look. With a shake of his head, he refocused and kept talking. "The queen tried to justify her case by saying that the AniMages had been planning to overthrow the crown. Eventually, the Mages realized it was she herself who had that plan all along. She told people they were aberrations, a race never meant to be born and an evil mix of uncontrollable animals lucky enough to have some Mage abilities. She convinced the Mages that if they continued to allow intermarriage between the races that one day their children would come out all animal, no Mage left. She actually had people believing that the AniMages' animal sides held the most control and they couldn't be considered actual people because they were first animals. The AniMages that stood up against her were thrown in prison and weakened until they couldn't shift out of their animal form anymore. They were collared and chained up. Hundreds of them."

A quick jolt shot through me, a visceral reaction spreading from the deep recesses where my power was hovering, sending rage and shock through me in waves. "She's a monster. Cole, I just don't understand how this happened. How is it that everyone just blindly believed her? That they turned on their friends and neighbors so quickly? How was she able to keep everyone from even discussing it? I can't believe all of our people were so blind and stupid." I was just flabbergasted to think we had allowed this to happen. But, it was fascinating how ignorant a collective people can be. History has shown us that time and time again.

He shook his head and I saw light green flow around the edges of his irises. My own power responded to the surge in his.

"The best I've been able to gather is that between Queen Julia and the Hunters, they had something on everyone with any sway. They blackmailed. They threatened. And, a lot of people did what mom and dad did, they just left. They refused to be a part of it, but they also refused to do anything about it. Most of the people who would actually talk to me were ones who walked away from it all and tried to start a new life. As long as the Mage's didn't cause a fuss, the queen just left them alone."

I pulled the bottom of my lip between my teeth and tried to breathe. "It just seems so cowardly. To walk away from something like this. Our people needed mom and the other Elders. They needed someone with power to fight for them, not to just walk away." I was getting worked up. So much emotion coursed through me — anger, sadness, the want to do something *right now* to change things. Electricity crackled in my veins and I could feel the throbbing at the base of my neck signaling a release I wouldn't be able to stop if I didn't calm down.

Cole reached out, laying his hand over mine, and I instantly felt relief. His power was a soothing balm over the frenzied and frantic pulses running through me. My nerves were slowly becoming less raw and ragged as my whole system calmed. It was one of the few times my magic wasn't angry for being tempered.

"Maybe that's why this happened to you, Ame. You are the last Elder for a reason," he said, looking far too hopeful. "Because you have the strength to do what no one else seemed to be able to do. You can marry the prince and fight for the right reasons. We just need to get you ready."

I hadn't ever thought of it that way. I could marry the prince like I was supposed to, yet have my own agenda. I had spent my life living a lie, trying to be someone I wasn't. How was this any different? Someday Queen Julia wouldn't be queen anymore and that would make me the queen. I would no longer be a pawn. I could change things. Life could be different if I could just learn to use what I had before I was sent to the castle and she had full access to what I was capable of. Pining away for what might have been with Aidan seemed so small in comparison to what I was up against.

I sat on the couch, attempting to care about homework but really thinking about Bethany. She wasn't avoiding me per say, but she wasn't being overly communicative either. I wanted to apologize again, but my own thoughts were a mess. It was as if an entire team was playing ping pong inside my skull. The thoughts rammed back and forth across the space, vaulting to one side and then the other.

I wonder what Aidan's doing?

Don't think about him.

What am I really supposed to do about a crazy queen?

You're gonna have to figure it out. You're the Elder.

Why me?

Quit with the pity party.

I was exhausted. I was lonely. I needed someone who got it.

I finally gave in to the instinct I'd been fighting for days and dialed Rynna's number. It was past time for a check in and I needed to know if dad had showed back up yet.

"Well, hello there, Amelia!" I always loved when Rynna answered the phone. She was always genuinely happy to be talking to me. I swear, I could feel her love and warmth through the phone, wrapping me up in hugs like she used to when I was home.

"Hey, Ryn! I've missed you. How are things?" I tried to project the happiness she made me feel, but it didn't quite make it to my voice.

"Things are fine, dear. But, you don't sound fine. Why don't you tell me what's wrong?" she asked.

I groaned, but was secretly happy to be so easily found out. "I suck at hiding things. That's what B always says, too. Except, she's mad at me, which seems to be the theme lately. I just keep pushing people away. Everyone I care about I have to keep at arm's length. I've just had it, Ryn. I've had it with the lying, and the power craziness, and always having to be the one giving things up for the good of the cause." I was whining and I knew it.

Rynna paused for a second, but I was used to her processing time. Every word was chosen carefully and she always thought every situation through. She was the voice of reason after too many of my father's tirades.

"I've been waiting for this, Amelia. It's what I was both afraid of and hopeful for when you left us," she said. There was a strange mix of pride and frustration in her voice.

"You've been waiting for me to call and say I feel like I have multi-personality disorder? That I can't control my power? That I lead a double-life and I question every day why the heck I'm doing all of this? Especially the more I learn about the wonderful and glorious Queen Julia?" Sarcasm laced my words, but tears filled my eyes. There was always someone who knew more than I did. I should just be used to it by now.

"Well, that is essentially true," she started. "But, what I truly hoped was that you would go out into the world and realize there was more to it than our little Immortal soap opera. Don't get me wrong, Amelia, what's happening in our realm is serious and has dire consequences for all of us, but you are a child in the scheme of things and your life was taken from you."

I was shocked at the force behind her words. The anger I heard in the timbre of her voice. Rynna was the strong and steady one. She believed in the system. Or, so I thought. "But, Ryn, this queen, she's a monster. And I'm supposed to marry her son. And I'm an Elder. The last Elder. Doesn't that make all of this my problem? It's on me to do something about all of this. Cole doesn't have what I have. That's what I keep hearing. That I'm the Elder and I'm the only one left who can change things. Or, at the very least, be able to stop her from using me for something terrible."

She sighed and it was a few moments more before she spoke again.

"Let me tell you a story, Amelia. I once knew another Elder with a very similar problem. She was beautiful, like you, with your independence, spirit, and power, too. Everyone loved this girl. She grew up privileged, with people always watching her everywhere she went. You'd think she would have let it all go to her head, but she didn't. She was kind and gracious and always thought of everyone else before herself."

"When she turned eighteen, she was also betrothed. But, by then, she had already met her one true love. Her parents told her it was for the good of the kingdom. That she had a duty to her family and her people. She tried to listen. She walked away from the boy she loved, spent all of her time at the castle buried in books and tribunals with the other Elder families. She tried her best to do her duty. But, all the while, her heart wasn't in it. She started to fade. Her internal fire dimmed. Her power wouldn't cooperate. She stopped smiling and she wandered around as if she were lost. She had only met her fiancée once and she was already a shadow of herself."

I hadn't moved from my original position on the bed, rapt with need for more of Rynna's words. I wasn't fading away yet, but it seemed as if I could. Like I could slowly lose the pieces of myself to this duty. Pieces I was only just finding and putting together.

"The boy she loved couldn't stand it. He also understood the duty that fell to her and tried his best to honor her wishes, but as he watched her wither away, he realized he couldn't do it any longer. So, one day as she walked her normal path to the castle, he hid in the bushes and snatched her off the path. She realized immediately who held her, as their magic had been too far apart for too long, and wept into his arms. He offered her two choices. He said that he would leave the village forever and let her do the duty she was bound to, or they could run away that very night. That she could choose love and the rest of the world would have to figure out how to save themselves. He told her that she couldn't sacrifice herself for others unless it was truly what she felt she wanted to do. That she was choosing her fate; that her heart knew her path and she needed to trust it."

Rynna paused again and I caught the sound of a sniffle on her end. She cleared her throat and ended her story with words I should have seen coming but was still shocked to hear.

"Your mother and father ran from our village that night and never returned, Amelia. They lived many blissfully happy years together and she never once voiced regret for choosing love. So, I want you to think about that. As you learn more about who you are and what you are capable of, know that you are not the first to walk this path and that the choices truly are yours. Your heart is yours to give, it is no ones to take. Not a queen. Not a prince. No one."

"Wait. Ryn, that means you know more, right? You know more about who I am and what I can do?" I was so hopeful to finally get answers from someone I trusted. Someone who could tell me the whole truth.

"Amelia, I've already said more than I should have. I have to go. But think about what I said. Choose your path." And with that, she hung up.

I stared at the disconnected phone in my hand, replaying her words in my head and connecting the dots from her words to my situation. Could I do that? Could I walk away from this? I didn't have someone I loved asking me to run away, but I had something. Well, maybe I had something if I hadn't ruined it completely already.

And, my mother. The mystery of a woman I knew so little about; she had been forced to make this same choice. I suddenly felt closer to her than I ever could have dreamed and found myself picturing her and my father in their younger days, in love and happy. Wishing I could have known those people for just a short time. I dropped back onto the bed and let my mind wander down paths it had never been. What could my life truly be like if it were my own choice?

It wasn't until much later that I realized Rynna had never answered my original question and I still had no idea where my father was or how he was doing.

Chapter 8

I circled our apartment for the fifteenth time, pacing the length of the living room and hallway, past the framed photos and cute decor we'd collected over the past few months. My mind was going in so many different directions, I just needed Bethany to get home already — before I changed my mind, yet again. Finally, I heard the entry door to the complex slam shut and her quick steps up the flight of stairs. I laughed a little at the shock on her face as I wrenched the door open. She stood on the other side wearing a look of surprise with her keys held up toward where the lock should have been.

I grabbed her by the shoulders and yanked her in for a hug. This time, she did laugh and asked into my shoulder, "What's gotten into you, chica?" I pulled away and couldn't stop my grin. "I need your help, B. I've been an idiot. You were right. I do want to date Aidan. I like him. I really like him. You've got to help me get him back."

That Cheshire smile was back as her eyes sparkled with mischief and she rubbed her palms together. "You've come to the right place, sugar. No one meddles in love lives better than a southern girl," she said, her accent heavily exaggerated. We couldn't stop the fit of laughter that brought on and collapsed onto opposite ends of the couch to make our plan.

I tugged at the bottom of my deep purple dress, already feeling uncomfortable with how short and fitted it was. Bethany came up behind me, smacking my hand. "Stop that now. You'll mess up my masterpiece!"

I was standing in front of the mirror, debating on the right shoes for my outfit, and honestly couldn't believe the miracle B had pulled off. She was still twirling and twisting the curls she'd spent an hour on, spraying hair spray here and there. As I continued to switch from one foot to the other, trying to make a decision, she finally let out a deeply exaggerated sigh and said, "The black ones. Good gravy, Amelia, if he's looking at your shoes I've failed at life." I couldn't help but laugh, yet it was cut short as panic set in.

"Are you sure this is a good plan, B? I mean, did you tell Micah what we're doing? Does he understand that we're just going to crash their man date?" She gave me a sideways glance and hid behind my hair.

"*Ohmygod!* You didn't tell him! B! This was *your plan*. I can't do this. This is stupid. He's going to think I'm an idiot." I kicked out my leg, effectively tossing the silver shoe I wasn't wearing across the room and feeling a measure of satisfaction at the sound of it smacking against my closet door. Only, now I had on one three-inch heel and not the other, so as I tried to glare at my best friend for being a deviant little coward, I looked and felt ridiculous. She stifled a laugh at my glare mixed with my odd posture, so I grabbed an old stuffed animal off the bed and chucked it at her head.

"I know. I *know!*" Bethany was laughing as she dodged the bear and held her hands up in surrender. "I know, girl. But, it's all part of the plan! I've been on him for days about how he was such a jerk to Aidan and Aidan doesn't seem to have many friends, so I subtly suggested they should check out Cole's gym." She shrugged, looking a little sheepish. "They're both into training, right? And then I might have also subtly suggested they get some food."

"B? Subtle? You're about as subtle as a shovel to the forehead." She shrugged again and smirked, giving me a wink. "Girl, I get things done. Now, put your damn shoe on and let's go."

As we pulled up to the restaurant where Micah told Bethany they'd be eating, she and I were still debating the intelligence of sending them to Cole's gym.

"B, you understand that my brother is going to freak out if he figures out I'm dating Aidan, right?" I groaned at the thought. "I've never dated anyone. You know how protective he is. You couldn't have sent them anywhere else?"

That was an understatement. When Cole figured out what I was doing, he was going to be furious. For so many reasons, not the least of which would be taking my focus off of wrangling my power. Which, at the moment, was pushing and shoving its way out of its box and into my system. Just to calm my nerves, I gave it a little push and let a small stream whiz through me. The eager anticipation it gave off at being close to Aidan again replaced the stone in my stomach and I was able to unbuckle my seatbelt and turn to Bethany.

She grabbed my hand, likely expecting my nerves. Squeezing it, she said, "Girl, I know you. You always do everything everyone else wants you to do. You've been a grown up your whole stinking life. It's great your brother is back in your life but don't you forget that he disappeared on you for years, leaving you on your own. Don't you let him make your decisions for you. College — no... life, Amelia, is about doing it your way. Even if all you do is date Aidan for the next two weeks and then decide there's someone else better on down the line, so be it. This is your life. Your choice. You make it."

It was the second time in as many days I'd gotten the same speech from two women I loved and trusted. Two women who knew me. As I let out the breath I'd been holding, I said, "You're right, B, as usual. It's my turn."

As we got out of her Jeep and walked around to head toward the front door, we both realized we had no idea what we were walking in to. Esmerelda's was something else. It was all dark red brick and looked more like it had been snatched off of the streets of London than built in a beach town in California. It was two stories with a peaked roof and wrought iron detailing. It sat at an angle on the square block, the front door facing the corner. Sitting above the door was a huge stone statue of a woman with long hair dressed in flowing robes, holding something in her hands I couldn't quite see. I forced a smile as I turned to Bethany. "Here goes nothing!"

The smile she returned was tentative as well, but she nodded and we walked inside.

It was dark and it took a moment for my eyes to adjust. The entry way was lit with low lighting and the walls were hung with ornate tapestries. This truly was the weirdest restaurant I'd ever been in. As we looked around, both trying to spot Micah and Aidan, a hostess approached.

Her eyes were cold and her tone clipped. "Excuse me. This is a private club and we don't just allow anyone in here." In her perfectly-tailored blazer and skirt, she looked more like a CEO than a hostess, but she stood behind the podium and made it clear that we had stumbled into the wrong place.

I started to speak, but my voice failed me. Bethany piped up instead, her voice louder than it needed to be. "Well, hiya! We actually were invited here. Micah Clair is expecting us."

Grabbing my hand and giving me a look that made her intention clear, Bethany led me straight past the Ice Queen and into the main dining room. "Excuse me. Excuse me! Girls!" It took the woman a minute to extricate herself from behind her podium and that moment was all Bethany needed to locate Micah and Aidan at a table in the back of the room. Her pace quickened and just as the woman caught up to us, she caught Micah's eye. "Well, hey there! Fancy meeting you boys here."

First, I saw panic. Then, a quick flash of red as he looked around the rest of the restaurant as if he were expecting someone else. In one more blink, he was all smiles for Bethany.

There was absolutely something off with that guy. I was starting to wonder if buddying up to him might have its advantages in other ways when I remembered that Aidan was also at the table. Just as Aidan was turning in his chair, Micah finally addressed the squawking hostess. "Natalia, it's fine. These ladies are my guests." With just a few words and a quick cold glance of his own, Natalia completely shut down, nodded, and walked away. But, not before attempting to kill us with her death glare, which Bethany returned with her own "bless your heart" smile.

As I turned back toward the table, I found myself eye-to-eye with Aidan. He had stood up and was simply staring. Looking me up and down, his gaze moved from surprise to smoldering in the span of a few short seconds. It stopped my breath to think I could affect someone like this. That just a little make-up, some hair spray, and a dress could make him speechless. I was powerful in a whole new way.

I allowed a slow smile to develop. "Hi." The Pop Rocks were back and the lid had busted off of the cage inside me. All I wanted him to do was touch me so I could feel that electricity between us.

"Well, hello yourself, doll." Aidan's voice was deep and thick.

Micah cleared his throat from behind us, reminding Aidan and I that we weren't alone and that we were actually standing in a very strange restaurant with our friends. We turned to find Micah with his arm around Bethany, both seated at the table. She couldn't stop smiling but he was doing a terrible job of trying to hide his scowl. "Won't you join us?" he asked, gesturing to the other two chairs. Aidan pulled one out for me and we both sat.

"To what do we owe the pleasure, ladies?" Micah asked, a positivity I didn't quite buy in his tone. "I don't think I realized that you were planning to join us, Bethany." He smiled as if he were amused but it didn't quite make it to his eyes.

"A girl has to keep you on your toes," she said with a laugh. "Besides, we figured you two would be bored after all that training talk, so we thought we could liven up the party. But, truly, Micah, honey, why are you eating here?" Her nose wrinkled as she looked around.

I allowed my gaze to roam and couldn't disagree. There really weren't any other patrons here and the whole place was dark and dreary. The paintings that hung on the walls looked like they'd been done hundreds of years ago. The brush strokes were thick, the paint colors dark like the rest of the décor, and the frames massive and gilded.

As I brought my gaze back around, I locked eyes with Aidan. He still hadn't said a word outside of our initial conversation and simply kept staring. This time though, his stare was questioning. I was sure he was wondering what my game was, but at this point I wasn't even sure. I just knew I wasn't ready to be out with it yet, so I looked up at him from under my lashes and did my best to silently flirt.

"My parents actually own this place, so I come here often. It's a private club though, which is why you had some issues up front," Micah explained.

"Oh, so it's like a country club? I've never been to a country club like this!" Bethany craned her neck to look around, as if she were expecting sunburned baby boomers to pop out in their polo shirts and ugly pants.

Micah continued, chuckling a little and shaking his head. "It's something like a country club, but not exactly. You simply needed to let me know and I could have made it easier for you to come in. If you'd prefer, we can head elsewhere." Thankfully, Micah had given his attention back to Bethany and they continued their conversation, deciding where we should go.

"Did you have fun today?" I asked quietly. We still hadn't looked away from each other. Aidan's dimple appeared as he smirked. "As much as I could, given the company. The gym we checked out is cool. I signed up. But, I'm not sure exactly why I'm here. Or, why you are." His eyes roamed again and I allowed mine to do the same. He had on a black button down, the sleeves rolled to his forearms, and the ever-present leather cuffs on his wrists. His hair was intentionally mussed and I wanted to reach up and run my fingers through it.

Instead, I shrugged, dragging out the game. "I wanted to see you."

His eyebrow rose and Aidan leaned in closer to me, allowing me to catch a whiff of his cologne — alternating scents of citrus and woods. I wanted to breathe it in and hold it forever.

"I thought you made it pretty clear you didn't want to see me." His words were low, barely above a whisper, and I countered with hushed words of my own. Never breaking eye contact, I leaned in even closer, very aware of where my lips and his lips were in relation to each other as I enunciated each word. "I was wrong." His pupils dilated in response and as close as we were, I saw his eyes shift from smoke to liquid metal as they darkened.

The screech of a chair being pulled back broke our trance and we both jerked away from each other, realizing both Micah and Bethany were getting up to leave.

"Let's head over to the beach. We can grab dinner on the pier," Bethany said as if we all had just been in random conversation and I hadn't been inches from my first real kiss. "I'll ride with Micah! You guys take the Jeep."

She tossed Aidan her keys, giving me a look that screamed, "See, told ya!" I smiled in return, but as I turned to Aidan and saw blatant desire mixed with his still-unanswered questions, I realized I might have bitten off a little more than I could chew.

In the few steps from the table out to the Jeep, I lost all of my bravado. I clutched my small purse in a death grip in an attempt to stop my shaking hands. I couldn't turn back now, I'd started this game. Doubt crept in and all I heard in my head was, *"What are you doing?"* Aidan was quiet until we pulled out to follow Micah and Bethany. I could see Micah laughing as he drove while Bethany was making crazy gestures and likely telling another one of her outrageous stories.

"I don't get you, Amelia. What are we doing?" I noticed his grip on the steering wheel, knuckles white with how tight he held on. His voice was tense. Frustrated. I hated that we were both thinking the same thing.

"I…uh…well, I don't know exactly what we're doing, Aidan." I was fumbling. In this whole planning process I never stopped to think about what I should actually say. "I just know I want to try this. I was, um, scared before."

I couldn't look at him. The words came out tiny and soft and I had lost any flirtation I'd held in the restaurant. I shifted in my seat and pulled at the length of my dress, anxious to be out from under his scrutinizing gaze. Most people wouldn't have admitted it outright like that, but the gnawing ache in my gut told me I just needed to put it out there. There was just something about him that made me want to tell the truth. Even that feeling told me I was probably causing myself more trouble in the long run, but right now, none of that mattered.

He was quiet the rest of the drive. Granted, it was only five minutes, but it was the longest five minutes of my life. I stared straight ahead, my nails likely doing permanent damage to my poor purse. As soon as Aidan put the car in park, I tried to launch myself out the door, but he grabbed my wrist. Instantly, his touch sparked a flame inside of me. My power popped and fizzed, filling every corner of me with happiness with just the imprint of his fingertips and the warmth of his palm seeping through my skin. I tried to keep my cool as I turned to face him — it would have been mortifying for him to understand the affect he had on me already.

For a second, Aidan just looked at me. Then, as he smiled, he slid his hand down my wrist and over my thumb, locking my palm in his. "Okay."

One word. That's all he said. One word and I couldn't stop the stupid grin from spreading from ear to ear. "Okay," I repeated back to him.

I expected dinner to be more awkward than it was, but everyone seemed to let their guard down and the four of us actually got along better than I imagined. Aidan had his arm around the back of my chair, grazing his fingertips up and down my shoulder the whole time, making it extremely difficult to think straight. I had to spend a considerable amount of effort containing my overly-zealous power, which he seemed to send into a frenzy by just breathing in my general vicinity.

"So, Amelia, I don't feel like I know much about you," Micah stated as we got our food. I stopped with my fork halfway to my mouth and wasn't sure how to respond.

Aidan actually interjected, adding, "That's true, Amelia. We've been listening to Bethany go on and on with her stories about raising chickens and being a rodeo princess, but you haven't said much."

He smiled and winked at B. She threw a chunk of breadstick at him in response. "You have no idea how complicated it is to stir up that much dust and still look like a pageant queen when you get off the horse. You don't see bull riders worrying about how dirty they are when their eight seconds are up, do you?" She straightened in her seat, the posture of a true queen, and looked down at him as if he were a mere commoner.

It was Micah who laughed the loudest. "You and my mother would get along fabulously, Bethany. You've both mastered the 'don't question me' look perfectly." The hope that lit into Bethany's eyes sent Micah back-pedaling faster than I'd ever seen and he choked on his own bite trying to speak. I decided to save him from himself and my surprisingly commitment-hungry best friend.

"I moved here from Northern California. My family lives in a small community there near Gualala. My brother lives here in Brighton now, which is why I decided to come here." I strategically omitted that they had just met my brother, unsure of how much I wanted these two parts of my life to intermingle.

"So, are you a mountains girl or an ocean girl?" Aidan's question caused me to sit back and ponder for a moment.

"Definitely ocean. My favorite is when I can be a part of both at the same time. Gualala was like that. Turn left and stare at the never-ending shoreline, turn right and watch the trees reaching for the sky all the way up the mountain. But, I've always been drawn more toward the water." Views entered my mind from the solitary walks I took to escape the realities of my life growing up. Standing with my palms on thick tree trunks, staring out into the breaking waves, feeling like everything else had dropped away.

Aidan just nodded as a small smile played at the corners of his mouth. Looking into his eyes, it was like we were the only two people at the table. I had to force myself to look around. As my gaze found Micah, the questions reflecting back at me made me sit back, instantly feeling uncomfortable. "What?" I asked.

He shook his head, seemingly surprised that I noticed his obvious expression. "Nothing. I'm sorry. My mind was elsewhere." He quickly changed the conversation toward how we all liked school and Brighton.

The evening finally came to a close and Aidan slowed our progression toward the cars, letting Bethany and Micah move ahead. Their hands were linked loosely and she was leaned into Micah, laughing. I took a few more steps before realizing Aidan had stopped completely.

"Sorry! I was just watching them. I'm really happy she's happy. He's kind of weird, but he makes her happy." I finally looked back at Aidan and was startled by the intensity in his eyes.

"Have lunch with me tomorrow," he said. It wasn't a command, but it wasn't a question either.

He waited a second before starting again. "Amelia, I know that whatever is going on with us has been…well, weird, to say the least. But, I'd really like to get to know you. Just us. No one else." His dimple appeared alongside a boyish grin. As he continued to look in my eyes, I once again got caught in his smoky stare. He brought his hand up, brushed the backs of his fingers along my cheek, and whispered, "I don't know what you've done to me, doll, but I can't help but want to know you."

Heat filled my cheeks and I brought my own hand up to remove his in an attempt to slow my frantic heartbeat, but I couldn't bring myself to. I gripped his wrist and found myself leaning further into his palm.

"Yes," I sighed, reveling in the warmth of him. "Aidan, I want time with just you, too." As I opened my eyes again, I couldn't help but smirk and finish with, "But you really have to stop annoying me all the time."

He chuckled, took my phone from my hand, and entered in his number. "I'll do my best, doll, but no promises." He gave me one last smile and turned toward Micah's SUV, tossing out, "Tomorrow. In the commons.

Lunch." The way that boy flipped from sweet to cocky never ceased to amaze me.

I stood staring for a minute, just watching him walk away. There was something to be said for a guy who knew how to pick a pair of jeans. His stride was relaxed but he exuded masculine strength — there was no denying it. Something about him just screamed "safe" to me.

I somehow knew that he was smiling to himself as he got to the car. I waited expectantly for him to turn around again and was surprised when he didn't. He just got in the car, Micah backed out, and they pulled away.

Oh, stop being such a girl, I berated myself as I pulled my way up and into the Jeep — which was not an easy task in a mini-dress. Bethany was already waiting, sneaking a peek through the side-mirrors. As I buckled my seatbelt, I finally looked up at her and she had the biggest grin on her face.

"You are in some serious trouble, girl," she said with a laugh. And, with that, she gave me a playful look, used her turquoise-painted nails to tap a button on her phone, and the latest Pop Diva love song came blaring through the speakers. "Subtle, B. Real subtle," I half-yelled over the music, while I laughed.

Chapter 9

I should have had happy and restful sleep after the amazing day I had, instead I tossed and turned all night. I still don't know exactly what it was that I was dreaming, but I heard that same melody as I got ready this morning. It haunted me. I found myself humming it, though the lyrics floated just outside my reach. I couldn't pin them down and the haze I felt was hard to shake no matter how much coffee I mainlined. It was just another night where it felt like I had been up all night watching movies instead of sleeping.

Knowing I had lunch with Aidan, I put a little extra effort in; pulling on my favorite dark skinny jeans, zipping up my brown ankle boots, and loving the flowing peasant top Bethany had talked me into during our last shopping trip. I left my hair down and a little wild.

Classes went by quickly and all too soon I stood in the commons, wondering where it was I was meeting him. I sent a few different texts and even called him once and had yet to receive a response. His phone had gone straight to voice mail, so I assumed it might be off, which was strange.

I stood off to the side tapping my foot and found myself getting irritated. Really irritated. Before I could pick up my bag and walk away, I saw him running across the grass. He scanned the crowds and finally landed on me. I jutted one hip out, balled my fist on it, and tossed the other hand in the air — making it clear from one-hundred feet that I wasn't impressed. As he finally skidded to a stop in front of me, actually huffing a bit — which I secretly appreciated since I hadn't worked out in forever — he tried to explain.

"Amelia, I am so sorry. I overslept, I missed all of my classes this morning and got here as soon as I could. Am I too late?" He looked around as if to make sure people were indeed still eating lunch. He was rubbing his hand through his hair as he scanned the crowd, looking like he hadn't fully woken up yet and too adorable for how irritated I wanted to be.

His clothes were a mess — wrinkled with a few visible stains. I would bet he either slept in them or dove straight into the laundry basket, not caring if they were clean or dirty. His hair went in all directions with a clear cowlick from where his head had been on the pillow. As I really looked at him, I laughed when I saw a sleep line on his right cheek. I could only shake my head and ask how soon we could eat.

With a bashful smile, he grabbed my hand and led me toward the outdoor food vendors, telling me to make my pick. As we stood in line at the Greek stand — gyros were my absolute favorite — neither of us said much. I couldn't think past the fact that he still hadn't let go of my hand and, instead, had interlaced his fingers with my own. His hand was warm and strong. As I stood enjoying the moment, I found myself people-watching and humming that same tune from my dream absentmindedly, not realizing I was doing it out loud. Before I could react, Aidan yanked me out of the line and pushed me backwards away from the crowd.

"Hey! Aidan! What the hell?" I tried to drop his hand but all that warmth and strength had turned to solid rock. The look in eyes was a little scary — he definitely wasn't sleepy anymore. Aidan finally stopped as he pulled me into an alcove.

"Where did you hear that song? How do you know that song?" His face was just inches from mine, his voice was menacing, and his eyes were so dark they looked black in the shadows of where we stood.

"Aidan, I…I don't even know. I woke up this morning and it was just there. I haven't been able to get it out of my head. I don't even know the words, I just keep hearing the music." I was talking fast, his reactions making me uncomfortable.

He brought his hand up and pointed his finger in my face, "Amelia, I need the truth. *Where* did you hear that song?"

I tried to calm the building hysterics in my own voice as I put my hand on his chest, both my eyes and my words pleading my ignorance. "Aidan, I'm really sorry, but I truly don't know how I know. I wish I could tell you, but it was just *there*. Sometimes I dream about things and I have no idea where they come from."

I watched him back away slightly, his posture slumping. I instantly felt responsible and kept talking. "Really, Aidan, I'm sorry. I wish I knew. Why? Do you know that song?"

"Yeah," he said, his voice laced with sorrow and his eyes pained. "I know that song. It's the song my mother used to sing to me before she put me to sleep. I haven't heard it in seventeen years." He backed away from me until his back hit the cinder block wall. "I haven't heard it since she died."

"Your mom died, too?" I asked quietly. I looked up into his surprised eyes and knew exactly what he was feeling. It was as if we were trading emotions. Or, at least acknowledging that someone else could understand the depths of a loss like that. A hole that permeated not only your heart but the essence of who you are.

He avoided my question, asking one of his own instead. "Wanna get outta here? I've got someplace I want to take you."

The look on his face was tired but hopeful. I had worn that look so many times myself, hoping my father would want to play with me or stay in the same room with me for more than two minutes. It was the look that said, "I don't want you to hurt me, but I'm willing to risk it." There was no way for me to say no to that.

"Sure. Let's do it. I've never ditched before," I answered.

That got a grin from him and his eyes lit up with mischief. "So, I truly am a bad influence then, huh?"

I laughed as I rolled my eyes. "Montgomery, you have no idea what you're getting yourself into with me."

As he grabbed my hand again and we walked toward the parking lot, he gave it a small squeeze. "Back atcha, doll."

The drive was actually pretty quiet. Aidan rolled the windows down and the air coming off the coast gushed in, bringing with it the taste of salt and the smell of earth as we got closer to the forest. I was content to put my feet on the dash of his Honda, lean back, and let it all drift past. It felt good — right, even — to have this companionable silence. The strains of a piano filtered through the speakers and I was surprised to realize there were no words. We were listening to classical music. There was still so much to learn about him.

After maybe an hour, Aidan pulled off. It was a pretty secluded parking area and he warned there would be a little hike to follow. I was glad I had gone with boots and not heels today. Aidan led the way up the thin, worn path, stopping every now and then to offer a hand or hold back branches. Just as I was about to comment on our "little hike", he pushed some branches out of the way and I was stunned by the view.

We were high above the water, on a cliff that jutted out and made me feel like I was suspended over the ocean. I didn't love heights, but the sound of the water bashing against the rocks instantly soothed me. I closed my eyes and heard the far-off barking of sea lions and squawks of the seagulls. The winds were light, seeming to wrap around me, engulfing me in the warm sea air. It occurred to me that he had been listening yesterday. He brought me to a place he knew I'd love.

"You really are beautiful, you know," he said. I turned to find him standing back near the tree line, arms crossed, and leaning against a larger tree trunk. Even with emotion still clouding his gray eyes, his gaze was intense and it was as if he could see straight through me.

I tried to laugh it off. "So you say, player. We'll just see how long my good looks keep you around." I gave him a wink of my own, hoping to lighten the mood a little. To stave off the intense reaction I was having at his gesture, both emotionally and in the small explosions that ricocheted around deep inside me.

He moved toward me, slowly, making me feel as if he were stalking his prey. "Amelia, that's no line. I don't have lines. I don't say things because they'll make you feel better. I say them because I want to. Or because they're true. Usually, both." I could feel the intensity coming from him. It was almost stifling, but made me stand at attention. The fizz of electricity zinged through my system as my power reacted in a way that it only did in Aidan's presence. I've never reacted to anyone like this, but I wasn't scared. I wanted him to come closer.

Just as Aidan closed the last few feet, looking at me like he might kiss me, I lost my nerve. I backed away, losing my footing. I started to stumble and heard my own shriek. Then, I was in his arms and being yanked back into the trees.

"Holy hell, Amelia - are you okay?!" He was pushing me away as he surveyed my whole body, looking for signs of damage. I couldn't speak. I just stood there, shaking, my power threatening to lash out in response to my fear and my racing heart. He crushed me against him again, whispering that I was okay as he pulled me back away from the edge, sounding like he was reassuring himself just as much as he was me.

We finally sat down with our backs against some smoother tree trunks. I continued trying to calm my frenzied power, glad Aidan couldn't feel the panic I did while he kept rubbing his hands over his face and then through his hair. Finally, with his elbows on his knees and his hands clasped, he looked over at me. "Are you really okay? I didn't mean to scare you. I always seem to make the wrong move with you."

I took another deep breath, let it out, and met his gaze, resolved to not let him take this on as well. "No, Aidan, I'm a klutz. These are the things I do. Someday, I'll introduce you to my brother and he'll be able to recount all of my best moments. On the other hand, don't ask him. Some things just don't need to be shared."

I gave him a sideways smile and was happy to have it returned, sort of. "Why don't you tell me why you brought me to this beautifully dangerous place?" I asked as I looked out over the water, trying to take some of the pressure off of us both.

That brought a sigh from him as he leaned his head back against the tree. I shouldn't have been thinking it given the circumstances, but he looked sexy as hell. It was like one of those cologne ads that makes no sense, but has you wondering if the men in them actually exist. They do. They so very much do.

"I had wanted to bring you here anyway, but after what you said last night, I knew it would be perfect. There are other reasons, but let's not go into that yet. Let's just talk about normal stuff," he said, looking away from me and up toward the sky. "Do you ever cloud watch?"

I almost snorted. "Cloud watch? The tattooed and mysterious Aidan wants to know if I cloud watch?" He feigned offense and took on a haughty tone. "Yes, Ms. Party Pooper. Cloud watching. Stop your judging and lay down." He pointed toward a patch of bright green grass and looked at me expectantly.

We both scooted out so that we were still under the trees but could see out over the water. Watching the giant puffs of clouds wafting through the air, they reminded me of ballerinas gracefully sliding across the sky in an effortless dance. There were a few feet between us and it took all of my self-control not to move closer to him. Before I could even make the middle school move of reaching my hand across the space between us, Aidan rolled on to his side to face me.

With his palm under his ear and his T-shirt sleeve riding up, I could see even more of his tattoo. Without thinking, I rolled myself toward him and traced the swirling lines. Between the captivating design I could still just partially see and the hardness of his bicep, I kind of lost myself. The fact that I reached out at all occurred to me like a glass of cold water tossed in my face and I snatched my hand away, instantly apologizing. Aidan just laughed, grabbing my hand again. "It's okay, doll. You're so skittish. You won't break me."

"But you might break me." The words slipped off my tongue, the filter between my brain and my mouth gone. The red creep of embarrassment flushed my face and I rolled away from him, throwing my arm over my eyes. Thankfully, he let my words go — but not my hand. Clearing his throat a little, Aidan brought us back to cloud watching.

"I used to do this when I was younger. I would find a patch of grass and stare at the sky for hours. I would watch the clouds and tell myself stories about the characters I met in the sky. People, animals, you name it, I brought them all into my stories. I... well, I used them to forget. What do you see?"

I dropped my arm back to my side. Even though every part of me wanted to look at Aidan, to see the pain I felt rolling off of him, I didn't allow myself to. I stared in the sky and analyzed the giant white puffs. "Uh…a dog?" I was terrible at this game. "No. A horse! That one, that one's a horse!" I found myself smiling as I turned to him for confirmation and he was smiling in return. "So, what's the horse's story?" he asked.

I looked around at the other clouds in the sky. "Well, there are all those other horses over there," I pointed to a cluster of clouds off to the right, "and he just wants to go be with them. But, there's that big fence, just there, so he can't. He's trying to find a way to get their attention to come knock it down so they can all run around together."

I was proud of my little made-up tale until I turned again to face Aidan. This time, the pain was visible everywhere. His jaw was set, lips in a thin line, brows furrowed. He was looking straight up at the sky but the emotion that invaded the air was thick and dark, angry and desperate. "Aidan? Did I do it wrong?"

Without looking back at me, he squeezed my hand tightly, his fingers pressing hard into the divots between the bones in my hand. He clutched at my hand as if I could keep him here, pull him away from the memories that overwhelmed him; that threatened to pull him down into a place I could feel he didn't want to go.

"You can tell me, but only if you want to." I put the words between us and let the silence follow. Turning back to stare at the sky, I gave him time to decide. I had no idea what he had been through, what he would say, but I understood what the darkness of truth could do to you if you let it.

"I don't know why, but I want to tell you, Amelia. It's insane because I never tell anyone this stuff. But, I want to tell you. Before this goes any further, I want you to know who I am." He still wasn't looking at me so while I saw him in my peripheral, I kept my gaze on the clouds. "Then, tell me," I said. Taking a deep breath, I finished with a surprising, "Tell me and I'll tell you."

The longer Aidan held my hand, the more I got used to the feel of my nerves being raw and the increased sensations that vibrated from our point of contact throughout the rest of my body. As I lay there, waiting for him to speak, he kept our hands locked, sliding his middle finger up and down in a slow rhythm over the back of my hand. I could feel callouses on his palm and the heat he radiated. It was soothing and, for once, I was truly in control, at least as far as my power was concerned. My heartbeat, however, raced triple time as I had time to realize that I was laying on the forest floor holding hands with Aidan Montgomery, waiting for him to unlock doors I hadn't known I wanted inside of. Someone I could give some of my truth to and who wanted to give me theirs in return.

"I don't remember what happened the night my parents died. I was only two. I remember them. People say I can't, or that I shouldn't be able to. That I was too young. But, I do. I remember the sound of her laugh and the smell of cigars and fir trees that would cling to his clothes when he would carry me to bed. It's harder now to see their faces, but I have a picture that I look at every day to make sure I don't forget. And the song, the one you were humming, it's one of the few true memories I still hold. Every single night my dad would carry me to bed and my mom would come in and sing that song. I would fall asleep to the sound of her voice."

We both continued to stare at the sky and he maintained the steady pace of running his finger up and down the top of my hand. "They tell me there was a break-in. That someone killed them during a burglary. Somehow, the burglars never found my room, and I never woke up. They told me how lucky I was to survive."

He laughed. It was dark and dry and held no humor. "Lucky. I was lucky to have no one who would come forward to take me. My parents had no records of their family and the state couldn't find anyone. I was *lucky* to spend my entire life bouncing from one foster home to the next. I was *lucky* enough to have a string of people constantly deciding I wasn't the kid for them and passing me on to the next person."

I couldn't help but squeeze his hand then. It was all I could do to stop myself from vaulting across the small space between us and pulling him into a hug. I knew what he was saying. What that kind of hurt did to a person. The blackness that leached into your soul and told you every day that no one loved you, no one wanted you… that you weren't good enough to make them stay. I knew he didn't want my pity, so instead I spoke my own truth and tried to show him that I understood.

"My mom died while having me. I never even knew her," I said. "I've seen pictures and my brother has told me about her, but she died minutes after I was born and my dad went crazy. Like, literally. He wouldn't come out of his office for days at a time. We had a nanny and she's the only reason I was fed or taken care of. When my dad would come out, he'd barely speak to me unless it was to yell at me for not following his rules and then lock me in my room again. My brother moved out when he turned eighteen, I was ten. He couldn't take it anymore. He...well, he had to. I get it, but he just left. And...and I have nightmares. I wake up crying, sometimes screaming. It seems like every night I dream terrible dreams that I can never remember, but still don't fully forget."

My own words were quiet. They seemed to float away on the breeze as I said them, making it easier to speak out loud about things I hadn't even shared with Bethany. Things that, until that moment, I didn't know I wanted to share with Aidan. But, he was right. I wanted him to know me, too.

He slowly slipped his fingers from mine and I instantly missed the connection. It only took a second before he moved behind me and pulled me back between his legs, my back leaning against his chest. There was a moment of panic as his arms slipped around me but it calmed as my power reacted with a sigh instead of a rebellion.

We sat there for a few minutes, nothing but the sounds of our breath and crash of the ocean waves below us. Then, Aidan leaned down and whispered, "I guess we're all a little broken, aren't we, doll?"

I could only nod as ill-timed tears filled my eyes. He wasn't supposed to do this. He wasn't supposed to see directly to the core of me and address my worst fears in one afternoon. He wasn't supposed to fill me with unspoken words and unknown emotions. I hadn't realized that making this choice to not walk away from him would literally change everything, but in the course of twenty-four hours, it had.

We sat there for a little while longer, but as the sun started to set, it was time to go. The drive back was just as quiet but Aidan never let go of my hand. As he dropped me at my car, I turned and asked, "Why do you call me doll?"

He tilted his head and I could tell he hadn't thought about it himself. "I don't know. Probably because that's what my dad called my mom. I have some of their old letters and he always called her doll."

I couldn't stop the blush that crept across my cheeks and the nerves that fluttered in my belly. It was both a compliment and a little too real to have our…situation…compared to the iconic love he saw in his parents. "Okay, then. See ya." I tripped over the words, shyness taking over.

As I went to push myself out the door, Aidan pulled me back toward him, my face stopping dangerously close to his. I looked from his eyes to his lips and back. They were swirling silver and projected exactly what he was feeling. He leaned in until our foreheads were touching.

"I'm not going to do it because I can tell you're still scared, but I want you to know that I *want* to kiss you, Amelia. I really want to." He so rarely said my name that, in that moment, his voice husky and deep, I wanted to let him. I wanted to move the extra half-inch to do it myself. But, it would take us somewhere that I *shouldn't* go.

I closed my eyes and took a deep breath as I nodded ever so slightly. "Okay." It was a tiny word. The same word that started everything, but now I used it to neither agree or disagree. "Okay," he replied, assuming my consent that the time would eventually come. "I'll be in touch, doll, you can count on it," he whispered. Again, I tried to smile, but I know it didn't go further than my lips. He looked confused as I fumbled my way out of the car and into my own.

I waved as he pulled away, trying to look as happy as I'd been just minutes before. As soon as he turned out of the parking lot, I burst into tears. I had made a selfish choice, thinking only about myself and the relationship I wanted. But, now I had fallen for someone. A human. A tortured yet amazing human who already saw too much of the person so few people had ever tried to know. And, I still didn't know what my final choice would be when the time came. There were just too many unanswered questions.

Chapter 10

I got home and found Bethany sitting on the couch, surrounded by notes and textbooks. "How's your new booooooyfriend?" she drawled out with a laugh, like we were in fifth grade and going to start talking about people kissing in trees.

I shook my head and dropped down beside her in the one place she hadn't covered in paper. "I don't know, B."

"Um, hello, girl? What do you mean you don't know? I saw you two love birds yesterday. You were almost drooling all over each other. What's not to know?" She looked completely baffled and I hated that I couldn't just be out with it.

"It just might be too much, too fast. He's just...intense, and I think it's moving more quickly than I'm ready for." I couldn't even look at her as I said the words. They weren't the truth and she'd know it.

"Ohhhh. I see exactly what's happening here." Bethany shoved her books and notebook to the floor and shifted so we faced each other. "You're scared. Honey, that's normal. Be scared. Enjoy being scared. He's new and scrumptious and scary. That's how it's supposed to be!"

"It's not that simple. He's been through a lot. What if I disappoint him like everyone else has? People did that to me. I can't do that to him." I felt so guilty already, just knowing that I would more than likely have to follow through with the betrothal. That there may very well be nothing I could do about any of it in the end.

"Is that your plan? Are you planning to string him along and then just drop him?" I looked up, surprised and shocked that she would even ask that. "Just what I thought," she said with a smirk. "Of course you aren't."

"Amelia, you've got to trust yourself a little more," she said, patting my knee. "Relax. Chill the heck out. It's not all life and death. What you feel right now could last forever or it could last three freaking days. Maybe you'll find out that he chews his food with his mouth open and you can't stand the sight of him anymore. Just let it be what it is." With that, she tapped my hand with her own and picked up her books again.

I spent the rest of the night stewing over that and finally decided she was right. I wasn't in love. This was all new. I needed to cut myself a break and just chill out. I grabbed my phone and sent Aidan a quick text.

Double date this weekend?

His response came minutes later.

I suppose Richie Rich isn't optional?

I laughed out loud as I responded.

They are a package deal, but he isn't that bad.

If it means I get to sit next to you, then I can handle him. ;)

I kept trying to think of clever responses but eventually gave up and just grinned as I stared at the screen.

We hadn't been able to have our double date over the weekend like I'd wanted, but the free time had given Aidan and I more one-on-one time and I wasn't complaining. We were in an easy rhythm that felt safe. Meeting for lunch, texting relentlessly, and finding out as many random factoids about each other as possible. His favorite color was blue. He loved alternative and hated country. He hated cold pizza. The one thing we didn't do was kiss. He had made a few attempts since our conversation in the car and I was able to circumvent each one. Not always gracefully, but it worked and he seemed to get the message because he backed off. I wanted to kiss him, but knowing deep down that I might have to leave him made me continue to pull back. Kissing meant commitment. I couldn't do commitment.

We finally managed to sync up schedules, so Aidan, Micah, Bethany, and I were sitting on an outdoor patio, eating appetizers, and chatting as the sun went down. People were everywhere along the boardwalk, enjoying what was left of the seventy-degree day. We were all laughing at a joke Micah had made — and a little at him.

He never seemed to realize just how prudish he could come across.

"But, really," he said as he tried to contain his long hair in the leather tie he miraculously always seemed to have, "don't you think the women of this country have something better to do than watch some ridiculous television show that proves exactly how impossible it is to fall in love in a matter of weeks?" Bethany instantly bristled. No one bashed reality TV in her presence and lived to tell the tale.

I rolled my eyes at Aidan and laughed as he shook his head. Listening to the deep rumble of his laugh had become one of my new favorite pastimes. I couldn't even pay attention to Bethany's lecture or Micah's continued skeptical questions because I didn't know how to stop staring at Aidan.

He sat there, watching me watch him, with a fire in his eyes I didn't want to acknowledge. I could see that he hadn't had a haircut since we met and the ends had started to curl. He had that barely-there five o'clock shadow I couldn't resist and I had to stop myself from reaching over to run my hand along his jaw. My eyes roamed to his broad chest, stretching his bright blue button-down. He had the sleeves rolled to his forearms and the muscles bulged as I noticed him flexing his fist. I finally raised my eyes back to his to find myself locked in his gaze. The bright blue flecks in his eyes stood out against the slate gray depths that were pulling me in and making promises again. Though I successfully managed to avoid any scenarios up to this point where he had another chance to kiss me, that didn't mean I didn't want it just as much as I was terrified by it.

I had laid in bed this morning, for the fourth morning in a row after another long, sleepless night, plagued by worse than normal nightmares, scolding myself for continuing this with Aidan. I warred with myself between Bethany and Rynna's words of encouragement and the realities of what I had learned from Cole about Julia. Would I be strong enough to just walk away? Was it fair to drag Aidan into this without him even being able to understand what was at stake? No matter what I felt for him, I couldn't justify hurting him. But, every time I convinced myself today would be the day I'd tell him it was over — whatever this was — he would give me that smile and look at me like I was the only person that mattered in the world. It was the thing I ached for; to be wanted for who I was. Aidan had no idea of what was happening to me and he never would. He had no idea what my actions would mean for our people in the future. He just knew a girl. A regular, normal girl.

"Hey. Hey, Ame, what's wrong?" Aidan leaned into me, whispering in my ear as he tucked me into his shoulder. "What's going on in that head of yours, doll? I just watched you run away without making a move." He pressed a kiss to my forehead that sent me into overload. I hadn't cried in a long time. My emotions and my power had been really level for a while now, but the fact that he saw me — that he read me and knew me enough already to know something was wrong — made it obvious that this was more real than I had ever allowed myself to acknowledge.

I tore myself from him, muttering about having to go to the bathroom. Through my lowered lashes and the dark curtain of hair I'd let fall into my face, I saw the look in his eyes and knew he had seen the well of tears in mine. His jaw tensed and his eyes asked questions I couldn't answer without the tears falling, so I walked away without a word. This was real. We were real. *What was I doing?*

I walked past the bathrooms and out the back door. I wasn't ready to face Bethany either and she would be sent after me. A sob built in my chest that I swallowed down. It always seemed to work this way; I would think I had it all under control and then one thing would snap me to pieces. What didn't make sense was that the farther I got from Aidan, the more my power rebelled. It had laid dormant while the realizations mounted, but it wasn't until I walked away that it pushed back. It pulled and shoved and pounded on me with every step I took until finally I stopped and leaned back against the wall, sliding down to the ground.

Aidan was everything I wanted and wasn't supposed to have. I sat there silently crying with my knees pulled to my chest and my head down on my arms. I heard someone running toward me, though it sounded as if the footsteps were in a cave. I could feel the emotion rolling off of them and before I could react, they reached down and grabbed me. I was instantly pissed, on top of being scared. When I looked up, I saw Micah get thrown back against the door I had just come out of, his whole body smashing against it with a force I'd never seen, actually leaving a dent in the old metal.

As he slid down and his feet finally touched the ground he whisper-yelled, "What the hell was that, Amelia? I've been calling your name and we've been searching for you for the last ten minutes. Aidan's losing his mind. You need to rein yourself in! I was able to follow your signature back here, which means other Mages could have, too."

Micah was dusting his perfectly-pressed khakis and polo off, shaking his limbs out. He closed his eyes and I watched him stand taller as he clearly used his power to ease the aches in his body from smashing against the door. He looked around, his expression oddly relieved.

I, on other hand, couldn't move. I sat there, stunned, with my mouth open, my open palms still held out in front of me and my rogue power humming through my system after being set free. It was that same feeling of being on the cliffs that night.

"Oh my," Micah said as he stooped down in front of me and took in my response to what had just happened. "You've never used force on someone before, have you? How far behind are you exactly, Amelia?" He cocked his head to the side and let out an audible sigh. "I've let you be, but I think it's time we have a conversation."

Before I could react or even laugh to myself over the fact that it was supposed to be me pushing Micah to help me, Aidan came running down the alley with Bethany struggling to keep up with his long strides. I didn't even have a chance to stand before he scooped me up as if I were a child and, without saying a word, stalked back out of the alley and to his car. I locked my arms around his neck and tucked myself deep into him as he walked, hiding my swollen eyes and the eyeliner that was running down my face. He marginally relaxed; his steps slowing. After he deposited me in the passenger seat and buckled me in, he touched his forehead to mine before slowly inhaling. He looked into my eyes and, in the most simultaneously controlled and violent tone I had ever heard, said, "You can't keep running from me, Amelia. You're scared, I can see that. But, next time, you *will* talk to me. Okay?" With wide eyes, the only thing I could do was nod.

It was time. Cole had been blowing up my cell for days because I had canceled our last two dinners and hadn't come down to the gym. We both knew I hadn't pushed the issue with Micah, but I didn't want to have to admit it — or why. And, I really didn't want to have to lie to anyone. So, instead, I called Micah and set up a time to meet to talk.

I was waiting on a bench near the beach, staring out at the water and trying not to think too hard about the complications of my life right now when he finally sat down beside me. We sat in silence for a few moments, as if daring the other to go first. I finally decided I had called this meeting so it was my show.

"You've already figured out I don't really know what I'm doing and I need help." Simple. Direct.

Micah snorted a little. "Well, that's an understatement, Amelia. Do you even know what you are? How did this happen?"

My blood pressure rose a little at his tone. I took a few deep breaths to keep myself calm. "I'm a Mage, Micah, just like you. And, my story doesn't matter. What matters is that I need to understand how to handle this. Can you help me or not?"

Instead of answering me, he stood and gestured out toward the water. "Let's walk a little," he said. I was annoyed that he wouldn't just answer me, but followed anyway. We walked out toward the rising tide, stopping far enough away that the water wouldn't reach us. He slid off his shoes and sat down in the sand, so I did the same. I looked at Micah sitting comfortably, albeit stiffly, on the beach next to me. He'd pulled his hair back but pieces of sun-bleached blond were floating in the breeze off the water. A Viking surfer, that's what he looked like. He was digging his toes farther and farther into the sand and I watched as he stared out at the ocean with the same intensity that I did.

"Does it touch you, too? Do you feel it?" I asked.

He looked at me a little shocked, but finally answered. "It does. I expect it's just the natural pull of the moon. Our power is strongest at night, making the moon more important to us than the sun, and the moon controls the tides. So, by proxy, the water is at the beck and call of our most powerful source of magic. And yes, I've always felt pulled to it."

I had never thought of it that way, or really even questioned my affinity for the ocean. As the sun was setting, I could feel a rise in Micah's magic. It wondered if it was a pep talk he was giving himself to start the conversation we both knew was coming. I laughed a little on the inside to think about the self-confident Micah being nervous around me.

Finally, still without looking away from the sea, he said, "You know, Amelia, it's so simple to see that you are capable of more than you realize. I'm not entirely sure how it is that you are so naive to the magic inside of you, or how anyone allowed you to be raised without proper precautions and then let you loose in a human area, but I believe that yes, I can help." He finally turned to me, all of the sincerity I had ever seen sitting in his eyes, and simply stated, "I wasn't raised with anyone like you — who didn't know how to control every ounce of their magic — but I believe that you should know how to use it. Your power is an extension of the woman you will become and, at the very least, I can teach you to control it and defend yourself, if that's what you want."

I sat staring into his bright blue eyes, seeing the hope hiding behind the doubt. I finally swallowed the lump of worry lodged in my throat and said, "I haven't had a lot of people in my life be up front about how to be what I am. I appreciate what you're offering and would like for you to help me. Obviously, Bethany doesn't know what we are, but she's the only person who has ever really been interested in being my friend. I hope we can be friends, too."

He nodded and gave me a small smile in return. "She is a beautifully positive creature, isn't she?" That made me laugh out loud. "Oh, Micah, you save that one for some night you're in trouble. That is sure to smooth a few things out." The grin I saw in return was priceless. Maybe he wasn't going to be so bad for her after all.

We got up, brushing the sand away, and I stood in front of Micah. "Alright, so we're doing this. When do we start?" I asked. I was a little leery about this part. I was ready to be pushed, but I still wasn't sure which abilities I should show Micah. I wasn't entirely sure of the abilities I even had lurking around inside me. So many things had only happened to me once and random things seemed to only happen when I completely lost control and my power reigned free. I was going to have to find a source that understood which powers belonged to Elders and which were only in Mages. Maybe Cole's people would be able to help.

I stood expectantly, nervously crossing my arms over my chest, trying to find peace in the waves crashing as the tide came in. I was very anxious all of a sudden and I could feel a similar nervous energy coming from Micah. I couldn't hear his thoughts directly, but his emotions hit me like the tides, flowing in and out as he also tried to contain himself.

"First things first. Time to give you a little test." With that, he threw me a wicked grin and took off running around a rock formation on the beach. I couldn't help but laugh and follow. Just as I rounded the corner, I saw a bolt of red magic coming at me. I dodged it and shot back with a purple dart of my own. We weren't truly aiming for each other, but I could tell that Micah wanted a gauge on what my magical defense looked like. It was liberating to use my power in a playful way and I was thankful human eyes couldn't detect the darts of color shooting in both directions.

This went on for a few minutes, him shooting larger bolts and me running behind him, face scrunched, willing something just half the size to come from my palms. I tried to channel the power I'd let loose on the cliffs, to really show him what I knew was inside me, but it was being stubborn today. The more I pushed, the less it reacted. What should have been thick bolts of power laced with violet and streaks of white were tiny streams that looked as if they were shot from a kid's water gun.

"Stop. Stop, Amelia." Micah jogged over to me. "Do you understand how to truly source your power? I feel like you're concentrating far harder on this than you should be. Your power is an extension of you. It is intermingled in your mind and your soul. It lies in every cell and each individual drop of blood. You cannot separate yourself from your power, so you should not have to try so hard to use it."

I cocked my head, completely confused. I understood what he was saying from the perspective of how it felt to lose control, but not in everyday use. I'd never *had* everyday use.

"Well. I… uh, have never used my power every day, so I don't know what you mean. I've actually spent more time telling it to sit down and shut up than using it." I glanced sideways at him, ashamed of how I grew up and how inadequate it made me in the scheme of things.

He stood there, mouth open, completely shocked. "Pardon?" was the only thing he could apparently say, though I got the feeling his mind had far more going on than was coming out his mouth.

"It's really not that big of deal. I mean, I just need you to show me how to do it. I'll be fine. I mean, you saw the freeze thing. And the thing in the alley. Clearly, I've got stuff to work with." I was embarrassed, but also a little annoyed that he was being so condescending. "Is this too much for you?" I asked, raising an eyebrow and allowing sarcasm to flood my tone.

"Certainly not. It's just…surprising. Let's move on." And with that, we moved into telekinesis. Moving things around would have been a dead giveaway, so even though I'd tested it a few times, I'd never spent any span of time on the skill. The exertion from pulling and yanking at my power for the last hour was grating on me and I could feel the headache starting. Not wanting to let Micah down, I pressed on. Various pieces of driftwood found new homes around our span of beach and I found myself sweating with the exertion of holding a rock the size of a basketball suspended in mid-air.

Micah was all business, standing with his arms crossed as he evaluated me. Nodding and giving instruction to put things here or there. He didn't ask again about what I could or couldn't do. For that, I was thankful. But as I stood there, a chunk of driftwood hovering over the water, my vision doubled and a sharp ache punched through my core. I dropped the log and fell to my knees, grateful we were on the beach and not concrete.

Micah was there in an instant, apologizing. "Are you okay? I'm so sorry. I should have realized what this would do to you. Sit down." He helped me back from my knees to sit on the sand and I could feel the top of my body actually moving in a circle as the rest of the world spun around me. Darkness threatened at the edges of my vision and I took deep breaths, willing myself to stay conscious. It took a few minutes but finally the world righted itself and it was only a dull throb thudding in the back of my skull.

"How about I drive you home?" Micah asked.

"No, just take me to the gym. Cole can help me." I realized as the words came out that Micah hadn't made that connection yet. I closed my eyes and exhaled in frustration. "He's my brother. Which also makes him a Mage. But, it's fine. He can help me. That's what he does."

Micah didn't ask questions. I was thankful he let it go and supported me as he led me up the beach and across the street to the gym. He let me go in alone, but wasn't happy about it.

As luck would have it, Cole wasn't actually at the gym, so I sat in his office for a while until my headache subsided. I was still exhausted, but I forced myself out to my car and navigated my way back to the apartment. I was asleep instantly and didn't move until the alarm went off the next morning. My only dreamless nights seemed to come after my body had been through the ringer.

Chapter 11

Over the next two weeks if I wasn't with Aidan, then I was with Micah. We changed locations often and, if the weather was bad and Bethany was working, we would just go to my apartment. I was kind of avoiding her because it was awkward to know I was spending all of this time with her boyfriend and we weren't telling her. It had been so much easier when I was hiding my power from everyone and the worst thing we had to discuss was where our next double date would take us. She was still my best friend, but I had to be honest with myself and realize that my *human* best friend just couldn't know, no matter how much I wanted her to.

In my sessions with Micah, we worked on so many things, but the biggest challenge and his biggest focal point was my mental defense. He wanted to make damn sure that I not only knew how to keep other Mages out, but that I could get in. This was some of the stuff Cole was most concerned about, too. He and I kept missing each other as he searched for more of his connections and I intentionally avoided having to talk to him and not explain about Aidan. But, we had texted and he was pacified to know that I was working on things. The problem, however, was that I just didn't get it. So, here we sat on the beach, yet again, as Micah explained the process.

"Okay, Amelia. We're going to try this a different way. Instead of you coming at me, I'm going to come at you. I'm going to do it slowly and we're going to talk through each step." His patient tone amazed me. I had all but given up on myself already. I sat up straight and forced myself to focus. So often in these sessions my mind drifted to Aidan and wished I were cuddled with him on my couch, watching a movie instead of sitting on a windy beach with my best friend's boyfriend. I opened my mouth and let out an audible exhale, trying to clear my head. I tilted my head toward my left shoulder and then my right. "Okay, Micah. Let's do this." I sounded more confident than I felt.

"This time, I want you to keep your eyes open," he directed. "Remember that humans can't see what we're doing here, so don't react to what you see. I'm trying to make this easier on you so I'm going to be very blatant about it. Watch me." Micah stared intently at me, his eyes slowly transitioning from their normal ice blue to red. It always freaked me out because he looked almost demonic — his blond hair, pale skin, and now bright red eyes. But as I watched him, I saw the tendrils of red start to float between us and knew my own eyes deepened to violet as my power rose in response. The red wisps spun and swirled, looking like smoke as they moved from him toward me. Suddenly, the smoke zipped quickly toward my face and it took all my strength to hold steady as people walked by on the beach. The smoke came to a dead stop right in front of my nose. I was almost cross-eyed as I stared into it, waiting for something to happen.

"Now, stop me." Micah gave me all of two seconds for that to sink in before he was pushing at my mind. It was as if a stranger were beating on my front door. Pounding furiously.

My hands went to my ears to stop the pounding. "What? Micah? What the hell?"

"Amelia. Stop doing that and *stop me*," he said through gritted teeth.

I closed my eyes and let the pressure in my mind extend throughout the rest of my body. When I felt that feeling of simmering electricity in every cell that was finally becoming familiar, I let my power seek out his. With a mental shove, I pushed at the red smoke. Not realizing I didn't need to push *that* hard, Micah and I both flew apart and back into the sand.

I sat back up, rubbing my temple, one eye closed and the other squinting across at him. His reaction was much the same as he scowled.

"Too much?" I asked. He gave a chuckle. "Too much, indeed. Let's try it again, except this time, I want you to let me in. Not far, but just far enough to open our lines of communication."

I took another deep breath and nodded as I repositioned myself on the sand and focused on Micah again.

"I'm not going to project the fact that I'm coming at you," he explained. "So, look for me. Find me. This is what I was talking about in the alley. We all have a signature and now that you've met mine, you can find it more easily." His directions seemed clear enough.

I closed my eyes, surprised to still see Micah in my mind. Though all I saw was red smoke sitting in front of me, it was obvious when he pushed his power toward me. He lightly knocked on the door of my mind. The pressure of him was there, just on the fringes, and I knew I had to decide if I could truly let him in — if it were smart to let him in. Quickly weighing the pros and cons, I decided he had been more of a friend to me in the last few weeks than most, so I took the chance. I allowed my power to meet his, the two swept around and around each other, tightening their loops until they resembled a twisted braid of color. They spun faster and faster until finally the braid was one single strand. Then, I heard him.

Looks like you finally figured out how to talk to me.

Hearing Micah in my head had to truly be the strangest happening yet. *I had no idea this was even possible.*

I heard his laugh as he said, *There's so much you don't know. But, we'll get there.*

With that, he left my mind. I opened my eyes to find both of us grinning at each other.

We sat there in silence for just a few moments and then Micah brought me back to the present with a muttered curse.

"What?" I asked. "Did I mess it up somehow?"

"No, I just realized that I am, yet again, late for a date with Bethany and she just might kill me this time." Micah sighed and stood, brushing himself off.

"Oh, no! We can pick this up another time," I said. "You need to take that girl out and have a good night. I'm sure she's missed you!"

He shrugged and helped me to my feet. "What we're doing here is very important. But, yes, she deserves better than this."

The sun had long gone down and the moon was just rising. We were basically alone on the beach and I'm sure to the average person looked like a couple coming up from a rendezvous. We were both quietly walking up toward the parking area with our shoes in our hands when a bolt of blue magic went shooting by us. Micah plowed into me, sending us both face first into the sand just as the next bolt came flying by.

"Shit! Amelia, we have to get to safety. Dammit! Where are they?"

He was crouched and looking in every direction, muttering to himself, "I should have been paying attention. I can't believe I wasn't paying attention!"

"What do you want me to do?" I whispered, bringing myself into a crouch as well.

"The best we can hope for is that we can run and shoot at the same time. Your aim has gotten much better and the blasts don't actually have to be big, just frequent," he said.

"The gym is just over the boardwalk. If we can make it to the back alley, then we can get inside," I explained. "Cole is always cleaning up around this time and props that back door open to empty the trash."

Micah nodded and we spoke in low voices for just a few minutes more, finalizing our plan. On "Three!" we were up and sprinting for the boardwalk. Even with magic coursing through our veins at top speed, I still had a hard time keeping my footing in the dense sand. As I shot purple blasts, thankfully larger now than they were at first, toward the direction of the blue bolts, Micah was also blasting them with large red bolts.

Trees were falling, sand was exploding everywhere, and the area was a mess. It was only as we hit the boardwalk and started around the corner that I saw bright blue eyes staring back at me. It suddenly hit me that I'd never seen or heard of blue power. Each Immortal race has their own signature and blue was never one we discussed. It was the same reason my father tried to keep me quarantined...violet eyes were rarely seen and he didn't want people asking questions.

I didn't have a chance to look again or process it further because another bolt came flying at me at the same time Micah hauled me around a corner and shoved me into the back door of Cole's gym.

The locker room was dark and we both fell against the door as we shoved it closed. We were panting and I realized I had left my shoes on the beach. So many thoughts were racing through my mind...*Who were those people? What did they want? How did they find us?* I turned to question Micah about these same things and couldn't help but laugh as I realized he had a huge chunk of seaweed in his hair. I was just reaching up to brush it away when I heard a voice say, "What the hell are you two doing?"

Aidan. Shit, shit, SHIT! It seemed like Micah and I started to speak at the same time, then stopped, looking at each other, then started again. Finally, I glared at him to shut him up and stepped toward Aidan.

"Looks like you caught us!" I tossed out, trying to sound like it was no big deal that he had walked into a scene that looked just about as bad as it actually was, but for completely different reasons. Aidan stood in front of me, still mostly in the shadows of the dark locker room. His stance and posture were exuding his rage at finding me with Micah. He had me reeling at the myriad of emotions that rolled off of him. Anger. Frustration. Hurt. I had to force myself to keep moving toward him, pushing through it all and knowing that there was absolutely no way around having to lie.

"I thought you would like it if I learned more about MMA, so I convinced Micah to start teaching me some of the moves and the lingo. I want to be able to understand what you're doing. I know it's important to you." I didn't bother to explain that I already held all of this knowledge and I could probably teach Micah a thing or two, even in the ring, because of Cole. I just prayed that Aidan wouldn't ask too many questions.

"You…asked Micah…to teach you about MMA?" The raised eyebrow and stone-cold expression made it obvious that he didn't believe a word I had said, but couldn't really dispute it. Without turning away from Aidan, I sent a message to Micah, *Tell him that you've been teaching me. Things like the proper way to defend an arm bar.*

I could feel Micah's confusion and hesitation, but he delivered the statement with utter confidence. Even adding that I was a better fighter than most would expect.

I puffed up a little, knowing that Cole's training would come in handy one day. He'd love hearing this story in a few years when I could admit to dating Aidan. I gave Aidan a big smile and challenged him, bouncing on the balls of my feet in a Southpaw stance.

"Whatcha got?!" I poked with a forced grin. He let out a little snort, snatching me up, bringing me flush with his body, and pressing a kiss to the top of my head. "Alright then, doll. You win. I'm not gonna fight you. But, I do need a minute with your training partner over there." I could feel him channel everything into protecting me — us — as he faced down Micah. I was certain he didn't believe a word I'd said. He wanted to, but there was just no way.

I kept my smile going, leaving them as if I had no reason to be concerned, though I was almost certain Aidan could probably dismantle Micah. Micah might have had a few inches, but Aidan had more muscle and certainly more emotion at this particular moment. I was lost in my own thoughts and didn't realize I had made my way to Cole's office. He looked up, surprised to see me, and instantly was up and around the desk. "Ame, what's up? I can feel it, some thing's wrong. What happened?"

Cole was giving me that look that was half "Dad", half "who can I beat up because I'm your big brother?"

I still didn't know how to explain the attack. It was only just now occurring to me what it could mean, so I didn't say anything. I just walked into his arms and buried myself in my big brother's chest. While I could feel his confusion over why I was so upset and his anger at whomever had caused it, he gave me a moment with his hand on the back of my head. Finally, I disengaged myself and stepped back.

"Cole, there's so much to say, so much that's been happening these last few weeks that I haven't had the chance to fill you in on. But, Aidan's going to be coming to find me soon and this is going to take a while to explain." I sighed, looking around for Aidan but knowing Cole wasn't going to let me off easy. He clearly wasn't happy with my build up and let down.

"Amelia, you come into my gym after dark with your power on full tilt, sand all over you, no shoes on, looking like hell, and you expect me to just let you walk away without an explanation because one of your *friends* is coming to look for you?" he asked.

It hadn't sounded so ridiculous in my head, but I also had no clue that I looked so terrible. Cole's face took on a pretty frightening expression; the one he reserved for the hoodlums who tried to infiltrate his gym... or when his sister stepped out of line.

Of course, Aidan decided at that moment to come around the corner and step into Cole's office. He actually wore a similar look to Cole.

"Amelia, you know Cole?" Aidan's shock was apparent. Then, he kept looking from me to Cole, and back. It wasn't really that hard to see the family resemblance when we were right next to each other, and I visibly knew the moment it clicked for him. I hadn't exactly hidden the fact that we were related, I just hadn't given it up willingly. I hoped that he didn't connect the fact that I might have already known the things Micah was supposedly teaching me. The lies just kept getting harder to maintain.

I gave Aidan a tentative smile but Cole didn't wait for him to verbalize the pieces he'd put together. He just stepped in front of me, crossed his arms over his chest, and said, "Yeah, she's my little sister. And, we've got stuff to deal with. So, I need you to beat it, Montgomery. I know you guys are friends, but we've got some family stuff."

"We're *friends*?" Aidan repeated slowly. From behind Cole, I nodded frantically at Aidan, trying to make him understand that the last thing I needed was to have that conversation now. In front of Cole. "Uh, yeah, we're…friends," he said, nodding at me. "Amelia, just call me later and you can finish filling me in on that *other thing*." Those last few words were punctuated with such an angry undercurrent, I shivered.

I had to be the only person on the planet capable of pissing off every guy in my life on the same day while managing to get them to all lie to each other — while lying to them myself. And, the fact that Aidan and Cole were giving me the exact same look did not bode well for my future.

Chapter 12

Aidan left the office and it took a moment for Cole to turn around to face me. I could tell from his stance that he was trying to control his temper. Finally, he turned and simply said, "Sit."

His tone had said enough. I sat.

"Would you like to tell me what in the hell is going on?" Cole's tone was patronizing as he leaned against his desk, his arms crossed.

"Well. The funny part about all of this is that I don't actually know." I wanted to play it off, but thoughts were bouncing around inside my head like someone had let every pinball loose in the machine. Every day just brought more information. More to think about. More questions. I had done an okay job of compartmentalizing everything up until now, but it all came crashing into me at once. Being the last Elder. Making friends with a Mage. Lying to my best friend and the guy I liked. Being attacked. *Being attacked.*

I looked up at Cole, my eyes filled with barely restrained hysteria, expecting to see anger. Instead, I saw empathy, frustration… sadness.

He sighed and sat down next to me. "Talk to me, Ame. We both know you've been avoiding me for weeks. Did I dump too much on you too fast? You know we can't just wait around for you to get comfortable, right? You're too far behind."

Anger replaced fear as he once again resorted to big brother behaviors. I stood, this time looking down at him. The emotion filling my chest choked my words, making them feel thick and hard to push out.

"Comfortable? You think I've just been hiding out in my room waiting until I can *handle* all of this, do you? You don't get it, Cole. You've been running around the country for last ten years. Granted, it was for me, but for you, too. Don't deny it. And, all the while, I've been dealing with Dad. With *this*."

I intentionally allowed my power to flood my system in a huge tidal wave that dropped my head back and sent crackling fever to my fingertips. I looked back down at him knowing my eyes were glowing, the iridescent purple likely giving me my own demonic quality. I held my hands up, watching the energy pulsing around them and losing myself for just a moment in the heady feeling of it all. I wanted to blow something up. Now.

I felt Cole coming toward me and before I could pull away he locked each of his hands around my wrists. "Calm down, Amelia. Don't do this." He stood nose to nose with me, looking more controlled than he probably should have. I'm sure I looked like a wild woman — wide-eyed and crazy. But, his energy immediately sapped away the hard edge of my power, placing layer after layer of smothering tranquility on top of the feral fire I had started.

The longer he held my wrists, the more I came back to myself. Instead of a powerful being, I was a scared girl who had just been attacked. All of the facade I had showed Aidan and the calm my power presented to Cole dropped away and I collapsed into him, sobbing into his chest as he hugged me and told me it would be okay. I pulled away, realizing we hadn't even had the worst part of the conversation yet.

Sniffling, I pushed back and sat back in my own chair. "I look like this because Micah and I were attacked. We were working on the beach and suddenly someone just started throwing bolts at us. Blue ones. None of our people have blue power! Mages have shades of green and red, and we talk about violet but few actually realize that's only Elders. What does that mean, Cole? Who are they?"

Cole was pale and quiet. He should have been ranting and raving at me for how stupid it was of us to be out in the open, or questioning the how's and why's of what had happened, but he just sat there with a glazed look, taking short, quick breaths.

"What aren't you telling me, Cole?" More secrets. More information I deserved to know but didn't.

He finally looked at me, saying, "I don't know yet. There were rumors but no one ever believed them. It's probably nothing. What about Micah? Does he know what happened? I think we need to get him in here. We need to talk about what happened and see if he saw something different from what you did."

"You're serious? You want me to just let that whole reaction go and then you want to bring Micah in so you can verify that I'm not just making all of this up? You're amazing." I stood up, shaking my head. "I need to go home."

He vaulted out of his chair. "No! I'm taking you home. You go nowhere alone. You are always with someone. We don't know what happened tonight or why it happened. Don't you get it, Amelia? They could be after *you*. Someone could know what you are. They could want you for all the same reasons the queen does."

I dropped back into the chair feeling like a bigger idiot than I had when Aidan caught Micah and me. "What should I do?" It came out much wimpier than I would have liked, but all of my bravado had been used up for the day.

Cole and I talked for a long time. We argued about whether or not we should talk to Rynna about everything. We talked about who those people could have possibly been and what they may have wanted with me. We talked and we argued until I was exhausted. It had been hours before either of us realized that we hadn't eaten and it was getting very late. Cole finally agreed it was safe enough to leave and he brought his car up to the front door so I could just run and dive right in. We went through a drive-thru and I demolished a giant burrito in record time.

As Cole dropped me at my apartment, he made me promise that I would set up a meeting between him, Micah, and me for the next evening to determine what Micah had seen and what he might know that we didn't. He hugged me tightly before letting me out of the car. "I love you, Amelia. Keep your phone on at all times and call me if anything weird happens."

I laughed. "I know, Cole, I'm on high alert. I won't go anywhere alone and I'll keep my eyes open. I don't think they would try anything in broad daylight and in public. At least, I hope not." He gave me a look that made it obvious he wasn't amused at my line of thinking. I gave his arm another squeeze and got out of the car. With one last wave, I went through the outer door and into my building.

My smile faded as I turned to find Aidan sitting on the steps leading up to my floor. His eyes were cold steel, none of the warmth and comfort I normally found in them, and I couldn't read his expression.

"Aidan. Um… hi." I had no idea what to say. Exhaustion was beating on my door, especially after that burrito. All I wanted to do was curl into bed and sleep for a week. Unfortunately, I had one very unhappy…boy? Friend? God, I don't even know what to call him, let alone how to handle his reaction today. There's no way I could be as honest with him as I was with Cole and I wasn't sure I could keep any more lies straight.

Aidan slowly rose from the steps and came toward me, his eyes never leaving mine. Just as I thought he was going to reach out, he spoke instead, "Come walk with me." Each word was enunciated, his tone making it obvious that it wasn't a choice.

He turned down the hall on the first floor without waiting for a response. I sighed and rolled my eyes at his back, sick of being told what to do. He led me out the back door of the complex toward the small park facing our building. There were a few little trails with some picnic tables and benches scattered throughout. He continued toward the first table and sat on the tabletop. It reminded me of that first night; his outline in the shadows, how dangerous but alluring I found him then.

Now, I was tired and mostly irritated. As I stood facing him, my irritation only grew as he glared at me, as if he were warning me. It was just too much and I found myself pacing in front of him. Nervous energy had me wringing my hands and I refused to look his direction as my voice dropped, the words strangled as I searched for ways to tell the truth without telling the whole truth.

"Aidan, I can't do this. I can't *do* this right now. I know you want answers and you don't understand what happened earlier today, but as much as I wish I could explain it, I just can't. It's complicated, it really has nothing to do with us and…I just *can't*. So, don't sit there, giving me your 'death stare', thinking that you're going to intimidate me into doing whatever you want." I finally pivoted on my heel and faced him as my frustration from the day poured out and onto the last person it should have. "You know what, on that note, I'm so sick and tired of the men around me thinking that they can just muscle me into doing whatever they want. Just screw you. All of you. I need a break. I need to breathe. There's a lot going on with me right now and it sucks! I just need…"

I didn't have a chance to finish my tirade before he grabbed me by both arms and crashed his lips to mine. Just like that, the entire world exploded. My power leapt, erupting through and around me with ferocity that rivaled my night on the cliffs, but it was all happening internally. I was so full of electricity and energy that I thought I might burst, but I didn't have time to analyze it because all I could feel were his lips. His passion crushing me while his lips melted against mine.

It wasn't even a thought as I opened my mouth to his and his tongue swirled and danced with my own. He let go of my arms to wrap his around me, pulling me between his legs and pressing me as close to him as he could get. I wrapped my arms around his neck, my fingers twisting in his thick hair. I was trapped between walls of muscle — between his legs, inside his arms — and for the first time in days, I felt absolutely safe. I gave myself wholly to a kiss that I knew would change everything. That was changing everything.

My power reached outside me and enveloped us both, wrapping around him. A second later, he shoved me away.

Shoved me so hard that I found myself looking up at him from the ground where I had landed. "What the hell, Aidan?" I stuttered, still reeling and confused about the literal pain in my butt as well as the fog in my brain.

He actually looked a little panicked. "Did you feel that? What happened?"

He was looking around, staring into the trees as if he expected someone to come rushing out.

"What are you talking about? The only thing I felt was the most amazing kiss of my life turn into me landing on my butt in a pile of sticks. What is your deal?" I asked as I tried to brush myself off and pick twigs from my hair. I wanted to throw something at his head I was so annoyed. He finally stood up, still looking around.

"Are you sure? I mean, it felt like…well, it was as if something was…never mind." He shook his head as he gave up trying and I suddenly realized it could have been me. I still didn't really know how to completely control my telepathy and I could have gotten inside his head. My anger turned to concern.

"Aidan, I don't know what's going on, but I'm sorry. And… uh, I'm sorry if the kiss wasn't as good for you as it was for me." I ducked my head a little, embarrassed that I was so inexperienced that he could be distracted — even if it was my Immortal voodoo freaking him out.

He stopped looking around and stared down at me. He didn't speak, just tilted my chin up to force our eyes to meet. He continued to hold my eyes, his gaze melting my insides. His lips met mine once more, and only then did he close them.

These kisses were slow and sweet, not near the heat of the first. He tilted and transitioned back and forth, from left to right, stopping to press kisses to my jawline and down my neck. I leaned back, hands in his hair once more as I sighed his name. Finally, he lingered one last time, slowly scrapping his teeth over my bottom lip as he pulled away.

He touched his forehead to mine and said, "Amelia, I don't think I ever want a kiss from anyone else again. I'm sorry for before. I don't really know what's happening, but I feel it, too. I can't explain it, but I feel like something is happening. And, I know you weren't doing anything wrong with Micah. I don't know why I know or why I can't stay mad about it, but some part of me knows that it's okay. I just hope that you decide that you can tell me the truth. But, I know all about secrets and I'm not going to push. For now."

He pulled me into his chest, pressing a kiss to the top of my head. I was confused. I was exhausted. I had just had the best kiss of my life. I could think about the rest tomorrow.

I woke up and laid staring at the wall for quite some time. There were dreams swirling in my head that I couldn't quite remember. The last tiny piece I could grasp before it floated away was running through the trees. That had been a theme lately — dreams in the forest. It was weird, but I had bigger issues than a random haunting dream. Those were the status quo.

My mind didn't know how to process everything that had happened yesterday. Micah, the attack, Aidan, telling Cole everything, kissing Aidan. *Kissing Aidan.*

Oh, I could have reminisced on that one forever. Touching my fingertips to my lips, I closed my eyes and lost myself in the feelings once again. Finally, I forced myself up. My clothes from yesterday were in a pile by the bed, my purse at the bottom of the pile. *Oh, crap!* Though I had promised Cole to stay close to my phone, I realized that I hadn't actually looked at it since he dropped me off yesterday. I dug into my purse, pulled it out, and unlocked the screen.

Twelve text messages

Three voicemails

Double crap!

I went through the text messages first, those were easier. A few from Bethany, but I could hear her out in the kitchen and would deal with that directly. Well, maybe after breakfast. And coffee. Lots of coffee.

A string of them were from Micah, asking if I was okay, asking to meet up last night to talk, getting a little more frantic to hear from me. I responded to him, letting him know that I was fine and asking to meet tonight at the gym.

He immediately responded.

Where have you been? Why do you have a phone you don't use? Do you know what I've been thinking the last twelve hours?! Why the gym?

I'll explain tonight. The gym is safe. Just meet me, OK?

Fine. The gym. 7. See you then.

There were quite a few from Aidan from before I saw him. Some were questioning. Some were angry. But, the only one that mattered was the one he must have sent after he walked me to my door.

I'm so glad I waited for you. It was the most amazing kiss of my life, too.

I smiled. I hadn't thought he was really listening to me at that point, but I guess he was.

Finally, there was one from Cole this morning asking about the meet. I confirmed with him that Micah would be there.

Now came the hard part. How to explain to my human best friend that my magic was out of control, her boyfriend was a Mage, but mine was human, my brother was also a Mage, someone had attacked Micah and me, we had no idea why, and…oh, yeah, not tell her any of that because she can't know Immortals even exist. Determined to fix my relationship with my best friend, I left the voicemails for later and opened my door to face the music.

I knew Bethany wasn't her normal self as soon as I walked into the kitchen and heard an acoustic ballad coming from the IPod dock. Typically, she always listened to something upbeat, whether it be Pop or Country. To hear this music meant she was accessing my play lists. The songs weren't necessarily sad, but their voices were haunting and the songs typically a little less happy and shiny. She was humming as she stirred her coffee, clearly lost in her own thoughts.

I stopped a few feet short of her, just outside the kitchen. "Hey." It was lame.

I had no idea where to start. She looked up at me, her face still clean of makeup and her hair pulled back in a low ponytail. Her over-sized sweatshirt dwarfed her tiny frame, making her look like a little girl, and her eyes were sad.

"Look, B, I know I owe you a huge apology for avoiding you lately. I've just had some stuff that I needed to work out for myself and I needed some space to think. I'm really sorry if I hurt your feelings." I stood in the doorway, fidgeting, waiting for her response.

"Amelia, honey, I love you, but not everything is about you." Bethany's words were just as sad as her eyes. She placed her spoon on the bright purple spoon rest on the counter, picked up her over-sized mug, and walked around me.

I had no idea what to do. For the past week, I had just assumed the looks she had been giving were because of me. It was clear I really didn't get how this whole best friend thing worked. I quickly pulled my act together and followed her to the living room. While I was gathering my thoughts, she had settled into the couch, pulling a worn quilt her Grandma had made over her lap.

Though Bethany never had any idea of what I was handling, from the first day we met I never questioned whether she would always have my back. She pushed me to not allow other people to define me and inspired me to not just be myself, but the best damn version of myself possible. "The world deserves it, Ame! You deserve it!" She would say. She also taught me that the best relationships were built on truth. And sometimes the truth was hard.

I sat down on the love seat across from her. "I have been a pretty crappy friend lately, haven't I?"

She didn't hesitate with, "Yeah, you pretty much have."

One of our rules was that we didn't sugarcoat, but it still hurt to be called on your crap.

"Talk to me, B. I know I'm late to the party, and it's no excuse that I was hiding from my own life, but I'm here and I want to listen. I really am sorry." I looked her in the eyes and tried to convey how sorry I truly was.

One of the things I really loved about Bethany was that once she forgave you, it was over. You knew she wasn't holding a grudge; it was truly over and she was moving on. I saw it cross her face, when she had officially decided to forgive me, and the slow inhale she took signaled that this was worse than I had imagined.

"I think Micah is seeing someone else," she said, her eyes brimming with tears. I couldn't hide my shock, my mouth falling open. "He's been really unavailable the last few weeks, not answering my messages or emails until much later and canceling our dates. I didn't realize that I liked him this much, but it's just been killing me."

I was stunned. I should have seen this coming; that his spending time teaching me meant he wouldn't be spending time with her, but it hadn't even occurred to me. Crappy Friend Sign #12!

"Oh, honey, no," I reassured her. "There's just no way he's seeing someone else. There has to be an explanation. Do you want me to see if Aidan can talk to him? Maybe we can set up a double? I know he's way into you, I'm just sure of it."

I had no clue how to get around the fact that I would see Micah tonight, but obviously I couldn't explain how or why to Bethany. It was breaking my heart to see her so upset.

"I'm sure this is just a misunderstanding," I continued when she didn't respond. "He probably just has a lot going on. And, you know guys are clueless — he probably just doesn't understand that this isn't acceptable."

"Are you sure, Amelia? I mean, really sure? Truth, remember?" Her words were like a knife — I was not built to be a liar. I could do it, but I hated every second.

"I don't want to get my hopes up and then get hurt. I hate how much this hurts already. I don't do this. I don't let boys do this," she said with a sniffle, swallowing back the break in her voice and blinking away the building tears. I hated myself just a little more watching her steel herself against what I knew she was feeling.

I stood strong in the truth that he wasn't seeing someone else and continued to reassure her, actually moving across the room and giving her a big hug.

"It's all going to work out, B, you'll see. Let's just give him a chance to explain. I'll talk to Aidan, we'll get this sorted out." She looked at me with relief and then I saw the change come over her.

"Okay, then. Enough wallowing. I'm going to pull myself together. The last thing he's going to see is that this has been bothering me."

With that, she threw the quilt aside and strode off with purpose. "Go get'em, B! Show him what he's been missing!" I hollered after her.

I jumped from the couch myself and changed the iPod back to pop. When I heard Bethany's low alto singing merrily along with the track, I knew it was going to be okay. Maybe Micah wasn't cheating, but I had no doubt she'd make him regret the last few weeks. I laughed a little to myself, realizing maybe I wasn't the only one with the issue of balancing two worlds.

Bethany headed out for class and I collapsed on the couch, exhausted though it was only eight in the morning. My phone dug into me from my back pocket and remembered that I still had voice mails to check.

Entering the appropriate passwords in, the string started. I deleted messages from Micah and Cole from last night, rolling my eyes at how similar both messages sounded. I was trying to befriend Micah so he could help me, I wasn't signing up for a second big brother.

Then, Rynna's soft voice came on and I couldn't stop the gasp that followed her words.

"Hi Amelia, honey. I'm sorry I had to cut you off the other night. There are just things I can't really talk about. I did want to let you know that your father came home and he seems just fine outside of being hungry. He has actually had a few really great days and even spoke to me a few times. Unfortunately, I've spent the last few hours trying to convince him that he shouldn't, but he's determined to visit an old friend. He believes this man has answers. He's going to go whether I want him to or not and there's not a lot I can do to stop him. I'm afraid that he might drop back into his normal state at any time, so I'm going to go along with him. We're leaving in the morning and heading up into the mountains, so I don't know what cell reception will be like. I'll try to call or text when I can, just know that I'll take care of him just like I took care of you. We'll talk soon."

Immediately, panic set in. Every alarm bell in my system went off at once. My hands shook and I dropped the phone. Swearing, I leaned down to pick it up to find both of my hands enveloped in violet pulsing light. I raised them in front of me, turning them front to back, shocked at how quickly my power had taken over, that I hadn't done anything or felt anything and yet, there it was, at my disposal.

Mentally berated myself for being so easily distracted, I sent an internal command to shut things down and my hands slowly faded back to normal. I dove for my phone and punched Rynna's speed dial in. It went straight to voicemail. *Dammit.* I tried again. Voicemail.

"Ryn, I just got your message. You need to call me." I tried to contain the fear, but no matter what, my Dad was the only parent I had left and it was literally impossible to guess how he might react in any given situation. "He shouldn't be doing this. Dad hasn't left town in years. I don't know that he can do this. Who is this guy? What answers does he have? Does this have to do with me? Ryn, I'm learning more about myself. I'm getting better at handling it all. He doesn't need to do this. Just call me."

I dropped back on the couch and dropped my arm over my eyes. Too much. The last twenty-four hours had just been too much. Taking a few deep breaths, I tried to calm the growing ache in the pit of my stomach that was telling me this was just the beginning.

Chapter 13

The day passed relatively slowly, my classes dragging and my lack of sleep making me even less attentive. My mind was lost between thoughts of my dad and Rynna, the attack, and how I was possibly going to keep up training in the midst of all of this chaos. I was in line for my second caramel latte of the day when I felt someone coming up behind me. Before I could decide to react to the feeling, hands slid over my eyes, a low voice whispered in my ear, and I breathed in the welcoming scent of citrus and woods.

"Well, there you are. I've been looking for you all day."

Warmth spread through me as Aidan's voice sent shivers across my skin. Immediately, some of my tension lessened and it was as if I could breathe again. His skin was warm as I pulled his hands from my eyes and turned around.

"Is that so?" I asked as I gave him my best flirty smile. "Well, a girl has to keep you guessing. I can't show you all of my tricks just yet."

Aidan wrapped his arms around me, pulling me to him, keeping his voice low and flirtatious. "Tricks, huh? I think I'd like to see more of your tricks."

His dark curls were falling across his forehead and it was obvious by the look in his eyes the kind of tricks he was talking about.

"Down, boy!" I said with a smack to his chest. I shimmied back into my spot in line and ordered my drink. I was thankful I'd spent a little more time on today's outfit, pairing an A-line summer dress with my favorite wedges. It had been in an attempt to convince myself I felt better than I did after yesterday's events, but the look on Aidan's face as he took me in was a definite side benefit. The half-smile that played at his lips and the look of obvious appreciation in his eyes as they traveled from my face to my bright pink toe nails made each extra minute worth it.

As we moved to the side to wait for my drink, I found his mouth next to my ear again.

"I'm going to kiss you again, Amelia. Soon. Very soon." I closed my eyes and smiled, reveling in his whispered promise. I could feel my power humming happily, reacting to the potential of it already. I turned around to throw another line his way only to find he had disappeared. I shook my head and laughed. Bethany was right...I was in some serious trouble.

I got to the gym a little early, wanting to talk to Cole without Micah. But, my being early meant I also ran into Aidan on his way out from his workout. Aidan didn't ask why I was there and I didn't offer. We chatted for a few moments, but his expression changed and a millisecond later I found myself being pulled into a training room.

The walls were red, covered in training mats in case the guys were tossing each other around a little too hard. Aidan held me captive against one of those mats, his forearms on each side of my head, his fingertips playing in the hair that splayed around me. It was dark in the room, just the light from a small window allowing the sun to peak in.

The only sound was our breathing. Mine a little more frantic than his. This proximity to Aidan narrowed my focus to only him — to the warm puffs of air he exhaled into my neck as he nuzzled that sensitive space — and I lost all coherent thought. After a nip to my earlobe, Aidan finally pulled back slightly. Though I needed that sliver of space, looking into his eyes made it perfectly clear what his intentions were. He silently dared me to object as his mouth got closer and closer to mine. I tilted my chin toward him a fraction of an inch before the reality of why I was at the gym sent an involuntary shiver up my spin. The attack. My power. *My damn duty.*

I sighed and that was enough to stop Aidan. He was hovering just a breath away.

"What is it?" he asked gruffly. His voice changed when we were in these situations. It was low and rough and so very sexy. I hated breaking up this perfect moment but the guilt weighing on me couldn't be stopped. I had started this. I told him I wanted to try. But, the attack changed things. At least until we understood what it was. What it meant. The last thing I could take was Aidan being hurt because of me.

"Aidan, I can't do this."

He yanked backward, all of the sweet softness of the last few minutes replaced with stiffness and a wary look.

"No, wait, that's not what I meant!" I rushed to try to salvage my choice of words, his reaction making me cringe.

"This is just so intense. It's just so…much. I just need to slow down." I had a hard time looking at him, knowing full well that I wanted to run full sprint into this. Even now, I wanted to jump into his arms, wrap my legs around his waist, and kiss him from here to moon, never even coming up for air. But, I couldn't. I couldn't keep making rash decisions and I couldn't put him in harm's way. If another attack came before Micah, Cole, and I could figure this out, and Aidan was hurt, I would never forgive myself.

He was suddenly wrapping me in his arms again. "Okay. Okay, doll. I'm sorry, I just can't help myself when I'm around you. It's like I can't stop; you're a magnet and I just want to be near you. To touch you. And, after the other night," he pulled back to show me that mischievous grin I loved, "kiss you. Again and again."

He pressed a kiss to the top of my head — it was starting to be one of my favorite things. A heartfelt reassurance that we were good and I hadn't completely messed this up. His grip was firm on the back of my neck as he pulled me in close for a long, hard hug. "I don't want you to be afraid of this, Amelia. Afraid of me. So, we'll go slow. I know I can be intense. I guess that's the foster kid in me. When I find someone worth it, I give it everything I've got."

I pulled back, words I couldn't say stuck on my tongue, not even sure how to make him understand what this meant to me. Simultaneously, I realized that even amid my lies, Aidan was being an amazing man. I didn't deserve him. I dove back into his chest, giving him my own hug, muttering a thank you, wishing I could stay there forever and just forget the rest of it. He and I both had so much baggage, I was worried we couldn't shoulder the load.

Aidan gave me a squeeze and then pulled away, looking down at me. "As much as I'd like to believe you were here for me, doll, I expect that your brother is waiting for you and I'd prefer to not end up being his punching bag during tomorrow's training. So, I'll see you later, 'kay? And don't think I'm going to let this go on much longer. The world is going to know we're together, including your brother."

He led me out of the room and gave me a little push toward Cole's office, trying to fake a brooding stare that completely failed.

"Is that right?" I asked, turning back toward him with my hands on my hips. "You've just decided for both of us, huh?" It was hard to keep the smile from pulling at my lips and he clearly didn't buy a word of my fake ire.

In a heartbeat, he had me pinned up against the wall and was lightly brushing my lips with his. I could feel his restraint thickening the air around me, intoxicating me into wanting to push us farther so he didn't have to. "I absolutely have decided for both of us, Amelia," he almost growled, his voice a low rumble that echoed throughout every part of me.

"Well then," I said, breathless. "I suppose I shouldn't argue."

With that, he pulled away, chucking me under the chin and throwing over his shoulder as he walked away, "That's right, woman. Know your place!" I laughed out loud. "Oh just get out of here, Montgomery!"

I watched him and Micah exchange a few words as they crossed paths and he gave me another smile and a wink as he left. I couldn't help but smile and shake my head, wondering what the heck I was going to do with him — or worse, without him.

I waited for Micah in the hallway and we went into Cole's office together. He wasn't there yet, he was finishing a training session with some of the younger boys before sending them home for supper. I don't envy the moms who have to feed boys who want to train in MMA — I can't even imagine the grocery bill. But, I suppose they'd rather buy groceries than pay court costs, and most of these kids would have been out running the streets if it weren't for Cole.

So, Amelia, what are you thinking? Do you have any ideas on who did this?

Ugh. None. I've been wracking my brain and I just don't understand why anyone would want to hurt us.

My eyes flew up to connect with Micah's. He was sitting in the opposite chair, smiling smugly, as he saw the realization of our unspoken conversation across my face.

Fun, huh?

Also weird, Micah. Wait, you can't just hear things, right? We have to connect each time?

He read my mind, though not literally. *No, Amelia, I have no interest in your X-rated thoughts about Aidan. We do have to connect each time, and truly, you should pay more attention to your surroundings and your power. You should have felt the connection. Just because you don't use your magic constantly doesn't mean you should ignore it.*

I rolled my eyes and sent him a glare across the room. *Oh, well, thank you, oh wise one. With everything else I'm dealing with right now, I'll make sure I'm on high alert for when you're sneaking into my head!*

You don't get it, Amelia. The fact that you aren't paying attention to your magic could be how they are finding us.

You're not tuned into it. You aren't hearing it, feeling it, reacting to what it's telling you. You need to LISTEN.

"What exactly are you two doing?" Cole was standing in the doorway, arms crossed and leaning on the door jam. "Wait, were you talking?" He stood between us, looking back and forth. "Can we do that? Can you teach me how to do that?"

I put my hands up, trying to stave him off. "Cole, just chill out. We have bigger issues than you letting Micah all up in your head. Believe me, he's a bigger pain than he's worth sometimes."

Ungrateful little viper. Micah's pompous demeanor didn't change even when he didn't actually speak out loud. I laughed and shot Micah a look to shut up. Then, I realized I could also control our exchange. I went inside and slammed the door to our connection shut. Micah jerked back in his seat, but gave me an approving smile.

"Well done, Amelia. I was waiting for you to figure that one out," he said.

Cole was still staring. "Sorry, Cole. We're done with that. Micah was just making a point. All conversation will be out loud from here on out. And, eventually, you and I can do some work on our own connection, but we have more pressing issues right now."

He looked back and forth between us again, as if he wasn't sure if we were truly done with our unspoken conversation, but finally walked around his desk to sit down.

"Okay," Cole started, clearing his throat and immediately taking on the controlling role. "Micah, thanks for coming down. I want to start with hearing how this happened from your perspective. Ame has already filled me in on a lot of what you guys have been up to, and I appreciate that you offered to help her, but I need to understand who these people were and what they were after."

Micah raised an eyebrow. "Oh, so you're leading this discussion? I assumed since it actually happened to us, Amelia and I were just doing you the brotherly favor of filling you in on the details."

I could feel the testosterone in the room building. "Oh, for goodness sakes, you two. Cut out the macho B.S. None of us have a clue what these people, or person, were after and we need each other right now. Micah, get over yourself and just tell Cole what happened. And, Cole, don't turn into Dad here." They turned to glower at me in tandem. I rolled my eyes blatantly at both of them and gestured at Micah to get to it.

"Well, since you asked so nicely, Amelia, I don't know how I could resist." Micah shot me one last look of irritation and turned to Cole to start relaying our story. His version didn't differ much from mine and the whole incident took place over maybe five minutes, so there wasn't that much to say. I kept waiting for Micah to bring up the color of our attacker's power...but he didn't. And Cole didn't call him on it. As I sat back and thought about it, I realized I was likely being played by them both. Each one had independently decided what they would and wouldn't share with the other and neither had bothered to loop me in. *Men. Sheesh.*

I had brought up the blue power to Cole, but hadn't mentioned the blue eyes I'd seen. It was common for an Immortal's eyes to match their power, so seeing blue eyes wasn't the weird part. It was the eyes themselves. I had only a split second to see them but I could have sworn they weren't human eyes — which didn't make any sense at all. I decided that I was just going to keep that to myself for now. If they wanted to play a game of secrets then fine, I could keep them, too.

"Alright. Let's just get to the heart of it." Cole took back control of the conversation, his tone authoritative as he stared Micah down. "Micah, do these people have any reason to want you? Do you have enemies?"

Micah paled just a fraction before his expression turned hostile and he laughed dismissively. "Me? You're concerned about me? What about her?" he questioned as he threw an arm out toward me, obviously frustrated with Cole's interrogation. "She's the one running around town completely inept at controlling her magic. Her aura is stronger than anyone I've ever come in contact with, and you're looking at *me*?"

I sat straight up in my chair. "My aura is *what*? ARGH! What is it with you two and the secrets?"

Micah looked at me, exasperated. "Amelia, I tried. I explained to you over and over again that you needed to control yourself — that you stood out. But you were so wrapped up in—"

"Work and school," I quickly interrupted, giving him a pointed stare and stopping him from mentioning Aidan in front of Cole. "But, really, Micah, you should try being more direct. Something like, 'Hey Amelia, you stand out like a lighthouse on a new moon' might have done the trick!" I wanted to stay annoyed, but I wanted answers more. So, as embarrassment sent red flushing through my cheeks, I asked the question burning in my mind. "So, what does it mean that my aura is that strong?"

"You have got to be joking," Micah muttered as Cole finally injected himself in the conversation again, at my defense, of course.

"Look, kid, my sister has had a rough road and I don't appreciate all of your 'I'm better than you' crap. She's obviously trying and there's something a heck of lot bigger than the three of us out there. We need to know what it is. How about you actually provide something helpful in the conversation?"

I could see Micah seething in the chair next to me. He responded slowly, his anger barely controlled. His eyes flashed red as he turned on Cole.

"Do not call me *kid*, Bradbury. It is quite unfortunate that I seem to be the only one here who understands the gravity of the situation we're in, and the fact that your 'little sister' is the flame to every other magical moth out there right now because she doesn't know how to tone it down." He turned to me. "Amelia, that is what I mean.

The aura you exude is like magical candy. Anyone within a certain radius of you is drawn to it. I don't actually understand why, because it surely isn't your sparkling personality, but your power just feels different to us."

No one said anything as we all mulled this over. Cole finally spoke, although much more respectfully, "And you're sure this attack has nothing to do with you?"

Micah sighed. "While I cannot absolutely guarantee it — I do come from means — it doesn't make sense. I've been here since before Amelia came. If someone were coming for me, wouldn't they have done it already?"

"Fine. Fine. So, Amelia, it's your power. You have got to lock it down. You've got to go back to the way it was when you first came." Cole spoke with such authority, like I could just snap my fingers and it would be that easy. I sat there, first feeling guilty because I knew I couldn't, then I got angry. It was happening *again*. The men in my life were just throwing out orders and I was expected to follow them without a word.

I vaulted myself out of the chair. "Oh, that is *it*!" I slammed my hands down on Cole's desk, causing both him and Micah to jump backwards in their chairs as a violet shower of sparks erupted in the room.

"I have *had it* with you guys! I've had it with being told where to go and what to do and what to think and how to feel and how to spend every damn minute of my life. I've just HAD IT. Cole, I hear what you're saying. I hear what Micah is saying. But, it isn't that easy. My power is bigger and stronger than it's ever been, since *someone* finally decided to help me do something with it," I said as I tossed my head toward Micah and simultaneously glared at my brother.

"It won't be pushed down and huddled up in some corner of my mind. It won't *let me* do that anymore." I could feel my power alternately raging and jumping with joy at my outburst. Lately, it felt even more like it was its own person, just trapped inside of me, and right now was definitely one of those moments. "It wants out, Cole. It wants to be used. If you want to protect me then you had better be okay with someone teaching me. The only way this is going to work is if I can figure out how to work with it, not against it."

As I finished my rant, I realized that both boys were staring open-mouthed at me.

"WHAT?" I half-yelled, completely agitated. As I followed Cole's wide eyes, I finally realized the issue. Everything in his office was floating. He hadn't had much furniture in the sparse room to start with, but as I stopped to really look around, I realized that it wasn't just his knick-knacks that were hovering. *Everything* was. Me. The desk with Cole in his chair. Micah in his chair. The whole room was suspended just a few inches in the air. I looked down at my own flip flops, still feeling the ground beneath my feet even though it wasn't there. I dropped my head back and groaned in frustration.

"Just...just...dammit!" I slapped my hands down on the desk again and with another eruption of sparks, everything came down in a crash. The furniture stayed upright, but the items from Cole's shelves toppled and scattered. "This has GOT to stop happening to me!" I exclaimed as I fell back into a chair, throwing my arm over my face.

Cole came rushing around the desk. "Ame, how did you do that? Have you always been able to do that?"

"Don't you get it, Cole?" Micah said, scowling. "She has no idea how she just did that. That's the problem. How are we supposed to teach her to control something she doesn't even understand? That we don't even understand?"

Unable to take any more of their constant bickering — or the continuous insults Micah didn't even realize he was hurting me with — I stood up and walked out of the room. I could hear them both yelling after me, but I just kept walking.

I walked out the front door, got into my car, and purposefully ignored their calls and messages all the way home. I completely disregarded everything Cole and I had discussed about never being alone because I needed to be alone right now. And, if someone came, so be it, I had enough power whizzing through my system I was sure I could take care of myself. I walked into the building but didn't go up to the apartment. Instead, I took the same path I had with Aidan and went to the picnic table.

I sat on the top, drawing my legs into my chest, pulling my dress skirt close, and laying my head on my knees. As I sat there, I tried everything I could to connect to my magic, but it seemed to only come out in reaction to someone else. I spoke to it — a lengthy inner monologue where I begged it to calm down and cooperate. I pleaded and even argued. Nothing. It just swirled around me and inside me, always reaching out as if it were looking for something. I had no idea how I was supposed to stay incognito while wearing a homing beacon I couldn't control or shut down, so I finally just gave up and went inside.

Thankfully, Bethany was working. *Oh, no!* I'd done it again. I'd been so wrapped up in my own drama that I'd forgotten to talk to Micah about the double date. I dug out my phone and swept my finger across the screen, realizing I had been outside for over two hours. It seemed like only minutes. It was still only 10:00 p.m., so I went ahead and called Micah anyway.

He wasn't exactly pleasant on the phone, but I suppose that's what I got for walking out on him and Cole, and then ignoring their constant calls and messages for the past two hours. But, he calmed down and shut up when I told him what was happening with Bethany. I really had come around about those two and he seemed like he did really like her. I made him promise to leave her a message asking to see her tomorrow and to set a real date if he didn't want to double with Aidan and me. We all needed a little normalcy for a night.

I heard Bethany come flying in the door about eleven, which was her normal time on the nights she closed the restaurant. She had to stay late to close out all of the other server's tabs, count down the drawers, and reconcile the night. I had left my door open and was sitting in my papasan, allowing my mind to wander as music played softly in the background.

I heard the thud of her purse hitting the counter and moments later she almost skipped into the room and dropped onto my bed. She bounced up and down, chanting, "He callled, we're going on a daaaate! On Frrrriday! And we're having breaaaakfast tomorrrrow!"

"Alright, B! See, I told you! I mean, you have to make sure to give him hell for what he's put you through, but letting a boy pamper you isn't the worst thing in the world!" I was genuinely excited for her and seeing the spark back in her personality was exactly what I needed. I had at least done one thing right this week.

I needed to be focused on Bethany and her good news, but Aidan's face was the only thing I could see. I could hear him in my head, telling me he'd go slow, that he didn't want me to be afraid. But, right now, that's all I could do — be afraid. I was spiraling out of control and all I wanted was to hold on to him, but I was so afraid I would just hurt us both. The attack made everything so real. It wasn't just Queen Julia out there, wanting me for her evil ways. Someone else was out there who knew what and who I was and they could just as easily go after Aidan.

"Amelia, honey, where'd you go? Girl, I know there's something going on that you aren't telling me about and I'm about at my wits end trying to sort it out myself. Just be out with it already. You were there for me; let me be there for you." Bethany's voice brought me out of my own head, but as the tears I held back for so long spilled down my cheeks, I had no idea what to say. It took all of my willpower to once again stop the truth from tumbling out of my mouth.

"Oh, B. It's all just a mess," I finally sputtered out. "Aidan is amazing, but I'm slowing things down one minute and jumping ahead of myself the next. I think I know what I want, but then I don't, and I keep changing my mind. I think I'm going to ruin this because I'm scared." It was the closest I could come to the truth.

"Argh. These boys will be the death of us, Ame." Bethany shook her head as she quickly exhaled a puff of air that pushed her bangs out of her eyes. "I know what you're saying about being scared, but Aidan isn't going to run away and I don't think he'll let you either. You've got to decide what's more important, lady — following your fear or following your heart. If you pick heart, you're gonna have to accept being scared to death, but what you get in the end could be better than you ever imagined."

I don't know why I was shocked to hear Bethany throw out such sage advice as simply as if she were telling me which shoes went best with my outfit. It was what she always did at the exact moment I needed it. Every single time I broke down, that girl showed up with a smile and a mop to clean up the mess.

"Now," she said, smacking her hands on her knees and standing up, "I do believe Fro-Yo is in order. There will be no more crying tonight. We are eating our weight in pineapple yogurt covered in sour gummy worms and strawberries, so move it, sister."

She walked out of my room, leaving me no choice but to wipe my eyes, shake my head, and follow her. As we got into her Jeep, she also added, "And, no more sad music. For goodness sakes, Amelia, let's at least convince ourselves we're the ones in charge of these crazy relationships." Her exaggerated sigh and eye roll had us both giggling, which was exactly what I needed.

We both knew the boys held the upper hand whether we wanted to admit it or not, but we still sang along to the radio, belting out lyrics about being "Stronger". I couldn't have been more thankful to have someone who could read me like a book and knew exactly how to pull me out of my own head. Well, that and a Fro-Yo spot that was open until midnight on campus.

Chapter 14

After that night, I kept to my word and didn't go anywhere alone. Micah and I kept up our sessions, focusing more and more on trying to control my unwilling power. Well, control probably isn't the right word, considering it had refused to do anything I wanted in days and seemed to constantly be raging at me. I could feel it beating against my mind, as if it were trying to tell me something, but we just weren't speaking the same language. It was frustrating and exhausting, all at once.

The only time my magic was cooperative was when Micah put me in almost threatening situations. He would deliberately come at me, his own power full-force, demanding a rise from mine. Only during those times did I have moments of complete dominance, where I was working in tandem with my power. I was able to lift larger and heavier items, take sneak peeks into the thoughts of my neighbors — since they were human and couldn't stop me — and my defense just kept getting better. I hadn't had any new issues pop up lately, and for that I was grateful.

Throughout that time, Aidan was my safe harbor. Being in close proximity to him was the only time my power seemed to take a backseat, stopping our constant clashing of wills. The fact that I couldn't stop staring at his lips and wanting him to kiss me probably had something to do with it, but I couldn't think about attacks or power surges, or anything really, when his breath would tickle my cheek as he murmured one of our growing inside jokes in my ear.

I was actually sad to see that my words at the gym had resonated. After that conversation — barring the last light kiss at the gym — he'd kept it all PG-13. We went to a movie and he even made sure to put the armrest down, sitting stoically next to me while holding my hand. I could feel the sexual tension buzzing between us, his aura a constant battle of passion against his desire to make me happy. It was my only saving grace, knowing that it wasn't just me being tortured. It took all of my own willpower to not jump him in the darkness of that theater. I allowed my mind to wander and it took me to places far past kissing. I wondered what he knew that I didn't. What experiences he'd had. He was the only boy I'd kissed and I was still fumbling, at best, to be flirtatious. It was uncomfortable, but made me want to go further, faster.

I kept sneaking looks at him for the entire two hours. I fantasized about what his five o'clock shadow would feel like against my cheek, his coarse hair threaded through my fingers. I played back the few kisses we'd shared in my mind, determined to make him do it again. I watched his profile as he laughed out loud at the actors on screen, the smile shining through his eyes. He laughed with utter abandonment and I loved it.

My knee bounced up and down as I tapped my foot, nervous energy filling me. It had been two weeks since our last kiss in the gym and he had remained annoyingly platonic. He was still playful and cocky, sweet and tender, but only with his words. My last conversation with Rynna echoed in my head, telling me my heart was mine to give. To choose my path.

So I did. I was done waiting and being the saint. I was learning to control my power, so I wasn't afraid of hurting Aidan again. We hadn't seen or heard anything from our random attackers, even with both Micah and Cole doing some discreet digging, and I just couldn't take it anymore. I spent the rest of the movie plotting my move.

It was always lurking in the back of my mind, the fact that things would likely have to change, that Aidan couldn't always be mine, but no matter how much I tried, I couldn't keep myself from him. I spent long nights having conversations with myself around all the reasons I shouldn't allow this to happen, but all it took was one look from him to root me right back to his side. The bottom line was that I was eighteen, I rationalized to myself. And, I was Immortal. I had years and years of life in front of me. Why did I owe anything to all of these people who had never tried to help me? After everything

I'd been through, I owed this to myself. I'd earned this time with Aidan.

We hadn't talked a lot about his past and the stories he told me that day on the cliffs, but from everything I knew, his fears of abandonment ran deep. His commitment to me was just as hard for him, in his own way. So, as we left the movie theater that night, I made a decision that I was all in. That whatever this was, I was meant to be here, living it. It was the first time in my life I'd made a decision that completely went against everything I'd been raised to be, a decision that was for no one else's good but my own. It was exhilarating. The fleeting thought that someday I could actually tell him who and what I was lit me up from the inside out. I was so buzzed with excitement that I was talking a mile a minute and yanking Aidan along with me as I bobbed and weaved through the crowd toward the front of the movie theater.

As I pushed through the double doors out into the parking lot, Aidan wrapped an arm around me, slowing my steps and interrupting my internal cheering squad. "What's gotten into you, doll? You've either got something exciting up in that brain of yours or you were sneaking Red Bull during the movie." He laughed as he tugged me into his chest and pressed a kiss to my temple. I looked up at him, returning his kiss with one just below his ear. "Let's go walk on the beach. I'm not ready to go home yet."

I had used my most suggestive tone and was praying it didn't come across as cheesy as it felt. I was still getting used to this seductive flirtation thing, but I could feel Aidan's emotions spike and his eyes went from smoke to liquid silver. I had hit the mark.

"It's your show, baby," he said with a low rumble to his voice. A voice I hadn't heard since our last real kiss. I closed my eyes and smiled to myself as I looped my arm around him, walking as one out to the beach.

It was a full moon and it gave us the perfect amount of light to walk on the beach away from the boardwalk. There were other couples walking as well, but it was clear that each of us were in our own worlds. Aidan and I kept ourselves intertwined as we walked. I loved how I fit just under his chin, the top of my head level with his shoulders. How I could feel his fingertips making swirling patterns on the small strip of exposed skin on my back between my jeans and my top as we walked silently, both just enjoying the quiet. I tugged him even closer to me and tried to decide where to start. Was I really ready to verbally commit to this? Could I look him in the eyes and tell him out loud that I didn't want to go slow, that I didn't want anyone else?

Aidan stopped and tilted my chin up, "You're brooding again. I swear, I can feel it when you start to get lost in your own head. What's up?" He looked down at me through hooded, questioning eyes. Looking up at him, his dark hair shining in the moonlight, strength and passion radiating from him, I was suddenly sure.

"Aidan, I want this. Whatever this is that we have, I want it." He cocked his head and as his smile spread, his adorable dimple appeared. "Well, that's probably good, since I want it, too."

I stepped back a little, trying to give myself some room to breathe, to stop him from intoxicating me into sounding like an idiot.

I pushed at the sand with my toe, suddenly feeling inexperienced and shy. "I don't really know what we're doing. I've never really had a boyfriend, so this is all new, and amazing, and scary. There are still parts of me that I can't share with you, but I hope to. Someday."

It was so hard to be honest without really being honest, but it was true. I hoped that someday I could actually explain it all to him. Right now, though, I hoped that he could see and hear how much I meant every word. I looked up and the grin was back. I could see him holding himself back, waiting for me to make the next move. The reality that I could make him feel that way had me soaring.

Aidan tried to speak but I held up my hand, asking for him to wait.

"I…uh…Aidan, I don't want you to be so nice. To go so slow." His eyes widened another fraction, his pupils dilating. "The truth is, the only thing I can think about is you kissing me. About you doing more than kissing me. It's all I can think about." I was shaking from the inside out, just wanting to be close to him. But, I stood still, digging my nails into my palms.

In two steps, he had me up and off the sand. I locked my legs around his waist as one of his hands came up my back and into my hair.

"Amelia," he breathed out in a whisper. "It's all I've been thinking about since that day. You have no idea how much I want this."

Then, all I could feel was Aidan. That stubble was just as rough and amazing and I thought it would be. He kissed me with all the passion I'd ever imagined. His tongue diving into my mouth, claiming it as his. There was nothing sweet or gentle about that kiss and it was exactly what I wanted. I wanted to be marked. I wanted to feel alive. I just wanted Aidan.

With my legs locked around his hips and his hands roaming all over me, I was breathless. He supported me, gripping my hips and then sliding under my butt. Aidan moved one hand up my back and around to cup my face as he continued to kiss me. Slipping it back and tangling it in my hair, he gently tugged at the long strands and I dropped my head back to allow him access to my throat. With a groan, he laid a trail of kisses from the base up to my ear lobe, nipping at the sensitive flesh and giving me goose bumps. His mouth left fire in its wake, igniting feelings in me I hadn't known existed. I had no idea it could be this intoxicating to simply have someone's hands on your body. I couldn't think and could only react to each new sensation Aidan brought out in me. We had gone from zero to sixty and I suddenly felt panicked by a myriad of emotions and feelings I didn't know what to do with. So, while no part of me wanted to, I told myself to slow down. To not go too far, too fast. We had time.

It took a few minutes to slow the pace as Aidan took his cues from me. Our kisses became more leisurely until he finally pulled back and kissed the tip of my nose as he set me back on the sand.

"Well, that was unexpected," he said with a cheeky grin. I couldn't help but beam back up at him. My lips felt swollen and my skin tender from all of his attention. I was shocked to realize it was the first time we hadn't had a magical flare during such a close interaction. I could only feel a content, gloating sigh coming from my sated power as it sat back and soaked in what had just happened. For once, we were on the same page.

I grabbed his hand, yanking on it a little to get us walking again, even though I could have skipped my way down the beach at this point. "Let's keep going, just a little farther," I said.

We walked the beach for another half an hour or so. When we realized it was close to midnight, we started back toward the car. Just as we were getting close to the parking lot of the theater, I felt it.

Each individual hair on the back of my neck shot to attention and every internal alarm I had was screaming.

She's here. I know she's here. We saw her walk off with that human.

I shook my head, shocked to hear someone's voice there. I'd only heard other people when I was intentionally trying to listen. No one had ever just shown up before. I quickly realized I had to get Aidan out of here.

Trying not to alert him, I started casually looking around as I sped up my pace.

They were just out on the beach. It's just her and the boy. This is the perfect time since she's away from the other Mage.

I looked around, realizing there was nowhere to hide. As we approached the theater, I grabbed Aidan and pulled him into the shadow of the building.

He grinned. "Didn't get your fill, huh? I'd be happy to oblige."

As Aidan brought his lips back to mine, I did my best to kiss him while I searched out the power of the people around us, trying to get a read on exactly where they were. Micah had me playing magical hide and seek with Cole a few different times last week so I had a good idea of how to follow their trail. It took a moment before I could source them, but as I reached out, I could feel their pulsing black auras not far away. I followed the first person's aura, but couldn't get anywhere. Their minds were locked up tight. The only thing that came through loud and clear was that they had been sent to find me and they couldn't fail.

It wasn't until I sighed at my lack of skill that I realized Aidan wasn't kissing me anymore. He was standing in front of me, arms crossed, looking rather perturbed.

"Okay, Amelia, really? What the hell is going on?" The hard edges of his jaw were set, his eyes dark and narrowed. How was I possibly going to explain this?

"I, uh, well...I think the popcorn isn't sitting well," I said, weakly.

His eyebrow arched. "Really? How many times do you think I'm going to let this stuff go, Amelia?"

"Stuff? What stuff?" I asked, my voice a little too high and shaking. I didn't have a clue what he actually thought was happening.

"Oh, I don't know, like your random migraines or your disappearing acts? Or your 'training' with Micah that I know for a fact you don't need because Cole has told me all about your MMA instruction. Or how you completely zone out sometimes and have no idea what's happening around you? Something is going on with you and I need to know what it is." He spat out the words with such intensity that I took a step back.

I had no response. I stood there, staring at him, willing myself to come up with some plausible excuse, but I had nothing. Aidan's wariness rolled off of him. I could feel the words he wouldn't say. The ones that questioned the truth of everything I'd just laid bare to him on the beach. I couldn't lie to him anymore, but what choice did I have?

At that moment, I didn't have to make a choice because a crackling blue bolt came shooting toward Aidan and the only thing I could do was scream as I shoved him aside. We both fell into a heap on the ground. He was instantly up and in a crouch. I had much less grace and began scrambling to get to my feet. We were both looking in all directions when the next bolt came flying at us. We dove apart and a chunk of the red brick theater wall ruptured into dust around us.

"What is going on? What the hell was that?" Aidan yelled. I was thinking as fast as I could.

"Do you trust me?" I asked, a plan forming.

My jeans were torn in a few places and my new sheer pink top was shredded along one arm where I had skidded into a heap on the concrete. My braid was half undone and I was crouched down behind a bush next to the theater like a fugitive. Aidan gaped at me from a few feet away, his yellow polo dirty and his cargo shorts also ripped. He was undecided and I hated that I had made him that way. Another bolt came flying at us, only missing by a few feet.

"Aidan! Do you trust me?" I smacked the concrete and was shocked to feel a little tremor shake the ground between us. Aidan's eyes widened and he nodded slowly.

"Okay, then. On three, we run. You parked around the back and we have to get to your car. I'll…I'll try to explain all of this eventually, but for now, we have to get away." I had made the decision that honesty was no longer a choice. He would know. I would tell him everything.

I was amazed that he didn't question me. The bolts of blue were getting larger and spraying dirt everywhere around us, which could only mean our attackers were getting closer. I tossed my head in the direction of the back of the building and gave a finger count. On three, we both leapt up and took off for the car. I forced Aidan to lead, hoping he would think he was protecting me while I was actually throwing down cover.

I shot my purple blasts as fast as I could to try to fend them off. I saw a man dodging my blasts between cars and almost tripped when I realized his eyes didn't look human. They looked like a cat. Bright blue and almond-shaped with just a sliver of black down the center. It didn't make sense, but I was certain that's what I saw. And, he looked familiar. But, I didn't have time for double-takes while I was dodging fire and running for my life.

I went skidding around the corner, expecting to have to catch up to Aidan. Instead, I ran straight into his back. I smacked into him with such force that he fell forward as I flew backward, landing on my back and tearing up my palms.

"How nice of you to join us, Amelia. We've been waiting so long to finally meet you."

My head flew up at the syrupy-sweet sound of her voice. I locked eyes with a beautiful woman wearing an evil sneer. Her long red hair fell in thick waves around her shoulders and the black leather she wore from head to toe only added to my fear factor. One hand hung loosely at her side, bright blue electricity pulsing around it. The other was held in front of her, a crackling orb bouncing up and down in her palm.

"We wouldn't want to harm your human friend, dear," she cooed. "So, if you'll just come with us, we can settle our issues properly. Away from those you care about."

Aidan had backed up and helped me stand by this point. At her words, he interlaced his hand with mine.

"I don't know what you think you're doing, lady, or what's going on, but Amelia isn't going with you." He sounded so confident, looked so sure. He took a small step forward, moving in front of me. Before I could pull him back, the woman shot a small, quick blast at him. It hit Aidan directly in the left shoulder, sending him reeling backwards.

I screamed his name, running to him. I kept looking over my shoulder and while I tried to assess the damage, I positioned myself shielding him but so that I could still see her. "Who are you? You don't have to do this. What do you want with me?" I threw the questions at her one after the other. My hands shook, both in fear and in anger.

"That," she said as she tossed her orb in the air a few times, "was a warning. He won't be hurt, Amelia, unless you force me to, or he does something stupid again. You need to come with me. I don't want to hurt you, but we have things we need to discuss. Don't make this harder than it has to be. You wouldn't want me seeking out your little human friend, Bethany, is it? Or your big brother, Cole?"

As I helped Aidan to his feet, I could feel my own rage building. I was terrified, but this woman was threatening the people I loved. She'd hurt Aidan. My power grew exponentially in response to her threats and it was pissed. I tried to hold on to Aidan, to use his presence to calm myself down and maintain control, but I couldn't stop it.

The pressure just kept building, higher than it ever had before.

"Amelia, I'm not playing with you. You have seconds to make your decision or I'm going to make it for you, and your little boy toy isn't going to like how it all turns out." The woman's laugh was shrill and it grated on me even further.

Aidan gripped my hand again, giving me a barely perceptible nod. My relief at his acceptance of what was happening was short lived as I had to make my move.

"Lady, I don't know who you are or what you want, but you picked the wrong girl on the wrong night." I straightened my shoulders, stood tall, held up my free hand, and just let loose. Dropping all of my walls in an instant, the release was an explosion bursting out of me. I gripped Aidan's hand, letting his presence give me strength, while purple lightning erupted from my palm and rocketed torward the woman in a tidal wave. After the night on the cliffs, I thought I knew what to expect when I let loose, but something was different. I felt the attack become less about defense and more about stopping the woman from ever coming back. Intense dark emotions filled my mind and I just wanted her gone.

I watched her sneer turn to fear as she tried to leap away. The ground where she was once standing exploded. The thought of her getting away fueled my fire and my next thought was that something needed to stop her. A tree branch tore from its trunk and shot into her path. She leapt over the branch and tried to run. Pride in my newfound skills filled me, and at that same moment, the wind picked up and starting throwing everything in her way: trees, trash cans, benches that weren't bolted down…anything that would move was blown toward her and around her.

The woman jumped and dodged, trying to use her own power to fight off the barrage of items that spun in the air, but it was no use. I stepped toward her — still holding onto Aidan's hand — as my hair whipped in the wind. I had to have looked like a madwoman — my eyes bright violet, my clothes shredded, and a scary smile on my face. I wanted her to leave us alone. To realize what I would do if she came back. And, with that thought, lightning struck the ground at her feet. She jumped and my smile only widened.

"AMELIA! STOP!" Aidan yanked on my arm, pulling me back to him. He put both of his hands on my cheeks and forced me to look into his eyes. "Just *stop*. Let's just go while we can. She can't do anything." I could barely understand him through my rage. My eyes narrowed as I look at him questioningly. I didn't initially understand his reaction to the glorious display I was putting on, but I saw that he was terrified. For me and of me. Still, he forced me to look at him as he tried to bring me back.

The woman stood in the middle of a swirling mess, the wind still roaring around her like a tornado. As items swirled in the air around her, I looked over Aidan's shoulder and our eyes connected again before a park bench broke our connection. She tried futilely to blow a hole in the growing barricade and her fear was evident on her face. She kicked and blasted, but to no avail. Not once had she aimed directly for me, but she kept trying to break free.

Aidan pulled me back to him. I looked into his eyes and felt the sweat of his palms on my face. The curtain in my mind opened a fraction and reality struck. My body responded to my commands to stop trying to move, but my power refused to end its attack on the woman. We had fought together for a brief moment, but an attack that I had only intended to use for defense had become a terrorist event that I couldn't control. I had to get away, to stop this and get Aidan out of there. I slowly became more myself and the darkness rebelled, pushing at me to continue our fight.

"Let's go, Aidan. Let's just go." My limbs were heavy and my thoughts sluggish. I pulled him with me as we started running toward his car. The whole time the onslaught on the woman didn't let up and it wasn't me doing it. I felt the pulsing anger driving the assault coming from deep inside me. I was divided and while one part of me fought to stop this, the other gloated in the power we held. The woman stood in the center of the pile just staring after me. Her red hair flew in every direction but the look on her face was one of awe and curiosity as items swirled around her.

We threw ourselves into the car and Aidan jammed the gear into drive. I couldn't stop myself from turning back one last time as my power finally settled back inside me, the malicious energy dissipating as quickly as it had overtaken me.

Just as the wind quieted and the objects all fell back to the ground I saw the woman's eyes pulse brightly as she dropped to all fours, fur rippling out across her body all at once and a deep howl piercing the air. A wolf with a coat of burnt red and ice blue eyes stood in her place. As we turned the corner that would remove her from sight, she let out another bone-chilling howl in my direction. It was a warning. I knew that much.

Aidan drove for what seemed like forever. His knuckles white as he gripped the wheel with both hands, glancing at me every now and then from the corner of his eyes. I could feel his confusion and hated the few feet between us. It seemed like miles. We didn't speak. Exhaustion was pulling me down and my skin felt too tight with all of the energy and mixed emotions pushing and shoving at each other. They were fighting — my power and myself at odds after the disturbing events that had just unfolded. My head was pounding and I wasn't sure how long I could keep the after-effects of the night at bay.

I looked out the window and tried to find the right words. To find any words. I had no idea how to even start to explain all of this to him — especially not what I had just become. I didn't even know given I'd never felt that level of fury. Aidan didn't even understand what an Immortal was, so how exactly was I supposed to explain to him that not only was I one, but that I had no idea what the hell was inside me or what had just happened?

I pulled my knees up to my chest and wrapped my arms around them. I pressed myself into the smallest ball possible, hoping I could just curl up and disappear. Aidan suddenly whipped into a parking lot and I almost fell into his lap as I sprawled across the console and tried to right myself. He threw the car into park and dove out, not even shutting the door. He took long, hurried strides away from the car. Away from me.

I scrambled to unhook my seatbelt and get out of the car, running after him.

"Aidan, wait! Let me…we need to…" I couldn't figure out what to say. I still had no idea what to tell him.

He rounded on me, coming back fast. I actually took a step back, the look in his eyes frantic and his stance aggressive. He stopped right in front of me, the toes of his shoes touching mine. He glared down at me, his dark hair wild and his eyes blazing.

"Amelia, I can't *do this* right now," he screamed at me. "I need you to go. Take my car. Just GO!"

As he roared that last word, he grabbed my shoulders and pushed me back toward the car. I was stupefied. I was already exhausted and stumbled over my own feet. I had expected him to ask questions. I expected him to be pissed and maybe tell me he never wanted to see me again. I never expected him to just leave me. Before I could force my brain cells to form a coherent sentence, Aidan had taken off running into the trees. I stood rooted to that spot in that parking lot for quite some time, staring at the trees and willing him to come back out.

It wasn't until the dinging of the alarm finally pierced my consciousness, reminding me his door was still open with the keys in the ignition. I knew I should just go. He wasn't coming back.

Chapter 15

That night, after the attack, I sent Aidan a text letting him know where his car was and that I'd put the keys under the mat. I wish I would have forced him to come to me for them, but it was three in the morning and I had struggled to even drive myself home as the after-effects of the fight sapped my energy. I was trembling, my legs barely holding me up as I walked into the apartment. As soon as my head hit the pillow, I was out cold. Aidan never responded, but the next day when I woke up, the car was gone.

It was all I could do to get out of bed later that morning. Every part of me hurt, I was exhausted and starving. I forced myself up and into semi-respectable clothes and made my way to the gym. My heart was racing triple time and I scanned every inch of the streets as I drove. I pushed my old Buick faster than it should have gone on the highway, not enjoying being alone after last night. I was certain that a big white van or black SUV was going to come careening around a corner, forcing me off the road to kidnap me at any moment.

I finally pulled up to the gym, shoved the car in park, and sprinted inside. Only when the door was closed behind me did I finally feel some of the panic recede.

As I approached, I heard Cole on the phone. "No, it's fine. I'm handling it. Her power is growing, but she's starting to control it." He paused and I assumed the other person was talking. "You don't have to do that. She's listening to me. She tells me everything and I'll make sure you know when I know."

I stood outside his door, just far enough that he couldn't see me through the glass. I leaned back against the wall, my eyes closed, hurt coursing through me. *Not Cole.*

He had always been my lifeline. Growing up, he was my protector. He was the one who dressed my skinned knees, ran the other kids off when they made fun of me, and helped make me feel like it would maybe, someday be okay. He was the only one who advocated for me coming to Brighton and I thought I could trust him. I couldn't do this today. Not after what I'd been through last night. Not after Aidan had run from me. I couldn't have my knees cut off *today.*

As I stood there, I felt that same dark energy emanating from my power. It spread through my deflated spirit and permeated my mind. I knew the moment Cole realized I was standing outside his door. He quickly hung up the phone and walked out to find me leaned against that wall.

But, my posture was not defeated as it had been moments before, it was furious. Defiant. The energy that filled me tensed my muscles and fed my anger.

My arms were crossed, my stance defensive. He could see the pain in my eyes just as easily as the fierce look on my face. He tried to explain, "Ame, you don't understand. It's not what you—"

I didn't even let him finish, I flung my palms toward him and watched him get tossed down the hall. It shouldn't have felt as good as it did to hurt my brother. Something inside me recognized that, but it was squashed by my need for retaliation. He landed more gracefully than I had hoped and stood up. He held his hands up in surrender, speaking quietly, though I could tell he was having a hard time maintaining control himself. His own power was spring-boarding inside him, waiting for the all-clear to take off at me. A part of me wanted him to let it out — to make this a fair fight.

"Amelia, this is not what you think," he said. "I'm on your side. I've always been on your side. That was Rynna. We're just trying to work together to help you. We've always done this, I've always kept in touch with her to make sure you were okay. Now, it's just my turn. On Mom's life, Amelia, I swear."

I stood there in the hall, clenching my fists, trying to quiet the warring sides of my brain. I wanted to believe him. He never brought up our mom unless things were serious, but it seemed like no one was who they seemed to be lately and I wanted to force the truth from him. To wring it from him like a dirty washcloth at the sink.

Cole took a few cautious steps toward me. "Amelia, I don't know what's happened, but I think you need to calm down. I... uh, I think you are going to hurt someone." I whipped my head back toward him and had the fastest thought that I wanted him to stop talking. Cole was suddenly whipping his head back and forth, clawing at his mouth, which had sealed closed. He was screaming but the sound was hollow, the noise barricaded in. For a moment, I simply tilted my head and watched him fight. I rocked back on my heels, awestruck at what I'd done. Then, Cole's eyes connected to mine — terrified and pulsing green, pleading with me for help as his magic tried and failed to fight off mine.

That look broke through the barrier and the black haze that had clouded my vision lifted. This time, when my mind connected to what I had truly done, I stumbled backwards, shrieking, "Stop — just STOP!" Knowing full well I was yelling at myself — my dark, twisted second self. I mentally lashed out at the rogue inside me and Cole was finally released. I slid down the wall as tears streamed down my cheeks. I pressed my forehead into my arms and balled myself up. All I wanted to do was disappear. What was happening to me? What was this *thing* inside of me?

When I could finally bring myself to look up, I found Cole sitting on the floor across from me.

"Do you want to tell me what that was all about?" His voice was low and steady, his fear of me palpable in the air around us. "What was that, Amelia? Because that wasn't you. I mean, I know it was, but I couldn't find you. I looked for your trace and there was nothing left." Cole was pale, his posture slumped over, and his head in his hands. Whatever I had done to him did more than just keep him quiet.

I pressed a hand to my mouth, balling it into a fist as I bit down on my knuckle. I was hanging on by a thread and the hysteria that hovered at the edges of my mind had been waiting for an entry point.

"I don't *know,* Cole." I was terrified and the words came out garbled, barely above a whisper. "I don't know what's happening to me. I don't know how to control it. It seems like most of the time it's controlling me. I'm there, but I'm not. I can see myself doing it, but I can't stop it." I looked up at him, regret and apologies on the tip of my tongue. But, in typical Cole fashion, he shook his head and scooted across the floor to me.

"I know, Ame," he said quietly as he circled his arm around my shoulder and pulled me in for a hug. "I could see it, feel it. I knew it wasn't you. There's something more here we don't understand." Even in his depleted condition, Cole was still able to take the edge off of my manic state.

"I just want to be normal," I choked out, trying to breathe and calm myself down further. "To go back to being the girl who didn't understand anything or try anything. I don't want to be the girl with the crazy power she can't control. I don't want to be the girl who gets attacked or who has to lie to her friends and boyfriend. I don't want to hurt the people I love. "

"Wait, boyfriend?" Cole pulled away from me, looking down as his eyebrow rose.

"Are you serious, Cole? I just went crazy ballistic nuts and you're worried about a guy?" I shoved at him lightly. The corner of his mouth quirked up as he replied, "Can't help it. Just comes with the gig."

I could only shake my head as I moved a few inches over and turned to face my brother. I pulled my knees to my chest and wrapped my arms around them tightly, trying to hold myself together in more ways than one. "Well, then, yes, I have been seeing Aidan. That's actually why I came." The knot in my stomach tightened but I continued. "Aidan and I were attacked last night outside the theater after a movie and he watched me basically go postal on some chick who wanted to kidnap me. What happened just now, it happened then, too. I lost it. I just lost it…"

The words trailed off as the night sped through my mind. I could pinpoint the moment when I was no longer me and when Aidan brought me back again. The memories played like I had watched them happen instead of made them happen. I was so lost in thought, I didn't realize Cole had been peppering me with questions.

His voice was distant in the background as it dawned on me that I no longer had the option of living in that brief moment of happiness I had with Aidan last night, where I was just a girl and he was just boy. That we could never "just be", that power would always stand between us. Mine or someone else's. It didn't matter how much I deluded myself, I couldn't expect him to accept what I was. To accept the consequences of being with me. I shouldn't even want him to.

Cole finally broke my train of thought as he gently grabbed my arm. My head shot up and the blatant fear in his eyes sent an embarrassed heat into my cheeks. "I'm so sorry, Cole. I—"

"No. No, Amelia. It's okay. I just need some time to process all of this. What just happened, what happened last night; everything is spiraling out of control and we need help. You need help. Let's go sit down." Cole nodded, seemingly agreeing with himself, before standing and helping me to do the same. He left for a few minutes to put a sign on the door that said the gym was closed for the day. In the meantime, I called Micah and asked him to come down. He was out for lunch with Bethany and would come in an hour or so. I was glad to hear he wasn't just blowing B off, at least someone around here deserved a normal relationship.

While I was waiting for Cole to come back, I ducked into the bathroom. I'd never seen myself look so bad. I had huge dark circles under my eyes, their normal hazel color was dulled and flat. I hadn't washed my face last night, so yesterday's mascara was running down my cheeks and caked around my eyes in a most unflattering way. My hair was a mess of tangles. I looked like hell.

I stood at the sink and splashed water on my face, using paper towels to clean myself up. I finger-combed my rat's nest into submission and braided it. Acknowledging that I may as well use some of my ability for good, I connected with my power and sent some healing energy through myself. I leaned in toward the mirror and stared at my reflection. I looked into my own eyes, expecting some obvious reaction to show me what was happening, but I couldn't feel the blackness anywhere, it was just my normal power. I sighed in relief as my frazzled anxiety calmed. When I opened my eyes, the circles were diminished, my skin was brighter, and my eyes had more luster. If only my internal heartache was as easily mended as my external appearance.

Cole was sitting at his desk when I came back and gestured for me to take a seat. I crossed my legs under me and huddled into the cushy over-sized chair.

"Start at the beginning, Amelia. I don't care about Aidan right now — though we'll come back to that," he warned. "I need to hear about this attack. About how it was like today." Cole dug into his drawer and pulled out a notepad. "I'm going to take notes so that we can compare this one to the last time."

I spoke quietly, seeing it all play out in my head again. I felt somewhat like I had then, like I was watching a scene instead of being part of it. I skipped past our time on the beach and the mind-blowing make-out session Aidan and I shared. I gave a detailed description of the men who had come after us and of the red-headed woman — down to her thick black eyeliner and her bright blue eyes. I explained how Aidan tried to protect me, only to be hurt for it, and then I got to the point where I lost control. Or, to be more accurate, completely rescinded my control.

"One second it was me using my power the way I have been for weeks and then the next, I was a spectator in my own body," I explained. "All I could feel was the hate I had for that woman and how much I wanted to hurt her. I was watching myself do these things, but at the same time, I was the one doing them. I lost myself in it…" I struggled to find the words to explain that, for a brief moment, I had reveled in what I'd felt. The feeling of power brimming over in my soul and knowing that I could do absolutely anything.

Cole scribbled furiously, looking up at me between statements, his brow furrowing more and more as I spoke. I swallowed down those last descriptions and instead tried to explain how, with only a thought, I'd been able to send items flying at this woman, how I sent lightning down from a cloudless sky. I talked and I talked, going over each little detail. Once I got to Aidan and me driving away, I just stopped.

My mind however, kept going, playing back the last conversation I'd had with Aidan. The last conversation I may ever have with Aidan.

There was more I should have told Cole. I should have explained the cat-like eyes of my attacker or that the woman was clearly an AniMage. I should have told him more about the darkness and how I wasn't sure I would be able to pull myself out of it if it happened again. That it had taken Aidan or him to do it these last two times. But, every time I opened my mouth to speak, warning bells went off and the words stuck in my throat.

"Amelia, I know Micah will be here soon, but you can't tell him any of this." Cole had taken that quiet moment as his opportunity to speak up.

"What?" I asked. "What do you mean, Cole? Micah's been in this with us since the beginning? You wanted him to help me and he is. He's my friend." I gripped the arms of the chair, digging my nails into the microfiber, trying to see where my brother was coming from.

"Tell him about the attack and the woman, but your power is too much to explain, Amelia. We can't just come out at tell him you're an Elder, though he might already have guessed depending on what he knows of our history. And, what I just saw out there — we surely can't explain that to him. We can't explain that to anyone, and we absolutely can't have him talking about you to anyone else. It's too dangerous," he finished.

I wanted to argue. I wanted to tell him he was wrong, but I knew he was right. "I understand what you're saying, Cole, but Micah has been the only other person who has ever been honest with me. God, he's even spent all this time trying to help me become a better Mage; to protect myself and learn how to use my powers. It just sucks to lie to him, too."

Cole came around the desk and sat in the chair opposite me. "I know, Ame," he said, grabbing my hand

and sending his peaceful energy into me. "I know this is hard, but you have to remember that you aren't a Mage. You're so much more than a Mage could ever hope to be and if Micah knows that — if he truly understands what you are — then he's another person in danger."

I sighed, feeling defeated once again. "Then what do we do, Cole? How do we find out what's happening to me?"

As I turned back toward him and met his eyes, I saw a sliver of hope that hadn't been there before. His eyes brightened as he said, "I've got a guy. It's not someone we're even supposed to know, and you can't tell *anyone* that we know about him, but he said he'd help us. I was going to tell you about him tonight anyway, but it's clear we need to get to him sooner than later." He squeezed my hand and stood up. "You trust me right, Amelia?"

I truly wasn't sure who I trusted, but of the options, my brother was the one I wanted, so I gave him the answer he needed. "Of course, Cole."

He walked back around the desk, his step a little lighter. "Let's talk about what we can actually tell Micah and then you and I are taking a road trip this weekend."

It was clear Cole wasn't going to give me any additional details now, so we spent the next twenty minutes deciding what we would and wouldn't tell Micah. Micah showed up right on time, which no one shocked by, and I went through the pre-approved story. I described the attack, including Aidan and the red-haired woman. But, outside of sending a bunch of stuff flying at her — which he already knew I could do — and blasting her to get away, I didn't tell him anything else. Micah claimed to have contacts through his parents who could track people down, so I gave him as much description as I could and left it at that. I continued to withhold what I knew were crucial details — the blue power, the shifting, and my inner battles. I'd never heard of anyone seeing an AniMage in years and I wasn't about to go blabbering on about the woman being one without somehow being sure.

Micah asked some questions and had me write down my descriptions of the people. His concern was obvious and he asked multiple times if I needed constant protection. I could read in his tone and body language that he was also worried for Bethany.

"Maybe I should stay with Cole for a while?" I asked, though it was the last thing I wanted to do. "I don't know how to explain it to B, but I can come up with something." Inwardly, I cringed at the prospect of living with Cole and not getting my girl time with Bethany. Of not being able to easily find and talk to Aidan.

Both Micah and Cole looked relieved at me bringing it up and them not having to convince or force me. "Yeah, that's probably the best plan, Ame. I don't want you alone," Cole said, who then suggested that I say I'm helping watch his "sick" dog since he's so busy at the gym.

It had been a long day and I didn't have the energy to talk anymore. We went through some additional logistics and Micah promised to get back to us as soon as he had more information. He also said he'd do his best to spend additional time with Bethany for a while, just to make sure she was protected as well.

Cole walked me to my car and gave me specific instructions to go home, pack a few bags, and come directly to his apartment. Do not pass go. Do not collect two-hundred dollars. Not even a drive-thru stop. If this was an inkling of what was to come, the next few weeks were going to be *so* spectacular.

I took my time packing. Bethany wasn't home so I connected my phone to the surround sound in the living room and let the music flow through our apartment. I didn't know what I wanted to hear but I needed an escape from the silence. I was pleased to hear an acoustic track start playing, so I got to work.

I packed up my books for class, tossing them into my backpack. As I picked up my notebook, a folded sheet of paper fell out and landed face-down on the carpet. I picked it up and opened it, curious because the paper didn't look like it had come from my notebook. A familiar scrawl stared back at me.

I don't know when you'll find this, but when you do, know that I'm thinking of you. I'm always thinking of you, doll. ~ A

I dropped onto my makeshift bed as a small whimper caught in my throat. I clutched the paper so tightly, my fingernails punctured it. I stared down at his words, realizing this could very well be the last memento I would have from our time together. That he ran away and I'd likely never be able to do anything to get him back. That, in all reality, I shouldn't do anything to get him back. Swallowing the tears I couldn't let loose right now, I shoved the paper deep into my backpack and walked out of my room.

Once my packing was complete, I stood in the center of the living room with my three bags on the floor at my feet. I felt like I was saying goodbye to my home and the sadness of it was unbearable. I looked around at all of the fun framed photos of Bethany and me that lined the walls. We spent every weekend for the first month taking photos all around town to decorate with. In the kitchen hung the giant fork and spoon she insisted we needed, though they were each three feet tall. I had had more laughs and more genuine happiness in this apartment in just a few months than I had had with my family in my entire life. But, I couldn't endanger someone I loved this much, so I grabbed my bags and headed out the front door.

I called Bethany from the road, knowing full well she was at work and wouldn't answer. I left her a voicemail letting her know that I'd be staying at Cole's for at least the next two weeks, but that we needed to set up some lunch dates in the interim. I also gave her a quick synopsis of the Aidan situation, just saying that we had a fight and I wasn't sure where it was going now. As I went to hang up, I found myself saying, "You know I love you, girl. Take care of yourself." It was if I were saying goodbye everywhere I went.

Chapter 16

Cole's apartment was a palace in comparison to mine. He lived just a few blocks from the gym and his living room was a wall of windows that faced the ocean. There were worse places to be stuck and I decided I should make the best of it. His dog, Charlie, a Great Dane, met me at the door. Charlie was absolutely a lover, not a fighter — even if he sat over three feet tall and weighed one-hundred and seventy pounds. He nosed his way into my arms, making me drop all of my bags as I laughed and gave him a full-on hug.

I knelt in front of him and loved him up, paying special attention to his ears, which he loved. Once I was covered in dog hair and slobber, I stood and told him to go lay down. Instead, Charlie promptly sat down and cocked his head at me. He was black and white spotted, but his head was all white except for the giant black spot covering his right eye and his big ears stood up in giant triangles. I couldn't help but tell him how pretty of a boy he was as I scratched his head again and took off for the guest bedroom.

By the time Cole got home, I was pretty settled in. I'd talked to Bethany, reassuring her that Charlie was fine, he just needed some shots every day for the next few weeks that Cole didn't have time for. I told her he was paying me to dog-sit and that she was welcome to come hang out. Since Cole had some protective measures in place, apparently an "I owe you" from someone he had met during his travels, he felt like his apartment was the safest place any of us could be right now. I'd caught up on my homework and checked my phone no fewer than forty times to see if I'd missed a message from Aidan. I couldn't bring myself to call or text him. After the way we'd ended things, he needed to be comfortable with telling me he was ready to see me again. If he ever was.

Cole kicked off our arrangement by reiterating all of his rules. *Again.*

"Do your own dishes. Don't throw towels on the floor. Keep your girly crap in your own space. Don't touch my PlayStation." I couldn't help but roll my eyes as he towered over me, ticking them off each of his fingers as he stood just in front of the couch.

"Really, Cole? I've been here before, and you're the one who wants me here, so chill out, okay?" He harrumphed and went to put in the frozen pizza we were sharing for dinner. I could tell he was trying to act normal, but there was still a definite wariness in him.

I followed him into the kitchen, leaning on the granite island countertop and fiddling with the vase filled with spatulas and other cooking utensils.

"So, are you ever going to tell me about your guy?" I tried to fake disinterest, but Cole saw right through me. "Nope. Sorry, Ame, but you get nothing. This is top secret and I'm not joking when I say that no one can know this guy exists. He's been off the radar for years."

I rolled my eyes. "This is all a little too cloak and dagger, don't you think?"

He stopped, the oven door half open. "I'm serious, Amelia. No one. Not even your little boyfriend, Aidan. Speaking of, what's the deal there? I'm afraid to ask, but I should probably know what he knows about you? I mean, not about *you*. You know what I mean!" He rushed through that last part, turning an adorable shade of red.

I couldn't help but egg him on. "Oh, you didn't want to know how our first kiss went? I mean, I can tell you exactly how he—"

"NO! BLECH. Just, no." Cole was walking around the kitchen, shaking himself out like he had caught cooties. Reacting to his weird antics, Charlie joined in the game, letting out thunderous *woofs* and jumping all over Cole.

"Good God. Down! Charlie, get down!" Cole was pushing at Charlie, which of course Charlie only saw as escalating the game. I, on the other hand, doubled over in laughter. Cole seemed so big and strong until his mammoth dog started to play games, too.

"Fine. I'll take your word for it, Cole, but I need to get out of here for a few minutes. Can I take Charlie out to the beach? He looks like he could use a good game of fetch." I put on my best pouting face and Cole gave in as I knew he would.

"Fine," he agreed. "After we eat. I'm going to sit out on the deck and watch to make sure nothing happens. Stay within yelling distance."

Just in time, the buzzer went off and our favorite sausage and green pepper thin crust pizza was done. I devoured my half, wishing he had stocked Cherry Pepsi, too.

Charlie couldn't have been more ecstatic when I grabbed his leash out of the hall closet. We stood facing each other and it was clear to me that we both understood the leash was a formality. Charlie could drag me along the boardwalk for a hundred miles and there was absolutely nothing I could do about it.

"Alright, dog, we have an understanding, but know that I could also turn you into a goldfish if you misbehave." Charlie actually snorted at me, as if to say, "Yeah right, lady. Nice try."

With that, I laughed and shook my head, clipped on his leash, and let him lead me down to the beach. Once we were fully out in the sand, I let him loose and started throwing his favorite Frisbee around. The sun was just setting and the water looked radiant. The oranges, reds, and purples shone across the ocean surface with only the white swells breaking the beautiful rainbow.

Charlie and I must have played for an hour. Finally, I sat in the sand and he laid down next to me. He crossed his two front paws, looking more regal than I'd ever seen, his ears alert and looking all over the beach. I looked back to see Cole on the deck — actually sitting somewhat similarly to Charlie — his posture rigid, his eyes scanning the beach. It felt good to feel safe and protected, even if I was lonely.

Cole let me go to school, but Micah had to walk me to and from each class. I felt ridiculous, but I wasn't there to learn. I was there to find Aidan. I needed to talk to him and I was becoming somewhat frantic. I alternated between feeling like I needed to spill it all and confess everything and completely ignoring him because it would be safer for him to never have met me. But, each time I walked into class, he wasn't there.

As I finished out the week, glad Bethany had never questioned why Micah was on campus every minute we were, I prayed Aidan would be sitting there. Even if all we did was ignore each other, he needed to be there so I knew that he was okay. The more I thought about it, I realized that, while his car was gone, I hadn't seen or heard from him since he took off into the woods. I had no idea if he was safe or dead. What if the red-haired woman somehow got to him and I wasn't home to get her ransom?

Good grief. Get it together, Amelia. I was annoying myself with all of the "what if's" rattling around my brain.

I refused to just ask Micah myself, instead I texted Bethany. What are best friends for, if not to stalk your maybe-ex and get details you aren't privy to? In just a few messages, she agreed to push Micah for some information on their dinner date tonight, not even questioning the situation further. There was something to be said for a friend that just acted without asking a zillion questions.

I was cuddling on the couch with Charlie late that night — which actually meant he was taking up three-fourths of the couch and I was relegated to the inside corner — watching King Arthur and distracting myself with the gorgeous Clive Owen, when Bethany messaged me back.

Hey, Ame! Talked to M. He said A is fine, just has "stuff" going on. Tried to dig further but didn't get anywhere. Boys. ;-)

I quickly responded. **OK, great! Thanks for checking.**

I know she wanted to keep digging, but Aidan's business was his. If I couldn't be honest with him, it wasn't fair to expect him to be honest with me.

I was lost in my own thoughts when Charlie suddenly bolted off the couch, barking non-stop. He ran in circles around the apartment as if he wasn't sure what he was upset with. I realized I was sitting in a living room surrounded on two sides by windows and switched off the lamp sitting next me while I slid to the ground. Before I had a chance to hit Cole's speed dial, I heard Micah's voice come from the other side of the door as he knocked.

"Amelia? I know you're here. It's Micah. Can you do something about that dreadful animal?" I stood up, turned the light back on, and mentally berated myself for being such a scaredy-cat.

I tried telling Charlie to stop barking, but he was still losing it, scratching at the front door relentlessly. There was no way I could move him myself, so I hollered to Micah to wait a minute. I tried pulling on his collar, yelling for him to lie down, and tossing treats into the living room. Finally, I'd had it and screamed his name as loud as I could, putting a little extra *oomph* behind it. Immediately, Charlie came and sat down in front of me. I stooped down, grabbed his collar, and looked him in the eyes. Without speaking out loud I said, *That's enough. Micah is our friend. Go lay down. Now.* He didn't hesitate, trotting off to his giant dog bed in the corner. I blew a strand of hair out of my face, briefly closed my eyes, and stood to open the door, finding Micah leaning against the frame, a smug smirk on his face.

"Well done, Amelia. I think you've got a magic-sensing creature living with you, but you handled him well enough for a newbie." I was still trying to comprehend what Micah had just said as he breezed past me and took a seat at the island.

"Come on in," I muttered to the empty space where he'd been standing. I closed the door and joined him in the kitchen.

"What brings you here? Weren't you on a date?" I grabbed a few bottles of water from the fridge and tossed him one. He slowed it down in the air and it landed gently on the counter in front of him.

"Show off," I said with a scowl.

He gave me a feisty grin as he twisted the cap off. "Indeed I was, but I just dropped Bethany at her apartment and wanted to speak with you as soon as possible. As we've talked about, I have been looking into these people who attacked you and Aidan. I haven't learned much, but it appears they are outcasts. They belong to groups of people who have rescinded themselves from the monarchy and now live in factions all over the world. It's unclear what their objectives are, but they hate the queen, that much I know."

"I suppose I can't blame them," I said with a shrug, forcing myself not to react with the disdain I had for the woman and her stupid betrothal. "She doesn't exactly seem like the nicest lady and she's got a pretty ridiculous agenda."

"Amelia, do you know anything about what the monarchy has been through? Do you have any idea what the queen has faced? Or do you judge her only based on the ramblings of some old Mage around your childhood campfire?" I watched Micah's face redden with anger and the aura of the room changed.

I bit my lip, trying to distract myself from the magical reaction I was having to his defensiveness. My breath stuck in my lungs and a nervous fear snaked its way into my system.

"Whoa, down boy!" I said as I raised both of my hands and backed away, trying to inject some sarcasm and lighten the mood for both of us. "Believe it or not, I've heard from a few more credible sources than that, but I'll admit to not being super-knowledgeable on the subject of the queen's issues. What's your deal? Are your parents BFF's with her or something? I've never seen you so fired up."

As I asked the question, he immediately started back-peddling. "Of course not, Amelia. I am merely pointing out that you shouldn't speak without a solid factual basis. You never know how your words could be construed or who is listening. If the queen truly is the tyrant you believe, then you could be jailed for even speaking against her." His smirk tried to tell me he was joking, but every other signal contradicted his attempt.

I nodded. "I suppose you're right. Anyway, did you figure out the mystery woman's name?" I wanted to get back on track. Though I was still curious about Micah's outburst, I had bigger issues.

"We believe her name is Melinda Carusso. I only had your brief description to go from, but that in combination with the magical abilities you detailed, fit with the profile of a woman who is a known rebel. She hates the queen, defies her at every turn, and isn't afraid to hurt people to make her point. She's very dangerous and you need to tell me right away if you hear from her again, Amelia. Do you understand?"

I paused, the water bottle mid-way to my mouth, and turned to face Micah. "To hurt people? And, by people, you mean *me*, right? You are telling me that this crazy chick hates the queen and has somehow decided hurting *me* is going to get her somewhere? Have you lost your mind? I'm nothing! And, why do you need to know? What aren't you telling me?" His demands made me sure he knew Melinda was an AniMage, but how could he possibly?

Micah just stared. For what felt like an entire minute, he just stared at me. I could feel our connection niggling at my mind and snapped at him, "If you have something to say, just say it. I'm not letting you in." His head snapped back a little, as if he were surprised I could feel his approach.

"Yes, Micah, I felt that," I said, scowling. "And I don't appreciate you trying to come in uninvited. So knock it off."

"Amelia, are you sure that you've told me everything that's happened?" Micah looked at me quizzically. Either he knew I knew about Melinda, or I wasn't supposed to feel him coming. Damn it all to hell, I was sick of not knowing which powers I was supposed to have and which ones I wasn't. I was sick of lying. I was sick of it all.

I groaned. "Yes, Micah," I said, trying my best to sound exasperated. It wasn't hard, he just didn't realize why I was so annoyed. "Why? What did I do now?"

He shook his head, but I could tell he wasn't pleased. "Nothing. Just…nothing. Look, I need to be going. Cole explained that you are leaving for the weekend. Take the dog. I don't know what he is, but it's clear he can sense power. It might come in handy since you both seem to have a hard time focusing."

"Uh, yeah, thanks. I'll make sure we do that." Of course, only Micah could be insulting while he was trying to be helpful.

I walked him to the door and as I went to close it behind him, Micah turned back and reached in to stop me, putting his hand on the door frame. "Amelia, I think there's more to this than we understand. I don't know what it is, but I'm going to find out. You need to pay attention. You need to be careful. You need to trust me."

His eyes were imploring. In that moment, I wanted to tell him everything. But, that meant truly trusting him and I couldn't take the chance. "I think so, too, Micah. And I do trust you — as much as I know how." I'd told him just a little about how I grew up, so my statement wasn't out of place. I put my hand over his on the door frame, hoping to convey that I was genuine even while internally questioning. He just gave me a small nod and walked away.

As I walked back into the living room and sat down on the couch, I realized that was the first time I'd gone for more than an hour without thinking of Aidan.

It was finally too much. I'd been sitting there, in the dark, staring at the wall for too long. Since I realized I hadn't been thinking of Aidan, it seemed like it was all I could do. I had picked up and set down my phone twenty times. I had gotten as far as opening our last text string but couldn't bring myself to type anything. What was there to say? But, I had to say something. So, I finally did. I held my breath the entire time.

Hi. I know you probably never want to see me again, but I wanted to tell you I'm sorry. I'm leaving with Cole this weekend. Take care.

There was so much more I could have told him. That I thought I could love him. That his arms were the safest place I'd ever been. That I'd give anything for him to kiss me — even if it were just good-bye.

I sat on the couch, buried under a flannel blanket with Charlie at my feet, and let the tears stream down my face. There were no sobs. There were no hysterics. I just cried for the things I would never have. For the reality that I could not choose my life and even though I kept trying to downplay the situation, it was serious. Someone was trying to hurt me. Still, Aidan was the only thing that mattered. I didn't want to want him, but it was like choosing not to breathe. It just wasn't possible. My soul kept fighting for him like my lungs would for air.

Chapter 17

Far too early for my liking, Cole was pounding on my door. "Up and at'em, Amelia! We've got places to go and people to see!"

He was way too damn happy for 6:00 a.m. on a Saturday.

"Come on, come on!" he yelled. I then heard massive paws thundering around the apartment. Clearly, Charlie took that command as a challenge and a fierce tug of war game had ensued. Realizing I would never win this battle — and that I wanted to meet this mystery man — I resigned to getting up.

I had packed my bags last night once I pulled myself together. I checked my phone again and there was still no response from Aidan. Not knowing who exactly we were meeting, I took a little more care with myself. I put on a flowing teal skirt, silver gladiator sandals, and a white sleeveless top. I sent a little zing through my system, trying to get my brain in gear while also removing the puffiness around my eyes from crying. It was only twenty minutes by the time I joined Cole, but he already had coffee in to-go mugs, our bags sitting by the door, Charlie's pail of food, and he promised me breakfast burritos on the way out of town.

"Are you ready for this?!" He gave me a poke in the shoulder, looking far too jovial for my non-caffeinated state. I took my first sip, showing no expression as I slowly swallowed, as if just that tiny bit of coffee would make all the difference. As if it could dull the ache that was slowly spreading through me, sapping any happiness one draining ounce at a time.

"I'm tired of half-truths and secrets, Cole. I'm tired of not knowing how to protect myself, or even how to keep from outing myself. I'm tired of feeling alone and having to push people away. I'm sick and damn tired of crying. So, if by 'ready for this' you mean do I want to know who this guy is and why he matters, then yes. I'm absolutely ready for this." I grabbed my girly weekender and stomped out of the apartment, leaving Cole muttering after me about how this should be fun. *Yeah, right.*

Clearly, the morning was off to a rough start. We'd gotten breakfast and headed east on I-80. Thankfully, Cole's car had Bluetooth and he let me have first pick of the music selection. I pulled up my music app and started an alternative radio station. I didn't need romance tracks, I needed change. I needed reassurance that sometimes you have to make the hard choice, that you might even have to run away from people you want to run toward in order to make the right choice.

Cole let me stew in my own thoughts for quite some time. It was something I appreciated about our relationship, the fact that he didn't need to take up my space. When I finally unfolded myself from the corner of the passenger side and reached back to love Charlie up a little, Cole finally spoke.

"I know I didn't fulfill my end of the bargain, Ame. And, I still haven't told you everything because I just can't. But, you know that no matter what happens, I've got your back in this. I'm not going to let you do it alone, or unprepared, if I can help it. I know you didn't get to choose this path, but there's a chance you can do something really amazing with what you've been handed. You could marry that prince, someday be Queen, and really change things for all of us." He looked so hopeful, his eyes alight with possibility and clearly feeling some sense of purpose I didn't.

"Shouldn't this be a choice though, Cole? Shouldn't it have been my *choice* to learn to use my Elder abilities, to master them and realize what I was capable of? Shouldn't I have been able to make a *choice* to understand exactly what had happened to our people and then *choose* to do something about it?" I struggled to stop my trembling hands, already feeling myself spinning out of control.

Cole laid a hand on mine and a sad understanding crossed between us as the weight on my chest lifted the tiniest bit. "It should have been a choice, Ame. You should have been prepared. But, life doesn't always hand you a choice. Sometimes it just picks you up and puts you where you need to be. And, I know you have this thing for Aidan, but you have to understand that in the scheme of things a human can never be for you. The queen would kill him in an instant if she understood what he meant to you."

He was right. I was being selfish. But, I also knew I was the only one faced with spending the rest of my life with a man I could very likely hate and being ruled by a tyrant I already knew I did. But, based on everything I'd learned, the danger to Aidan was as real as anything else I'd faced. There was no right answer. There was no way out of it and I didn't have a choice.

"I just need more," I resigned. "I need more of life that's mine. I need more information about who and what I am. I'd even love to know who this mysterious prince is that I'm supposedly marrying. Dad has kept me isolated from our entire world and even Ryn won't help. More than anything, right now, I need to know how to control what's happening to me and who these people are. Why they want me. So, is it time for you to spill the beans, big brother, or what? Who is this guy?"

"Not yet," he said with smile that seemed far too excited. "I promised I'd let him introduce himself. It's only a few more hours, just stick with me."

I rolled my eyes, reclined my seat, and let Charlie put his head on the headrest next to mine. I let his soft snorts of breath calm my own breathing and restless power, and fell asleep.

I woke up as the car came to a stop. We were in the woods. Not just woods — trees the likes of General Sherman. Trees with bigger trunks than a car.

Cole and Charlie were already out of the car and romping around, trying to get out some of Charlie's pent up energy, and all I could do was stare at our surroundings. I looked behind us at a dirt road that resembled more of a path and wondered how I possibly slept through the ruts I could see. I got out of the car, smoothing my skirt and making sure my braid was still intact.

"Hey, Cole? Why are we parked at a dead end in the middle of the forest?" I tried to sound like that was no big deal, but I couldn't help but be a little freaked out. It was the middle of the day and the trees cast such a shadow, it was as if the sun was setting even though it was only late morning. There was a quiet rustling of leaves that made me feel surrounded on all sides, causing my internal panic to slowly grow.

As if on cue, Charlie bolted. Just went tearing off into the woods at full speed. Even Cole, in perfect shape with a little magical push, couldn't have attempted to keep up with a dog the size of a small horse. I was screaming at him to come back, running toward him, when Cole grabbed my arm and stopped me.

"What are you doing, Cole? We can't let Charlie run off like that! He could get hurt, he could get lost. What are you doing?" I wrenched my arm from his grasp and my power leapt out, searching for Charlie itself. Ever since our "conversation" the other night, I could always get a decent read on where he was. I was frantically following his mental signature when Cole grabbed me again, this time with both hands and a good shake. "God, Amelia. STOP. Charlie's fine. He knows where he is."

I narrowed my eyes. Cole was still smiling while my scowl only deepened and my frustration grew.

I crossed my arms and glared. "Explain. Now."

He let me go and I stepped back, putting some space between us. "Well, he—"

Suddenly a voice came from behind me, deep and melodic, sounding all too familiar. "Charlie is quite comfortable here because this is where he was born. He's currently playing with his brother, Onyx. They are having quite the time."

I turned to find a tall man striding toward me through the trees as I heard deep, happy barks and yips in the distance. He wore his dark hair long and pulled back, had to be at least six-foot-three, and looked like a lumberjack. He was even wearing a red, plaid button-down with dark jeans and hiking boots. He had a thick beard but even that couldn't hide his giant smile. Cole almost ran to him, giving him a huge hug. When they turned back to me again, the man's arm slung over Cole's shoulders, he finally let the bomb drop.

"Hi, Amelia. I've wanted to meet you for many years. I'm Derreck — your uncle."

I leaned in as if I didn't hear him correctly. "My *what*? What did you say?""

Derreck smiled, looking triumphantly at Cole and then back at me. "Your uncle. Your mother's brother."

Standing back, my hands clenched so tightly I could feel the press of my nails into my palms, I focused all of my attention on Cole.

With barely restrained fury, I yelled, "My UNCLE, Cole? You've been hiding our *uncle*? You thought it best not to share that little tidbit with me?"

My power blasted through me and a whole new state of pissed-off found its home inside of me.

I stalked toward Cole, yelling, "Don't you *think,* oh big brother of mine, that I might have appreciated knowing him? That maybe in all the years Dad was berating me and in no way preparing me for a life I hadn't even chosen, that maybe I could have used someone? That because I didn't even *get* time with mom, I might have benefited from him?"

I threw my hand out at Derreck, just trying to make a point, but unfortunately my unrestrained power had other plans. The two men were standing there, mouths slacked and looking stupefied, when suddenly they were both on their backs on the forest floor.

"God DAMMIT! I'm sick of this." I stamped my foot, sending a tremor through the ground as I hissed in anger and walked over to help them up. I did a quick scan and this time it was actually me, not the scary part of me, lashing out. Even as livid as I was, they didn't deserve that low blow. Cole was already halfway up and I extended my hand out to Derreck. I finally looked in his eyes and all I could see was the photo of my mother in my mind. They had the same eyes. The same smile. As our hands connected and Derreck met my eyes, I watched him wince a little.

Once he was on his feet, he explained, "That's, uh, quite a punch you've got there, Amelia. I think maybe it's time we talked about how to control it."

"Give it your best shot, buddy. I've been trying for months." The sarcasm was dripping from my words but again, all he did was smile.

I turned to Cole, who still hadn't spoken. "Is this guy where you get the non-stop smiles, because damn it if you both aren't driving me crazy with the smiling and the optimism." I got the desired effect and he broke out into a grin. I returned his smile with a hesitant one of my own, feeling better about putting us back on equal footing. I hadn't forgiven either of them, but there was a possibility of answers and I wanted them.

"Are one of you going to tell me where we're actually going? I didn't dress up to hang out in the forest all day," I asked flippantly.

With another giant smile and a laugh, Derreck pointed off in the distance. "This way, it isn't far."

I was shocked at how "not far" it was. We only walked for maybe five minutes and then his giant log cabin was just *there*. "Wait a minute…that wasn't there. I would have seen it as we were walking."

I was turning in circles, thoroughly confused, as Charlie and another giant Dane that had to be Onyx, came bounding up.

"Magic, my dear. It can do far more than you realize," Derreck said with a grin that was still too similar to Cole's for me to be comfortable with.

Charlie head-butted my hand, breaking my train of thought and running in circles around me as Onyx joined him. I could tell he wanted me to meet his brother, his mind was a repeating image of me petting Onyx and playing fetch with them both.

I laughed and squatted down. I didn't even have the chance to say his name before Onyx came to a skidding stop in front of me. He was jet black with eyes so dark, they blended in with his shiny coat. He was gorgeous and only slightly smaller than Charlie. I cautiously reached out to establish a connection as I also stretched my hand to take his lifted paw, sending reassuring vibes as I did both, though he looked all too happy to interact. As soon as I touched his mind, he immediately flooded me with images.

He dipped his head into my hand and I found him squatting between my legs as he wiggled in as close to me as possible, his thick tail thumping a quick rhythm in the dry dirt. I couldn't focus as he assaulted me with every memory he had of his brother — from being a puppy and playing with Charlie, to how sad he was when he left, to

Cole bringing Charlie to visit. It was clear that the best days were when Charlie was "home" with him, and that Cole had been here often.

I couldn't believe all of the emotion he conveyed. I gave him a hug, sending him my own images of me and Charlie cuddled on the couch and how good it felt to have him with me. Then, I stood up, intending to send him off to play, but before I could, Onyx lifted a massive paw and dropped it onto my thigh. With that deliberate connection by him, the images from his mind hit me harder than they had previously. Instead of flitting through my head like a movie reel, his thoughts slammed into my head and took over.

Suddenly, my father's image filled my head. I expected this to be some kind of memory from years ago, realizing it was only logical for my father and uncle to have known each other. Yet, as the memory played, I realized that I wasn't seeing a younger version of my father, that it was him, now, recently. As he walked away, I also caught Rynna in the background, laughing at something Derreck was saying. She was leaned in closely to him, her hand on his arm.

"Onyx, down! No! I told you to keep things to yourself, you mangy brat." Derreck's booming voice filled my ears as Onyx was pulled away from me, our connection breaking, and with it, the vision of my father disappeared. I was still crouched on the ground, my head feeling fuzzy, as I looked up at my uncle. He held Onyx by the collar, glaring down at him. The dog tucked his head sheepishly behind his master's leg, sneaking a look around and at me. I swear, in my head, I heard him whisper, *You needed to know.*

I tried to stand up, but was assaulted by spinning nausea and dropped back to my hands and knees.

"I'm sorry, Amelia. Sometimes Onyx comes on a little strong. He's only really used to me and Cole being around." Derreck grasped my biceps and helped to steady me as I stood. As soon as I had righted myself and the world stopped spinning around me, I yanked away and stepped back.

"How about my dad? Is he used to him? Or Rynna? She looked pretty comfortable with you. Does Onyx know her, too? It's great that your dog is telling me things you aren't. Very reassuring." My words were biting. I spat them out coated in angry venom, so completely sick of the lies that followed me everywhere.

Derreck's shoulders slumped and he didn't even bother with a rebuttal as he pulled a hand through his hair and wrapped it around the back of his neck in obvious frustration. Cole had been standing just behind him, leaned on the deck railing, but when he heard my accusations, came to stand beside me.

"I thought you were supposed to different, *Uncle,*" I said with contempt. "You were supposed to help, but you're no different than everyone else." I stood my ground, feeling strong with Cole beside me.

"Why was he here? Rynna told me he wanted to go see someone who had answers. What answers do you have?" I asked, swallowing the lump in my throat. I hadn't expected the emotion that lodged itself there. Cole put his hand on my shoulder and the constriction in my chest let up the tiniest bit. My eyes glowed brightly but I was able to quell the waves into ripples as my power stretched itself through me.

"Is what Onyx showed her true, Uncle? Why didn't you tell me?" I felt the hurt before I looked over at my brother, his expression pained.

At that exact moment, Charlie came bounding around the house and skidded to a stop next to me. A low growl hummed in his throat as he took one step toward Derreck, feeling the animosity radiating from both Cole and me.

Derreck's head snapped back in surprise. "Charlie, it's okay. It's just me." He held his hands up and looked over at Cole and me, questioning what we had done. Without breaking eye contact, I laid my hand on Charlie's scruff and silently told him to heel. He stepped back beside me and sat down, though the quiet growls continued.

I quirked an eyebrow at Derreck, still waiting for a response.

"Alright. Yes. Your father and Rynna were here. He did come to me for answers. He thought I could help break the spell the Hunters had put on him for good." Derreck's words were quiet and calm but his eyes were filled with shame.

Cole and I turned to each other, and then back to him, saying at the same time, "What spell?"

Derreck took a deep breath, forcefully blowing the air out of his mouth as he tried to control his own reaction to his words. A flash of green in his eyes was all that truly gave away his internal struggle. The thought that I was jealous of his control deepened that scowl I was already wearing.

"There is so much you two don't understand. So much we've tried to protect you from in various ways, but we can't do it anymore. The time is coming and from what Cole has told me, they've realized who you are, Amelia. Let's go inside, this may take some time." Derreck turned and walked up the wooden stairs into the cabin. He took dragging steps, his boots making a distinct *thud* on each one, as if the weight of the world rested on his shoulders. In minutes, he seemed to have aged hours, all the joy and happiness he'd shown me earlier erased.

I closed my eyes and tried to understand what was happening.

My father has been under a spell?

Rynna knew?

I have an uncle?

Cole knew Derreck all these years? What else isn't he telling me?

There were more unanswered questions than I had even realized and it seemed like the more I asked, the less I knew. I took a few steps forward until I realized Cole was still standing where I'd left him.

"Hey. We need to go inside. We need to find out what's going on, Cole." I stood in front of him, looking into his glazed and unfocused eyes, and finally waved a hand in front of his face. "Cole!" I shouted.

He slowly blinked and focused a now angry stare on me. "He's been lying to me, Amelia. All these years."

I couldn't stop my bitter laugh. "Welcome to the club, big brother. This is how it's always been. I wish I could say you get used to it." I lightly smacked him on the chest twice, punctuating my words, and turned away. "The only thing you can do is listen when people talk and decide later what was worth hearing."

As I walked up the stairs and toward the front door of the cabin, the pit in my stomach grew, along with the inescapable feeling that in just a few steps nothing would ever be the same.

Chapter 18

I stepped across the threshold of Derreck's home and was surprised by what I found. I was surrounded by sleek black appliances, dark granite counter tops, exposed piping, black leather furniture, and modern art. I stood in the center of the very open floor plan and turned in a slow circle.

"You were expecting animal heads and an old brown recliner?" There was a hint of smile playing on Derreck's lips as he put a tea kettle on to boil. I looked away, embarrassed to realize I had expected just that.

"It's…um, nice. Really nice." I fumbled for words and was glad when Cole stepped quietly through the door. Just having him here, realizing that I wasn't the only one people had been holding out on, gave me strength. The last few weeks had been hell and I was ready for it to end. I just didn't feel like tonight was the night. No, tonight was just the beginning.

I paced the length of the living room and back. Charlie and Onyx sat on opposite ends and I let my hand drop to absently caress their heads as I walked past. I chewed on my lip, deep in thought about what it all could mean. What would happen if I sat down and let Derreck speak? Would he be the one who could tell me the truth? Or would he only tell me the parts he wanted to share like everyone else had done? Would I find out exactly what it all means? Or would he just lead me down another path I hated more?

Aidan's face flashed in my mind and the ache in my chest deepened. That sent me down a whole other line of thinking.

I could walk away. Right now. I could walk away, find Aidan, and do what my mom had done. I could leave the truth and the drama behind and be happy. I could live the life I chose.

But, could I?

"You're going to wear a path, Amelia. Sit down."

My head flew up and I realized that both Cole and Derreck were sitting on the black leather couches in the living room. Cole's jaw was locked, a muscle ticking in frustration, as he struggled with his own emotions. Derreck simply sat back, sipping his tea, not really looking at either of us directly.

I took quick steps to the overstuffed chair and pulled the blanket from the back over myself, suddenly needing comfort of any kind. As the thought entered and left, Charlie appeared beside me, whimpering as he licked my palm. I scratched behind his ears and left my hand on his scruff as he sat beside my chair, his big head sitting taller than the armrest. I threaded my fingers through his course fur, preparing myself for what was to come.

I couldn't walk away. I had been waiting for the truth for longer than I could remember. My mother lived with the truth her whole life. She got to make an educated decision. If I wanted to do the same, I needed all of the facts, however I could get them.

"Okay. Go." I wanted to get back up and go sit by Cole; I had a feeling I would need him. But, someday I was going to have to be able to handle this stuff myself, so I stayed in my chair.

Derreck set his tea cup on the table and put his elbows on his knees, clasping his hands in front of him. He looked intently between Cole and I, but his gaze returned to Cole.

"Cole, before I start, I want you to understand that I was trying to help you. To make the right choices to protect you. I never got to be a part of Amelia's life and honestly, I wasn't supposed to be part of yours. That was the agreement we all made. So, please, listen to me before you judge me. That's all I ask."

Derreck sat and waited. Cole eventually lifted his eyes and met Derreck's. So many emotions and unspoken words traveled between them in mere seconds but even I could see the pain and apology etched in Uncle Derreck's features. Finally, Cole simply nodded and Derreck's face relaxed in relief, some of the tension visibly draining from his rigid posture.

"Okay." He took a deep breath. "I'm not sure exactly where to start, but you need to understand what's really happening.

"First, most importantly, you both need to know that your parents loved you more than anything." He looked at me. "You, especially, Amelia, need to understand that. You didn't get time with your mother like Cole did, but know this — she loved you from the very moment she felt your light inside of her to the moment hers was snuffed out by that *Hunter*." The snarl that accompanied that last word changed his every feature. His mouth twisted, his nostrils flared, and his eyes narrowed to slits.

"So, our dad isn't crazy? She really was murdered?" I asked. It had been a possibility, but having it confirmed challenged everything I thought I knew. My father's delusions were legendary and this one always seemed so far-fetched.

Derreck's eyes glowed an iridescent green, like the glow of the green flash you could sometimes catch just as the sun set over the ocean. Against his dark features and the black leather of the couch, he looked scary.

"Oh, yes, Amelia. Your mother was absolutely murdered." Derreck's eyes glittered with hate, the green glowing brighter and brighter. "The queen sent her most ruthless Hunter specifically to find your mother. It was only dumb luck that he found her giving birth to you, and his own good sense to make the deal he did to keep you

251

alive. Julia would have likely preferred he wiped out the whole line, but the Hunter, Rhi, understood immediately what you would be capable of. That you were the one."

"The one what? I know I'm an Elder but there have been hundreds of Elders over the years. There is nothing special about me, Uncle Derreck, except the fact that I'm the last female and have absolutely no idea how to handle the crazy power I've got." I shook my head at him, trying to make him understand that if they were pinning any hopes and dreams on me, it wasn't a safe bet. And, given what had been happening lately, there was no way he wanted to put my dual personalities in charge of saving anyone.

Cole kept quiet as I looked at him, waiting for some back-up, but I got nothing. "Really, Cole? You know how much of a disaster I've been. I'm nobody's *one* anything," I muttered those last few words to myself. We had agreed not to bring up my alter ego until Uncle Derreck had showed his hand, but I wanted help. I wanted to just spill it all.

Derreck reacted to my conflicted expression by thrusting himself off the couch and taking three purposeful strides over to me. Crouching in front of the chair, he put his hands on my knees.

"Amelia, you absolutely are our *one*. You are the one who can kill Julia. You're the only one who can stop her devastating reign and right our world again. Under no circumstances can you go to that castle. You have to get away, Amelia. She can't ever have access to you. And, before the time comes when she expects you, we have to find your mate. He's the only one who can bring out the real power you hold, and the only one who can help you control it."

I tried to stand but was tangled in the blanket. The current that jolted through me was so strong, I thought it would split my head in half. I tore the blanket from my legs and tossed it across the room, diving out of the chair and almost toppling Derreck in the process. My hair floated around me and the violet smoke I had come to love swept in and around each of my fingers, encompassing my hands as it built and gathered.

"I have a WHAT? What the hell is a mate? It's bad enough I'm already betrothed to one guy and now you're telling me there's another one out there expecting me? What exactly do you people think, that it's okay to pimp a girl out to the highest bidder? Does anyone around here give one crap about what I want?" I balled my fists, trying to contain the rapidly spiraling power that was radiating in and around me. I expected Cole to stand up and help me slow the waves rippling off my body, but he just sat there, staring. The dark energy was back. The black seeping into my internal violet power, blotting out the brightness and sending my emotions through the roof as my desperation for answers trumped anything else I was feeling.

I took measured steps toward my uncle, feeling the change as a stronger, more dominant side of me took control. "You still haven't told me what I am. Why I'm *the one.* All Elders have power. What makes me different? What is so special about *me*?"

He actually stumbled as he tried to back away from me. "Amelia, you need to calm down. I told you I had answers, but you have to be able to hear them." He looked around as the framed art on the walls started to shake, his hands out, as if he could slow my progress. I cocked my head, looking at him, making it perfectly evident that I wasn't calming down in the slightest. I was lost in the haze of power and energy. There was nothing he could do to stop me.

"You. Need. To. Tell. ME!" Derreck's eyes widened as he lifted off the ground and floated in front of me. "I won't ask again, Uncle. I don't know exactly what I could do to you, but you probably don't want to find out." The cold, flat tone of my voice seemed foreign to my own ears.

It was a heady feeling as the energy built around me. I had no idea where it was coming from and I didn't care. I just wanted answers. I was done waiting.

With a flick of my hand, I sent Derreck flying across the room, stopping him inches from the wall. "NOW!" I screamed the word and it was at that point Charlie's barking broke into my thoughts as he barreled into back of my knees. He was running between Cole and me, bellowing at us both as he tried to get a reaction from either of us. My brother sat there, still as a statue, refusing to make eye contact with me.

I closed my eyes and tried to breathe. It was in control, though. With its destructive energy and single-minded focus, the rogue part of me was enjoying this too much. It didn't want to stop playing with Derreck. It wanted to force him in whatever way we needed to. I heard its thoughts as clearly as my own, but mine were telling me to stop this, to calm Charlie, to let Uncle Derreck go. The two halves fought inside my head until I couldn't take it anymore.

"STOP! JUST STOP IT!" I dropped to the floor, covering my ears with my hands, and continuing to whisper, "Just stop. Please stop." I rocked back and forth and all at once, the rattling of frames stopped, Derreck dropped to the ground, and Cole was by my side.

Cole pulled me into his lap and I stayed a tight ball, trying to understand what had just happened as I let him smother the fury that had infiltrated my veins. As my body reacted to what had just happened, I was pulled under. In the most far off voice, the last thing I heard was, "That's what you are, Amelia. You are a Keeper. You are our Keeper."

I woke up to a pounding head and a dark room. Through tiny slits, I saw light coming around the window shade and knew it was still the same day. I closed my eyes again and searched myself for my destructive power. As much as I wanted to forget it was there, what had just happened made it very obvious that I was not truly the one controlling my power. Inside of me was something else entirely. I could see my own inner light, the part of my power that was truly mine to own and control. But, there was also this other piece that I couldn't name and didn't feel like it belonged to me.

The tight ball of power that wasn't truly mine sat back in the corner of my mind, a vibrant flame of shimmering black light. I could feel its smug pleasure and it made me sad. What I had just done to my uncle wasn't who I wanted to be. I dragged myself off the bed and out into the main room. With each step, my head pounded more viciously. I struggled to move with any speed or grace, my whole body still reeling from what had happened.

Derreck and Cole were back on their individual couches, talking in hushed tones. Both stopped as they saw me, wary looks in their eyes.

"It's just me. No crazy woman here. She's back in her hidey-hole." I tried to inject some humor, but the words didn't quite have the playfulness I had hoped.

Derreck gestured to the chair I'd been in earlier. "Take a seat, Amelia. We should probably pick up where we left off. There really isn't time to waste given what I just witnessed."

I sat gingerly, trying to move as little as possible as my head continued to throb. "Are you okay, Ame? Really?" Cole asked. "Do you need me?"

"Amelia. Help yourself. You can undo exactly what you've done, you just need to focus." Derreck actually sounded a little irked to have to explain it, but I didn't care. I'd thought of helping myself, it was what I usually did, but after what had just happened, I was afraid to use even an ounce of my power. I would have much rather had Cole's help, but now I didn't feel like I could.

"It's fine. I'll be fine. Just talk." I let my own irritation come to the surface and with a huff, Derreck got back to business.

"Things got a little convoluted back there and I feel like you only got half of a few different stories. I want to start with your father, which was where I tried to start."

I wanted to say something snarky about all of the half-stories, but I just didn't have the energy.

Derreck continued. "What I was trying to explain was that the day you were born, the day your mother died and you were betrothed, the Hunter, Rhi, also put a spell on your Father. Rhi initially wanted to take you right then. He wanted to take you back to the queen and force you to live your life out at the castle. But your father, even amid all his grief, thought faster than Rhi. He offered to allow Rhi access to his mind, to allow him to monitor you, so long as you were allowed to stay with him until you were twenty-one. Your father wanted the opportunity to be with you, to watch his beloved daughter grow up. Rhi agreed, but your father didn't force Rhi to be specific enough in his oath. He wanted the ability to allow Rhi to see you when he chose to. Instead, the oath allowed Rhi to access his mind any time the queen wanted to see you or see your progress. All Rhi had to do was say a specific command and he could see whatever your father could see. Any moment of the day or night, your father would be a spy for the queen."

This time, it was Cole that spoke before I did. "You're telling us that not only was he not crazy and that mom was really murdered, but that what he did to us — what he did to Amelia — was all because the Hunters really were everywhere? Do you understand what that means? What knowing that could have changed?" His voice cracked as he spoke and I felt the wounds inside of him rip open once more.

Derreck was quiet for a moment. "I'm sorry, Cole. It wasn't my choice and it wasn't my place. Your father made the decision that he needed to protect your sister, to try to do his best to stop her from becoming what they wanted her to be. Or, if she did, to make damn sure they never knew it. You were an innocent bystander, but he also needed you. You helped contain her. Your leaving was hard on him in so many ways, but I was watching, too. I followed you from town to town and I saw what you were trying to do, how you were trying to help Amelia. You were going to get yourself killed doing it the way you had. And, I felt your pain, your loneliness. Your mother would have never forgiven me if I had let you face all of that alone."

I had never seen my brother cry, but as the two men sat staring at each other, Cole's eyes shone with unshed tears. Probably tears he should have cried many times over the years and never did. The tears that came from feeling betrayed not once, but many times — by family. But, there was also understanding.

Blinking them back yet again, Cole composed himself. "At least you were there. I'm glad you were there," he said, his voice thick.

As I had watched the conversation progress between Cole and Uncle Derreck, my mind was reeling at all of the information. All the times my dad had yelled at me about control and locked me in my room. They hadn't been about me failing him. He had been protecting me. He hid in his office so they couldn't see me. So that he wouldn't accidentally show them something. My throat clogged with emotion and my own tears fell in silent drops, leaving trails of regret in their wake.

"Where is he, Uncle Derreck? Where is our dad? We need to see him. He needs to know we know." An urgency I hadn't felt through any of this raced through me. There was so much I needed to say to my father.

Derreck shook his head, his answer a mix of patience and misery. "I'm sorry, Amelia. He's gone. I couldn't help him and there was only one person I could even think of that could. I can't tell you where he's gone or how long, I don't know where the man I sent him to is. And, you can't see him anyway. They would be able to see you. Rhi is still inside of his head. Until someone can break that bond, he'll always be in his head."

Defeat sucked the urgency and the fervor straight out of me. "Then tell me, what is a Keeper?" I had to keep going. I had to know it all. It had been hard enough being an Elder, the idea that I was still something else entirely was almost more than my mind could handle.

"What you need to understand is that there is not more than one. You are it, Amelia. You alone are the Keeper and what you are has never been and can never be again. You are a combination of all of the power held by the Elders who were still living when your mother got pregnant. You have the normal Elder power you should, but you also hold power from all five families. You are the only one to ever hold this power. The first thing the queen did when she moved to take over was separate the five families from each other. She knew that alone they could never do the damage they could together when their powers were linked and fed off of each other. That is what you have inside you. You have their power. You are the Keeper of our future."

I sat back in my chair in stunned silence, Derreck's words rolling over and over in my head. It should have been harder to understand, but at least now I could give a name to the darkness in me. It was a she. Many of them. How could I explain to him that it was evil? That this supposedly-wonderful Keeper power took me over and did nothing but damage? That it wouldn't listen to me or be guided by me? I needed more time to think, so I just sat quietly.

"And, her mate? What does that even mean?" Cole asked. "Did Rhi do that, too?"

"No," Derreck responded. "Rhi had nothing to do with anything Amelia is or isn't. That was all your mother. She had foreseen what was to come and took action of her own accord. She was one of the strongest Elders we had and knew she could handle the pregnancy and that her daughter could handle the power. No one knows who Amelia's mate is." Derreck paused for a moment before leaning in, his palms together and his fingers steepled.

"The oldest living Elder from the high council prophecised the end of Queen Julia's reign. From what I know, she told her that, 'A day would come when inside her the five families would merge and only a man who was both king and companion could tame the wild and set her free.' I've heard that there could be more to the prophecy, but that was all your mother was sure of. She passed it on to me the same day she explained the choice that she'd made. Of course, she thought she would be here to help guide you, to help you learn to control it all and rise to greatness. Your father didn't even know until it was too late. He would have never arranged your betrothal had he understood what you were to become."

Derreck fell back onto the couch, relief visible on his face, as if a weight had been lifted from him by sharing his story. The problem was that that weight had been transferred to me. I dropped my head back and closed my eyes. My mind was racing and I couldn't begin to sort through the madness. My life had been a lie. Everything I thought I knew was false. No one was who they seemed.

Who was I? All of my hopes for real answers were gone — dashed in an instant as Uncle Derreck's words sunk in and the reality emerged that not only was this so much bigger than I had imagined, but that no one truly knew the truth.

A huge crash brought me out of my contemplative trance. I shot up as both dogs started barking and Derreck leapt from the couch. I was shocked to find Cole in a rage. He was upending side tables and sweeping the contents of shelves to the ground. His eyes burned a deep green and he tossed a kitchen table chair as he roared, "WHY?" He rounded on Derreck and stalked toward him.

"WHY? You had so many opportunities to tell me the truth. You found me when I was twenty. I had been out on my own for two years trying to find a way to help my sister. To get her away from my crazy dad and stop this betrothal. You *knew* I'd spent my life protecting her and that I'd spend the rest of my life doing it. You *told me* you were going to help me. Did you? Did you really help me, Uncle Derreck? You could have helped me by telling me THE TRUTH!" Cole's words were like thunder, echoing throughout the cavernous cabin.

Derreck stood his ground. As I watched the green fire build around Cole's body, starting at his hands and rippling out until it surrounded him, I kept expecting Derreck to back down. To walk away. To apologize. But, he didn't. He just stood there, in the center of the room, breathing deeply as he did his best to control the natural reaction to Cole's explosion. A trickle of electricity swept through me as my eyes changed and she came to life. I tried to push her down, but she was elated to have a reason to come out to play.

Both dogs were hunkered down on either side of me, inherently protective. The stand-off between Cole and

Uncle Derreck was intense, both literally radiating power and emotion. While Cole wanted to be angry, I felt his pain as acutely as if it were my own. The sharp bite of the blade of betrayal. Whether that's truly what it was or not, that's what it felt like. I hated that he knew that feeling, that we had that in common now.

Derreck stood stoic, limbs down but rigid at his sides. Cole faced him in a fighter's stance with clenched fists and a fierce stare. He took short breaths in and out of his mouth, just waiting for the excuse. I couldn't take it anymore, so I pushed my way between them.

"Stop it! Just stop it!" I shouted. I shoved a hand to each of their chests. Not that my one-hundred and fifty pounds was going to do much against two walls of muscle, but it was worth a shot. I looked back and forth between them as heat radiated from their chests into my palms.

"You want to make this about me, Cole, then make it about me," I commanded. "Whole truth or not, Uncle Derreck has told us more now than we've ever known. But, even with everything we do know, there's still so much we don't. Who else is going to help us? We need him. We need his information." I stared my brother directly in the eyes until the burn faded to the shine of fresh grass and eventually back to brown. Then, I turned on my uncle. "And, you. Right now we need to be convinced that we can trust you. So, convince us."

The rogue in me added a little jolt to that last word and Derreck took a step back, rubbing his chest. "Fine!

Deal! As much as I can tell you, I will." He turned away muttering, "Now, was that entirely necessary?"

Chapter 19

"What about the attacks? Twice Amelia has been targeted. We don't know who they are or what they want. All we know is that the woman is associated with a rebel faction that hates the queen. There has to be more than one group of people that hate that woman, so that doesn't narrow it down much for us." Cole looked to Derreck for confirmation.

Derreck nodded, saying, "We can assume these people at least understand that Amelia is an Elder — they may even have the notion that she's the last one given no one's seen an Elder in years. That in and of itself is enough for them to want to use her for her power. I think it's time I make a visit to Brighton to see what's happening. It would also help to get a better scope of Amelia's skills when she's actually using them herself." Derreck turned to me. "We need to teach you some control and I'm not even sure how to do that, given what's inside you." He didn't look nearly as confident as I wanted him to.

Derreck went on to give us more background; explanations Cole had already given me around the history and how Julia came to power. It was good to be able to say, "I knew that!" instead of constantly questioning everything. My frustration resumed when we got back to the issue of me having a "mate".

"You have to have some idea who this guy is, don't you? I mean, who really just throws something like that out there with no extra information?" I was having a bit of a tantrum. I was beat tired, my head was throbbing, and Derreck just kept telling me I needed to be out there looking for my mate. That I needed to give up school, my job, my friends, my life, and go.

"Amelia, you're asleep with your eyes open. There is no use going in circles right now. It's time for bed." Derreck stood and the look he gave me made it perfectly clear that the conversation was over for tonight. I wondered if that look would have been the same one my mom would have given me had she still been alive.

"Fine," I said with an extended yawn. "But I still have questions."

"Understood," he agreed. Then, he stopped next to me as I stood and spoke in low, unyielding tones. "Understand this though, Amelia, whatever you have with Aidan Montgomery ends today."

Had I been holding anything, I would have dropped it. As it was, my mouth fell open and I couldn't speak. When my voice finally came, I could only sputter at him. "Excuse me, what?"

The look on Derreck's face was one of cold, steel determination. "You heard me correctly, Amelia. You will not see that human again. He is a liability and he is not your kind. You need to be focused on finding and building the relationship with your mate."

How did he even know? I turned to Cole and he refused to meet my eyes.

My heart physically hurt, but I refused to allow the emotion to overtake me. I had already known that Aidan and I weren't meant to be, but having it put into words, as a proclamation from the only man who could explain who and what I was, was like seeing small pieces of my heart crumble and then be crushed under the thick soles of his boots. How could fate be so cruel to put Aidan in my path, to let me fall for him, to let me feel loved for just being myself for the first time, and then rip him from me so quickly? I blinked back the tears that kept threatening and nodded, which was truly the only thing I could do.

I sat back down and stared out into the room, looking at nothing and wondering where Aidan was and what he was doing. I wondered if he had missed me, or if he was worried. My phone had died on the way here while it kept searching for service, so I hadn't even had the ability to check it. I didn't understand why my mind wouldn't let him go. But, it wasn't just my mind — my soul ached for him. For the safety of his arms and the soothing tone of his voice. If I closed my eyes and sat still enough, I could even smell him. Citrus and trees. Summer. I could feel myself pressed into his warm chest with his arms around me.

But these thoughts would do me no good. I had to make a clean break. I had to sever all ties. This was too real. What Derreck was saying was too much for Aidan to have to deal with. He wasn't of my people and that could get him killed. Derreck and Cole were still talking as I abruptly stood, resolute in the fact that Aidan and I had to be over. I turned to them and said, "I want to leave tomorrow. I'm going to bed." I went through my nightly rituals, put on my favorite sweatshirt and yoga pants, and laid down in the over-sized guest bed.

I thought I would lay awake for hours, but I was out in an instant and slept hard until I awoke screaming. Cole came banging through my bedroom door, Charlie barking his head off not far behind. "Hey….are you okay? Amelia? Amelia!" he shouted.

I was sitting straight up in the center of the king-sized bed with the covers tangled around me, looking around with wild eyes. I was awake, but I wasn't seeing the room.

I was seeing the woods. I was running through the woods, but I wasn't me. I was far too close to the ground. The last thing I heard before Cole shook me to my senses was howling.

Derreck and Cole grilled me over breakfast, yet again, about my dream. Something about it felt so weird and personal that I decided to hold back. I told them I had no idea what the dream was about or why I was screaming. Neither of them seemed to believe me, but they also didn't argue, which I appreciated. I was collecting a vat of my own secrets, I just needed some time to piece it all together.

Before we hit the road, Derreck decided we needed to have one more discussion — in private. Cole gave him an odd look, but shrugged and went out with the dogs.

As Derreck sipped his tea, I squirmed, feeling scrutinized under his gaze.

"You know, we can't keep doing this thing," I said as I flapped my hand between us. "This thing where you just stare at me and make me feel like I'm either in trouble or you're about to drop another bomb. You've had enough time to figure out what to say to me all these years you were ignoring me, so just spit it out already." I sank back in my chair, feeling smug.

"Has anyone ever told you that you are far too honest?" Derreck questioned with a smirk.

"Huh," I grunted. "Only like every day."

He chuckled a little. "Well, you are your mother's daughter, that's clear enough." That got a genuine smile from me as my heart warmed a little. No one but Rynna had ever compared me to my mother.

"Well, Amelia, this is another one of those things you aren't going to love hearing, but it's been said to every Elder and so it will also be said to you. Your mother should have been the one having the discussion with you, that's how this is typically done. But, since I am technically an Elder, though just a lowly male, I can do the honors. Your case is especially different, given you are the Keeper, but this is a rite of passage I won't deny you. You wanted the whole truth and so you shall have it." He set his cup down and leaned toward me.

I couldn't help but lean in as well. I was a little apprehensive, but finally being a part of something and not feeling alone was something I couldn't hold back from. No matter what he had to say.

Seeing he had my full attention, Derreck continued. "There will come a time, Amelia, where you must choose love or duty. You have a duty to your people — not just Mages, but to all of our people — Mages, Hunters, and AniMages, alike. Your duty is to protect them, to honor their ways and to heal their hearts. You are a symbol of all that is good and right. Your magic is a gift, not only the gift that all women of your line carry, but a gift that holds the power of all five families. This gift allows you to rise above those who would tear our people apart and make them weak. Your strength is their strength. Your love is their love. But, they must come first. That's not to say you won't love, because you will, but you will love your people first. Do you understand?"

"I think so," I said weakly.

Derreck shook his head. "No, I don't think you do. Amelia, this life you yearn to understand and the woman you want to become will always be ruled by the needs of the people. You are last. Always. This will not fully make sense to you for some time, but it needs to sit in the back of your mind. You need to seek these words and remember why we are here. Elders are needed to keep the balance and maintain order. The queen must be stopped and you are our only hope."

It was decided that Derreck would come visit the following weekend. That he would leave his self-imposed solitude to come to Brighton and help me work on my skills, as well as start taking me on trips to visit other areas. I truly had no interest in finding my supposed mate, but at this point I didn't know how to argue about it either. His words kept repeating over in my head.

You will love, but you will love your people first. You will always be last.

I couldn't argue with what he was saying, but my mind couldn't truly grasp the magnitude of what I had just been handed. So many dots were connecting in my mind. My father's odd behaviors. Why I could never even begin to control my own power. The fact that my mother had trusted me with this. She had chosen me for this.

What a mind job.

As soon as we got in the car, I plugged my phone in to charge, but I hadn't actually turned it on. About mid-way through the drive, when I couldn't even stand being inside my own head anymore, I realized it and powered the phone up. With a swipe across the screen, I was suddenly inundated with all the beeps and buzzes that meant I had messages from every angle. There were texts, missed calls, and voicemails. I was a little overwhelmed because I'd told both Micah and Bethany where I was going — sort of. They both knew I was heading out with Cole for the weekend.

I started with the text messages since they were the easiest to get through. A few benign ones from Bethany on Friday, telling me she hoped I had a great weekend with Cole and that she was thinking about poor Charlie and his shots. One from Micah that only said: **Call me when you get this. Immediately.**

Then, there was one from Aidan. My phone wasn't showing me a preview and I couldn't bring myself to touch his name on the screen. I closed my eyes and took a deep inhale. After I'd emptied my lungs, I pressed my index finger to the screen and watched his message appear under the last one I'd sent.

Leaving? What do you mean leaving? Please don't leave me, Amelia. We need to talk first.

The broken pieces of my heart split and fractured yet again. I could have handled it better if he had told me he never wanted to see me again. I could have even taken being called a freak that he didn't want to be associated with. I could not, however, take this. I saw his pleading eyes in the back of my mind. I heard his voice as if he stood in front of me saying the words, and the pain reverberated through me. I closed my eyes and leaned my head against the window, staring back out at the coast.

"It was Aidan, wasn't it?" Cole's quiet question broke the silence.

"Was it that obvious?" I responded with a groan.

"I know you don't want to do this, Ame, but you've got to cut the poor guy loose. If for no other reason than he could really get hurt. I know you care about him, probably more than you should. I've seen how happy he makes you, but you know it's for the best."

I groaned yet again. "I know, Cole. My head knows all the reasons, my heart just isn't interested in the conversation." He grunted, as if to say he knew exactly what I meant, and we left it at that.

My phone let out another reminder beep, letting me know the unheard voicemails were still sitting there waiting for me. I put the phone to my ear and hit the button. Micah was suddenly screaming into it.

I shot up in the seat and in the process dropped the phone. Scrambling around, trying to dig between the seats, all I could say was, "No, no, no, no, no."

Cole finally pulled over to the side of the road when I wouldn't answer his third "What?" and grabbed me by the shoulders. "AMELIA — WHAT HAPPENED?" he bellowed.

I could only whimper Bethany's name. "They took her, Cole. They took Bethany." The roar he let out and the magic that came with it set Charlie howling.

"This has nothing to do with her. Dammit! She can't handle this crap," he yelled. I wanted to tell him she was stronger than he gave her credit for, but instead I sat mutely, trembling, apologies I couldn't give her burning in the back of my throat.

Cole immediately sprang into action. He had Micah on speaker phone in less than ten seconds.

"Where in the hell have you two been?" Micah greeted.

"You're on speaker. We were out of cell range trying to get some space and sort some things out. What happened? Where's Bethany? Why weren't you protecting her?" Cole was screaming at the phone and looked like he might shatter it in his hand. I slowly wrapped my hand around his wrist to get his attention and took the phone. He slammed himself back in the seat as Micah responded.

"Do not even go there with me. I'm not the one who ran off. And I couldn't be expected to be with her every second. If I hadn't kicked in her apartment door last night, we wouldn't even know what happened since you both abandoned her!" I could hear the anger and the fear in Micah's voice.

"Just explain, Micah. We don't need to point fingers. We need to know what happened and what we can do," I said, my voice surprisingly strong as I tried to take control of the situation, though my hand was shaking so badly I could hardly hold the phone myself.

My best friend. They took my best friend.

If I weren't completely terrified, I would have laughed at the stereotypical nature of it all. How could I have possibly imagined that by leaving her alone, I would actually protect her?

"All I know right now is that she's gone and the red-haired woman is Melinda, as I predicted. She left a note saying to stay near your phone, so I would appreciate it if you'd keep the damn thing charged and on."

I felt a nudging on my shoulder and Charlie was there with my phone in his mouth. Giving him a scratch behind the ears, I took it and wiped the slobber off on my jeans. "I've got it here, Micah. I had more voicemails than yours, let me listen to them. Just a sec."

The fear inside me was almost paralyzing, but she — my dark power — raged inside me as well. She was pissed. I was pissed. How dare these people hurt Bethany? One of the few people I loved. I stabbed at the voicemail button again and skipped past Micah's message. Left only an hour ago was one from Bethany herself. I listened to it, trying to hold back a scream of my own, and then replayed it on speaker for the boys.

"Um...hi, Ame, it's me. I...uh...I have to tell you some things. First, these people kidnapped me from the parking lot after work last night and they...um...told me to tell you that (sniffle) if you don't come to them (sniffle) they, will...oh, honey, they say they're gonna kill me. What the hell is going on, Amelia? Who are these people?"

Then she screamed. Not in pain, but someone clearly did something to her.

"Goddamnit. That was unnecessary and that was MY HAIR. Amelia, this red-haired witch just singed my hair with a damn lightning bolt that came from her hand. She isn't messing around."

275

I couldn't help the tiny satisfied smile that played at my lips. Only Bethany would toughen up over her hair being damaged.

"They know you aren't home yet, but they said you had to meet them at midnight tonight in the woods behind our apartment. Way back. They said to go where you went before."

The phone made a bunch of garbled noises and then Melinda came on the line as Bethany shouted in the background. I would recognize her voice anywhere.

"I told you, sugar, I will do what I have to in order to get your attention. You shouldn't have played with me. Your little human is fine right now, she's actually quite the feisty one. But, she won't stay this spirited for long if you don't do what I've asked. Come to the woods and come alone. We'll know if you don't. Go until you see the tree marked with a slash and then head south. We'll find you."

Cole was the first to speak, his voice hardened steel. "Be at the gym in a half an hour. We'll be there. We don't have long before midnight and we need a plan."

"Fine." Micah disconnected.

I started to speak and Cole merely held up his hand. I closed my mouth and sat back. Charlie whimpered in the back as both of our magic raged inside and around us in the car. Cole finally picked his phone back up and explained the situation to Uncle Derreck. He was jumping in the car as soon as possible and would meet us later. He had been off the grid for so long, he didn't want to expose himself to anyone else so he wouldn't meet us at the gym.

My thoughts were racing. I wanted to break things. I wanted to cry. I wanted to call Aidan and hide in his arms. I wanted to rewind my life and not even choose to come to Brighton, effectively stopping all of this from happening — or at least keeping the humans I loved out of it. But, instead, I sat back and opened myself up to the severely pissed off dark power flowing through my veins, letting it penetrate every cell and fill me with frenzied anger instead of fear. If this chick wanted to pick a fight, she came to the right place. At this point, neither of us truly knew what I was capable of.

Chapter 20

The gym was dark and Micah was already sitting in Cole's office when we arrived. All three of us were on full tilt and Charlie was just as agitated by the magical overload. He paced back and forth in the hallway, emitting a short growl every few steps, his ears pricked. Cole motioned to Micah and we went out into the training area. It felt good to be in an open space again after all that time in the car. I looked haggard in old ripped jeans and a sweatshirt with my hair in a knot on top of my head. Cole and I had both been so worked up, we hadn't even talked about what we would or wouldn't discuss with Micah. I let him take the lead in the conversation.

None of us sat down as we came to the center of the room and stared at each other. The only sounds were Charlie's nails clicking on the cement on the outer edge of the training room as he continued to pace.

"Micah, I'm sorry we weren't here and you couldn't find us." Cole's apology caught both Micah and me by surprise.

Micah's eyes widened just a fraction before he nodded. "I know. And I shouldn't have blamed you. But, what are we going to do? We clearly cannot allow Amelia to go meet them alone. You know she's who they want." He ran a hand back through his hair and I could see his pained expression. We were all worried about what Bethany was going through.

I harrumphed a little, "Well, normally I'd be offended by that, but I don't particularly want to go out there alone. I just don't see a way around it."

Both men turned and started yelling at me at the same time. It took a supreme amount of control not to lay them both out on the mats and leave them pinned there. I was sure I could do it, especially right now. So, instead, I put some power behind my voice and yelled, "JUST STOP IT!"

They both shut up and took a step back. Before they could come at me again, I started talking.

"Let's get real, guys. These people want me. Not you. Me. And they have Bethany. I can defend myself. She can't. I can defend both of us. This isn't a choice and you both know it. On top of that, you both care about her, just like I do." I sent Cole a look that said "You know you do so just shut it" and he looked back at me a little sheepishly.

"Micah, you and I can open our connection so that I can keep you both updated on what's happening. Even where they take me, if they do. You'll come for me, right? If it comes down to it, you'll find me?" Those last words came out far more quietly and with less strength than I had hoped.

The fear was sneaking in again, but I wouldn't have it. This was for Bethany. I stood up straight and sent a ripple of electricity running through me once again. As I had calmed down, I pushed the darkness back into its corner, making promises that she would get her chance. When I lifted my eyes to Cole's, and then to Micah's, I saw what I needed to see. Cold determination.

We decided we would meet back at my apartment to finalize the plan. Micah said he had some potential reinforcements he might tap into, so he went his way and Cole and I went ours. Once we were in the confines of the car, I turned to him.

"What if I can't stop her, Cole? When I lose it, she takes over, and I can't always stop her." I had taken to referring to my power source as her own being, at least to Uncle Derreck and Cole, who understood what she actually was. "If they've hurt B, I won't be able to stop her. I won't want to."

Cole turned to me and placed his hand over mine, reassurance and strength filling the void my fear had left when I forced it out. "You can't, Amelia. You can't let them know who you are — what you are. They can think you're an Elder, that's fine. But we don't even understand what being a Keeper means for you. If they figure that out, you'll never get out and you have to. It's not a choice, Amelia."

Looking into my brother's eyes, I saw no fear, only confidence. He was faking it, I could feel his warring emotions, but I appreciated the attempt. "Okay, Cole. You're right. I can do this."

Internally, I stared down the pulsing orb of dark light inside me and told her the same thing. *She's more important. You have to do this. We have to do this.* The quiet hum of satisfaction was all I felt. At least we were on the same page this time.

When we got to the apartment, I asked Cole to wait outside for a little bit. "I'll make it very obvious if there's a problem," I told him with a smile. "I just need some time in there alone to get my head right."

He argued for a brief minute and then just shooed me out of the car, muttering something about his boneheaded little sister that would drive him to drink. Melinda and her crew knew I'd be there tonight, so it was a long-shot that anyone would be waiting to ambush me. As I walked into the entryway of the building, my thoughts were focused on Bethany. If that wench had done anything more than singe Bethany's hair, I was going to kill her myself. I'd never killed anything bigger than a spider, but for Bethany, I would.

My mind wasn't focused and she reacted first, letting out a relieved sigh that filled my lungs and expanded through every inch of me. He was the last person I had expected to see. It took a moment to register Aidan sitting on the steps, just as he had been the night of the first attack. This time though, he didn't look strong and determined. He looked as tired and beat-down as I felt.

At my gasp, he looked up and his eyes brightened. "You're here. Thank God, Amelia, I've been waiting for hours."

He stood up and closed the distance between us in a heartbeat. Before I could do anything, he had me in his arms, pressing his lips to my hair, forehead, cheek, and eventually, my mouth. I should have stopped him, but instead I tucked my head under his chin and gave myself that one last embrace. I put every ounce of the love I had for Aidan into that hug and when he pulled away slightly, I pushed the same emotion into a last kiss. Tears I hadn't allowed since I found out about Bethany welled in my eyes and I stepped back away from him.

Aidan looked at me confused. "What's happening, Amelia? I know I don't completely understand what's happening, but I'm not scared of you. In fact—"

"Aidan, just stop," I interrupted, shaking my head. "I'm sorry, but we can't do this. I can't do this. You have to go. You just have to go and never see me again." I tried to push past him and up to my door when I felt his hand on my arm and his rage in the air.

"What?" It was one word but it came out with deadly force. "That's it? After all of this, that's all I get? After that kiss? You're just going to walk away and think I'm going to let you?"

It took every shred of my willpower to look up into his steeled gray eyes and lie through my teeth. "I wanted to kiss you goodbye. This was fun, Aidan, but it's not anymore, and I'm over it. It was good while it lasted, but you don't mean as much as I thought you did. This is just a complication I don't need right now."

He winced away from me and the pain he exuded stabbed me directly in the heart. I have no idea how I managed to maintain his stare until he finally dropped my arm like it was bag of overflowing trash and back away from me, shaking his head slowly back and forth. As Aidan continued to back away from me, still not speaking, I quietly said, "Goodbye, Aidan," and turned away.

As I shut the door to my apartment, I slid down the wall and wept noiseless tears. She was pounding on me from the inside as I ached, feeling beaten from the outside. It took all my remaining willpower to shove her down and stop the spillway from opening. The throbbing had already grown to a dull roar building in every artery and vein, but now wasn't the time.

I thought he would leave, but within seconds, Aidan was pounding on the door, screaming, "Amelia, open the door. Damn it, Amelia. I'm not leaving! I know you don't mean it! I know there's more to this. There has to be."

He pounded and pounded. It had to be five full minutes he pounded on the door, yelling my name. Then, it was silent. I kept swallowing down the cries I wanted to release. I had wrapped myself in a ball on the floor to keep from running to him. I thought he was gone when I heard his soft words.

"Amelia, this isn't over. I won't let it be. You changed everything. I love you." I don't know if he knew I could hear his hoarse whisper or not, but his words unraveled me. I dove for the door, but before I could wrench it open, I heard Cole. "What the hell are you doing here, Montgomery? Didn't my sister break it off with you?"

I could almost picture Cole's puffed up stature as I listened through the door. Aidan's anger rose again and I heard a loud *thunk*.

"You listen to me, Bradbury. Amelia and I are not done. Not by a long shot. You're part of whatever this is and you need to know that I'll die before I let her go. She's everything. This isn't over."

I heard the entry door slam and then Cole was knocking. I unlocked the door and walked away as I opened it, not wanting him to see what the encounter had done to me. Typical Cole, he wouldn't let it go.

He strode right to me, turned me around, and crushed me to his chest. "Damn, Ame, you had to go and actually pick a good one, didn't you?" he muttered into my hair.

That set off a fresh wave of tears. I gave myself one more minute to let my heart howl in agony before I pulled back and started to wipe my eyes.

"I can't do this right now. He can't matter right now. Right now is about Bethany. You have to keep me focused. You have to help me get her back." I stood there, staring into my brother's eyes as the transformation came over both of us.

His jaw tensed, his eyes darkened, and his posture stiffened. My own magic rose to meet his, making my eyes change to luminescent violet and my sorrow get buried in the back corner of my mind. This wasn't the time for me to wallow in my broken heart. Maybe what Derreck told me was already happening — I was already choosing duty over love. It wasn't even a choice, it was just how it had to be.

Micah showed up not long after Aidan left. Cole and I were talking quietly when he walked in. We had already decided that we were not sharing anything with him about my Keeper status. There were far too many unknowns at this point. Midnight was only an hour away and we went over our very simple plan, time and time again. I basically knew where I was going. I would slowly build my power levels as I hiked, making sure I could instantly protect Bethany and myself if it came to it.

Micah and I would open communication lines right before I left. He would see everything, including how I got there so he and Cole could find us if need be. We still hadn't heard from Uncle Derreck and his phone was going straight to voicemail. Hopefully, he would show up soon. We could use his expertise on this one.

If all hell broke loose, they would get to us as fast as they could, which was pretty fast. My job was to protect Bethany, get us the hell out of there, and to try to keep my rogue power in check so that the AniMages didn't understand more about me than they needed to. I realized as I reran the plan through my mind that I still hadn't told them what I knew.

I cleared my throat, suddenly feeling like a bit of traitor for holding out on them. "Um, you guys should probably know that I'm pretty sure they're AniMages. The people who have Bethany. I mean, I know they are. I watched Melinda shift at the theater." I squirmed a little in my seat, knowing just what was coming.

Both Cole and Micah started yelling at the same time. It was a combination of "Why didn't you tell us?" and "What the hell are you talking about?" and five or six other jumbled questions and swear words overlapping each other.

I stood and spread my hands out, trying to shush them both. "I get it! I should have told you! Do you guys want to know what I know, or what?" They both shut up, glaring daggers at me. Micah looked down at his watch, making it clear I was wasting time.

I sat back down. "You know, I don't need either of your hostility. It's been a hell of a few days and I've got a lot on my plate. Bottom line is, the blue power we saw coming at us on the beach that day was AniMage power.

Did you know that, Micah?" My tone was accusing, but deep down I hoped he hadn't.

Much to my dismay, he averted his eyes. "Ha — gotcha! See? You knew. And you didn't say anything either." I pointed an angry finger at him, waiting for his defense.

"No, Amelia, I didn't say anything," he said with a scowl. "But, it wasn't because I knew then, I didn't know until today. Just tonight after I left you and talked to my people, that's when I knew. I wasn't withholding information, like some people." He narrowed his eyes, glaring as I rolled my own.

"Whatever. Either way, I saw Melinda at the last second before we got away shift into a huge, dark red wolf. I don't know if all of her people are AniMages, or what this rebel group is all about, but I wouldn't be surprised. From what you've told me, Cole, they got the crappy end of Julia's wrath."

I saw Micah tense at the same time that Cole eyes darkened. "They sure did, which makes them even more dangerous, Ame. Dammit, I should be going with you." That set the boys off on another heated argument.

I found myself reassuring them, when in all reality, I know it should have been the opposite. An eerie calm had come over me, my magic was a whisper in every cell. Not pumping through my veins as it had been lately, it made itself known in other ways. My stride was faster. My hugs to them before I left more fierce. My eyes shone like night lights. Even my hair floated a bit around me. This was how I had felt at the theater. Like I could do anything.

I was going to get my best friend back.

Chapter 21

I let the back door slam after I shoved my way through it, convincing myself I could do this. I walked up the trail and at the tree marked with a slash, I deviated and started pushing through the brush. I didn't go far before I came to a clearing. Micah was in my head; I could feel him sitting in the back of mind, trying to be quiet, but his anxiety radiated into my subconscious.

As I pushed the last of the tiny tree branches out of my path, I saw him. Across the grass-covered oasis stood a man that had to be six-foot-five. Even from my distance, I could see the rigidity of his muscles as he stood facing me, his arms crossed. What I couldn't see was his face as the trees cast a shadow over him.

We both stood facing each other, silent. Finally, I opened my mouth to ask where Bethany was when he spoke first.

"Get him out," he said. His tone was dry and impatient.

"Who out?" I asked, wondering how he could possibly know.

"We all have our gifts, Amelia," he said with a smirk. "I found his trace as easily as I found yours, it was only as you approached that I realized he wasn't physically here. So, again, get him out. We had an agreement." Only his mouth moved as he spoke. He didn't fidget. I couldn't even tell if he was breathing.

I closed my eyes and whispered a quick apology to Micah. His anger exploded just as I kicked him out of my head and shut the door behind him.

"He's gone," I said, immediately feeling fear flood my system as I realized I was truly alone. But, it melted into determination just as quickly. Bethany was here. I had to get her back.

The man finally stepped out into the clearing, the full moon's light shining down on him. He took sure strides to the center, still a good fifteen feet from me. I was surprised to find he had bright red hair, thick and wavy.

"I am Elias. It's nice to meet you, Amelia. We've been waiting a long time to find you," he said, a genuine smile transforming his chiseled face from menacing to boyish charm.

I couldn't believe how easily he transitioned to being conversational. Like we were here to get to know each other instead of freeing my imprisoned best friend.

"You know, I don't really give a crap who you are. All I want to know is where Bethany is and what exactly you're expecting from me to get her back," I snapped, impatient and eager all at once.

"Fair question. She's here." With breaking eye contact he said, "Bring her out." He clearly wasn't talking to me.

Bethany stumbled out of the tree line behind Elias, flanked by a large wolf on each side. I saw the burnt red coat of the wolf on the right and knew it was Melinda. I had no idea about the one on the left, but it wasn't just two wolves who accompanied her — animals streamed out from the forest. Wolves, panthers, mountain lions, owls…there had to be at least ten of them. The animals surrounded Elias, making a semi-circle. He still hadn't broken eye contact or changed his stance.

"Let her go," I said. My hands were starting to shake as my power rose to meet the surge of magic around me. All of this power in one place was more than I could handle but I couldn't show my hand. He couldn't know what or who I was. It was the one promise I'd made my brother, I wouldn't give myself away. So, I pushed, shoved, and scolded myself internally, while trying to stand relaxed and poised in front of a mass of AniMages.

"We will let her go, but first, you and I need to have a discussion. There are things we need to get straight, Amelia. Information you need." I hated the cocky certainty in his tone. How he was controlling the situation. I was surprised that my fear hadn't returned, but for whatever reason, I was sure Elias didn't want to hurt me. I was at least glad to know my internal alarms were back in action.

I had kept myself from looking at Bethany, trying to maintain eye contact with Elias and hold my ground, but I couldn't stop any longer. She stood stick straight, and even with her hair a mess of tangles, her makeup streaming down her face from dried tears, and a wrinkled and dirty dress, she held an uninterested stare until her eyes connected to mine. As soon as we locked, the fear was evident. The panic she had been containing came to the surface as her eyes filled.

A lump lodged itself in my throat at seeing my best friend like that. I glared at Elias. "Are you afraid of a little southern girl, Elias? You think she's a match for your crew?" I tossed my head toward his minions. "I think it's a safe bet that she can stand next to me and we can still talk, don't you?"

A small smile played at his lips and he nodded. "Go," he said, gesturing to me. Bethany took a few steps forward, maintaining a perfect pageant stride until Melinda let out a low growl and nipped at her heels. Bethany let out a squeal as she sprinted to my side. I enveloped her in a hug, crushing her to me as I finally exhaled.

"You okay, B?" I asked into her hair. "Huh," she snorted weakly, "and I thought I was the bad influence on you." I couldn't help but smile, relieved that she was okay enough to make jokes while we were being stared down by a hoard of Immortals.

We parted and I kept her hand locked in mine, standing just in front of her. They wouldn't come close to her again.

I turned myself back to Elias. "You wanted to talk. Talk. And, while you're at it, control your animals." Melinda took a step toward me, her eyes a disconcerting shade of iridescent blue. A deep growl built in her throat before Elias broke in. "Stop. Melinda, shift. Now."

His words were even. He never raised his voice or changed his tone. In just four words he had tamed the beast. In the blink of an eye, I was staring at a red-haired Melinda crouched down in front of him. She was completely naked and didn't seem to mind at all. She stayed in her crouch as she shook her head and her hair fell around her shoulders, providing modest cover.

"My apologies, Amelia. Some of us are a little more passionate about the cause than others. Melinda will control herself." He looked down at her without moving his head and she nodded in grim submission.

I nodded, still waiting to know why I was here.

"You are here because you have been lied to your whole life, Amelia. Yes, I heard that." He clearly saw the question in my eyes. "By your father, your nanny, your schools, and your friends. We've seen you. We know who you are. What you are. And you need to know that we are the people you need to fight with. To fight for. We are the exiled, we are the ones who were tortured and held captive. We endured the worst of Julia's reign and you can help put us back in our rightful place. Only you." His eyes were as pained as they were hopeful.

"I apologize for the means in which we had to get you here, away from the rest of them, but there are things you need to know. We couldn't risk anyone else knowing we were here."

I put my hand up. "I know all of that. I've been told about what the queen did. How she treated you, the Elders, and any Mages who didn't fall in line. I know what happened."

In an instant, he was two inches in front of me. Bethany gasped and stepped backward, still holding my hand and forcing me to twist toward her and into Elias.

"Do you now?" he whispered. Looking into his deep blue eyes was like staring into the depths of transparent ocean water as they swirled and churned. His hand cupped my cheek and I dropped straight into Elias's own personal hell.

I stood in the center of a small log cabin. All around me, people were throwing things into bags, moving quickly here and there. People were running in the front door and out the back. I couldn't move as the action never stopped around me. Finally, I heard someone speak. A woman turned to a young man, who I immediately recognized as a young Elias, and said, "Are you sure? Are you sure they're coming for us? We know nothing. Why would the queen do this?"

She was young, maybe in her twenties. Fear etched panic lines in her face. Her lips were a tight line and her eyes shone with unshed tears. Elias reached out and pulled her to him, embracing her as he whispered in her ear. I almost smiled at the sweetness of his gesture. It was clear that he loved this woman.

Their loving moment didn't last long though as another man came barreling into the room. "They're coming! John is up in the sky and he said they are close. We have to go. Elias, we have to go now!"

Elias grabbed the woman's arm and the backpack she had been holding. "Come, Nell. We have to shift. We have to go now." She pulled her hand from his and it immediately dropped to her stomach. "But, Elias, we don't know what that will do. I was told not to shift…" her voice drifted off as the tears dripped in a steady stream down her cheeks. Elias's breathing was becoming shallower by the minute.

"Nell, honey, I can feel them. I can hear what's in their heads. They won't spare anyone. Not even a pregnant woman. You're going to have to shift. Please, Nell." The other man looked back and forth between them, clearly torn, before he wished them luck and ran out the back. Elias pulled Nell outside. "Shift, Nell. Now. We can have another baby."

She silently shook her head. "You don't know that, Elias. A new AniMage hasn't been born in years. We have no idea why, but our people need this baby."

"But, Nell, I need you." Elias crushed her to him, wrapping her inside his giant arms. He pulled back and looked down at her, heartache in his eyes. "You won't shift, will you?" The sadness of his words pierced my heart. Nell shook her head. The heartache in his eyes was replaced by unwavering resolve. "You aren't going to leave, so I'm not either. We'll do this together. You and me, Nell. Just like it's always has been."

The tears continued to fall as she nodded and reached up to press a kiss to his lips. It was not a romantic kiss, it was desperate, scared — it was a good-bye kiss, and they both knew it.

I stood back with tears falling as I watched the moving scene. In the depths of my mind, I knew what was coming, what had to be coming. But, nothing could have prepared me for the storm of Hunters that swept into the area. There had to be a dozen of them, orange eyes blazing, bright white and orange balls of fire erupting from their palms. Elias shoved Nell behind him and with a roar, shifted into his bear form. I hadn't a clue what his native form would be, but a mammoth black bear stood protectively in front of the love of his life. She shot her own small blue blasts from around him, but it was clear to me that magic was not their strong suit.

Elias fought valiantly, attempting to slice Hunters open from root to tip when he was able to get his huge paws close enough. Within minutes, the group suddenly stopped and parted, allowing the largest Hunter I'd ever seen to walk between them and stop just feet in front of Elias.

"You think that your stinking bear hide means anything to me, vermin? You are not part of us. You don't belong here or anywhere. I will be damned if I allow you to weaken our race and pollute our people with your vile ways." The man stood at least seven feet tall. He wore black leather from head to toe, the only things in contrast being his bright white hair and the silver collar he wore around his neck, signifying his oath and allegiance to Queen Julia.

Nell took that moment of silence as her opportunity to try to hurt the Hunter and shot a blue flame in his direction. The Hunter laughed an evil, booming laugh and with a wave of his hand, the flame dissipated in mid-air.

"You are nothing to me, half-breed. I see you cowering behind your mate. Do you think he can keep you from me? And, I hear that little heartbeat. You will die together, as a family." The Hunter was so focused on intimidating Nell that he didn't see Elias jump, shifting yet again, this time into a black panther and slashing him across the face. The Hunter roared in pain as blood dripped from his cheek. In the same instant, he froze Elias in mid-air and then pinned him to the side of the cabin with nothing more than a flick of his wrist.

"For that, vermin, you will watch. You won't die today. You will live to remember what your worthlessness caused." The Hunters eyes glittered with evil joy and a sick smile replaced his scowl as he turned back to Nell. Without moving from his position, he lifted her from the ground. She screamed in agony as welts appeared on her arms and legs and blood dripped from wounds no one had physically made. The Hunter was torturing her without moving a muscle. In his panther form, Elias shrieked as if he were being beaten himself. Elias struggled against the power, scrambling for any kind of purchase against the coarse cabin exterior. He yowled and screamed, suddenly shifting back and forth between human and panther.

The Hunter simply laughed as Nell whimpered from above him. Elias hurled curses and vengeful promises in his direction. "I wish I had time to draw this out, but I have places to be. So, beast, remember my face and what I've done. Remember this feeling because it is the feeling I will evoke in every single one of your kind. Go and tell them that Rhi the Hunter stole your woman and babe. Tell them how you couldn't move an inch to save her broken, battered body."

I was thankful the scene went dark before I had to watch the rest. I couldn't let myself imagine what that Hunter had done to poor Nell. What he had said echoed in my mind. That was Rhi — the same Hunter who murdered my mother.

When Elias removed his hand from my cheek it was all I could do to not crumple to the ground. Bethany caught me as I bent over. The hurt, pain, and despair that cascaded through me was more than I could handle. Elias's leftover emotions charred my heart as I tried to separate myself from him. I reached up to place my hand where his had been only to realize I couldn't move as the sobs wracked my body. I cried for that poor woman and Elias's heartbreak. When I looked up at him, the tears were falling from his eyes in slow rivers. He didn't move to wipe them away and neither did I.

"Is that what you knew?" he asked, sorrow seeping from his words as the blood had from her wounds. I could only shake my head. Nothing Cole had told me prepared me for what I had just witnessed. I, too, would never be able to erase her screams from my mind.

"There is more, Amelia. So much more. I hold so many truths that you need regarding how to control what's inside you. About the prophecy. About your mother."

My head cleared at his mention of my mother and the power I had done my best to hide. My curiosity peaked, but I had no reason to believe he knew anything more than Derreck had. "And, why is it that I'm supposed to trust you, Elias? You just finished telling me how everyone lies to me. Constantly. Why would I trust anything you say over them? Your story is terrible and I am so sorry for what you went through, but what makes you different?" I leaned heavily on Bethany as I finally stood tall and fixed my stare on his.

His tone was grim, but determined. The tears gone. "Because I started our relationship with truth. I haven't lied to you. I manipulated you to get you here, but I didn't lie. I don't lie."

He stepped back from me a few paces and gestured to the beasts around him. "These are all people, Amelia. People who have been running their whole lives. Who, like me, watched their friends and family murdered, or worse. I am not Julia. I don't want to use you. I want to help you. I want you to help me — us. But, the choice is yours. You can always find one of us here, in this place. I know that you cut off the communications to your brother and the prince, and they are likely to come for you soon. You should go."

Bethany and I reacted simultaneously. "The what?" I yelped at the same time that she said, "Who's a prince? Prince of what?"

Elias smirked and looked far too smug for my liking. "Another half-truth, Amelia. Ask him. You know exactly who I'm talking about. I just thought you realized. Ask him why he's really here, Amelia. Then, come back and we'll talk some more. Just be careful with what you share. He, like so many others, is not what he seems."

Bethany and I watched, our hands still gripping each other's, as Elias, Melinda, and all of the animals melted back into the tree line. In mere seconds, it was as if they'd never existed. Bethany turned to me to say something and I interrupted her before she could ask. "Not yet. There's so much I have to tell you, and I will. Just give me a minute, okay?" She swallowed and nodded, standing silently next to me while I tried to slow my racing heart and make sense of what had just unfolded.

Thankfully, Bethany was quiet as we made our way back toward the apartment. My mind was swimming. Micah was the prince. He had to be. There weren't any other options. That meant I was betrothed to Micah. And, judging from what Elias had just said, Micah knew it.

I felt the dark magic rising within me and forced my thoughts away from Micah and back to Elias. To his words, his excruciating memory, and the promises he had made me. He used the only thing he knew would sway me — the allure of truth. And it was working. I wanted to deposit Bethany in the apartment and run back to where he had stood. I had so many questions. Everything I'd learned in the last twenty-four hours was a convoluted mess in my brain. It seemed like the only thing anyone agreed on was the fact that I couldn't go to the castle. I couldn't play into the queen's plan. But, outside of that, no one seemed to agree on anything.

Uncle Derreck wanted me to find my mate. Elias wanted me to help the AniMages. And, then, there was Bethany, to whom I owed a lengthy explanation. Everywhere I turned, someone needed something from me. What I needed, was time to think. To sort all of the madness out in my head. I needed more than just a few minutes between catastrophes. Somewhere in this mess was a choice I had to make, but at this point I didn't have a clue on where to find it.

As we neared the complex, Cole and Micah burst from the back door. Bethany went running for Micah and he swept her into his arms. For a millisecond, I was happy for them, then Elias's words came back and squashed any joy I held for my friend. Cole came toward me a little more tentatively.

"Ame? What's wrong? I can't get a read on you, there's too much going on." He gave me a sideways look that said he could tell that she was taking hold of me. "What happened up there? Why did you shut us out?" I could only stare over his shoulder at Micah. Pure, unadulterated hate was all I had for him. I had trusted him. I had thought we were friends. My limbs started to tremble. I made the conscious decision to stop fighting her off and stood taller as the layered effect of her power gave me the necessary strength.

"Amelia," Cole said slowly. "What is going on? I can feel it. This isn't good. Talk to me, Ame." He tried to reach for me and I flinched away, shaking my head.

"I need to talk to Micah. Alone. Now."

Micah pulled his head up from being bent into Bethany and his eyes widened when he met mine. I saw the instant he realized I knew. Apologies reflected back at me, but I wouldn't acknowledge them. I wanted him to feel badly about what he'd done.

Cole looked between us, and when Micah asked him to take Bethany inside he agreed, but didn't look happy about it. He took a step toward me. "I'll be just in there, Amelia." I nodded, my eyes never leaving Micah's. "Stay in there." I waited for Cole and Bethany to go inside before I spoke.

I found it hard to form the words; to put the accusations into syllables that would make sentences. I opened and closed my mouth a few times before I could even do it.

"You lied to me. You've been lying to me from the beginning, haven't you? You never wanted to be my friend. You asked me to trust you and *I did!*" The more I spoke, the stronger my voice became. My violet smoke surrounded me. My breaths became shallow and the pressure inside me quickly became too much to bear. I couldn't stop the eruption. After everything I'd just been through, I wanted someone to pay. To feel as beaten and twisted and tortured as I felt in that moment. I had no idea which way was up or what I was supposed to do. So, I funneled all of that into Micah.

"I thought we were FRIENDS!" I shot a blast at him, not giving it everything, but trying to give myself a release. He was ready for it. Sadly, he understood my power probably better than I did, at least the parts he had seen, and he countered. Red and violet crashed into each other, electricity popping and snapping as the two magic's battled between us. I held both hands up in front of me, pushing at him, wanting him to do something. To say something.

Sweat popped on his brow as Micah finally yelled over the sound, "We are friends, Amelia. I came for you, but not for the reasons you think. I came to help you. To protect you."

That only set me off further and I pushed harder, forcing Micah to take a few steps back. "To protect me? How? By figuring out exactly what I could do so you could report it back to your demented mother? I'm nothing but a puppet to her. A means to an end. I won't do it, Micah. She doesn't understand what I am. No one does."

Suddenly, I was exhausted. Drained of hope and will and the energy to even hate Micah the way I wanted to. I slowly backed myself down and Micah did the same. I doubled over, my hands on my knees as I fought for air. I looked up at him from under a curtain of hair, happy that he was at least visibly exhausted, too.

"Amelia, it isn't what you think. Really." He coughed out between deep breaths.

"Isn't it, though, Micah? Is that even your name? Who are you really?"

A deep voice came from behind me, sending chills up my spine. "He is Prince Mikail. You would do well to remember that, girl. Keeper or not, he is your prince."

I turned around. At the sight of him, my world spun. Standing feet from me was Rhi. The Hunter who murdered my mother and Nell. Elias's scar still remained a thick line running from his temple to his chin. I should have killed him. I should have maimed him. There were so many things I should have done. Instead, I passed out.

Chapter 22

I woke up on the couch in the living room of my apartment. As I squinted my eyes open, sending a little jet through me to dull the pain in my head and the aches in my body, I saw Cole and Bethany sitting at the kitchen table. I looked around and Micah was gone. Or Prince Mikail, I suppose.

As soon as Bethany saw my partially-opened eyes she was next to me, helping me sit up. "Hey there, girl. What can I get you? Tea?" I nodded weakly and she disappeared into the kitchen. I turned myself so that I wasn't taking up the entire couch and found myself eye-to-eye with my very irritated brother.

"Would you like to explain what the hell just happened, Amelia?" His anger was at new heights, but I didn't have the energy for the argument.

I laughed a broken laugh. "Only if I knew where to start, Cole. I wish I could."

"Well, honey, why don't you start with what you've been hiding from your best friend?" Bethany stood in the kitchen, filling my mug with water and refusing to look at me. "Then, you can tell me what in goodness gracious I just witnessed out there, and you can end with why you were trying to kill my boyfriend! After that, we can get to why he brought you in here comatose before he disappeared. Those are really the high points we need, isn't that right, Cole?" Her sarcasm was tinged with hurt and it killed me to know that I had done that.

I stood up from the couch and took a few steps toward Bethany, taking the tea mugs from her and then yanking her in for a hug. I held on for dear life, for my sanity, and to try to show my friend in some small way that none of this was to hurt her. The realization that I had done exactly what had been done to me — lied to protect her — was a bitter taste in my mouth.

I finally let go, picking up our mugs and taking them to the couch.

"This is the short version, B, because it would take days to explain the long version. It's probably pretty clear that we have some...uh, different abilities than you do."

She snorted, "Really, Ame? Abilities? Your crazy magic business pretty much takes the cake."

I laughed at little. "Well, you seem to be rolling with it pretty well. Yes, we have some crazy magic business. Both Cole and I. Mine is a little different from his. I'm...uh, special. And I have some power other people don't. The people who took you are AniMages. They are a kind of

Mage that has less power, but the ability to shift into animals. You saw what they can do."

"And they want your help? Who forced them out? Why? That Elias man seemed decent enough, but I'll tell you what, you scared the beejesus out of me when you went blank out there. What was that?" She was tapping her nail against the ceramic cup, the tiny *ping-ping* in rhythm with her foot tapping on floor. I was so impressed that she hadn't had her own meltdown. I could only imagine that there weren't many humans who could walk away from this ordeal without losing it.

I put my hand on her leg to stop the bouncing. "Too much, B. I'm going to skip some questions for now. The AniMages do want my help, and Elias showed me a very painful memory of his past." I looked up at Cole, whose concern was etched in the furrow of his brow, his lips pursed, and worry lines around his eyes. At my mention of sharing memories, sadness filled his eyes. Yet another dark piece of a limitless puzzle we now shared.

"And Micah? What happened between you two?" she asked.

I couldn't explain that to her without Cole going ballistic, so I didn't. "I won't lie to you again, B, but I can't tell you that yet. I will, but Cole and I need to talk first." She pulled back from me, hurt again.

"Oh. Well, then." She stood up and I grabbed her hand, stopping her exit. "Hey, look at me." She stared straight ahead for a moment but finally looked down at me.

"This is a lot, B. It's a lot for me. So much has happened in the last day that I don't even know how to talk about it. I don't know what it means or what's going to happen. But, they've come for you once. I don't want them to do it again. Just give me time, okay? Pinky swear, you'll get the full story. I just need time." I held out my hand, pinky extended.

She sighed in acceptance. "Okay, girl. But, you hear me now. In the last twenty-four hours I've been snatched from a parking lot, stared down a wolf that I watched turn into a demon woman, had my hair burnt, watched my best friend light up like a damn glow stick, and my boyfriend spit red fire from his hands. I won't say I haven't cried, but all in all, I've kept my shit together pretty well. No more holding out on me. Got it? We are *best friends* and I'm in this for better or for worse. I deserve the truth." With her hands on her hips and scowl on her face, I'd never loved my best friend more.

I got up and hugged her again. "Deal. Now, go pack a bag. We've got to get to Cole's. It's safer there."

She looked down at herself and wrinkled her nose. Her dress looked like it had been dunked in a mud puddle and her hair was in knots. "Can I at least shower? This is just unacceptable." I laughed and looked up at Cole for confirmation.

"Twenty minutes, princess, and we're out the door. Make it happen." She rolled her eyes and sauntered toward her room. "Oh ye of little faith, I only need ten."

As soon as the water started, Cole was next to me.

"What aren't you telling her?" His words were hushed, but I wasn't sure they would stay that way. I gave him the short version of what happened with Elias. He nodded and asked a few questions, but didn't seem overly shocked.

"I knew there were AniMages out there, I just don't know how they found you. Or knew about all of this? You know we need to talk to them, don't you?" He was rubbing his face, the last few days wearing on him as well.

"I know, Cole, but we have bigger problems. Elias also told me that Micah is the prince. Prince Mikail, to be accurate. I passed out because when we were arguing, Rhi showed up. His Hunter. The Hunter. The one who killed mom."

That sent fire into my brother's eyes. They lit up like bar neon, glowing green. "Prince? You're telling me the guy we've been trusting, the one who has been helping us and dating your best friend, is the *prince*? As in, the one you are betrothed to?"

This time, it was me putting my hand on his. "You've got to calm down, Cole. I don't know how to explain this to Bethany. I don't even know what it means." I wasn't sure how I had become the voice of reason, but I couldn't stop myself. "He says he was here to help me, to protect me. I think we have to hear him out. I don't understand how that Hunter fits into all of this, but there are too many players in the game. I don't know who to trust. I don't know what to think. So, we just have to hear them all out and make a choice. Don't you think?"

He huffed in response. "How did you become the rational one?"

I smiled. "Trust me, I've made enough impulsive decisions lately to last a lifetime. I just don't see another option." It occurred to me I still hadn't seen our uncle. "Hey, where's Derreck? Shouldn't he be here? It'd be really nice to hear his take on all of this."

Cole shook his head. "I don't know. I've called and called. He's not answering, so I told him just to meet us at my place in my last voicemail. Speaking of, her ten minutes is—"

At that second, Bethany emerged from her room, toting an overnight bag. "Looking for me, honey?" Her smile was syrupy-sweet and victory shone in her eyes. I couldn't stop the laughter that bubbled over as my brother stared open-mouthed at her perfect hair and make-up, shaking his head in disbelief.

He snapped his mouth shut. "Let's go. In the car, everybody. Now."

He went first and I gave B a silent high five as I grabbed my own bag and headed out the door.

I crashed hard once we got to Cole's. I was planning to eat and take a shower once we got there, but as I laid down to close my eyes for a few minutes, I was out cold. Then, the howling started again.

I don't know how to explain it, other than to say that I knew I wasn't in my own body. Everything was sharper; more crisp. I could smell the soil beneath my feet, the different plants and animals, even the ocean air — all of it taking on a different taste than anything I'd ever experienced. I ran and ran, trees whipping by and barely glancing off of me. The howling varied. Sometimes long, eerie wailing and then furious-sounding baying.

It took a long time for me to realize those noises were coming from me.

I awoke with a start, once again sitting straight up in bed. I was covered in sweat, my hair matted and sticking to the back of my neck. I kept looking left and right, expecting to be surrounded by trees. It didn't make sense. Why would I be howling? Why would I be dreaming about being something that could howl? Had Elias done something to me when we merged?

As I laid back, I groaned at the realization that it was another day that likely held more questions than answers.

I rubbed my eyes, feeling the film of yesterday's events still on my skin, and decided it was time for my shower. I could see light through the shades. Why not get the next potentially life-threatening day going already?

I mean, really, there's positivity and then there's realism.

After my shower, I found myself alone in the kitchen. Charlie lumbered in, his gigantic paws landing in my lap as I sat at the bar counter. He nuzzled and whimpered, licking my hands and diving his head into the crook of my arm. I tried to send him reassuring thoughts but instead was assailed with all of his worry from last night. He was not pleased to have been left at home and was trying to show me how he could have patrolled and helped me. He also showed me how he had slept outside my door all night and heard my dream. Apparently, I was making quite a bit of noise as the lone wolf was howling its way around the woods. I dropped my head to Charlie's and scratched behind his ears. All I could do was tell him I was okay. He dropped down and plopped a few feet away on his humongous dog bed, letting out an indignant *woof.*

I couldn't blame him. I didn't even believe myself when I said I was okay. I was nowhere near the continent of being alright. As I tried to mentally rewind through the last few days and weeks, it was exhausting to even try to think of everything I'd been through. I felt like one of those investigative reporters that had an entire wall filled with post-its and strings tying the various pieces together. Except, it was all a jumbled mess inside of my head.

Bethany found me sitting at that kitchen counter with my arms crossed and my head down. "It's too early, honey. You can't be trying to solve the world's problems until you've been properly caffeinated. Don't make life any harder than it already is."

I snorted, trying to keep quiet as her words struck me as utterly hilarious. Only a half-asleep Bethany, wearing Cole's XXL Matchbox Twenty T-shirt and my too-tall yoga pants, could throw out that kind of wisdom at 7:00 a.m. the day after she'd been held captive by a group of rebellious, crazy town Immortals.

I couldn't stop myself from getting up and wrapping her in a hug. I told her I loved her between a laugh and a cry, as I realized how lucky we'd been that Elias had never truly wanted to hurt her.

"Alright, lady," she said with a pat to the back of my head. "It's especially too early for tears. We don't cry before breakfast. Mamma's rules." In a small whisper, she added, "I'm okay, Ame. You got me. They didn't hurt me. I'm okay."

I let out a breath I didn't realize I was holding and nodded into her hair. I turned and starting pulling coffee supplies from the cupboard. There was still one piece of information I didn't know how to share, but I needed to do it soon.

Bethany and I were facing each other, with our backs against each arm of the couch. We were sharing a blanket and sipping our coffee as we talked. I was doing most of the talking, actually, and as I'd promised, I started at the beginning. I explained everything from the circumstances of my birth up through the events of last night. I tried to give background on our races and how I came to be betrothed to a prince I'd never met — conveniently leaving out that I now knew that prince was Micah. I just wasn't ready for that part yet.

I tried not to talk about Aidan, but that seemed to be where Bethany wanted to focus. The memory of our break-up seemed like a lifetime ago but she kept peppering me with questions about how I felt about him and how I could just walk away. That I needed to fight the betrothal because I deserved something in my life to make me happy given everything else. Finally, I couldn't take it anymore.

"This isn't a movie, B. There is no happy ending for me and Aidan. Don't you get it?" I tore the blankets away from my legs and with very little grace, scrambled over her to get off the couch.

Once I found my footing, I turned back to her glowering. "I. Don't. Have. A. Choice. If I don't marry this prince, there's a solid chance the queen will kill my family and everyone I love. That's what she does. If I don't let this bitch use me and my power, everyone who's ever even known me is at risk. But, there's also a whole group of Immortals who need my help. Who think I can stop her and make everything right again…whatever that means. And, then, to top the whole damn cake off, apparently I also have a mate wandering around out there. Someone I'm actually meant to be with. So, no, it doesn't *matter* how I *feel* about Aidan."

I wanted to keep being angry, but saying those words out loud and hearing them in my own mind caused my strong walls to crumble. I stood in the center of Cole's gorgeous living room completely rigid, trying to compel myself to regain control. The sobs started deep in my chest as I squeezed my eyes shut as tight as I could and begged myself to get a grip. Arms encircled me, the smell of vanilla and brown sugar filling my nostrils. She hadn't made a sound, but Bethany had come over and wrapped me in a hug.

"I don't understand what you're going through, Ame, but I know heartbreak when I see it. It's okay to miss him. It's okay for all of this to be too much. It's just me, honey."

I felt her sincerity to the bottom of my soul and I let go. Part of me was so sick of crying, but the rest knew that if I didn't, there was a good chance I'd end up blowing something up. I couldn't *really* be expected to handle all of this well, right? I was standing at a fork in the road that had a lot more than two options and none of them looked appealing. There were lives at stake. A power struggle not only within me, but using me. Oh yeah, I deserved a good cry.

Eventually, the crying stopped and Bethany and I pulled ourselves together. It took a minute to realize it was Monday and we had both missed class. Bethany did some damage control at work and explained away her absences. Cole showed back up at the house looking pretty beat down early in the afternoon. He'd spent the day out looking for Uncle Derreck, but had still not heard anything from him.

"I think I'm going to head back out to his place tomorrow," he explained. "There's no way he'd leave Onyx to fend for himself. If nothing else, I'll bring him back with me. But, hopefully I'll catch him there, or at least get some kind of clue as to what his game plan was."

Cole and I were sitting at the kitchen island, both eating in an amicable silence while Bethany was napping. I was lost in my own thoughts when I realized he was staring at me.

"What," I grumbled, my mouth half-full. I thought he would roll his eyes at my less-than-ladylike behavior, but his stony look remained.

"We need to talk about all of this," he said. "We need a plan. Do you think we should try to find Dad and Rynna?"

I was shocked that he brought up our father. I had been trying to decide how to bring him up. "I was thinking that, too. Let me grab my phone."

I dialed Rynna and was shocked to hear it ring. It had been going straight to voicemail for days. On the fourth ring, she finally picked up.

"Amelia?" she asked.

"Rynna? What's wrong?" The hairs on the back of my neck stood up. I knew something wasn't right.

Rynna was quiet for a moment. "We've been traveling for days, hiking and driving and searching. I know your uncle told you what we've been doing and, Amelia, I'm sorry I couldn't tell you myself. Your father made us all swear an oath that we wouldn't tell you. He didn't annul it until we saw your uncle last week. We finally found the man Derreck sent us to, hoping he could break the spell, but nothing works. He tried everything. Your father isn't doing well. He's been through too much. We're going home, Amelia. I have to go, he's calling out again, but we'll be home soon. I'm sorry."

She disconnected and it took me a moment to comprehend what had just happened. I relayed the message to Cole and his shoulders sagged. We both had held out a silent hope that we might get our father back.

I sat across from Cole, my breathing rapid and my frustration growing. I needed out of this apartment, but there was so much we needed to talk about and decide on.

We needed to decide if Cole was going to Uncle Derreck's. We needed to talk about whether I should go back and talk to Elias. We needed to probably have a screaming match about whether we should talk to Micah and how we were going to explain this latest wrinkle to Bethany. But, none of that was anything I could handle at this particular moment with all of my childhood insecurities running rampant in my head. The bottom line was that we were alone in this. Technically, it was all on me.

So, instead, I shoved away from the island and called for Charlie. "I'm taking Charlie down to the beach. I need some air."

Cole was looking dejectedly at me, a deep sadness in his eyes. Charlie bounded up and gave a happy *woof* when I grabbed his leash and the handle to the front door. I turned back to my brother, understanding exactly how deep the pain went. "We have each other, Cole. At least we have that."

He nodded and gave me a small smile. "Don't go far, and keep Charlie with you. Got it?"

I gave a mini-salute, trying to lighten the mood. "Aye aye, captain."

Cole rolled his eyes and chuckled as I was yanked out the door by one overly-excited Great Dane.

Chapter 23

I hadn't remembered a hair tie and my hair was blowing everywhere in the strong wind coming off of the water. The waves were intense, leaping over each other and capped in white foam. The surfers were out in droves, hovering in packs in the distance. I would never grow tired of seeing them against the never-ending water with the sun at their backs.

Charlie and I had been walking for about an hour. I needed to go back, but I could finally breathe. The only sounds were Charlie's small snorts and the crash of the waves. The beach was pretty empty since most people were at work or school. As we kept walking, I realized I had made my way to the stretch of beach where Aidan and I had been on our date. I was standing fairly close to where we'd been when I told him I was in. That I wanted whatever we were becoming.

I stood in the sand, my face tilted up into the sun and my eyes closed, as I relived those few moments in my mind. How his eyes lit up. The way he picked me up and made me feel like I weighed nothing at all. How his arms locked around me and his hand fisted my hair. The stormy look in his smoky eyes before he kissed me. That kiss would be burned into the back of my brain for the rest of eternity.

I wanted to live in that moment just a little longer. Total calm spread throughout my system. Not only could I breathe, but I was genuinely happy. The anxiety that was a constant pit in my stomach had all but disappeared and all of my power sat back, a peaceful murmur in my mind. It was a welcome change from the constant buzzing and swirling I typically endured.

As I went to open my eyes, I had that niggling in the back of my mind that someone was there while Charlie let out a low growl. As I slowly turned around, I unclipped Charlie from his leash while pushing the message to him to stay unless I said otherwise. I was hyperaware of everything in those few seconds.

The sand under my feet was coarser. The humidity in the air settled on my skin and I tasted the salt in my mouth. As I lifted my eyes to gauge the latest threat, I also brought my power to the surface. Something was off though, she wasn't listening. In fact, she seemed happy, not angry. Then I saw him. Standing just fifty feet away, his body rigid and his mouth hanging open, was Aidan.

Well, just damn it all.

"Hi," I breathed out. It was utterly lame and literally the only thing I could come up with. Aidan just stood there. He was wearing sunglasses, so I couldn't see his expression. A muscle ticked in his jaw and he pressed his lips together in a tight line. He looked as if he couldn't decide if he should run toward me or from me.

Charlie continued to growl and I quietly commanded him to stop. He gave me a look that made it obvious he wasn't pleased with not being able to do anything but stand there. It seemed like an eternity that Aidan and I stood there staring at each other. Finally, I couldn't do it anymore. "Okay, well, it was…uh…nice to see you. So, I gotta go." I didn't want to go. I didn't want to move. But, I needed to go.

"Please don't." I didn't so much hear his whisper as I felt it. Those two words reverberated through my soul. My head dropped to my chest. That's what I wanted to hear him say, but I also knew it was the worst thing he could've said. There was no way I could walk away from Aidan right now. Not when I craved the safety of him, though I knew how foolish it was to indulge in it. I walked slowly toward him. Charlie stayed in step with me as Aidan met us halfway.

"What are you doing here, Amelia? Where have you been? Why?" He just stopped after that last word. We both knew what he wanted to ask. Why did I say those things? Why didn't I answer the door? Any of his messages? I couldn't answer any of these questions, so I just silently shook my head without looking up at him.

"I'm just walking Cole's dog. This is Charlie." I absently stroked Charlie's head as I spoke, trying to keep my hands steady as she reached out for Aidan. *Traitor*, I internally reprimanded.

Just because he made me feel alive didn't mean I was going to be able to love him. But, every part of me wanted to do the same. I wanted to wrap my arms around his neck and find myself buried in that small crook of space between his chin and his chest. I wanted to feel his hands in my hair and his arms around me. I wanted to hide inside of him until this all went away. Instead, I continued to pet Charlie and avoided looking directly at him.

"You're not going to tell me, are you?" I heard the plea in his voice. He wanted me to trust him. Needed me to. But, I had already endangered one human I cared about, I wasn't going to do it again.

"I can't, Aidan. I just can't. You don't understand. You can't." His frustration permeated the air around us.

"Can you just come with me for a few minutes?" He was gritting out the words as if it pained him to say them. Something was wrong.

"Are you okay?" I took a step forward as he took one back. I paused, confused.

"Amelia. Please. Just follow me." He looked tired as he turned and walked away.

I had a hard time keeping up and Charlie kept assaulting me with his version of a warning. I mentally hushed him as I half-ran to catch up with Aidan as he left the beach. I found myself between two buildings in a deserted alley.

"Aidan, what's going on? Why are we here?" He walked back toward the edge of the buildings and the street, looking around before coming back to me. Charlie started growling again.

"Dammit, Charlie. Just stop it. Aidan isn't going to hurt us," I scolded. Aidan stood directly in front of me. Sweat was building on his forehead and he was pale.

"Aidan—" He held up his hand. I assumed it was to get me to stop talking, so I did. What I didn't expect was an iridescent ball of bright blue magic to form and shoot past me, blasting the trash can fifty feet back into smithereens.

I looked from him to the trash can and back. And back again. "But? How did you? Where did you? How? You're human!" I was sputtering nonsense.

I turned to fully face Aidan and for the first time, he gave me a tentative smile. I saw that adorable dimple appear and the little gap between his front teeth that I loved. "I thought so, too. But, I guess not." As he finished his sentence, he took off his sunglasses. I was staring at eyes the same brilliant blue as his magic.

I couldn't breathe. No wonder Charlie had been having a panic attack. It wasn't that he thought Aidan was a threat, he recognized his power. But, why couldn't I? And his eyes, they were blue. His power was blue. Was he an AniMage?

I had been keeping my own power on such a tight leash. In a spur-of-the-moment response, I let it loose. My traitorous power leapt out and dove straight for Aidan's.

We were standing just feet apart but as soon as our magic found each other, I felt it in every fiber of my body. It was one giant exhale. Small, happy tremors went through me and I was alive. His love, pain, and anger filled every part of me. I found myself smiling, an uncontrollable grin taking up my face.

"Is that you," he asked, looking around, obviously confused. I laughed. "It's us. It must be our powers getting acquainted. Apparently they like each other."

He smiled and even through the endless blue of his eyes, I could see the smoldering change. "They aren't the only ones who like each other. Amelia, this changes things, right? You don't have to run from me. I can help. Whatever is happening, I can help. I'm…uh, still figuring this out, but I won't let you leave me again." Those last words weren't just a statement, they were a promise. I felt his conviction in the depths of my heart and it only made it ache.

"Let's not do this. Not yet. Let's talk, okay? For just a few minutes, can we talk and not get into the rest of it?" I was almost begging.

I couldn't even process what I had just learned because it did change everything, but at the same time, it changed nothing. He gave me a sideways look that questioned, gave permission, and promised we weren't done yet. I nodded for both of us and led the way back to the beach. Neither of us spoke as we walked down a little ways and then sat. Charlie stood sentry next to me, his huge body sitting tall and his head constantly scanning the rest of the beach, as if telling me that I could do what I needed to and he would keep watch.

Aidan sat down on the other side of me. He sat so close that our bodies were almost touching. It was a fight to stay still. Part of me wanted to scoot away and create more space, and the other wanted to leap into his lap and spill my guts. So, instead, I stood, turned, and sat down in the same position just facing him instead of next to him. This way, we could see each other and were still close — our feet and legs just inches apart. He smirked knowingly. I couldn't stop myself from laughing a little and shaking my head. He knew me too well.

"So," I started, "are you going to tell me what this is all about? Last time I checked, you were human. Unless we've both been hiding things?" I quirked an eyebrow and gave him a joking look. It felt better than I'd imagined to actually speak openly to him.

In typical Aidan fashion, he started with a shrug. "I thought I was just a human. I'd been noticing some weird stuff happening, but it wasn't until after that night at the theater that it really got weird."

"Define 'weird stuff,'" I requested, my anxiety spiking.

"I would feel this pressure inside of my head. It would get stronger and stronger until, finally, I couldn't take it anymore and then the release would be one of those blue balls that decimated anything it came in contact with."

"Has there been anything else, Aidan? Have you noticed any other weird stuff?" There wasn't an easy way to ask if he'd ever randomly turned into an animal.

He shook head. "No, not really. I mean, I've been having some really weird dreams. But, until I saw you that night at the theater, I didn't know what was happening. I thought I was losing my mind. That's what I was trying to tell you that night at your apartment, Amelia. I was trying to tell you that I understood. And, that I needed help."

I had to look away when he brought up that night. It still hurt in a way nothing ever had. He stayed silent and waited for me to bring my gaze back to his. I saw the same pain reflected in his eyes and I heard those whispered words in the deepest parts of my soul. *I love you.* My own set of pressure started building in my chest — this was panic, not power. Lately, the distinction was becoming clearer.

What was I thinking? None of this mattered. So what if Aidan had magic? I was still betrothed to Micah. There still wasn't a choice.

Was there?

I felt guilty for not hearing him out that night, not helping him to learn about his own power and this world. Damn it, I knew what it was like to be kept out of the loop on your own life. The worst was knowing that I broke his heart, as well as my own, by walking away. There was so much working against us, but him not being human did change the game at least a little, right? He wasn't human. He could learn to protect himself. We could take care of each other. Hope was a bright light bursting from my heart into my head as an idea suddenly formed.

I had no idea if it would work, but I could try. If it didn't work, I was no worse off than I was now, staring at the boy I wanted to love but kept running from. I smiled my first genuine smile in days.

The words gushed from my mouth. I couldn't say them fast enough. "Aidan, we have so much to talk about. I have so many things to tell you, but things are just really complicated. I need you to trust me. I need you to try to keep a low profile and wait for me to contact you, okay? There's something I have to do and it could change things."

I started to stand but Aidan grabbed my hand, sending all-too-familiar sensations pinging through my system. "Amelia, don't go yet. You can't go already."

Against my better judgment, I leaned down and pressed a quick kiss to his lips. I wanted to linger and savor it, but if I fell into Aidan, I wouldn't be able to climb back out. "I have to go, Aidan. I'll be able to explain it all soon. Just give me some time. I'll find you. Don't worry."

Charlie and I started to walk away, but I had to look back. He sat there, in the same position I'd left him, staring at me. I tried to give him a reassuring smile but I had no idea if what I was about to do was going to be a new beginning or a disastrous end. I just knew I had to try.

Chapter 24

I crashed into the apartment, hollering for Cole. Bethany came out from the spare bedroom instead. "Where's the fire, Ame? Cole isn't here. He told me to tell you he was going to Derreck's to get Onyx and see if there were any clues. He'll be back tomorrow and we're supposed to stay close to the apartment."

I hadn't put Charlie back on his leash, so he ambled off into the other room. I was standing in the middle of the entry way, getting sand everywhere, trying to process all of that at once. With a shake, I realized that I didn't care about any of it.

"B, do you want to help me get my happy-ever-after, and yours, too?" I was wearing an ear-to-ear grin and I couldn't stop it.

With a cock of her hip and a raise of her eyebrow, Bethany replied, "Oh, honey, I'm from the south. Every girl grows up knowing about Prince Charming. You just tell me what I can do to get you and Mr. Beautiful Smoky

Eyes back together so I can get back to my own prince." I swept her up in a huge hug and then pulled her to the counter. She had no idea how true her words were. I was still holding her hand as I started in on what was going to be difficult information for her to understand, but a plan that could give us both what we wanted.

"Okay, B, I'm just going to lay it all out there," I said. "You wanted full disclosure. Well, last night I learned something I hadn't known before and I wasn't sure how to tell you. The night I was born, which I told you about, the only way my father was able to stop the Hunter from killing me was to betroth me to the queen's son."

"The bitchy queen? The one we don't like? I can't believe your dad was such a moron. How could he possibly—"

"B. Stay focused," I interrupted as her face took on the exasperated look that meant she was building up to a full-on tirade. "The guy was going to kill me."

She nodded and shrugged, acquiescing to the logic. "Okay, so the agreement was that I would have until I was twenty-one and then I would have to move to the palace and marry the prince. By marrying him, the queen hoped to use my power to solidify her family's ability to hold the throne and continue to terrorize my people. But, here's the tricky part, I need you to stay calm and remember when I tell you this part that I have a plan. Okay?"

Again, she nodded, looking a little less enthusiastic.

"No, B. Out loud," I said. "Pinky swear you're going to hear me out, okay?" I held up my pinky and though it

329

was obvious she didn't like the blind agreement, she did the same. We linked up and I spoke, hoping she wasn't going to completely lose it.

"So, what I found out from Elias last night is that the Hunter who killed my mother and betrothed me to the prince works for Micah. Micah is the prince. Micah is the one I'm betrothed to."

"YOU'RE WHAT?" The stool toppled as Bethany jumped to her feet, shrieking at the top of her lungs. I quickly started doing damage control.

"B. Calm down. Pinky swear, right? Just listen." I couldn't talk fast enough. "I didn't know. I had no idea who Micah was. I told you how he was helping me with my abilities, but I didn't know. What matters is that I have a plan for you to keep your guy and me to keep mine. Are you in?" I had to keep yelling over her as she let out a very un-southernly string of curse words.

Finally, she stopped pacing and was standing in the kitchen looking shell-shocked. I couldn't blame her, but I wasn't sure really how much time we were going to have.

"B? If we're going to do this, we need to move. This is in no way a Cole-approved exercise." I was impatient myself and afraid I would lose the gumption if this didn't happen soon.

She sighed, clenching and unclenching her fists at her sides. "Let me get this straight. You're almost-kinda-sorta in love with Aidan but are currently betrothed to my magical actual prince of a boyfriend that I might also almost-kinda-sorta love, and you have a plan that's going to get his wretched queen mother to let us all have what we want?" I nodded enthusiastically, still smiling.

"Huh," she snorted, "well, when you put it like that, how's a girl supposed to say no?" I lunged in and gave her another huge hug. "Here's what I'm thinking," I started to fill her in on the details and we solidified the plan.

I had no idea if this was going to work, but it was the best I could come up with and knowing I could have a future with Aidan was enough to make it not a choice at all.

At this point, the queen knew I was here. She knew I had met Micah and was likely going to want me to accept the betrothal early. It didn't take a rocket scientist to figure that much out. Knowing that Rhi had shown up and seen me fighting with Micah, I was sure the queen would be here soon if she weren't already. Bethany didn't love my plan, but I was going to set a meeting with Micah and try to get him on board to help me convince his mother to give me more time. It was out in the open now. I knew who I was. She knew who I was. Just let me have until my twenty-first birthday like everyone had agreed. In that time, I could go back to Elias and find out how to control my Keeper power and truly fight Queen Julia. I could also help Aidan acclimate to his new abilities and hopefully repair the damage I'd done.

It was a long shot. It was probably a really stupid plan. But, after seeing Aidan on that beach, after my reactions to him in heart, mind, and soul, I had to try. I just had to.

I called Micah. He answered on the first ring.

"I need to see you," I said. "Soon."

"That is fantastic, Amelia. We need to talk. I want to explain." He sounded way more relieved than I wanted him to. I was still burned by his lies, but I wanted to believe he was a good guy. I had to. For this plan to work, I needed his help.

"Where are you?" I asked.

"I'm at Esmerelda's, but—"

"Micah, I need your help," I interrupted. "I need you to help me convince your mother that I need time. That she needs to honor the terms of the betrothal. I'm coming to you. I'll be there in fifteen minutes."

He tried to say something but I was already losing my nerve so I hung up. We'd figure it out when I got there.

I was in the parking lot in ten minutes. Bethany sat next to me and, for the fifth time, asked if I was sure that she shouldn't come in.

"B, thank you. I really appreciate the offer, but I need to do this on my own," I said. "I need to talk to Micah and figure out what to do. Honestly, I'm not even sure exactly what I'm walking into here. I don't want you to get hurt again."

"Okay, girl, but I'm waiting right here. I'm not moving this Jeep until you're sitting next to me again. And, you make sure he knows that this is going to take a hell of a lot of making up." We laughed together. It was strained, both of us obviously scared, but it was welcome.

I blew out a breath and shook the tremble out of my hands. "Here I go. I'll be back out in no time. Don't you worry. It's just Micah." She nodded, looking past me to the bleak exterior of Esmerelda's. "I know, girl. This place just creeps me out," she said grimly.

I reached over, gave her a quick hug, and then jumped down out of the Jeep. As I mounted the steps and walked through the doors of Esmerelda's, my inner alarm bells went crazy. *You're just nervous. Calm down,* I reprimanded myself and approached the host stand. The same small, pinched-face woman stood at the desk, glancing at me with complete disinterest.

"Yes?" she asked in an annoyingly clipped tone.

"I'm here to see Micah…um, Prince Mikail, he's expecting me. Please take me to him." She didn't respond, instead she picked up the phone and queried the person on the other end. With a surprising smile, she nodded and led me to an elevator.

She rode down with me, saying nothing until the doors opened again. "Follow the hallway. Third set of doors on your right." I was struggling to maintain my power, feeling her agitated and antsy in the back of my mind. I had already had about ten mental conversations where I tried to explain why she had to stay quiet. To stay hidden. It was a strange thing, talking to yourself, but the more I embraced the fact that the Keeper power was its own being within me, the easier things seemed to go.

I wasn't sure exactly how to enter, so instead of knocking, I decided to make a statement and just open the door myself. I was shocked at how light the large wooden doors were, it flew open and slammed against the wall, making a loud *thud*. I shocked myself with the sound, thinking the door was going to be much heavier. Once I had gotten my bearings and turned back to the room in front of me, I found myself staring directly into the eyes of Queen Julia. Well, her and about twenty Hunters who seemed only too happy to display their bouncing balls of crackling orange magic and wicked stares.

It took me a second to absorb the scene. The queen was sitting on a large throne. Next to her was a smaller ornate chair that Micah held. I refused to show them my fear, so I straightened my posture and strode into the room as if the eyes and magic that followed me didn't exist. I imagined the pressure of Aidan's hand against my lower back, giving me the feeling of safety I'd never known until him. Aidan was the reason I was here. Even though this wasn't the meeting I had signed up for, it was what I had to do.

The Hunters had started out in a single group in front of Queen Julia and Micah, but they separated into two groups and allowed me to walk through their ranks. I stopped about ten feet from the upraised platform that held their chairs and met Micah's eyes. I could see the apologies already. This was absolutely not going to go well.

I urged my own power to slowly creep through me; building and rising to the surface, while reminding her to stay silent but ready. I looked straight into Micah's eyes and sent a very clear thought his way: *Traitor.*

He winced. That brought me a small smile.

As I shifted my focus back to the queen, I couldn't believe how much Micah resembled her. Julia had thick, blond hair that was tied back severely at her nape. Her crown dripped with diamonds and her dress was black lace over black silk. I expected her to be older, but her skin was porcelain and she looked beautiful. Her features were softer than Micah's and it wasn't until I reached her eyes that I truly saw the difference. This woman was pure evil. Her eyes were cold and empty.

I was staggering under the weight of her stare when the queen finally spoke. "So, the Keeper has finally come home. You didn't tell me she was also beautiful, son. It may not be so terrible to have this one on your arm. Though, we will have a discussion later on how exactly it is you came to know each other." Julia quirked a thin, angular eyebrow at Micah and I watched him shrink in his seat. Apparently it was intentioned by both of our parents that we not be exposed to each other.

I couldn't stop my visible, shocked response and the words came tumbling from my mouth. "Um. Excuse me? First, I'm right here and my name is Amelia. Second, the whole reason I'm here is because there were terms to this betrothal. Terms you have to honor. I thought I was going to be having a conversation with Micah, who has clearly been keeping us all in the dark, but I suppose since you're here, we can all just do this together."

Somehow, the queen's stare actually became frostier and the smirk she'd held flattened. Her words were quiet but her barbs were sharp. "Have you no respect, little girl? How dare you address me and my son so casually? Though, your father hasn't been himself in years and I suppose you didn't have your mother to instill in you proper respect for the crown, did you, dear?"

I immediately opened my mouth to respond when Micah jumped in and cut me off. "Mother, please. That's not necessary. Amelia is to be my wife. You need not poke at her immediately. You know she grew up in a remote area. We need to acclimate her to the court — to our ways."

I could hear Micah in my head as he spoke to his mother.

Amelia, you must watch yourself. I don't know what you think you're doing here, but you can't do it like this.

I wanted to talk to you, you know, like friends. But, it's clear you have your own agenda.

With that, I slammed the door closed on our connection and saw a second wince that again brought me a measure of pleasure. There was no way I was allowing that jerk in my head now.

"That is a fair point, son. Exactly what is it you would like to discuss, child?" She was patronizing me, but it gave me an opening to speak. This time, I tried to formulate my sentences in my head before I just let them spew from my mouth.

"Thank you, your…highness." I had no idea what the proper terminology was. "It's clear to me that Mi — Prince Mikail and I were not supposed to know each other yet. But, we do, and that's okay. I just want to confirm that you will abide by the terms set by the betrothal you demanded. I will have until I'm twenty-one. Those were the terms and I believe they should hold true."

I tried my best to sound confident in my words but deferential in my tone. I thought I might have succeeded as Julia sat and tapped her long red nails on the armrest of her throne. Then, she spoke.

"You have come into my court, interrupted my day, insulted my son, and believe you can tell me what I will and will not do?" The queen somehow sat even straighter in her chair, pointing her finger at me while her shrill voice grew louder. "Do you expect me to believe that after everything I know of your mother and her devious ways, that her little plan didn't succeed? That the prophecy I have spent years waiting for is a lie? Do you honestly think you can tell a queen what rules she will abide by?"

"No. No…um, your highness." I had to back pedal, quickly. "I didn't say anything about the prophecy. I don't even understand the prophecy. I just want the time that was promised to me." I didn't have to lie, the prophecy made zero sense to me.

Her eyes narrowed as they blazed red. "I believe there is more to you than it seems, Amelia. And, from what I understand, you just need a little incentive." The bitterness in her voice sent fear racing through me. I looked to Micah and he wouldn't meet my gaze. Cursing myself, I realized that I was stupid. This was stupid. I wasn't going anywhere. I was just lucky I was more valuable alive than dead.

Chapter 25

Julia stepped down from her chair and walked toward me, gliding across the floor silently. It took all of my willpower to not step back, but I refused to show her weakness. She looked over my head and nodded. As I turned to look around, someone pinned my arms. I was struggling against the unknown Hunters, still trying to control the raging Keeper power inside of me, when fingers gripped my chin and I found myself eye to eye with the queen. The look in her eyes stopped me from doing anything. I could barely breathe as I watched red creep into her irises, like blood spreading across an ice cube. From inches away, she said, "You know nothing, you say? Are you quite sure of that, little one?"

She didn't even give me a chance to respond before she pulled my face all the way to the right and I almost fainted as I saw Bethany unconscious in Rhi's arms. I wanted to look at Micah, but Julia wouldn't allow me to move. She held my face, the pads of her fingers burning my skin while she forced me to stare at the limp body of my best friend held in the arms of my mother's murderer. There was nothing random about this. Realizing, slowly, that Micah had been a part of all of this, a whole new fire came alive in me. As the queen brought my face back to hers, she saw it, too.

"You didn't tell me she had violet eyes, Mikail. My, my, you are just the picture of your mother. I've never known anyone else to have those particular violet eyes. You are quite the prize, indeed." I opened my mouth to argue, to tell her off, to finally take a stand, and instead found her finger across my lips.

I gritted my teeth and bit the inside of my cheek as she continued to speak, my control waning and anger spiraling. "You see her? She is just a fragile little human. Do you see? LOOK AT HER!"

I had refused to keep staring at Bethany's slack form, but Julia turned my face back to her and held it until I opened my eyes.

She laughed. "This is my court. My kingdom. I make the rules here. If you want her to live, to go back to her happy little human life, then you'll tell me the truth. Do you have the Keeper power? Are you coming for me?"

With every ounce of pain, hatred, and anger I had, I removed all barriers from the Keeper magic that sat ready and waiting, and let her do her worst.

"YES!" I screamed, the single word echoing from every inch of the cavernous room as the queen and her Hunters were blasted away from me. No one saw it coming and I took the moment to my advantage. I dove for Bethany, hoping I could do some kind of damage to Rhi to free her from his arms. The balls of electric energy pulsed around my hands as I ran to him. Rhi hadn't moved, though a slow smile crept over his face. "Your little Keeper is no match for me, girl. Your mother should have known that." I wanted to end him for so many reasons, but he was holding Bethany.

"Give her to me. She doesn't need to be a part of this. You don't want to fight me," I warned him. I looked around and saw the Hunters closing ranks. Julia had righted herself and Micah still hadn't moved from his chair. His face paled further while his eyes never left Bethany. What a coward.

Rhi laughed at the same moment the other Hunters converged on me. I pushed outward with everything I had, at the same moment calling on the elements that had aided me at the theater. *Blow them over.* The wind storm that erupted split the ranks of Hunters and slammed them against the walls. I blasted at them as well, sending them flying into heaps. I kept moving toward Rhi. He stood staring at me, looking pleasantly surprised by my show of ability. He still held the prize though, and we both knew it. I kept blasting and pushing, and only when I got within feet of them, did the queen join the party again.

"THAT'S IT!" she screeched. Then, I was floating ten feet up in the air and couldn't breathe. I was gasping for air and clawing at my throat, trying to pull in oxygen from somewhere. There was nothing.

"I AM THE QUEEN. YOU WILL DO AS I COMMAND. YOU ARE NOTHING TO ME. I OWN YOU." Her words reverberated off of the stone walls and the Hunters had to steady themselves against the shifting ground. I would have been more scared if I wasn't so concerned with breathing.

"Mother!" I finally heard Micah yell. "She can't help us if she's dead. Mother, stop! Let me deal with her."

With a wave of her hand, I dropped to the ground in a heap and could do nothing but gasp in huge breaths of air. "You do that, Mikail," she snapped. "I expect to see a marked improvement the next time we meet."

I could barely focus on Julia as she strode out of the room, followed by the majority of the Hunters and Rhi who was still holding Bethany. I couldn't begin to think about moving and I soon felt myself being pulled into someone's arms. I immediately started to struggle until Micah spoke, "Amelia. It's me. Let me help you."

I wasn't able to do anything more than collapse into Micah's arms as I lost consciousness. The last thought I had was *I'm sorry,* but I couldn't decide whom exactly the apology was meant for.

I awoke with a start and darted up. It was dark in the room with only a small lamp on in the corner. It took me a moment to realize what had happened and where I was. Actually, I had no idea where I was, outside of sitting in the middle of an ornately-decorated four-poster bed. I saw

Micah slumped in the chair across from me and was sad to realize it hadn't been another of my nightmares.

I slowly laid back down and dropped my arm over my face. What had I been thinking? How could I have possibly thought it would be logical to believe I could just walk in and convince a power-hungry tormentor to just let me go have my happily-ever-after? *Idiot.*

Cole would have never let me do this. *Oh, no. Cole.* My next thought sent fear to my core. *Bethany.* I shot back up.

"Bethany! Where's Bethany?!" I tried to scream but my voice was still hoarse so it came out a garbled whisper.

Micah came awake with grunt. "What? What?" He rubbed his eyes as I tried to yell again. "Micah, where is she? Where is Bethany?"

"She's next door. I can't believe you brought her here. I can't believe you endangered her like this. What in the hell were you thinking?" He stood over me now, fully awake and yelling. I chucked back the covers and scrambled to my feet. "Don't you dare make this my fault, *Prince Mikail.* I told you I was coming and you let me walk into this ambush blind. How could *you* do *this*? How could you let your mother *use her*?"

"Me? *ME?* Did you actually think you could walk in here and convince my mother to just let you walk away and come back in three years? Have you lost your mind, Amelia? Her Hunter has been in your father's head your whole life. She knows exactly what you are." I started to explain about Aidan but realized that probably wasn't information Micah needed at this point.

I crossed my arms over my now rumpled dress and glared at him. "You are the liar," I hissed. "You are the one who played us all for a fool. You are going to break Bethany's heart and I will never trust you again. Why are you even here? Get out. Just, GET OUT!"

"You don't understand, Amelia. I was trying to help you."

"I understand everything I need to, *Prince*. Get out." This time the words were measured and cold.

I sat down on the bed and stared at the wall. I refused to acknowledge him. It was childish, but it wasn't like I could be the one who left. Finally, Micah left the room with a slam of the door. I ran to it once I heard his footsteps go down the hall. As I expected, it was locked.

I decided there was no way I was hanging around for whatever they had in mind. I tried to build up my magic so I could blast my way out, but there was nothing. I searched and searched, but I couldn't find one shred of power anywhere in my body.

I did everything I've done my whole life. I searched myself for the familiar tingle and hum, it was gone. I started to panic. I had never been without my power. Even when I didn't know how to use it or was suppressing it, I always knew it was there.

I started beating on the door and yelling for Micah, or Prince Mikail, or anybody. Over and over, I yelled and pounded. Finally, I gave up and fell down onto the bed. I wanted to cry. The tears were there to be had, I just couldn't. Micah was right on one count. I had walked myself and Bethany right into this disaster with my naivety. I couldn't expect anyone else to get me out of it.

I laid there for what had to be hours, staring at the ceiling. I thought about all the ways I could kill Julia. Maim Micah. I thought about Bethany and wondered if she was scared. If they were feeding her. I thought about Cole and how worried he would be once he knew we were gone.

I realized I had no idea what time it was since there were no windows. Even after all of those things, I refused to think about Aidan. His face, his words, his beautiful blue Immortal eyes kept finding their way into my mind and I had to force them out again. I had to be brave. I had to find a way out of this, even if just for Bethany.

I fell asleep for a while, waking when I heard the door opening. Unfortunately, I was too tangled in covers to get out of bed fast enough to stand up. When I finally righted myself, I found Micah standing at the edge of the bed with a tray of food.

"I don't want that." I crossed my arms again and stepped back. "What did your mother do to me? Why is my power gone? Did she steal it?" The last question came out weakly. It was the last thought I was focused on before I fell asleep and I was terrified it was the truth.

Micah laughed. "There is so much you don't know, Amelia." His condescending tone grated on my nerves and made me even hungrier for the power I was missing.

"No, of course she didn't steal it," he continued. "That's not possible, it's just something the old women like to scare children with. This room has been enchanted and your power is bound while you're in here. She knows what you're capable of and I didn't want you to hurt yourself or anyone else." The way he said "anyone else" and looked to the right made me realize exactly what he meant.

"Did you feed her? Is she okay? Can I see her?" I peppered him with questions and Micah sighed. "No, you can't see her. But yes, they took her food. She's not very happy and won't speak to me, but she seems okay." He looked sad but I shoved down the compassion that snuck up on me. He didn't deserve it.

"Will you let her go?" I wanted it to come out strong but the words were anything but. The longer I stayed in this room, the more I realized how much of an idiot I really was.

"I don't know, Amelia. It's not really up to me, now is it?" Micah snarled the words and shoved the tray across the covers. "You have to eat. You're going to have to deal with my mother again soon and you'll need your energy. Can you please stop insulting her and just pretend to have some amount of respect for her? It will only end badly if you don't."

Micah turned to walk away but there was one last question I had to ask. "Why, Micah?" I asked his back. His shoulders sagged. "Why did you find me? Why did you date my best friend? Why did you pretend to be my friend?"

He didn't even turn around. "Because no one knows better than I do what she's capable of and I knew you weren't ready to take her on. I knew you were doomed if she got to you before I did. She was never going to wait the full term. She's been looking for you ever since you left the protection of your father's home."

This time the door closed with a whisper. I wanted to throw the tray of food against the wall but Micah's words rang in my ears. Julia had been looking for me. My home had been protected. If he was telling the truth, then Micah really had been trying to help me.

I dropped onto the bed and curled up into a ball. I would eat. I would eat and I would think and I would find a way out of here.

Chapter 26

I counted the days by the meals. It had been three days. Micah brought me a tray three times a day. We would have short conversations but he wouldn't say much and flat out refused to answer my questions. On the third day, I asked him if Cole knew where I was. "Yes. He knows. Your father has made quite a scene at the club a few times now trying to secure your release."

That came as a shock. The last I had heard from Rynna my father hadn't been well.

"Is he okay? My father?" I asked.

Micah nodded. "Yes. Luckily, my mother found it humorous that he would go to such lengths." Micah started to leave and stopped at the door. "Amelia, I'll be back soon with a dress and some make-up. You and Bethany will be coming to dinner. Please be on your best behavior. If you are, there is a chance she will let Bethany go. So, please, Amelia?" His eyes were pleading with more emotion than I had assumed he held for Bethany.

"Fine, Micah. But it's for her, not for you," I said indignantly. He nodded, his relief obvious, and was gone again. I wanted to trust him, but at this point I didn't think I could trust anyone.

I went into the small bathroom to take a shower. They had brought me sweats and T-shirts the first day but nothing else. I had been confined to this room for three days and the prospect of getting out was more exciting than I had thought it would be. And, if I could just keep it together, at least Bethany could leave. Hopefully. I smiled for the first time since waking up that first day and started the water.

When I came out, the dress was waiting. I didn't know what I was expecting, but a full-length, white, gauzy dress fit for a Roman goddess, wasn't it. The dress was one-shouldered and had a thick, ropey silver belt around the waist. It was beautiful and set off my dark hair. My eyes were their normal hazel since I was devoid of power, but I could only imagine what they would look like once I had my magic back.

I used the hair dryer and curling iron and was sliding on the gladiator sandals I'd found on the floor when Micah knocked. I told him to come in and was happy to see the surprise when he took in my appearance.

It felt good to laugh at little at his sputtering before he finally spit out, "You look lovely, Amelia. Please, come with me." I expected him to get Bethany as well but he gestured me in the other direction. I stopped in front of her door and gave him a quizzical look. "She's already been taken to the dining room," he said. That brought on a pout. I had hoped to get just a minute alone with her.

Sullen, I took Micah's offered arm and let him lead me down the hallway and into a massive dining hall. This wasn't a "room", this was a ballroom. Queen Julia sat in a tall, silver chair at the end of the table. Hunters were stationed around the room and Bethany was trying to hide her shaking with rigid posture. She wore a similar gown to mine and looked breathtaking. I was relieved when Micah led me to the chair next to hers. As soon as I was seated, she grasped my hand. We entwined our fingers and gave each other a quick look before focusing back on the table in front of us. Micah had been specific that we shouldn't look the queen in the eyes and that we should be as quiet as possible.

I kept waiting for that familiar feeling of my magic to come back, but it still wasn't happening. I thought Micah had said just that room? Inwardly sighing, I realized that was a question for later.

The room was quiet as the four of us sat without speaking, Micah sitting just to the left of his mother. Then, the main doors opened. They were at least ten feet tall and similar to the doors I had pushed through days ago to try to make the speech that should have changed everything. So much for that great plan.

I was mentally berating myself again when shock took over as Cole and my father walked in. Both were in similar tuxes to Micah's. Cole's hair was smoothed back and he looked relieved to see Bethany and me next to each other.

It had been months since I'd last seen my father, but he looked as if he had aged ten years. What I remembered to be salt and pepper was now purely silver hair. His eyes were tired and his steps were carefully taken. Cole saw my concern and returned it with a troubled look of his own. I had so much I wanted to say to my father; instead, I just sat and stared into his eyes, trying to apologize for all of the things I never knew and everything he chose not to share. He wore a pained expression, like it physically hurt him to be in the room with me.

Cole and my father had taken seats next to Micah after murmuring their respectful "thank you's" to Julia for being invited to dinner. The queen nodded and kept us all in awkward silence for another minute or so.

"I believe it's clear to everyone why we are all here. Nathaniel, your daughter has proven to be quite willful and very disrespectful. You know I don't take well to either of those." Her gloating sneer made me think there was more to those words than I understood.

My father merely nodded and began apologizing. "Your grace, I don't know where those traits grew from. I've always taught Amelia proper etiquette and impressed upon her the benevolence of our queen."

I couldn't believe the words I was hearing. I opened my mouth and was kicked from under the table. Cole had been seated across from me and was glaring. *Oh*. I was being a moron again. Of course, he was just saying what needed to be said.

I endured an agonizing conversation for the next five minutes, the queen deconstructing me and my father apologizing for every fault she listed. Finally, Julia got to the point. "I don't feel that her human friend has a part to play in all of this, Nathaniel. If your daughter will agree to stop fighting our arrangement and embrace her role as my son's fiancée, then I see no reason to continue to hold the human."

I started to nod enthusiastically when she dropped the next bomb. "Of course, given the circumstances, I do believe that the dates will have to be adjusted. Due to what my Hunter has reported and the display in my chamber a few days ago, she clearly has more power than we even hoped. I will expect her to leave with us immediately."

My nodding stopped as the queen's words sunk in and my panicked eyes met the pure delight in hers. This time though, Bethany beat me to the punch.

"She will not! She will not be your little magic puppet! How dare you think you can treat people this way? You...you...BITCH!" Bethany slammed her hand down on the table as she yelled that last word. If I weren't so scared for what would happen, I would have laughed at the red that flooded Julia's face. Micah jumped to his feet at the same time Cole shoved back his chair.

"Mother. I'm sorry, Mother," Micah rushed out. "She doesn't understand who you are. She's just a simple human. Please, excuse her ignorance. Let's just get her out of here so that Amelia and I can focus on ourselves."

I hated Micah in that moment. I realized exactly what he was doing and how he was protecting Bethany, but I hated him for the pain that flooded her eyes and the tears that filled them just seconds later. She fell back in her chair and I could see the emotion that pulled her down.

I heard Derreck's words in my mind. *Your people will always come first. Always.*

It dawned on me suddenly that Bethany was my people. She had stood by me, accepted me, been kidnapped for me. I didn't give a damn if she was Immortal or not. She was mine.

Before I fully knew what I was saying, the words tumbled from my mouth. "Please, your majesty. Please just let her leave with my family. I'll do it. I'll do what you want. I'll marry Prince Mikail and go now."

My words were quiet and my eyes were down. I couldn't keep watching the pain I inflicted on everyone around me. I had known this was my path for eighteen years; I just had to accept it. At least for now, I had to make the choices that would keep my people safe.

When I looked up, the shock on Micah, Cole, and my father's faces was no match for the anger I found in Bethany's. She was livid. Her eyes said what her lips couldn't. The same word I had just thrown at Micah. *Traitor.*

I paced the bedroom for the millionth time. It had taken some extra pleading from everyone at the table, but Julia finally allowed Bethany to leave with Cole.

She had taken me in a hard hug and I barely caught the words, "I won't let this happen. This wasn't how it was supposed to go."

I quietly responded with, "You have to," and sat back down.

I didn't look at her, Cole, or my father as they left. My eyes stayed on my plate until I was also dismissed and Micah walked me to the bedroom. We had never even eaten dinner. Before he closed the door, his last words were, "Thank you, Amelia. And, I'm sorry, but we leave in two days."

Based on sleeping and meals, it had to be late the next afternoon. I wasn't expecting anyone when a light knock came through the door. "Come in," I answered. I was sitting on the bed, flipping through the same book for the third time when Micah slipped in. He looked back out into the hallway as he quietly shut the door.

"What's going on?" I asked. "You know I volunteered for this. You don't have to act like we aren't stuck together."

He set a small duffel bag on the bed, not acknowledging my snarky comments. "I'm coming back for you later, once everyone is asleep. Make sure you're wearing all of this and your hair is up." With those few words, he was back out the door again.

I lunged for the bag and was confused to find my own black jeans, a black Henley, and a black zip hoodie. In the bottom, I found my favorite black tennis shoes. As I dug around, I found a small zip pocket and in it held the true treasure. Mom's bracelet. Only Cole knew that I kept our mother's infinity bracelet in my top drawer in a small velvet pouch. I never wore it for fear of losing it, but it was the only thing I had of hers and I loved it more than anything. I hadn't even opened the pouch in years because it hurt too much.

As I slipped it out, I grazed my fingertips over the symbols that coated the cuff bracelet. Instantly, there was a measure of peace in holding something that had been my mother's favorite. I'd asked my father once to explain the symbols to me and he had told me he would explain when I was older. *Thanks, Dad,* I thought sarcastically.

After changing into the clothes in the duffel as Micah had directed, I laid back on the bed. I continued rubbing back and forth over the cuff, wishing I could find even a spark of my power and wondering how I was going to get myself out of my current mess. My impulsive decisions had surely gotten me in deeper than I'd ever thought possible.

I stared off into space, once again searching every corner of myself for my power. I clutched the cuff as I hunted. Where was it? Who was I without it? *COME BACK!* I screamed inside my head. Without warning, a jolt shot through me and I felt it. I was back. She was back. We were back!

But, how? I stared down at the bracelet and sent up a prayer of thanks to my mother, wherever she was. I heard a light knock and quickly shoved the bracelet into its pouch and then my hoodie pocket. I tamped down my ecstatic power so that Micah hopefully wouldn't realize what had happened.

I didn't have to worry though because he wasn't there for chit chat. Micah wasted no time beckoning me out into the hallway. He was dressed similarly and had a dark beanie covering the majority of his bright blond hair. We hardly made a sound as we sprinted through the halls and up what I guessed were back stairs. It wasn't until we had actually made it outside and into his waiting Acura, that I finally took a deep breath and started badgering him with questions.

"What's going on, Micah? Where are we going? Why are you doing this?" I couldn't bring myself to fully trust him. "Are you letting me go?" The last question was much more eager than the first three and I grasped his arm as I asked. He had been smiling during my initial inquisition, but it faded.

"I'm sorry, Amelia. I can't let you go," he said, the guilt and pity evident in his drawn features and quiet words. "There would be severe consequences involved for everyone. Me. You. Your family. Bethany. I can't take that chance. But, I don't agree with what my mother has done, so I'm trying to give you a small measure of happiness before we leave. I know I am not who you wanted."

I didn't know what to say. I wanted to say so many things. I wanted to keep asking questions. I wanted to scream at him about how unfair it all was. But, he was right. *Damn it, he was right.* I had to stop making snap decisions that did nothing but hurt everyone. So, instead of saying anything, I just sat silently and watched as the side streets of Brighton passed me by, probably for the last time.

We drove for quite a while down the coast and I realized that the scenery was one I recognized. As we pulled into the same secluded parking lot I had been in with Aidan months before, the day we ditched, I could only stare at Micah. He half-smiled and gestured for me to get out. "He's there, just off in the trees. I asked him to stay hidden in case we were followed, but I don't see anyone. Go, Amelia. Say your goodbyes."

Part of me wanted to sob, but the larger part couldn't stop the excitement. As we had driven farther and farther away from Esmeralda's, I let my power slowly build back up so that Micah wouldn't notice. It was impatient for me to find Aidan. I jumped from the Acura and took off running for the tree line. As I got to the edge, Aidan stepped out and I leapt into his arms. Our magic crashed together in complete bliss as we wrapped ourselves around each other, both physically and spiritually. He carried me back into the trees.

I was hugging him as if my life depended on it. I had myself completely tucked into the safest place on earth. He smelled like ocean water and fir trees. He pulled me back a little and I pulled his head down and brought his lips to mine, not giving him the chance to talk as I presumed was his intention. It was as if stars were colliding. I could feel our magic completely intertwine. I could feel his confusion and relief. I could feel his love. *His love.*

I gave just as much as I got, trying to convey to him everything that he brought out in me. How he had made me feel truly loved for the first time. I pushed every ounce of my passion and love for him back in those few moments as we did so much more than simply kiss. In that brief interlude, we were as whole as we could ever be. Aidan had captured my heart, and with him it would stay, even when I walked away.

As our kisses slowed down and we finally pulled apart, I opened my violet eyes to find myself staring directly into his bright blue ones.

"Hi," I whispered, feeling shy suddenly.

"Hey there, doll," he returned, his voice low and thick.

I slid to the ground and steadied myself, still not letting him go. Realizing just how bright his eyes were, I looked around. "Does Micah know?" Aidan shook his head. "No, that's why I pulled you back here. I didn't want to give myself away."

Aidan took my hand and led me to a bench just a few feet away. It was amazing how just the feeling of his strong hands holding my small ones made everything seem a little less scary. I batted away the fears and realities that were swirling in my mind. For just a minute, this was what I needed.

"I thought you had a plan, Ame. Why did Micah set this up? What's going on? It's been almost a week since I saw you. You've completely fallen off the grid." His anger and frustration of not knowing and not being able to control himself to try to help was seeping through.

"Stop, Aidan. Don't beat yourself up." I hung my head a little. "There's so much you don't know. So much I doubt I have time to explain. I was so stupid." Seconds ago, I was on a high like no other. Now, I was falling faster than a comet plummeting to the earth, just waiting to create a giant explosion. Just like a comet, I had no idea exactly how much damage I would leave in my wake.

I looked up to find Aidan patiently waiting. "Oh, no. Don't do this, Aidan. Don't be good to me. Don't trust me. You're going to hate me." I choked on the last words. Tears filled my eyes, blurring his face ever so slightly.

"Hey," he whispered as he tilted my chin up with his finger and pressed a kiss to my lips. "I could never hate you, Amelia. I love you." I was staring into eyes the color of the brightest blue sky and hearing the words I'd longed for my whole life, but I didn't deserve them. I couldn't have them.

I pulled my hands from his and stood. He winced and dropped his hands to his sides when I didn't return the sentiment. I had tried, so hard, during our reunion to show him exactly how I felt, but I couldn't give voice to it. I knew what lay ahead and it would crush me to say those words knowing I could never act on them. That they could never be truly mine to give him.

I started to pace in front of Aidan, finally stopping to help in the only way I could before I crushed him completely. "Aidan, no matter what else you hear tonight, I want you to remember to go to Cole. Go to him and show him what you are. He'll help you, okay? Are you hearing me?"

He sat staring at me and then stood, stopping my pacing by placing his hands on both of my shoulders.

"Amelia," he said, emotion choking his voice. "My life has been completely turned upside down since I met you. I have something inside me I can't control and know nothing about. I know how you feel about me, but you won't say it. Micah Clair is driving you to me in the middle of the night and you're dressed like you're on a spy mission. You are the absolute best part of my life, I promise I won't hate you, but I need you to just say it."

The tears were back. I stood there, looking up at him, knowing these words were going to ruin the only perfect thing I'd ever had.

"Aidan." I dug my nails into my palms, reminding myself that I was strong and could take the pain. Then, I let the words fall out. "When I was born, I was betrothed to the prince in the Immortal court. I am an Elder, a Keeper if you want to be completely accurate. I found out five days ago that Micah is that prince. I tried to stop it. That was my stupid, grand plan, but the only thing I did was piss off his very psychotic mother who also happens to be our queen. So, tomorrow, I leave with Micah. As his fiancée."

Chapter 27

There were so many reactions I expected but what I got was none of those. He simply looked at me and said, "No."

I watched him shake his head. His power rising in tandem with his emotions. My own power — both of them — beat on me from the inside out, screaming in my head. Wordless wailing assaulting me from all sides.

I had to explain. To make him understand. "Aidan. Please. You are the best thing that has ever happened to me. It wasn't fair of me to start this thing with you knowing my destiny, but I couldn't stop it. I couldn't stop how I felt. How I still feel. But, I can't stop this. No one can. You have to let me go, Aidan." I was grasping at his forearms and pleading with him. Finally, the tears started to fall as he backed away from me.

"No," he said again. "This can't be happening. You can't do this. They can't *make* you do this."

I watched in awe as his eyes became even more iridescent than before. He stood straighter and seemed to grow taller before my eyes. I ran to him. "Aidan. Whatever is happening, please stop it. Just stop it!" I was sure I knew what was happening, but it couldn't happen here. Not now.

I put my hands on his cheeks and pulled him down to me, smashing our lips together. His power was nothing I'd ever encountered. It wasn't like Elias or Melinda, and it wasn't like Micah or Cole's. It seemed like it was overtaking my own and his fear was penetrating both of us. He stood still at first and it was like kissing a statue. I kept murmuring for him to come back to me and he slowly relaxed and started to kiss me back. Finally, everything felt normal. Just as I was about to breathe a sigh of relief, Micah stepped into the clearing.

"I'm sorry to interrupt, but we've already been gone far too long. We need to get back before anyone realizes and the guards change for the morning shift."

Aidan looked as if he might kill Micah where he stood. "GUARDS?" He yelled, his tone alarming. He almost shoved me away as he stalked toward Micah. "You have her guarded? Is that how you treat your friends, *Prince*? You think you can just take her from me? Maybe you could have, but not now."

I saw Micah's face as soon as he registered the brightness of Aidan's eyes. You couldn't miss them. He looked at me, bewildered and I just shrugged. The next look I saw was panic because the blue ball of magic building in Aidan's palm was aimed at Micah. I screamed his name as I rushed at Aidan and leapt at him right before he let loose. The magic blast took out a few trees, but missed Micah as he dove the opposite direction.

I landed on top of Aidan and was immediately pleading with him to stop. "Please, Aidan. You just have to let me go. If you hurt him, the queen will find you. They'll hurt my family. They'll kill you."

My fear had turned my tears to sobs and I heard the release of his breath as he pulled me closer and tucked me into his chest. As we stood and righted ourselves, I thought I had finally gotten through. Instead, Aidan held me at arm's length. He caressed my cheek and I leaned into his palm, savoring the warmth of him. As I opened my eyes and he dropped his hand, I could see that I wasn't going to like what came next.

Aidan took three steps back. I was standing the same distance from him as I was from Micah, positioned at the tip of our triangle. Aidan glared at Micah and his expression only softened slightly when it came back to me. Micah still hadn't spoken and seemed to understand that he should just stand there.

"Amelia," Aidan started. "You didn't choose this. You don't have to go with him. We're already this far. We can run and I can protect you. We can get Bethany and Cole and your dad and we can just go. They can't hurt us if they can't find us." His love wrapped around me as his power still intertwined with mine, pulling and pleading internally as he did externally. I wanted him to be right. I wanted it to be that easy. The last intact parts of my own heart broke and crumbled as he begged me to go.

I choked up as the tears clogged my throat. I tried to use my own power to strengthen my resolve but it rebelled against the very idea of what I was about to do, abandoning me to my own demise. Everything in me wanted to go to him, but I couldn't. It would only make it worse. I rooted myself to the spot I was in. I couldn't look away from Aidan. I could see Micah in my peripheral, but he was just staying quiet as he stood, waiting.

"Aidan, I'm sorry." My words came out much stronger than I thought possible. "It's just not that simple. You haven't lived in this world and you don't understand. This woman is evil. I don't have a choice, no matter how I feel about you. I have to go."

I started to turn to Micah as I heard his quiet words. "Pick me, Amelia. Please, pick me. Be the one who finally picks me." My whole body seemed to cave in on itself as my soul ripped in half.

Everything inside of me bellowed for me to run to him and let this love carry us as far as we could go, but I couldn't make another selfish decision. I didn't allow myself to turn back around and face him as I whispered myself, "I can't. I'm so sorry. Goodbye, Aidan."

I walked to where Micah was standing and followed him from the clearing. My uncle Derreck had been right all along. The moment had come and I had chosen duty over love. Just as I had for Bethany.

My destiny had been dictated from the very beginning and I would always have to choose my people over myself. The further I got from Aidan, the more it felt like very best parts of me were being shredded to pieces as our powers were forced to separate. The tears slowly fell and rolled down my cheeks. I didn't bother to wipe them away. I swore to myself that these would be the last tears I cried, so I just let them come for all the days I would wish I had them back.

As we got in the Acura and Micah backed out, I saw blue eyes shining from the trees. Moments later, I heard the most bone-chilling howl. I couldn't stop the audible gasp and from my peripheral, I saw Micah's eyes flash as we watched Aidan drop to all fours.

Neither of us looked away, but the red of Micah's eyes shone in the dim lights of the interior as his power reacted to the perceived threat.

"Did you know?" It wasn't accusatory. It was barely a whisper between us in the dark. I could only shake my head as Aidan completed his shift, snarled in our direction, and loped away. I had wondered. I had guessed. But I hadn't known. I could only hope he had heard what I said. That he wouldn't try to go it alone.

I finally turned to look at Micah as he said, "Then no one else needs to."

Amelia's journey is just beginning. Stay tuned for the next installment in the "Bound" series.

Acknowledgments

Abe — From the first day I brought up the crazy idea that I wanted to write a book, you were nothing but supportive. This book would not exist without you. Thank you for reading it in secret, even when I told you that you didn't have to, and knowing what I needed in the process — even when I didn't know myself. Muah.

Renee — You read the first chapter and told me it was good. You built my self-esteem and told me I could actually do this. Thank you, lovely. Thank you.

My Betas — I can't believe all I put you through! Shannon, Callie, Kristin, Christina, Natalie, Carrie and Renee…you read draft after draft. You were nicer to me than you should have been. You cheered me on and let me freak out along the way. I love you, ladies. For real.

Kristin — You get a special note, because you truly took this book to the next level. I cursed your name at first but the drafts that came from your edits were a Phoenix rising from the ashes. You saw the bones of the story I really wanted to tell and you made me tell it. Thank you. From the absolute bottom of my heart.

The Rebel Writers — Oh, ladies. I haven't gotten to meet a single one of you in person and yet you are among my dearest friends. You kept me sane, you pushed me to keep going and you believed in me when I didn't. You shared your secrets and made me better. And you made me laugh, constantly. The Rebels will truly take over the world — I have no doubt.

Toni — For not laughing at me when I told you about the crazy book I was writing and how I needed a designer but couldn't pay much. For getting so excited about this book and designing a gorgeous cover that will do just as much for me as the words on the page. And for putting up with my, "Just one more edit" emails and "Did you see my email?" text messages. You're the best.

Monica — You took my words and made them shine. And you put up with all of my grammar questions. You're wonderful and I can't wait to put book two in your hands.

Rachel Higginson, Tracey Garvis-Graves and Jessica Park — For answering my incessant questions about being an author, the process and the realities. For the ridiculous amounts of Facebook messages, texts and phone calls you allowed me. Your books and your professionalism inspired me and I wouldn't have come this far without you.

Mom — I love books and words because of you. I befriend every character as if I knew them personally because you showed me how someone else's world can become your own. You fostered the mind and passion that made this book possible. I love you.

For every person over the past year that congratulated me, encouraged me and got so excited about what I was doing. You kept me honest and pushed me forward. I appreciate your words, your gestures and your willingness to let me gush about my baby more than you will ever know.

And last — but most important — thank YOU, dear reader. For buying this book, for getting to the last page and supporting my dreams. I hope you enjoyed the world I created. I would love to hear what you thought, good or bad, so that I can make the next one even better.

About the Author

Stormy Smith calls Iowa's capital home now, but was raised in a tiny town in the Southeast corner of the state. She grew to love books honestly, having a mom that read voraciously and instilled that same love in her. She knew quickly that stories of fantasy were her favorite, and even as an adult gravitates toward paranormal stories in any form.

Writing a book had never been an aspiration, but suddenly the story was there and couldn't be stopped. When she isn't working on or thinking about her books, Stormy's favorite places include bar patios, live music shows, her yoga mat, or anywhere she can relax with her husband or girlfriends.

Okay, enough with the third person!

Where you can find me

If you'd like to be alerted when my next book will release, sign up for my mailing list at http://eepurl.com/WLlq1. I promise, you will *only* get new release emails. Pinky swear.

Website: www.stormysmith.com

Facebook: www.facebook.com/authorstormysmith

Twitter: @stormysmith

GoodReads: www.goodreads.com/stormysmith

Email: authorstormysmith@gmail.com

A note about reviews

Whether you loved it, hated it or were completely ambivalent, your review will help others decide if they would like to read my book. Please consider leaving just a few words on the site you purchased from and/or GoodReads. Every review matters and I read them all.

Keep reading for a sneak peak at REGAN CLAIRE'S recent release, *Gathering Water*!

GATHERING WATER

REGAN CLAIRE

CHAPTER ONE

Eighteen. We all expect our lives to change when that number finally hits us. It is, after all, the year you are finally an adult, finally in charge of your own life. Most people wake up on that monumental birthday and run to the mirror, convinced that they were magically transformed during their 8 hours of sleep into a *bona-fide* adult. Others just lie in bed, thinking about the momentous changes that are sure to be coming.

I'm sure there are some people who just go about their day as if nothing were different and usually nothing really is. I like to think that those are the people who are most content with their lives… The people who have no unanswered questions, no haunting pasts, and no uncertainty about their futures.

When my 18th birthday arrived I didn't rush to the mirror eager to see my grownup self. And being in the foster system since birth kept me from seeing that day as if it were any other.

I probably lay in bed for 10 minutes before my alarm finally convinced me to get up. 18 was huge. It was a birthday I had waited impatiently and anxiously for. It meant I was legally an adult and for foster kids like myself that's a big deal; it meant that I was no longer a ward of the state. Finally, it meant control. I didn't have to worry about getting a new family if I made a mistake. No more psych evaluations, no more child services, no more any of that kind of stuff that made up my life. I was free!

It also meant that I was, suddenly, responsible for myself.

Just the day before I had a team of people to answer to; people that fed me, clothed me, told me what to do and when to do it. If I had felt like a prisoner to the system before, I felt as if I were adrift at sea now.

After getting out of bed I gingerly stepped over my two duffel bags' worth of clothes out into the hallway and made my way downstairs. Most of my room was already packed. I didn't have many personal belongings, which would make moving that much easier since Margaret, my foster mother, was no longer responsible for providing me with a room.

Margaret was, as always, already up when I walked into the kitchen. She was an early riser and was usually drinking her second cup of coffee by the time I rolled out of bed. The previous eight months had actually been pretty decent because of her. She was an elderly woman, with salt and pepper hair and a disapproving mouth; not exactly warm and cuddly, but she treated me well enough.

She kept mostly to herself except at mealtimes, when she insisted that we be together. I'd had worse rules. I think she appreciated my company since her own children so rarely visited, only twice since I moved in.

Though my world already felt so different, that morning's routine continued as it usually did. Margaret finished making her oatmeal and started on the coffee while I poured milk into my Lucky Charms, then we both sat down to eat in companionable silence at the beige card table she kept in the kitchen. When the meal was finished I grabbed our mismatched dishes and brought them to the sink, before lathering them up with lemon scented dish soap and playing the part of dishwasher, as I always did. When I reached for the flamingo-decorated dishtowel to start drying, I was surprised to find that Margaret had already started on the job.

"I can finish this up, Margaret."

"I don't doubt your abilities Della, but I can at least dry the dishes on your birthday." Not knowing what else to do I thanked her, then turned to go back down the hallway into my soon-to-be former room, but was stopped by a tentative touch on my arm.

"Della, the new kid isn't supposed to be here for another couple of weeks. You're welcome to stay here until then," Margaret said, surprising me completely. I knew that she was going to get another ward soon; she'd been fostering consistently for the past 10 years and was a way station of sorts, only holding on to a kid for a few months until a better place was found.

"Um, thanks Margaret, but I'm already packed and it won't take that long to move my things into the apartment above the convenience store."

My job at that store had been a lifeline. I mean, the pay wasn't exactly great, but in a smaller town the job options were limited, especially since school was out. My boss Marv was letting me rent the small room above it for cheap in exchange for fixing it up and making the space livable, since it barely fit that bill.

After thanking her for the offer I went on to my room. I was supposed to meet one last time with my social worker that morning, and even though she no longer had any say in my life, old habits die hard and I put on my nicest sundress and made sure my mousy brown hair was properly subdued.

The meeting really should have been before my birthday, to see how I was preparing for the transition, but things kept getting held up. Sara was by far the best social worker I'd had, mostly because she hadn't been doing the job long enough to become disenchanted with it; she still cared. She was the one who got me placed with Margaret instead of in another group home.

I didn't hear her car pull up, but I knew when she arrived all the same. I always had good, even uncanny instincts for that type of thing, and I was at the door by the time she was up the steps. This would be the last time I saw her, but I wasn't expecting this particular visit to affect my life in any way—I thought that meeting represented the end of my old life, but really it marked the beginning of my new one.

CHAPTER TWO

We sat in the only café the town had to offer. Sara always insisted on meeting in a 'neutral' place so that I would feel comfortable. Usually Margaret would be at another table reading a newspaper until she was called over for her own part of our meeting, but I guess since I was now 18, Sara didn't need to speak to my former guardian any more.

She spent the first few minutes sipping her black redeye, which was just a fancy way of saying coffee with a shot of espresso; having a caffeine addiction must be part of the job description for social workers. I had my usual raspberry hot chocolate with extra whipped cream even though it was really just fancy chocolate milk, since I ordered it iced over the summer months.

As my entire existence had been unpredictable, I liked the comfort of having something in my life being unchanged, even if that something was only a sugary drink.

I decided to jumpstart the conversation right when the silence was beginning to turn awkward.

"I've already packed everything, and Margaret said I could borrow her car to move my things and go shopping for the necessities later on. There's an old pickup that's been for sale for as long as I've been here and I think I have enough money to buy it, but I didn't want to use all of my money right away. I mean, the store is right down the street from-"

"Della, I know. We've already talked about all of this. Really, I believe you. This isn't really an official meeting. I took an early lunch break so I could see you today. You remember the promise I made you when we first met?"

Ah, the promise. I remembered it. It was the week after Thanksgiving and I had just been kicked out of another foster home and was staying in a group home, I thought until my birthday.

Group homes can be all right sometimes, but this one wasn't. There were too many other teenagers, and those of us who've lived in the system our whole lives, well, we're kinda hard to live with. I didn't do so well with other people and I was an easy target for some of the other kids, and by kids I mean guys.

I had just spent another sleepless night guarding myself from the creeps in the house. Most of the other girls would help each other out and take turns keeping watch, but I didn't make friends very easily, so I was on my own.

On this day, in walks Sara, yet another Social Worker who had been thrust upon me. I don't know if they get to trade us kids like baseball cards or what, but I rarely had workers stay with me for more than a year or two before throwing their hands up. Maybe they all just quit after working with me, I don't know. Anyway, you could tell Sara was new on the job because she carried a shiny new briefcase and there were no discernible grey hairs.

I grudgingly sat in the room they used for private meetings and listened to her drone on and on about how she was going to help me and how I should think of her as a friend, and how friends trust each other.

Well, after she hinted about the 10th time for me to open up, I did... big time!

I plea temporary insanity. I just wanted her to be quiet- this was the only time I could sneak off to sleep without worrying too much about being... ahem... *bothered*, and I hated her for interrupting that. It was like an out-of-body experience and I could only sit there and watch myself blubber about how there was no place for me. That I never did anything wrong and people still couldn't stand to be around me. That I didn't even have a single living relative and how that must be proof of how innately *wrong* I was.

Basically, I told her about every foster kid's worst fears.

When I finally got to the part about how sleep-deprived I was because I didn't want to be woken in the middle of the night again by some creep sticking his hand up my shirt, I came to my senses, wiped my face, and refused to make eye contact for the rest of the meeting.

Right before she left, after unsuccessfully hugging me (I'm not a hugger), she took my hand and told me she'd help me. She promised to help me find my place.

The next day I was placed with Margaret, an ideal home for a kid like me; a place that had locks on the doors. As far as I was concerned she *had* kept her promise, even though she would have been the first person to do so in my entire life. So when she asked me if I remembered, I was kinda wondering if she wanted me to return the favor or something. I just nodded my head and stirred the now gross-looking whipped cream into my iced chocolate milk.

"Well, it's taken me a little longer than I anticipated and when I did find it I had to wait until you were 18 to give you the details, which is why I had to cancel our last meeting. I mean, it was hard enough not telling you over the phone."

She seemed to realize that she wasn't making any sense, took a deep breath, and tried again. "I found it. Well, I found something."

"You found what?" At this point I was pretty confused.

"I found your place! I mean, I found where you come from, and your family, and well, everything!"

Now I just thought she was being cruel. "I don't know what you mean. I was told my mother died giving birth to me, that she was a Jane Doe," I pointed out.

"Well, she did and she was. But, I got hold of her personal effects and was going to give them to you for your birthday. Here." She pulled out a manila folder and slid it across the table.

"It turns out that some detective a few years ago got into some trouble and was put on desk duty, and one of his case files was finding out who your mother was! Her name was Gabriella Deare from North Carolina. There are some things that go to you," she said as she tapped the folder. "So, take a look."

Numbly, I opened the folder and tipped the contents out, barely registering the clink of metal that hit the table with all the paper. If I had ever had a surreal moment, this was definitely one.

I didn't look at the copy of the police report; in the state of shock I was in I knew I wouldn't be able to make any sense out of it. There was a cheap journal that had been a vibrant red at some point, but many years' worth of fading turned it into a dull pink. Flipping through it I saw a looping scrawl of what must have been my mother's handwriting, since her name was carefully written on the front cover. There were more papers there, but I couldn't make my brain function enough to understand the writing that covered them, though I could tell that they were probably important documents by the multiple signatures that appeared at the bottom of most of them.

Sara quietly observed me through all of it, tactfully not commenting on the amount of shaking my hands did as I very nervously organized the papers so that all the sides lined up perfectly and slipped them back into the folder. Left on the table was an ornate key, nearly black, and when I picked it up I saw the top of it was worked into one of those interlooping knots. It looked familiar to me and I realized it was the same as the power of three symbol from a show that one of my foster mothers used to watch. There was a long chain looped through the top, which I started wrapping and unwrapping around my fist as I looked up at Sara, too overwhelmed to talk.

"There's a lot to take in there, I know. And I'm sure someone would have notified you soon anyway about all of this, now that you're of age. I just wanted you to have it today. I wanted to be able to hand it to you and offer my help, as a friend." She paused for two whole seconds, and her exuberance made me see her for the first time as someone more than my jailer; she was a person and probably only a few years older than I.

"Are you going to go there? I mean, it's quite a long way away - North Carolina is literally on the other side of the country, but you still have family there. And a house!" She picked up the folder that was laying on the table and waved it, as if there were a house inside. "Your grandmother left you a house too. I'm not really sure how that works since you weren't even born when she died, but it's been held in trust for your mother's daughter all these years; there's a lawyer who's been in charge of keeping up with the taxes and insurance, so all you need to do is prove who your mother is and you're all set," she took a big gulp of her coffee, then continued.

"Also, there are a couple of bonds that were your mother's. They were easy to track down once I had her name and social security number. They are being held in a safety-deposit box close to where she lived, and they go to you now as well. About six thousand dollars in all, and they're fully matured." She took a deep breath, since she'd been talking so fast, then went on destroying my world-view.

"They wouldn't mail them to me, said they had to be picked up by the deposit owner, which is you, in person. There might be some other things in there as well; they couldn't tell me. You'll need to update your birth certificate so that it has your mother's name on it, and just bring that and her death certificate, which is in the police file, to prove that you are who you say you are. I have all the necessary paperwork in the folder for you. They were really friendly on the phone. I'm sure they won't make it difficult for you once you get there."

I had no idea what to say, or what to do. All I could do was stare at her, too dumbstruck to say anything. How was I even supposed to feel in this type of situation? Actually, I started feeling a little angry. That anger helped me find my voice.

"You mentioned family? I have living, breathing family there?"

"Yes, I can't believe I was going on and on about a house when I should've been telling you about your family! Your mother's father still lives there, and I believe she had a brother, and there's probably some extended family." She sounded really excited at the prospect and completely unaware that I wasn't.

"The police had to contact them about my mom right? To identify her or something? Do they know about me?" I knew the answer: of course they did.

"Well, I'm sure they know about you." I could tell the exact moment that it dawned on her what it meant that they must have known about me for years now, if the police report was correct, and that I was just learning about them. We orphans are usually shipped off and adopted by any living relatives, or at least fostered by them. The only exceptions are if they're unfit or unwilling to take us on. Even if they hadn't learned of my existence until a few years ago, they still would have been notified and asked to take me in.

I could see the pity seep into her face. Since I wasn't in the mood for the pep talk she was probably about to give me, I gathered the folder and stood up. I was already clutching the key in my hand so hard that my fingers were tingling from lack of blood flow.

"Yeah, well. Thanks for giving me all this. I've got to go though, still got a lot of stuff I need to do and well, I think Margaret wanted me to eat lunch with her today before I left."

As far as excuses went, mine was pretty lame. I just had to get away from her, get away from other people for a few minutes. I walked off with my hands full before Sara could really react. I heard her stand up and call my name, but I didn't look back and she didn't come after me; I think she knew I needed some time alone.

I walked the two miles back to Margaret's, going back and forth between mad, hurt, and excited to learn all these new things about myself. Mad and hurt seemed to win over excited, and after I let myself into the house, I went to my room and shoved the folder into one of my still open bags, then told myself that nothing in my life was different because of it; I was determined to forget all about it.

Margaret, with her perfect timing, was just finishing up my favorite lunch when I walked in: grilled cheese and tomato soup. We were going to eat on the patio, and I was instructed to wait at the two-person table while she brought out our plates.

I didn't realize that I still had the key and chain wrapped in my fist until I went in for my first bite. I put it down and tried to ignore it, but every few moments I'd realize that I'd stopped eating and was tracing the imprint left in my palm and staring idly at the offending key.

"Is everything okay, Della? How was your talk with Sara?" As a rule, Margaret and I didn't talk about things, not real things anyway, but she must have noticed that something was up with me and was trying out her very rusty maternal instincts.

"It was good I guess. Very informative." I muttered the last bit, but not really softly enough to not be heard.

"That's a pretty necklace. I don't remember seeing it before. Did Sara give that to you for your birthday?" She gestured towards the key sitting innocently next to my bowl.

"Well, kind of. Apparently it belonged to my mother. They found out who she was. I guess she left me some stuff back where she lived. Not like I'll go and get it or anything. Her stupid family can just keep it." I rarely acted the part of a surly teenager, but exceptional circumstances are cause for exceptional behavior, or something like that.

"Della, they know who your mother was? She has family? Child, that means that you have family! That's something to be happy about!"

"Yeah, but they knew about me! They knew where I was. They didn't just find out, they've known for years. I could have had a home, Margaret; they could have been my family. They didn't even contact me and let me know they existed. They could have, you know. Even if they didn't take me on, the courts would have let them contact me. I know tons of other kids in the system who at least get a birthday card from their birth family, even if they're being fostered," I told her, even though she was well aware of that fact. Then, when she didn't say anything, I went on with my rant.

"They didn't even want to know me. Why would I go there for some stupid house that's probably run down, and some stupid family that doesn't care if I exist? I've gone my whole life without whatever's out there and I don't see why I need it now. I just want to forget about it all and get on with my life!"

Margaret sat back with her hands in her lap for a few minutes, but I knew she wasn't going to drop it since she got a certain look in her eye when she knew she was right about something. It was a look that she usually reserved for trivia game shows, something she was both obsessed with and brilliant with.

"Well, it seems like it would be a little difficult to move towards your future if you don't know your past." She wiped invisible crumbs from her mouth with her paper-towel napkin. "Della, even if you don't see these people at all, you need to go back and find out about your mother. You said she left you a house? That seems like a pretty good way to start a new life, which is exactly what you have been planning to do, isn't it? Why shouldn't you start that new life in a place where you can find some answers rather than above some old convenience store?" she asked in her no-nonsense manner.

"It's not that simple, Margaret. Even if I wanted to go, the house is in North Carolina. I've never even left California. I can't go all the way to the opposite side of the country just because of some empty house and some relatives who don't want to know me. How would I even get there? What am I supposed to do there? It's better that I just forget the whole thing and move on with my life, don't you think?" My argument sounded weak even to my ears.

"Well, I suppose you could do that, but if it were me I'd want to know. I'd want to know where I came from, and know who my family was. I'd even want to know the worthless relatives who didn't want to know me, because you can't find any answers if you don't ask any questions. But I guess I'm just more inquisitive than you are. Those questions would burn at me and keep me up at night. To each her own, though."

Obviously satisfied with planting the seeds she knew would take root in my thoughts, Margaret kept the conversation light for the rest of lunch. She did, however, seem really pleased with herself and was uncommonly cheerful for a woman who never smiled. After lunch she insisted on cleaning up again, and I excused myself for a run.

Now, I am by no means an athlete. I don't go to the gym or play team sports, but there is something about running that is extremely satisfying. I usually only take my runs when it's raining outside, one oddity of mine from a long list of them. I also like to run barefoot. I've had my share of stubbed toes as a result, but the feeling of my bare feet hitting the earth is just exhilarating to me.

I took the trail behind the elementary school I had found my first week in town. It was a dirt path that wound through a semi-wooded area to a clearing with a picnic table and a few sandboxes. I always made a beeline for the huge redwood tree that seemed to watch over this little family spot; it was a lonely reminder that this entire area was once a huge forest. I sat down with my back to the tree, dug my toes a little into the dirt and grass that surround the roots, and let myself absorb the calm that the tree offered with my head back and my eyes closed.

I'd been doing that a lot, going to that redwood and thinking about my future, and thought I had figured out which path my life would take. I would work at the convenience store, buy the old beat-up truck, rent out the tiny loft apartment, and save up for community college. I had only vague plans after that since I wasn't in the habit of making long-term plans, never having been in one place long enough to make them.

My plan, which only that morning seemed exciting and fulfilling, was now lacking. I wasn't exactly sure what it was missing, but I was sure that I could no longer be satisfied with that life, with any life really, at least not until I put my curiosity to rest. I guess I wasn't too surprised that I'd come to that conclusion. Margaret's seed had taken root and was sprouting.

I had managed to save nearly a thousand dollars working part-time at the convenience store, but I knew that wouldn't last long. Airfare would take up a big chunk of that and, for once, I was really glad that I didn't have that many things. Everything I owned could easily be packed into a couple of suitcases. It wasn't as if there were anything keeping me here. If I went to North Carolina and it didn't work out, I could just go somewhere else, start over in a place where nobody knew who I was, where I could be whoever I wanted to be. Besides there was a little money waiting for me, more than enough to replenish what I would spend getting there, and if the house belonged to me, then there wasn't anything that anybody could say about my living there.

Who said I even had to see the supposed family that lived in the area? I figured I could ignore them quite as well as they had ignored me over the past few years. Better, in fact. I ended up being so very wrong, but at the time the thought comforted me and helped me steel my will toward a new direction.

I stayed a good deal longer under that tree, making mental to-do lists and planning my next few days. I didn't think about what I would do once I got to my mother's house, didn't think about the family that still lived in the area. Instead, I kept my thoughts filled with the few things I could control: the details of what I needed to do the next day to claim my inheritance.

Before going back to Margaret's house I stopped by the convenience store to talk to my boss and let him know that there was going to be a change of plans. He was disappointed when I told him I would be moving away and would be unable to work that summer, but he wished me luck and gave me a gruff hug before I left to walk, still barefoot, back down the road to Margaret's house. It was a strange walk, everything looked different to me, as if it were the last time I would see that road. I was thinking about how vastly different my life would be from then on. I felt that I was on the verge of becoming a new person; that I was about to be reborn.

Available now!